2003

Read by:
Bart Holmes
Mary Holmes
Wayne Thompson

ALSO BY NINO RICCI

Lives of the Saints

In a Glass House

Where She Has Gone

NINO RICCI

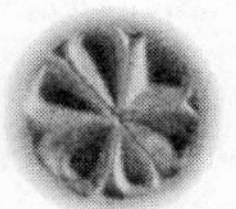

TESTAMENT

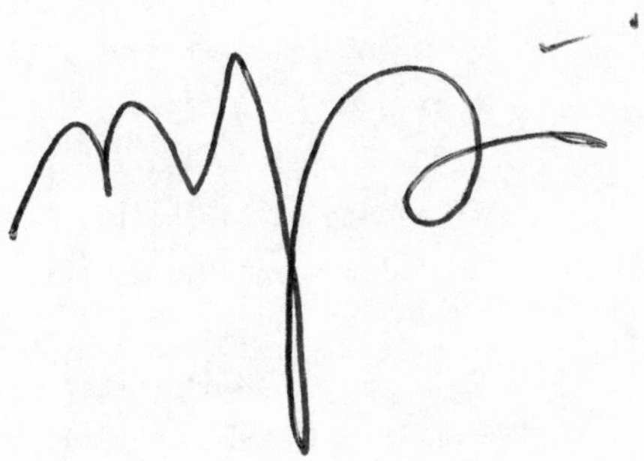

DOUBLEDAY CANADA

National Library of Canada Cataloguing in Publication Data

Ricci, Nino, 1959–

Testament

ISBN 0-385-65854-0

I. Title.

PS8585.I126 48 2002   C813′.54   C2001-904046-6

PR9199.3.R512T48 2002

Text design: CS Richardson

Printed and bound in the USA

Published in Canada by

Doubleday Canada, a division of

Random House of Canada Limited

Visit Random House of Canada Limited's website: www.randomhouse.ca

BVG 10 9 8 7 6 5 4 3 2 1

for Sarah
for Virginia
for Luca

BOOK I

YIHUDA OF QIRYAT

I FIRST SAW HIM in the winter of that year at En Melakh, a town of a few hundred just north of the Salt Sea. He had come in out of the desert, people said—from the look of him, his blistered face and the way his skin hung from his bones, he'd passed a good while there. He had set himself up now just off the square, squatting in the shade of an old fig tree; I had a good view of him from the porch of the tavern I'd put up in across the way. Some of the townspeople, no doubt taking him for a holy man, dropped bits of food in front of him from time to time, which he accepted with a nod of his head but more often than not couldn't seem to bring himself to stomach, letting them sit there in the dirt for the flies to collect on or the dogs to snatch away.

Though the town lay on the Roman side of the frontier, the soldiers of Herod Antipas often passed that way when they travelled up from his southern territories. At the time, I was awaiting an informant we had among Herod's men on his way back to the court from the Macherus fortress. The holy man had appeared perhaps the third day of my wait, simply there beneath the fig tree when I awoke; from the joyless look of him I thought he might have been cast out from one of the desert cults, the way they did sometimes if some bit of food should touch your hand before you'd washed it or if you missed some pause or half-word in your prayers. His hair and beard were scraggly and short as if recently shaved for a vow—they gave him a boyish appearance but couldn't however quite take the dignity from him, which seemed to sit on him like some mantle someone had laid over him.

He wasn't wearing any sandals or cloak. I thought surely he'd had some cave out there to hole up in, and some brush for fire, or he would have frozen to death in the cold. Even here in the valley the nights had been bitter, the little heat the sun built up over the day through the winter haze vanishing the instant dusk fell. I waited to see if he planned to weather the night in the open or repair to some cranny when darkness set in. But the sun dropped and he didn't move. My tavern-keeper, a mangy sort with an open sore on one of his knuckles, brought a lamp out to the porch and a bit of the gruel he passed off as food.

"He's a quiet one, that one," he said, with his low, vulgar laugh, trying to ingratiate himself. "Nearly dead, from the look of it."

Not ten strides from the man some of the boys of the town, coming out after their suppers, began to get up a bit of a fire, spitting and holding their hands up to the flames and keeping their talk low lest the holy man overhear them. The orange haze their fire threw out just reached the man where he was, making him seem like someone at a threshold, someone turned away from the room of light the fire formed. Get up and warm yourself, I wanted to say to him, feeling I was out there with him in the cold, with the wind at my ankles and just a few bits of bread in my belly. But still he sat. It occurred to me that he was perhaps simply too enfeebled to rise, that his hapless look was his own hunger-dimmed wonder that he could sit there as his life ebbed away and not be able to lift a finger to save himself.

I had half-resolved to go out and offer him my cloak when I was headed off by a woman who was apparently the mother of one of the boys in the square, and who came out chastising the lot of them.

"Animals! Didn't one of you think to give him a bit of fire?"

And she proceeded to purloin some of the precious faggots of wood the boys had no doubt scrounged for all afternoon in the brush and to build a little fire in front of the man. When she'd got a blaze going she took off her own shawl and draped it over his shoulders, then took her son by the ear and dragged him off home. Within minutes the rest of the boys, thus humiliated, had begun to disperse as well, the last two or three lingering defiantly a bit before finally quenching their own fire and shamefacedly dropping their remaining handfuls of wood into that of the holy man.

The holy man, for his part, had seemed oblivious to all of this. But when the boys had gone I detected a bit of movement in him, a slight drawing in towards the fire as if towards some secret it might whisper to him. I thought I ought to assure myself that he at least had his wits about him, and so, with the excuse of further stoking his fire, I took a few twigs from the small bundle that the tavern-keeper kept near his gate and walked out to him. It was only when I got close to him that I saw what his body had been giving in to: he had fallen asleep. I wavered a moment over tending to him—it was always my instinct then in situations of that kind to err on the side of indifference, as the way of drawing the least attention to myself. But seeing him helpless like that in his sleep, and even more hopelessly frail than he had seemed from a distance, I shored up his fire a bit and then for good measure draped my cloak over his shawl, knowing that I could beg an extra blanket off the tavern-keeper for my own lice-infested bed. What struck me as I draped the cloak over him was how peculiar this act of charity felt, how alien to my nature, as if I had now truly become a man whom I'd thought I merely feigned to be.

The group I formed part of was based in Jerusalem, and had among it a few members of the aristocracy from which it derived funds, but also shopkeepers and clerks, bakers and common labourers, though I had never been certain in the several years of my own involvement with it how far its network extended. The truth was that we were not encouraged to know one another, against the chance of capture and betrayal, and in my own case I could not have named with certainty more than a few dozen of my co-conspirators, although there were many others, of course, whom I had met in one way or another or whom I knew only by aliases. I myself had been recruited during my days as a recorder at the temple, where I had taken refuge after the death of my parents. At the time it had been rage that moved me, and a young man's passion, though afterwards I also had cause to be grateful for the years of boredom I had been saved copying out the rolls for the temple tax.

Like the Zealots, we worked for Rome's overthrow though, unlike them, we did not imagine that only God was our commander or that it was profanement to know more than what was written in the Torah. So we had a few men of experience amongst us, at least, who understood how the world worked and the forces we were up against. But many of those who had joined us in the hope of imminent revolt had, over time, lost patience with our leaders' caution and our lack of progress. It was our strategy, for instance, that we stir up unrest in the entire region before risking any action of our own. Yet the fact was that we did not have the contacts for proper embassies abroad, and that outside our borders we had won to our cause only the most minor of tribal lords. So our grand hope of a revolution that would spread across the whole of the empire, and be unquenchable, appeared increasingly the merest fantasy. In the meantime we had begun to descend into factions, and even those who ought to have been our allies often proved, over some point of doctrine, our fiercest enemies. The Zealots, for instance, considered us cowards and collaborationists because we did not protest every smallest infringement of Jewish law; yet they thus wasted in a thousand little outbursts the resources that ought to have gone to a single great conflagration.

In the face of our failures abroad we had begun to put our energies instead into infiltrating the Palestinian outposts, not only those in Judea, which the Romans controlled directly, but also those in the territories of their vassals Herod Antipas and Herod Philip, on the reasoning that in the event of revolt we would need to take the outlying fortresses at once if we were to stand any chance of holding back the Roman legions based in Syria. Most of us were kept in the dark, of course, about our actual strength, going about our little tasks with hardly any sense of the whole we formed part of, not only because our leaders so arranged it but because even amongst ourselves we did not dare to confide in one another or pool our knowledge, for fear of spies. In my own case there were two men I reported to, one a teacher and grain merchant who lived near the stadium, and the other a lawyer who worked in the city administration; outside these I spoke to no one except in the most general terms. For my work, I ran a shop just beneath the Antonia fortress where I sold phylacteries and also various foreign texts, and where I offered services as a scribe. It was in this latter office that I made myself useful to our group—the soldiers from the fortress often came to me to prepare their letters home, and so I learned the comings and goings of the procurator and the movements of the troops and so on. In the beginning, because I had been raised in Ephesus and knew something of the world, I had also a number of times been sent abroad, even once as far as Rome. But eventually it grew clear that I did not have the character for diplomacy. So I was given other duties, though from time to time was still sent on small assignments outside the city, which I increasingly welcomed as the atmosphere among us in Jerusalem grew more and more oppressive.

En Melakh was barely a day's journey from Jerusalem but seemed much further, at the bottom of the long, bleak road that led down from the city to the Jordan plain. I had left Jerusalem under clear skies, but here a dust-filled wind had daily blown across the flats like the Almighty's angry breath, blocking the sun and dropping grit in every nook and crevice. The morning after the holy man's arrival, however, dawned clear. During the night I had hardly been able to sleep for the thought of him sitting out there in the cold—I did not know why my mind had so fixed on him except that he seemed an obscure sort of challenge to me, to my own smug sense of mission, sitting there half-dead yet asking for nothing.

When I awoke, just past daybreak, I did not take the trouble to so much as wash my hands before going out to check on him. My heart sank when I saw he was missing from his spot beneath the fig tree—my first thought was that he had died in the night and had already been carted away, to prevent the desecration of buzzards alighting there in the middle of the town. But then I caught sight of him amidst the early morning traffic a little ways from the square, padding along in the dim red of sunrise towards the stable that served to house the pack animals and goats of the local market. It was a shock to see him fully upright, all skin and bones the way he was, little more than a wraith against the dawn, walking with that strange light-footedness of the very thin and the very frail that makes them look almost lively and spry even when they are at death's door.

At the stables he ducked into one of the stalls and squatted to ease himself. It was only when he had emerged and had begun to move back towards the square that I noticed he was no longer wearing my cloak, only the shawl he'd been given, which gave him a slightly comical, womanly air despite his wisps of beard; and I saw now that my cloak in fact lay neatly draped over the low mud wall of the tavern's porch. Clearly his wits were sharper than I had imagined them, if he had known enough to track me down. But rather than being pleased that the thing had been returned to me, I felt a prick of injury at how speedily he had seemed to wish to rid himself of it, as if it were some curse that had been laid on him.

He took up his place beneath the fig tree again. There was a little more life in his eyes than there had been the day before—it seemed he had crossed back, after all, to the land of the living. From somewhere he'd got hold of a gourd that he'd filled with water and now he set about doing his ablutions, with the careful frugality of a seasoned desert-dweller, a few drops for his hands, his forearms, his face, a few more for his ankles and feet. When he had finished he leaned in low on his haunches, arms outspread, to say his prayers.

It seemed shameful to watch him while he prayed. I took my cloak up and drew it over me against the lingering cold and went into the courtyard, where the tavern-keeper's daughter, Adah, a girl of fourteen or so, was preparing some porridge at the bit of fire there. She was a strange girl, as unblemished as her father was vile but also not quite present somehow, a bit simple perhaps. Sometimes her father would send her half-undressed to my room to bring me my meals or wine, with a conniving that chilled me.

"I never see you go out to the market like the other girls," I said to her. "Maybe your husband's there."

But she misunderstood.

"I don't have a husband," she said with a panicked look, then hurried off to bring her father his breakfast.

I was accustomed enough to biding my time in those days but the holy man had made me restless—simply that he was there, fired by a sense of purpose different from mine, or perhaps the waste that I saw then in his sort of devotion. I went out after I'd eaten and he was still sitting beneath his tree, the sun just rising above the houses behind him to cast his shadow all along the length of the square. Without quite knowing what I intended, I walked out to where he was.

I tossed a coin on the ground in front of him.

"For your breakfast," I said. But he didn't pick it up. Up close I saw he still had a dulled look, his eyes sunken, the skin sagging against his bones.

"Bread would be better," he said.

His voice was stronger than I would have imagined it, seeming to echo in the hollow places in him.

"With a coin you can buy bread."

"All the same."

There didn't seem any arrogance in this, only stubbornness—I thought perhaps it was part of his vow, to abjure any coinage, or that he was one of those who wouldn't touch coins on account of the images there. I bent to collect the thing and went at once into the market, where I bought a bit of stew that I brought back to him. He thanked me roughly and set into it with a barely controlled vehemence, his appetite clearly returned.

"I lent you my cloak," I said.

He didn't look up from his food.

"I recognized it."

And yet did not think to thank me. So it seemed I must wrestle him for my blessing.

"And you returned it. For which I'm grateful."

"It seemed so fine I thought you'd miss it."

"But you haven't returned the shawl you were given."

"It's less fine. I thought it would be less missed."

He put me in mind of those barefooted Greeks I'd seen as a boy in the squares of Ephesus, who lived on air and made it their job to poke fun at the least hint of pretension.

He had finished his food.

"Should I send another bowl?" I said.

"If you like."

I paid a boy to bring out more stew, then moved on through the market. En Melakh was one of the towns that the madman Cassius had razed when he was in Syria, for failing to pay him tribute, and it had been rebuilt in crude Greek style with an open market just inside the gates. There wasn't much of interest to be had in it—a bit of coloured wool from the coast, a few trinkets and hair combs, some dried meat and fruits. At the back, where the concessions gave way to the narrow alleys of a bazaar, an old woman ran a shop out of her house that I'd noticed people hurrying from carrying secret parcels wrapped in sackcloth: potions and charms. A carved figurine of three wise men wrapped in fish skins stood in a niche above the woman's lintel. These were our God-fearing Jews, I thought, hedging their bets, worshipping icons of old men dressed up as fish.

As I was coming out of the far end of the market there was a commotion near the town gates. Some sort of detachment was coming into town—Romans, I thought at first, but then I recognized the standards of Herod Antipas. I made my way through the gawkers who had already lined the street to get a better view. They were a bit of a rabble, it seemed, around a dozen in all, arranged in rough formation around their captain, a bearded colossus who was the only rider. It took me a moment to see what it was that had caused such a stir: they had a prisoner in tow. He was being pulled along, virtually dragged, by a rope attached to the captain's saddle, though because of the soldiers and the crowd I could not get a good view of him. Then a gap opened up and I saw his face and was stopped dead, for though he was badly beaten I recognized him at once as my contact.

I did not know how to react. The truth was that nothing in my experience had prepared me for a situation of this sort, so that it seemed as if what had been merely trifling until then, playing a part, had become suddenly real. I moved to the back of the crowd to be out of the soldiers' path, afraid some look or glance from the man might give me away. But he looked too far ruined for that. Both eyes were swelled to slits from whatever beatings he had got; one of his ears had been cut away, but crudely, so that there were still ragged bits of flesh left hanging, encrusted black with flies and dried blood. As he went past he stumbled and fell and did not get up again, so that he ended by being hauled along the street on his backside while one of the town dogs ran barking half-crazed around him and the townspeople laughed, no doubt taking him for a simple criminal.

His name was Ezekias. He was not much more than a boy, a messenger for the court in Tiberias who had been scouted out because of his position and then recruited during a visit to Jerusalem for one of the feasts. My only dealings with him had been a short encounter in the city at the time of his recruitment and a further one in Jericho some months later—he had struck me then as young, loyal, earnest, and entirely unaware of the danger he had entered into. It seemed more and more we relied on this sort, who could be easily replaced; indeed, I myself had not been so different when I had joined.

His use to us had been that he was often able to bring us news from the Macherus fortress, which was second only to Masada in impregnability, and with it formed the backbone of the southern defences of the Palestinian territories. We had been working to infiltrate the place for some time, in which task we had some reason to feel hope since, unlike at many of the other outposts, there was a large contingent of Jews among the company there. But there were also many Edomites, whose lands lay nearby and from whom Antipas's father had descended, and who therefore could not be trusted. The Edomites held all the positions of command, and found every means of keeping the Jews subordinate. Yet there were one or two Jews who by dint of sheer perseverance and faultless service had got ahead, and these were the ones to whom we had directed ourselves and so gained a foothold.

The soldiers had come to a stop in the middle of the square. There were a couple of hitching stones there, near the well; they tied the captain's horse to one and bound Ezekias to the other with the rope he'd been dragged by, haphazardly, as if he were a sheaf of wheat they were binding. After they'd drawn up their own fill from the well, they watered the horse but left Ezekias untended, not so much out of malice, it seemed, but more as if he were something they'd lost interest in, in the oafish way of boys who tired of some creature they'd caught. Ezekias, however, seemed aware neither that water was near nor that he was being denied it, his head drooped and his body straining against the rope that bound him so that it seemed the only thing that held him upright.

After the days of cloud and dust the clear sky now seemed an assault, the sun already beating down like a hammer. I stood there in the street but could not form a plan, felt only a general outrage as if some trick had been played on me. I could not know what Ezekias's capture meant or who else had been implicated by it; I reasoned the soldiers knew nothing of our meeting or they would not have come into town so openly, but even that wasn't certain. They had moved off now towards the tavern where I was staying, the tavern-keeper hurrying out to greet them, putting on his most servile of appearances, smiling and bowing and scraping and promising wine and meat, which I myself had hardly seen a trace of in my days there; and meanwhile the townspeople were still lingering uncertainly about the square, in the hope, perhaps, of some sort of violence.

I looked to Ezekias again and thought, He must be killed, for his own sake and for the sake of those he might name, when the king's men in Tiberias put their wits to his torture. Then once the idea had entered my head, there was no putting it out, because of its logic. All of us had heard the stories of those who'd been taken and the things that were done to them, and how sometimes, for instance, to make them name their accomplices, their children or wives were brought before them and their fingers severed one by one or their eyes gouged out. So it was not simply a matter of sparing Ezekias—my own life stood at risk if I did nothing, for surely I would be among the first he would give up, if he had not already done so.

I had a dagger in my room that I always carried among my things. In all the time since my recruitment I had never had cause to use it; it seemed a great irony to me that its first victim would now be a member of my own cause. Thus, even as it grew clear that I must attempt the thing, it seemed a sort of joke, not the least part of which was that I would need to find the courage to slit my own throat if I was caught, or I would merely have put myself in the place of Ezekias. So I stood there in the street and did not know how to begin, and the sun grew hotter and the flies continued to cluster around Ezekias's bloodied face. Twenty paces from him the holy man still sat beneath his tree—next to Ezekias he seemed diminished somehow, though I saw how he had watched the soldiers' progress closely.

The company had been too large to fit in the tavern-keeper's courtyard so he'd had his sons set up awnings in front of the porch and lay out carpets there. When the group had finally settled itself he sent Adah out, arms bared, to serve the wine, with the predictable result that the soldiers, lethargic and dull until then, grew suddenly animated, slipping their hands on poor Adah's backside as she passed and laughing at her frightened retreat from them. While their attention was thus diverted I made my way past them in order to get to my room. Only the tavern-keeper showed any particular awareness of me as I went in, catching my eye dismissively as if to say he was sorry, he had more important matters than me to attend to at the moment.

I got the knife from my things. I had a scabbard for it but had never been in the habit of wearing it. Strapping it on now I felt like a child dressing up for a game of assassin. It made a bulge beneath my cloak when I had it in place that I imagined would make my intentions plain to anyone who laid eyes on me.

I went through my sack then, since I did not think I would be returning to my room. But other than a bit of cheese and stale bread from the trip down from Jerusalem there were only some underthings and a dirtied shirt, which I left there.

Stepping out to the porch from the courtyard, I ran full into Adah as she was hurrying in. The force of the collision sent the jug she was carrying smashing against the ground and sent Adah herself sprawling backwards practically into the laps of the soldiers, who at once were in an uproar, half-drunk by now and pleased beyond reckoning at the mishap.

"I'm sorry," Adah stammered, "I'm sorry," scrambling to collect up the broken jug before fleeing back into the courtyard.

The soldiers, meanwhile, had now decided that they must make me their good friend and pulled me down to join them at their libations, with that brutal jocularity soldiers had, that you knew could turn against you at the slightest whim. I was worried they would ask me my business—I had put it out to the tavern-keeper that I was expecting some traders from Nabatea—and would catch me out in some mistake, since I did not know very well the movements of the traders in those parts. But they did not seem to have much interest in anything outside their own crude humour. I saw now that there wasn't a Jew among them—they were mainly Syrians, it seemed, except for the captain, who was clearly an Edomite.

Because my cloak had fallen open one of the soldiers noticed my dagger, which had a jewelled handle. He was one of the younger ones, whose provenance I could not make out, since he spoke neither Aramaic nor even Greek very well. Without asking my leave he pulled the knife from its sheath and then with a grin made as if to stab me with it, the whole company bursting into laughter when I started back. He then pulled out his own knife, which had a curved blade and a handle of tooled leather, and offered it in exchange. I was afraid this was some custom of his that I would be forced to honour.

"It was my father's," I said of my own, which was the truth and which seemed to satisfy him, since he returned the thing to me.

With each moment I sat there, it seemed increasingly far-fetched that I should carry my plan through; and indeed there was that part of me that was happy I had been compelled to stop there. The thing was simple enough—I lacked the courage. Or perhaps for a moment I did not see the point, of Ezekias's death or my own, the useless pile of bones we would amount to.

I asked as casually as I could manage after their prisoner.

"We always carry a Jew to draw off the dogs," the captain said, his first words to me.

The soldiers at once broke into laughter, not bothering to restrain themselves in the least on my account, so that I felt sickened to have sat down amongst them. I started to rise but one of them held me back, clapping an aggressive arm around me, until I thought I must draw my dagger then and there. In the meanwhile, however, the captain's attention had been drawn to the square. I looked out to see that a small crowd had gathered there near Ezekias—it seemed the holy man, while the soldiers had been busy with me, had gone to the well to get a scoop of water to bring over to him, and people had gathered around now to see if he would get away with the thing.

The captain had one of his men out there in an instant, who snatched the scoop away and sent the water spilling, in the process practically knocking the holy man over. Some of the crowd jeered him at that, for it was one thing to torture a prisoner but another to slight a Jewish holy man; and then someone, it wasn't clear who, threw a stone at him. The soldier drew his cutlass then and it seemed for a moment that there would be a riot, which however would have suited me very well. But the captain at once roused his men and hurried them out into the square, where they stood with their hands on their swords until the crowd had backed off.

In all this I had quietly made my way back to the edge of the market, still awaiting a chance if one should present itself. But in a moment it grew clear that my plan had been truly foiled now, for the captain had apparently had enough of the place and had begun rounding up his men to resume their march. He sent one of the soldiers back to pay the tavern-keeper, lest he lodge a complaint and the Romans bar Antipas from their roads; some of the others prepared his horse. But when they went to loose Ezekias from his post, he simply slumped to the ground and did not move.

The captain squatted down to him and held a hand out to feel for his breath. After a moment he stood and kicked the slumped body over angrily, then for good measure pulled out his cutlass and stuck it into Ezekias's side. A trickle of blood seeped up through the wound.

"Leave him," the captain said, and abandoned him there by the hitching post.

The captain wasted no time now in taking up his march again, and in a matter of minutes he and his men were already out the gates. I stood there in the square and could not believe the way the thing had ended, nor could I say if it showed the Lord's mercy or his spite.

The crowd around Ezekias had grown again but no one dared to touch him, fearing who knew what defilement. There were mumbles of confusion, then the question of what should be done with the body; I cut off debate by undertaking to look after it. Of the entire crowd the only one who came forward to offer to help was the holy man.

"I can manage it," I said, given his state. But he had already moved to take Ezekias's feet.

We carried him out through the gates. The holy man proved surprisingly agile, keeping up a brisk pace without complaint. We were silent until we were a little way beyond the town, but then we needed to discuss how best the body could be disposed of. It would take a day's work to dig a hole in the rock-hard earth outside the town there. But I could not bear the thought of simply burying Ezekias beneath a pile of stones like a common criminal.

"There are some caves in the hills," the holy man said. "Not far."

But it was two miles or more of barren plain before the hills began, and the sun still climbing.

"You'll be all right?" I said.

"If not, there are caves enough for all of us."

It was past mid-morning before we reached the hills. The sun was relentless; beneath it the landscape looked utterly transformed from the previous days, stark and deathly and unreal. Ezekias's body was sending up a terrible stink—from the slit in his side, mainly, though it seemed also that he had soiled himself at some point.

It took all our effort to make our way up the scree of the first hills. But the holy man knew his way around, leading us to a small promontory beneath which were sheltered a few natural caves. A bit of careful manoeuvring got us down to one of them and we set Ezekias's body inside. The holy man pulled a waterskin from under his shirt then, and wetting his sleeve he wiped some of the grime and blood from Ezekias's face. It was only now that I allowed myself to truly look at it, so mangled, though it had once been quite handsome. The jaw looked broken, perhaps the nose as well; the hair was matted with blood where his ear had been severed. But under the holy man's ministrations the face began to look human again.

"You knew him?" the holy man said.

"No." But it bothered me to lie to him, nor did he seem to believe me.

When we had laid the body out and wrapped my cloak around it as a shroud, we set about closing up the mouth of the cave, heaping rubble down from the slope above it and scrounging what rocks we could from the hillside. The work took an hour or more, in a heat that was like a wall bearing down on us. Afterwards we sat on the ledge that came out from the cave and drank what remained of the holy man's water. From where we sat we had a view of the Jordan plain, with the palms of Jericho to the north and the intimation of the Salt Sea to the southeast. En Melakh, directly ahead of us, looked almost indistinguishable from the rubbled plain it rose out of—it was a town that defied logic, sitting nearly undefended like that at the frontier, with its houses of unbaked mud that a few good rains would wash to nothing. If it were ever abandoned, the desert would have erased every trace of it inside of a year.

"Will you spend the night in the town again?" I said.

"I think I'll go on to Jericho."

We sat talking, in the tired, laconic way that came of our fatigue and of the gravity of the task we had shared. His name was Yehoshua; when I asked him what had brought him to En Melakh, he told me, with surprising frankness, that he had been an acolyte of the prophet Yohanan, whose camp had been nearby. It was not two months then since Yohanan had been arrested, by Herod Antipas, though everyone knew it was the Romans who had put him up to it.

"We heard Yohanan's acolytes had been killed," I said.

"Not all of them." Though he wouldn't look at me when he said this.

Things were clearer now: he had shaved his head to hide from the soldiers, since it was a mark of Yohanan and his men that they went unshorn. So we were both of us outlaws, it seemed, joined in that way if no other. In fact our movement had followed Yohanan's arrest closely, to see if we could find the way to turn his supporters to us; but in the end we had found them too leaderless and fanatical and dispersed. In my own view the Romans had been wrong to see in Yohanan a political threat, for all the numbers he drew—rather he had been a boon to them, by diverting to mysticism those who might otherwise have put their energies to burning Roman garrisons.

With the mention of Yohanan, Yehoshua's mood had turned—it weighed on him, as I guessed, to have deserted him. He seemed tired to me, and embittered, like someone at the end of a road.

"If you left him it was to save your life," I said, "so that you might put it to good use." But the words sounded empty—I was not some wise man to tell him such a thing, nor even, it seemed, more certain of myself.

He didn't take offence, however, but made light of the thing, saying, "He's better off than the man in the cave, at least."

It was Yehoshua, before we set out, who said a prayer for poor Ezekias, asking the Lord to look to him. Then, where the hills gave way to the chalky plain again, we took our leave of each other. He handed me the shawl he'd been given in En Melakh, and which he'd been using as his headgear, and asked me if I might return it to its owner. I could not say why it so moved me that he should make this request of me.

"I'll find her," I said.

I watched him as he melted into the barrens, not imagining I should see him again but feeling still bound to him, because he had shared with me the contamination of Ezekias's death. I thought of the story of the priest who saw a dying man by the road and passed him by, for fear of uncleanness—at least that was not the school that Yohanan had raised him in. It was to prepare God's way that Yohanan taught, as I'd heard it, though his acolyte seemed to have lost his own. No doubt his courage had failed when the soldiers had come and he'd run; yet I could not say I would not have done the same.

He had already disappeared in the haze off the desert when I turned back towards En Melakh. A wind had come up by then and the dust was rising. By the time I reached the town it had blocked the sun again.

The purge that followed the discovery of our infiltration at Macherus was a great setback to us and indeed seemed to threaten to undermine the whole of our movement. At the fort itself it was not only our leaders who were discovered but also their handful of recruits, all of them summarily executed, so that our strength there was wiped out. But by far the greater blow to us was that the Romans and the Herods were quick to use the thing to their own ends, joining forces to rid themselves of anyone who had ever been the least trouble to them, and in the process ferreting out by chance many of our own people. In Jerusalem there was such a stink from the rotting corpses outside the Gennath Gate that the members of the council, as I heard it, sent a protest to the emperor, no doubt imagining that they had thus stood strong against our Roman oppressors and showed the dignity of the Jews.

I myself had gone quietly back to Jerusalem after Ezekias's death but did not dare to speak to anyone, for fear I was being watched. Then a few days after my return, I learned that the teacher in the city I had reported to had been arrested. I did not waste any time then but at once packed away all the goods I had in my shop and then collected what money remained from my inheritance and left the city. For a number of days I took refuge with a cousin I had at Joppa, though I told him nothing, of course, of my situation. But Roman battalions often passed through the town on their way from Caesarea Maritima up the coast, which the Romans had set up as their capital, so I grew afraid of bringing him into risk and moved on.

In the end I crossed the northern frontier and went on to Tyre, having heard we had a group there. I had passed through Tyre with my father several times as a child and had thought it a great city, with its grand causeway and port and its many temples. But it now seemed a vulgar and lawless place, full of beggars and scoundrels. It took me many days to track down our group, since there was much suspicion and fear even there at the time, and then what I found were half a dozen aging rebels who still hearkened back to Yihuda the Galilean and who had been so long absent from our country as to have lost all sense of the realities facing us. As a result, my relations with them were strained from the start. As others of our party began to filter into the city with more news of the reprisals against us, the members of the Tyrian group grew puffed up with the delusion that the leadership of the movement would now somehow come to rest with them. So the rest of us began to avoid them out of fear they would compromise us in some way, with the Roman authorities or with our own leadership. For my part, since I had heard of no warrant against me in Jerusalem, I began to think seriously of leaving the city, though I knew also that a few of those close to me had been arrested and shipped off into slavery.

Through all this I had hardly given another thought to Yehoshua. But one day after I'd been in the city a matter of months I came across a gathering of some twenty or so near the city gates and there he stood addressing it, though changed in appearance now, fair and well-groomed and well-fed so that he seemed almost a Greek, and changed, too, in his manner, with an air of authority I had not seen in him at En Melakh. Nonetheless he did not seem to be making much headway with the crowd, who were badgering him because he had slighted the Tyrian gods.

"You should keep your ideas for the Jews," someone said to him.

"Is that what your teachers tell you? That there's a truth for Tyrians and another for Jews?"

"You say so yourselves!"

Soon enough the crowd broke up. A few rough-looking attendants who had been hovering near him in stony silence huddled around him now speaking in muted Aramaic. But when I approached him his eye went to me at once.

"I saw you in the crowd," he said. "I was happy to see a friend in it."

It was getting on to dark and so I invited him and his men to take their supper with me at the inn where I was staying near the port, run by an old Jew sympathetic to our cause. The whole way there he grilled me in a fairly lively way on the customs of the city, in Greek, leaving his colleagues, who obviously spoke no Greek and in fact looked like the roughest sort of hirelings, entirely out of the conversation. At the time this did not strike me as remarkable, but later I saw how he sometimes consulted them for the smallest things, so that my first impression of them as mere bodyguards or servants seemed mistaken.

Then at one point, taking me by surprise, he said, "I heard the arrest of that man at En Melakh was because of a plot."

"Ah," I said, and didn't pursue the matter. But in this way he made clear to me that he'd guessed the reason for my presence there in Tyre.

At supper we switched to Aramaic, though his men—there were three of them, Yaqob and Yohanan and then the apparent leader, Shimon, whom Yehoshua, however, no doubt because of his hulking frame, called Kephas, the Rock—mainly kept up their brooding silence. From their accents I'd gathered they were Galileans, which went some way towards explaining their manner, since that race was not known for wasting its words. They addressed their master by the shortened Yeshua, which made him seem common. But later I learned that that had been his given name and it was only the prophet Yohanan who had named him more formally, when he had purified him, as was his practice.

Though he had been Yohanan's acolyte, his notions did not seem to accord much with what I knew of Yohanan's. Yohanan had preached the imminent end of days, like the desert cults; but Yeshua did not seem in such a hurry. As he put it, Yohanan was right to make us feel each day was our last, so we might be woken up to our mortality. But in so saying he showed he didn't agree with him. For his own part, he seemed to think more in the manner of a Greek than a Jew, finding recourse for his arguments in logic rather than scripture; thus I wasn't surprised to learn that as a child he had lived in Alexandria.

I couldn't quite gather what it was that had brought him to Tyre and wondered if the reason wasn't so different from my own, having heard that the matter of Yohanan had not yet been settled. But it wasn't entirely unknown for Jews to proselytize in that region, so he might merely have come in search of converts. Also, as I learned, he had been there only a matter of weeks, and planned to return the following day to Kefar Nahum in Galilee, where it seemed he was now based. I made some comment half in jest then of how I would gladly be rid of Tyre as well, and he said I was welcome to travel with him if I wished. But I could not tell if the invitation was made casually or in earnest.

I asked the group if they wanted to put up at the inn for the night. But Kephas, who was clearly wary of me, said, "We sleep in the open. We have no money with us."

This seemed a point of honour with him. I remembered Yeshua's rejection of the coin I had offered in En Melakh.

"Then how do you eat?"

"The Lord provides," Kephas said.

I was tempted to ask if it was the Lord who was paying for his supper, but said only, "You will stay as my guests, of course," so they could not refuse me.

Our meeting might have ended there with Yeshua and me going our separate ways the next day if not for an occurrence later that evening that considerably sharpened my interest in him. A Phoenician woman from the countryside appeared at the inn in search of him, having somehow managed to track him down; and she had along with her a daughter whom she held literally leashed to her by a cord tied around the girl's waist and who looked like some wild animal she had captured, dirtied and dishevelled, her face covered in scratches and scabs. The girl's hands were bound in rags that she was constantly gnawing at to free herself, all the while emitting long howls and moans, eerie and guttural, that seemed to border on speech without quite becoming it.

I had stayed down in the parlour after supper and was one of the first to speak to the woman when she showed up in the courtyard. She said word of Yeshua's power had reached her after he had passed through a village near hers the previous day and cured a child there, and she had brought her own daughter in the hope he might cure her as well. The rags, she said, were to keep the girl, who had several times tried to take her own life, from doing any further injury to herself.

I was surprised to learn that Yeshua enjoyed this renown as a healer. A boy was sent up to his room to fetch him and a few minutes later he appeared in the courtyard with his men. A curious and almost comic thing happened then: at the sight of Kephas, the girl, who despite her rantings had appeared relatively harmless until that moment, suddenly lunged at the poor man and began hitting at him with her rag-covered fists. It took both Yaqob and Yohanan to pull her off him.

The mother, by this point, was practically prostrate with apology.

"Master, please," she said, nearly incoherent, "master."

Yeshua had wisely been holding himself back a bit from the fray. But now he came forward to put a hand on the girl's forehead. The gesture seemed to calm her.

"Bring her into the sitting room," he said.

His men sat her on a bench in the parlour. She was still mumbling in her indecipherable speech but seemed to have retreated into herself, staring out glassy-eyed as if entirely unaware of us or her surroundings. At Yeshua's instructions the servant boy brought a basin of water and a cloth, and Yeshua proceeded to dab at the grime on the girl's face and at the streaks of dried blood from her scratches. I remembered how he had tended to Ezekias in this way, how he had made him seem human again; and somehow he managed to work this same effect now with the girl. From out of that demonic visage of grime and blood there emerged suddenly a child, an innocent. He ran his cloth over her hair as well, bringing it back to rough order; then he began to unwrap her hands. All the while the girl grew increasingly placid, until her ramblings had died down to a whisper.

"Bring her something to eat," Yeshua said, after he had her hands free, and when a bowl of soup was brought out she set into it like someone famished.

From a pouch on his belt Yeshua pulled out some bits of herb and told the girl's mother to make a brew from it to help calm the girl if she should suffer another attack.

"Is it a demon, master?" the woman asked.

"The girl is pregnant. When you find who's responsible, you'll have your demon."

The woman was instantly silenced by this, as were we all—the girl was no more than nine or ten. But it was immediately clear that Yeshua was right, both from the woman's guilty silence and from the small bulge in the girl's dress that grew obvious now that our attention had been drawn to it.

The girl was quietly licking her bowl to get the dregs of the soup.

"Take her home and look after her," Yeshua said.

There had been nothing miraculous in any of this, yet the whole incident affected me deeply. The vision of that young girl's face, called back, it seemed, from some precipice as if indeed by a kind of magic, had seared itself into my mind. I had seen instances of this kind of possession before, if that was what it could be called, and also "cures" of varying degrees of success (on more than one occasion staged, I was sure, to win over a credulous audience). But while usually these cases were handled with all manner of obfuscation and subterfuge, with chants and potions and charms or countless animal sacrifices that usually ended up on the doctor's supper table without any appreciable benefit to the patient, Yeshua had held true throughout to the plainest and simplest of observations and gestures, and in so doing had brought about an improvement that, if not permanent, had at least the great virtue of being honest. That he had taken the trouble of examining the girl's condition from the point of view of physical causes already set him apart from the usual run of physicians and healers, who leapt at once to the mystical in order to cover their own lack of understanding.

Afterwards I held Yeshua back on the pretext of speaking to him of his education, which he told me he'd received during his time in Alexandria. But in fact a notion had taken hold of me: I had begun to think of his earlier offer to join him. I reasoned to myself that he would provide cover for my return to our own territories, even if at bottom he wasn't much less a fugitive than I was; and also that in Galilee I could move freely, being unknown there. I had it in mind, or so I said to myself, that I might look to building our movement there, since as far as I knew we had no strength in the region. But the truth was simply that I was drawn to Yeshua. I had seen something in him, the mark of a leader, and was loath to let him slip from me.

We sat talking there for an hour or more, long after his men had returned to their room. As he presented himself, it seemed he was merely an itinerant teacher of the sort that was common enough even in Judea, with a little following there in the Galilee that supported him. Yet he did not much resemble the teachers I had known when I'd studied in Jerusalem, whose minds were like windowless rooms circumscribed on every side by the law, while Yeshua's was curious and quick. The innkeeper had joined us and brought wine, which Yeshua did not abstain from, and soon we were drawn into political arguments and to talk of the emperor Tiberius and his strange retreat to the isle of Capri, where it was said he indulged every lust and gave no thought to the affairs of state. The innkeeper saw hopes for our independence in this, saying surely his house must crumble if he did not look to it. But Yeshua, cutting to the heart of the matter, said, "I'm sure he has servants enough to tend to his house if he doesn't," which indeed proved prescient, for it wasn't long afterwards that we began to hear how Sejanus had wormed his way into power, managing things with greater brutality and rigour than ever Tiberius had.

At one point Yeshua asked after my own schooling and I was quick to mention Ephesus, as if I was anxious not to seem to him some mere Pharisee, who had read nothing outside of the scriptures.

"So we're both Greeks, then," he said to me, joking. Yet the truth was that even in Ephesus my father had sent me only to the Jews of our own quarter, since he himself had been raised in the Negeb and was hardly worldly. What larger education I had got then had come mainly from scrounging the occasional text from the market and from wandering the streets, and it had always seemed to me that our little quarter was like some island we lived on, the tiny realm of the familiar, hemmed in on every side by the great, dark swell of the unknown.

I asked him if he had ever seen Ephesus and he said once, in passing, before he had joined Yohanan.

"It seemed to me there were many wonders there," he said.

But in fact it still pained me to speak of the place since my parents' death there.

"Surely there were more in Alexandria."

He laughed at that.

"Maybe so. But not every wonder is a boon."

Before we retired I finally put it to him that I might take up his offer to share the road. I was afraid he might surmise I was merely using him for my own ends and take offence. But if he was troubled by the notion of travelling with someone he had by now surely gathered to be a rebel, he did not show it.

"Of course you're welcome with us, as I told you," he said, and seemed sincere in this.

So it was set that I would leave with him and his men the following day. I asked the innkeeper to pass on word to my Tyrian colleagues that I had gone, but I did not imagine that I would be missed.

We set out the next morning not long after dawn, travelling cross country towards the frontier at Gush Halav, though it meant a hard trek over the mountains. There was only the odd village along the road, rough assemblages of stone shacks with perhaps some pasture nearby or some rocky patches of field carved out of the forest; the rest was dark cypress woods for as far as the eye could see, forbidding and without interest. Despite the sun the air was cool because of the hills and because of a wind that blew against us the entire day, so that it seemed the distance we travelled was doubled and the slope we rose against twice as steep. As the road was deserted except for the occasional villager who tried to sell us some bit of handiwork or food, we were left to our own company, which however suited me well.

Yeshua, no doubt sensing the uneasiness of his men at having me included among them, seemed therefore to throw us together, for much of the journey walking some paces ahead of us and out of hearing so that we were forced to make our way with one another. For their part, his men, after the first awkwardness, made a genuine effort to integrate me into their party, and regaled me with stories—some of them, however, utterly fantastical—of the great works that Yeshua had already wrought in Galilee. (Later, of course, I would hear them recount in these same exaggerated tones the story of Yeshua's treatment of the young girl in Tyre.) Even Kephas, in the end, maintained the strictest civility, passing his flask first to me whenever we stopped to drink and in the evening, when we set up camp at the side of the road, carefully portioning out the bits of food he had in his pack—I, assuming we would be having our supper in Gush Halav, had neither brought my own provisions nor purchased any along the way—so that everything was perfectly equitable.

In amidst the tales Yeshua's men passed on to me I was able to pick out that Yeshua had come to Kefar Nahum early that spring, which would have been not long after we'd met in En Melakh. The men were very mysterious about how he had ended up there and how they had come to be his followers, saying only that he had called them, giving to the words that special weight with which converts invested their particular terminology. I thought perhaps he had chosen the place for the refuge offered by the hills in the area should he need to flee, since as far as I knew it was otherwise without distinctions or charms. But it came out he had family nearby in Notzerah, a town just outside of Sepphoris, the former Galilean capital. I was surprised when his men said they had never met with any of his family; it appeared, however, that they had little to do with Yeshua's past, nor indeed did they seem curious of it.

We crossed the frontier at Gush Halav not long after dawn the following day, getting through without incident. I immediately felt my blood quicken at stepping back onto native soil. It was just coming on to the end of the summer and the grape harvest was in progress, the vineyards already alive with workers and the air rife with the sweet, half-fermented smell of must. After the gloomy woods that had lined the road to Gush Halav, it was a relief to see open fields again and signs of human presence. I had never been in that part of the country before or indeed spent more than a matter of days in the Galilee and so was surprised at the level of cultivation, not only in the valleys but even on the hilltops, which were covered in olive groves. I imagined it was the Jews who had so tamed the place, in the generations since the Maccabees had won it back for us, though many of the olive trees we passed looked so gnarled and old they might have gone back to the ancient Canaanites.

It seemed that Yeshua and his men livened up as well when we crossed the frontier, perhaps at the prospect of returning home. But it turned out there was more to it than that—they were recognized here. In each village we passed there was someone who knew them, and came quietly offering homage; in one town, where we stopped for our midday rest, there seemed a whole little colony of Yeshua's followers, who came slowly filtering in to pay their respects at the house where we'd put up. Yeshua appeared different among them than he had among the crowd in Tyre, more at ease, though it wasn't the elders or even the men of standing who came to see him but the merest peasants and the like.

It was twilight by the time we reached Kefar Nahum. The town lay along the Damascus road and the caravansary outside the walls gave off the noise and stench of animals and men. But the town itself had a dulled, neglected air. Just outside the gates we found a little crowd who had heard of Yeshua's approach and had come to await him, most with some particular ailment they wished him to minister to. For the better part of an hour, until it grew too dark to see, Yeshua tended to those gathered. There was one boy, writhing in pain, who'd been brought to him with a broken shin bone, the fractured end of it protruding through the skin; Yeshua, with a few smooth motions, massaged the bone back into place, so that with a splint affixed the boy was practically able to leave on his own two feet. Surely it was more than simple learning that Yeshua brought to this work; he had a gift. You saw it in the concentration that came over him like a possession, the way every fibre in him seemed devoted to the task at hand.

Afterwards we made our way to Kephas's house, where Yeshua stayed. It was a small compound just off the main street, dank and cramped and swarming with animals and children. There we had our supper, which was ample enough, and then Yaqob and Yohanan—who were brothers, it turned out, a point no one had mentioned before—returned to their own home. Kephas invited me to sleep on his roof, which hardly seemed fit to hold my weight. But in fact the late summer heat sent several of the children and a couple of the men of the household up there as well, though not Yeshua, who apparently had his own little closet to sleep in at a back corner of the compound.

One of those who came up to the roof was Kephas's brother Andreas, who had taken a strange liking to me at supper, leaving his own place to come sit at my feet like a dog in search of a scrap. It had taken me a moment to realize he was simple—as I later learned, he had suffered some accident as a child. The others seemed uncomfortable when he came to me but did not really try to stop him. So for the rest of the evening he stayed close by, and then that night came up to the roof, setting his mat close to mine and giving me a huge child's grin. The truth was I took comfort in his attachment to me—it was such a guileless thing, and so undemanding, that it made me feel welcome there, among strangers though I was, in a way that the mere protocols of hospitality could never have done.

It was not until the following morning, when I awoke there on Kephas's rooftop, that I had a chance for a proper view of Kefar Nahum and its situation. My impulse then was to revise my original harsh judgement at Yeshua's choosing it as his base. The town itself—a city, Yeshua's men had called it, though it had the most makeshift of walls and no battlements of any sort—did not amount to much, just a straggle of compounds similar to Kephas's stretching along its few streets, all in the coarse black stone of the area and each looking as forbidding and cramped as the next; and then to the south the harbour, which was large enough but built with a confusing disarray of jetties and quays and crammed with every sort of ramshackle craft. It was the prospect, however, that struck me, the view out over the whole of the Sea of Kinneret, which seen from there—unlike from Tiberias, where it seemed merely a backdrop laid out for the king's amusement—appeared truly to merit the name of sea, not from its size, perhaps, but from the sense of being in some way on a distant shore. Jerusalem felt very far from here, in another world; Rome, non-existent. Of course, all this was perhaps no more than the feeling one often got in the provinces, the illusory sense that nothing beyond the immediate was important or real.

I was surprised, however, to make out just a couple of miles east of town what looked like a military camp, with Roman eagles flying. I had not heard of the place and wondered how it had come to be there, and that Antipas allowed it. Since the household had not yet come fully to life, I took the chance to slip away and make my way out to it, imagining I might learn something of use that I could then bring back to Jerusalem to show my superiors I had not been idle.

The camp lay right at the Jordan, which fed into the lake there and formed the frontier of Herod Philip's territory. It looked large enough to house perhaps a hundred men, and stood watch over a sizeable customs house that controlled the border crossing. A sleepy-eyed guard, a young Cilician, told me the Romans had set the place up a number of years before to deal with the brigands in the hills—freedom fighters, I took him to mean, though it was true that many of them were no better than thieves—after Antipas and Philip had shown themselves unable to. The so-called brigands had been more or less eradicated, but the camp had remained; no doubt the Romans were happy to use it to keep an eye on their client kings, and on the revenues coming in from the customs house. At the moment only a meagre twenty-five men were stationed there, commanded by a captain who was apparently quite well liked by the local population and who in fact had recently married a girl from Kefar Nahum.

I made my way back to Kephas's house. It was still not an hour past daybreak and so I was surprised to find a small crowd had already gathered in the narrow street outside his gate, imagining them to be supplicants for Yeshua's attentions. But there were no ill with them, nor indeed did they seem there for instruction, for there was a tension among them and an angry murmuring that died down only when I came near and they saw I was a stranger.

I asked one of them what had brought them there and he said bluntly, "They've killed the prophet Yohanan."

I was shocked. As we'd heard, even in Tyre, Yohanan had lately been taken down to the fortress at Macherus, to rot there, we assumed, until he was forgotten; but this was unexpected. There had been no trial, not even a charge—the Romans would at least have taken the trouble of that, though perhaps that was why they had left the job to Antipas. No doubt Antipas had assumed he might simply append Yohanan's execution to the recent spate of political ones, not reckoning how much greater was the affection Jews felt for their prophets than their insurrectionists.

The crowd continued to grow. I could see how he'd been loved even this far along the lake, many of those who came looking stricken as if one of their own family had died. At one point a wail of mourning started up, and slowly filled the street; but still Yeshua did not come out. I could not tell what the crowd wanted of him, simple condolence or something more—there was that peasant anger to them that I'd seen elsewhere, born of helplessness but more dangerous for that, if it found an object.

When Yeshua finally did emerge, however, he looked so naked in his own mourning, his robe torn and his forehead blackened with ash, that the crowd seemed instantly quelled. For a few minutes he talked, though without great conviction, I thought, of how Yohanan's death merely confirmed his greatness, invoking the usual scripture and the familiar stories of the rejected prophets. The speech appeared to have less the effect of reassuring the crowd than of bringing home to them their loss. Yet in this way the threat of violence that had been palpable moments before seemed to dissipate.

As he finished, there was a commotion at the far end of the street: a contingent of soldiers had arrived from the military camp. They'd clearly been roused in a hurry, given that there hadn't been any sign of activity when I'd been out there not a half-hour before. The captain—Ventidius, I'd learned his name was, after the famous general—left his men at the back of the crowd and made his way through it to Kephas's door. He was a man of forty perhaps, not young at any rate, and too old surely to be commanding such a forgotten outpost. But he had a natural dignity to him and carried authority, to judge by the ungrudging way the crowd let him through. He addressed himself at once to Yeshua, with an intensity and familiarity that surprised me.

"I assure you Rome had no hand in this," he said.

He seemed almost to believe this, though it couldn't have been true. Yohanan's only crime against Antipas had been to denounce his lusts, which in any event were well known.

To his credit now, Yeshua said only, "The Romans have many hands besides their own."

Whatever the case, it was obvious that Ventidius had been caught off guard, and also that he was angry not merely at having been left in the dark but at the actual outrage of Yohanan's death. Later I learned he was a God-fearer, as they called them, one of those sympathetic to the Jews.

He stood there awkwardly an instant, not able to look Yeshua in the eye, then faced the crowd and asked it to disperse. Everything had gone strangely quiet, and it seemed for a moment that things might turn again. At the foot of the street the soldiers stood by uneasily, seeming to hem the crowd in because of the narrowness of the space. But Yeshua, for his part, did nothing to relieve the tension, turning and retreating without another word back through Kephas's gate. A kind of panic seemed to go through the crowd then at being left suddenly leaderless. But finally this too passed and people began to drift away, until Ventidius gathered up his men and led them off without further ceremony.

In the end only a small group remained there in the street, huddled outside Kephas's gate. Seeing that the brothers Yaqob and Yohanan were part of it, I went over and Yohanan, the younger of the two and the more friendly, introduced me around to the rest of the group. The men were mainly fishermen and labourers, from the look of them; there were a few women as well, to whom I was introduced, however, with the same blunt lack of formality as to the men. I was amazed when Yohanan said that all these, too, were among those whom Yeshua had called to be his intimates, for it was clear at once that there was not a person of education or of standing among them. The whole group of them looked chastened and subdued with the news of Yohanan's death, and I sensed as well a measure of fear in them.

Soon Kephas came out. We followed him around the corner to the harbour and from there out through one of the town gates and onto the lakeshore. Yeshua was already there by the water, still in his torn robe; he had apparently slipped out of the house by a back way. The barest of greetings were exchanged, and then a couple of the women set about preparing a cooking fire, into which some fish were heaped with some onions and leeks. One of the women had brought bread; for water, Kephas filled a flask directly from the lake. When the meal was ready everyone sat in a circle right there on the stones and a little ritual of deferment was played out, the disciples first offering the food to Yeshua who in turn offered it back to them, so that in the end it was Kephas who broke the fast.

It was not until we had eaten that anyone broached the subject of Yohanan's death. Yaqob—I took it that he and his brother were thought the hotheads of the group, by the group's measure—was of the opinion that a protest should be lodged directly with the governor in Damascus, or with Caesar himself. But a few of the others felt rather that they should remain quiet for the time and perhaps even disband.

"Fools!" Yeshua said. "Haven't you learned anything from Yohanan's death? Don't you understand it's the same road we're on?"

Everyone was taken aback at this. There was an awkward silence and then someone timidly asked if he thought then that they should follow Yaqob's advice and protest to the governor.

"What's the governor to us, who wouldn't have been fit to touch Yohanan's sleeve? Try to think what I've taught you when you say things."

He was out of patience. It was clear Yohanan's death had unsettled him.

There was another long silence.

"Teacher," one of the men said, and you could see it was what they were all thinking, "will Herod come to arrest us now?"

Yeshua relented.

"No," he said, "no. We have no fight with Herod."

Not long afterwards the group broke up. Kephas and I were left alone with Yeshua on the beach.

"Are you so sure of Herod?" I said to him.

"We're nothing to him. You can see for yourself."

And it seemed true enough, seeing him there with his little band of peasants. Yet he talked like someone who would bow to no one.

Kephas was busy clearing away the remnants of our meal.

"You think I've surrounded myself with simpletons and cowards," Yeshua said to me, though it wasn't clear if Kephas had heard.

"It's not for me to judge."

"When you look at us, you probably imagine only how we would seem to your friends in Jerusalem. But in the end the people you're trying to save are these same ones you might look down on. And without them, who is left? Without them, what is the point?"

He said this although I hadn't spoken to him in anything but the most guarded terms of my work. Yet he appeared truly to believe what he was saying, though in my experience it had always seemed that the vast mass of men were expendable, and had little to redeem them.

Yaqob and Yohanan had brought a boat out from the harbour up near the shore where we were sitting, apparently setting out for a day's fishing despite their mourning. They called out for Kephas to join them.

"You're welcome to stay with us for a time if you wish," Yeshua said to me. But I couldn't tell if he meant this merely as an offer of refuge.

Kephas was still lingering nearby.

"I have affairs—" I started.

"Of course."

And yet I knew in that moment that I would stay. The truth was I had no other plan, nor could I bear the thought then of returning to Jerusalem to the fear and distrust I was certain to find there.

Only now did Kephas finally take his leave, giving his respects to Yeshua and me and then hiking up his tunic and wading out to the awaiting boat. In a matter of minutes the boat was already far out onto the lake and I could make out merely the dark speck of its hull amidst a dozen others. So I had thrown my lot in with fishermen, it seemed. But it appeared honest enough work, something to put against all the empty gestures and talk I had left behind in Jerusalem.

From the outset it was clear that I was not well accepted by the others in Yeshua's inner circle. My education marked me, and my accent; but chiefly it was my willingness to challenge

Yeshua's views, which Yeshua applauded, saying it kept his mind sharp for his critics, but which in the men of the group brought out a brooding discomfort and in the women a fairly open hostility. The women—there were several of them who hovered around Yeshua like the Greek furies, and whom I could hardly tell apart—were in fact not much more than girls, and were a source of considerable dissension, as I learned, within Yeshua's following. But because he treated them with a measure of parity with the men and suffered them to be among his intimates, they imagined themselves his protectors, and showed me an arrogance I would never have countenanced in them if not for Yeshua's sake. There was one of them, a plain thing thin as a reed who was the daughter of a fish merchant, who seemed to make it her sole work to resist any competing claim I might make to his attention, travelling several miles from her village every morning at the crack of dawn to make sure she was present the instant he rose from his bed. It did not always appear to me that Yeshua quite understood the effect he had on these women; otherwise he might have taken greater care to keep a distance from them, which, as it later fell out, would have saved him much grief.

Apart from Andreas, then, whose artless attachment to me even the women had been unable to undermine, only Yohanan showed me anything like friendliness. He had apparently taken to me on our trip in from Tyre, and his natural liveliness and curiosity made him see in me a window onto the world. He often asked me about my travels and about life outside the Galilee, the wonders I had seen and the different customs and beliefs; he was a bright young man, and the only handsome one of the lot, and I suspected that if Yeshua hadn't taken him in, he would have found a way to make a name for himself in Tiberias or Jerusalem. His father was a successful fisherman in the town, with one of the larger residences; and eventually, unable to bear any more the congestion at Kephas's house and the tension that my presence there seemed to arouse, I took up Yohanan's offer to repair to his, where I had a little canopy of my own off the courtyard and was left more or less to myself.

There was something else that set me apart from the rest of the group: I was one of the few who carried a purse. I was never certain how the original injunction against money had come to assert itself among them—with some of the group I was sure it was mere superstition, and predated Yeshua, since I'd heard there were still many in those parts who believed that demons lived in coins. But Yeshua, it appeared, had some program in mind. It was nothing so plain, say, as the simple eschewing of greed; it seemed rather a kind of surrender, a means of stripping away the usual barriers between people. Often enough we would arrive in a town with not a scrap of food with us and not a penny in our purse, and then somehow it would seem that exactly because we had nothing, what we needed would come to us, and a meal would be offered and a roof put over our heads.

As time went on it happened more and more, however, that we could not exist entirely outside the usual systems of exchange. For one thing, as Yeshua's popularity grew, a few of his wealthier patrons were forever urging donations on him, to help with the purchase of medicines or to distribute to the poor; and even before I came to them they had appointed one of their number, Matthaios, who worked at the customs house, to carry the common purse. Gradually, however, that role came somehow to devolve upon me, partly, it seemed, as Yeshua's way of showing the others that I could be trusted. The others appeared happy enough to let me have the thing—I was their scapegoat, bearing the taint of lucre so they needn't. In fact, not a little of the money that we took in came from the most dubious of sources, publicans and collaborationists and the like, people shunned by the local populace but openly welcomed by Yeshua, who neither refused their money nor asked them where it came from. If it had been taken from the poor, he said, then all the better that we should have the chance to return it to them; and if from the rich, then we would surely put it to better use than they would have themselves.

It seemed to me that Yeshua was often in danger of contradicting himself in this way, championing the poor in the morning, then sitting down to supper with the local tax collector at night. Coming from Judea, where we were in the habit of seeing every act as a political one, I was shocked at first by such vacillations. But many of Yeshua's notions, I came to learn, were not the sort that could be reduced to simple principles; rather they had to be felt, as it were, and lived out, so that it was only the experience of them that could bring you to understanding. In the beginning I often lacked the patience to follow him in this logic, particularly as regarded his talk of God's kingdom, a notion he had borrowed from Yohanan but had adapted to his own ends. He had developed many analogies and stories to explain the nature of this kingdom; yet each seemed as obscure as the next, nor was it clear if the place was in heaven or on earth, or if it had a governor or was ruled solely by God, the way the Zealots preached. The first time I heard him speak of the thing to his followers I imagined he might be a secret ally, and taught revolt, and only cloaked his message to escape arrest. But then in private it grew clear I'd been mistaken. As far as I could gather, his kingdom was of an entirely unpolitical nature, a philosophical rather than physical state, requiring no revolution. I complained to him that it seemed then a mere salve to make more bearable the yoke of an oppressor.

"You want to change things yet you're incapable of changing such a simple thing as your own mind," he said to me then.

And indeed there was that part of me that felt he was right in his assessment of me, and that it was the rigidity of my own notions that made it hard for me to follow his. For if the kingdom, in my way of reckoning things, was merely a sort of dream he had invented, yet he seemed to live in it; and I often had the sense with him that where I saw the world in shadow and grey, he saw it rich in colour.

Though not overly given to ritual like many of the cults, Yeshua had nonetheless established a routine with his followers that he stuck to fairly closely, perhaps because it provided a level of stability and order for what was otherwise a somewhat amorphous movement. Generally he met with his inner circle every morning at Kefar Nahum, except when his travels had taken him too far afield; and there we would take our meal together, either on the beach or in Kephas's house. Afterwards, if he did not go out on the lake with his men, he would take a small group of us and make his visits to his disciples in the surrounding towns, usually following the schedule of the rotating market days of the region. Given the terrain of the Galilee with its deep valleys and precipitous hills, so that sometimes a dozen ridges separated towns only a stone's throw from one another, it often amazed me the ground he covered and how far afield his followers were spread. Nonetheless, the Sea of Kinneret remained the heart of his ministry, and it was rare for him to travel further than Sennabris to the south or Cana to the west. I noticed that he avoided Tiberias and Sepphoris, the only cities of note in the region, though perhaps this was because of the cool reception he had had in Tyre. At any rate, Antipas had so Hellenized these cities and so packed them with foreigners that for the mass of Galileans they might as well have been in different countries; and indeed they were generally regarded as cursed, Tiberias because it had been built on the site of a burial ground and Sepphoris because for many years Jews had been all but banned from it, on account of the revolt there at the time that Antipas came to power.

Yeshua's usual practice when he arrived in a town was to go to the house of one of his disciples and share a bit of food or wine there while word of his presence was sent around to any other followers he might have in the place. When people began to gather he would tend first to any sick who had come, then settle in his host's courtyard to do his teaching or perhaps repair to some field outside of town. His methods were very informal—usually he simply sat in amongst his disciples and answered the queries they put to him, often turning the question back onto the questioner in the manner of the ancient Greek philosophers. Much of what he conveyed in this way was no more than what one heard in the assembly houses: follow the commandments; give alms to the poor; believe in the one true God. But he had a way of making these notions seem new again, and vital, while most teachers intoned them as if they were the remotest arcana of a forgotten era.

What truly struck me in these sessions, however, was how he did not condescend to his pupils, or consider anything above their understanding; and this amazed me, for when it came to the core of his teaching, and to those notions that were distinctive to him like that of the kingdom, it often seemed to me that not Hillel himself could have followed the nuance of his thought. Like the Pharisees he subscribed, or so it seemed, to the idea of resurrection, believing no god would have set us to suffer on this earth, where the wicked prospered and the just were punished, without the chance of a final reckoning. Yet he would not say it was the body that rose into the heavens at death, when clearly it went to the worms, nor would he say the soul, as the Greeks did, but rather that we must not think in such ways as life and death, or body and soul, as if one was distinct from the other; for in that way we would only come to value one at the other's expense, and live as gluttons and libertines, not thinking of death, or live as ascetics, and so miss our lives. For my part, I thought it coyness at first that he did not put the thing more clearly, or a sign that he himself had not worked it through. But over time I came to see a wisdom in his approach, and the folly of putting into words notions that by their very nature, like God himself, must exceed our understanding.

It was not surprising, however, that such views, which were easily twisted, should lead him into conflict with some of his counterparts, and indeed I soon learned that he had already amassed an impressive group of enemies. At Kefar Nahum, for instance, I had wondered from the start why he did not avail himself of the assembly house to meet with his followers, avoiding it even on the sabbath, when instead we met for our prayers on the beach; and it came out he had actually been barred from the place by the town's teacher, an old Sadducee named Gioras. No doubt Gioras had felt provoked by Yeshua's preaching resurrection, which was anathema to the Sadducees. But it was a different question that had brought them to public confrontation—it seemed Yeshua had treated a sick child on sabbath day and Gioras had accused him of breaking the sabbath, since the illness had apparently not been life-threatening.

The matter might have ended there except that Yeshua had insisted on confronting his accuser in the assembly house the following week. Instead of broaching the matter directly, he told the story of two teachers who were each visited on the sabbath by a man in extreme hunger. The first, believing the man who'd come would survive until the following day, sent him off, saying he could not break the sabbath by preparing food for him. That night the man died, but the teacher was deemed by the scholars and priests to have acted correctly, since he could not have foreseen the death. The second teacher, however, finding at his door a man who was clearly suffering, invited him in and made him a meal. But this one was deemed to have sinned, since he could not have been certain the man's hunger was life-threatening, and so was sentenced to death.

The story was such an obvious parody of Gioras's charge that Gioras had been outraged, and had rallied the other leaders in the town to have Yeshua banned from the assembly house. By the time of my own arrival, the town was polarized between Gioras and his camp and Yeshua and his, with the mass of people, however, letting caution guide them and giving open allegiance to neither. The story was the same throughout the region: in any given town there seemed always a handful among the leadership who truly despised Yeshua and worked actively for his downfall. All manner of accusation was levelled against him—that he encouraged the young to turn against their parents, that he was possessed of demons, even that he was not a Jew at all but a pagan trying to trick the people into following a foreign god. Because he had lived in Egypt, he was everywhere dogged by the charge of magic, on account of his cures; and because he would not hold his tongue but always spoke his mind, it seemed he had more than once come close to stirring violence. At Tsef, for instance, he had apparently intervened in a land dispute on the side of those whom the Galileans mistakenly called the Syrians, the descendants of the line that dated back to the Assyrian conquest and that had been forcibly converted under the Maccabees. A good deal of enmity still existed between this group and the Jews whose ancestors had come to the Galilee as colonists, as well as many disputes over property; that Yeshua had taken the Syrians' side had nearly got him stoned. Some said he had done this merely to increase his following among the group, which indeed had been the result, for there were many Syrians now who were among his fiercest supporters.

So Yeshua had gained a reputation as a rabble-rouser, though in his teachings he counselled disarming one's enemies with kindness and forgiving even those who flogged you, the way the Cynic philosophers did. I had at first discounted this type of statement as mere rhetoric or even a calculated sort of insolence, just as some of the Zealots, when they were arrested, would at once confess their crimes as a way of showing their contempt for their captors. Yet I had heard that early in his ministry there was a faction, led by one

Aram of Kinneret, that had split with him precisely over the issue of force. For my part, I had never quite been able to bring myself to broach this particular subject with him. I told myself it was simply that I did not wish to start down a road that must inevitably lead to a break between us should we disagree. But that was not quite the whole of the matter—there was also that part of me that did not wish to expose to his scrutiny views that defined me so deeply.

Once it happened that we argued over his friendliness towards the tallyman at the docks in Kefar Nahum, a stunted half-pagan they called Rakiil, the Babbler, who worked tabulating the catches the fishermen brought in so they could be assessed for tax. In Galilee, it seemed the tax collectors were not nearly so hated as in Judea, where they worked directly for the Romans; yet neither were they embraced, nor free from corruption. Rakiil was a figure of ridicule at the docks, because of his deformities and his work—the local boys tormented him, intoning his name in a mocking cry like a gull's that would send him chasing after them red-faced with anger. But he had a streak of petty baseness in him that made it hard to feel any sympathy for him, seldom missing a chance to inflate a tally or to set a fine, if he could find the excuse for one.

Yeshua, however, had somehow got it into his head to make Rakiil his friend, and never neglected to greet him and exchange a word with him when he passed through the docks. Now, if Rakiil had responded to his overtures by becoming suddenly merciful and fair, I might have been the first to see the wisdom in his actions. But in fact he continued as mean-spirited as before, regarding Yeshua's friendliness with suspicion and going out of his way to impose the stiffest possible tallies on Yeshua's men, to show he had not been duped. I could not fathom, therefore, why Yeshua continued in his kindnesses and did not simply condemn him as an ingrate and a churl, who took pleasure in extorting from the poor rather than simply doing his job, as even Yeshua's master Yohanan had taught.

When I made this argument with Yeshua, however, he said, "How honest would my kindness to him be if it were only a means of seeking more favourable treatment from him?"

This sort of logic infuriated me.

"By that reckoning we might just as well embrace even the Romans, and make an end of it."

"You hate him because he's a tax collector," Yeshua said.

He was trying to bring the thing around to my politics, so that he might say, Did not even Solomon collect taxes, so why take it out on miserable Rakiil, and what did it matter what yoke you were under since there was always a yoke. But this was not an argument I cared to engage.

"I hate him because he's vile."

"Will your hatred make him any less so?"

"No more than your love will."

I knew that to follow him to the logical end of his reasoning must lead where I could not go, for if I must love even my oppressor, then how could I ever muster my forces against him. Yet the fact was that there was something in Yeshua's stance in this matter that I admired, perhaps because it reminded me of my own youthful contrariness, that he seemed always to embrace exactly those who were universally despised, as if to show how little he cared for the opinions of the world. Indeed, it was almost axiomatic with him that he reverse the usual order of things, giving the smallest heed to those of highest standing while always finding the way to raise up those whom no one else took into account. In this he showed himself exactly the opposite of a collaborationist, since he did not profit in any way from his behaviour, but rather often opened himself up to censure.

Nowhere was this clearer than in the matter of the lepers. The Galilee was even more hopelessly backward than Judea in its treatment of lepers, subscribing to the usual Levitical proscriptions and refusing to acknowledge any medical basis to the condition; and since none of the towns had any adequate authority for sorting the more serious cases from common boils or sores, they turned people out at the first hint of an eruption, with the result that the leper colonies were filled to overflowing and that many who entered them with some minor ailment ended up condemned along with the rest. Yeshua had apparently understood this situation and addressed himself to it, going out to the colonies to sort out the curable from the truly diseased and treating the former so that they might be allowed to return home.

All this might have been seen as a great public good if not for the outcry of his detractors, who claimed that it was nothing more than devilry to attempt to cure an affliction that the Lord had ordained and that Yeshua's true intention was rather to render unclean the whole of the population. The situation was compounded by the lepers themselves, who began to hear rumours of miraculous cures and so stole out from their colonies, which were poorly guarded, to mass outside the towns that Yeshua was known to frequent. For the local townspeople, the sight of dozens of lepers huddled outside their gates, people who heretofore had taken all necessary care to hide their uncleanness from the world, provoked great concern, and indeed made them fear that perhaps Yeshua had come to visit a pestilence on them.

It was at Korazin that we were first turned away on this account: we arrived there one morning from Kefar Nahum, half a dozen of us, to find several armed men already warned of our approach, standing at the gate to bar our entry. What surprised us was that they were not the henchmen of the local leader, a landowner named Matthias who held most of the townspeople in thrall in one way or another and whose avarice Yeshua had often publicly ridiculed, but rather common peasants, men who a week or a month before had no doubt been among those who had come for Yeshua's sermons or cures. They looked awkward barring our way, refusing to meet Yeshua's eye.

"Why are you coming with weapons against me?" Yeshua said, though the truth was they had only a few sticks among them and maybe a dagger or two, still in their sheaths.

"We have to think of our families," one of the men said. "We don't say you mean us any harm. But you're always with the lepers. The law tells us that makes you polluted like them."

"It's what's inside you that pollutes you, not what's outside," Yeshua said.

But the men held their ground.

Kephas was with us and seemed ready to come to blows with them.

"Has our master ever lied to you?" he said to them. "Has Matthias ever told you the truth?"

But Yeshua merely bid the men good morning and motioned us on our way.

Clearly Matthias had found the way to turn the townspeople against us. But from the sullen stubbornness of the men at the gate it seemed he had done so more by persuasion than coercion. When the word spread that even the common people of Korazin had gone against Yeshua, his reception in other towns grew cooler, and it began to happen from time to time, coming to a new town, that the authorities had heard of his reputation and did not permit us to enter. Some of his followers began to beg him then to cease visiting the lepers, lest he end up barred from every town in the region. But their arguments only hardened him.

"What kind of a doctor ignores the sick?" he said. As for being barred from the towns, he said if it came to that, then he would preach in the wilderness the way Yohanan had done.

I was inclined to agree at first that he abandon his missions to the lepers, since for the handful he saved among them, he risked losing his entire following. But when I put this to him, he said that if I could make such an argument then I'd understood nothing of his work. The following day, to make his point, he took me with him to visit the colony at Arbela. Normally he made these visits alone, or took along a group of us but left us outside the walls while he went in to do his rounds. But on this day he passed me off as a fellow doctor to the guards and brought me in with him, assuring me that there would be no risk to me. Such was the faith I had begun to put in him by then that I believed him.

The camp was not nearly as ramshackle a place as I'd expected, having been built not by Antipas but by the Romans, with their typical efficiency and precision. They had been motivated in this less by philanthropy than by strategy: the colony was set on the promontory that stood over the Arbela caves, and was a way of keeping the caves, which were accessible only from above, out of the hands of the rebels and bandits who normally inhabited them. Several barracks-style dormitories ran along the length of the promontory, with a courtyard and common kitchen at the centre of them. Apparently before the Romans had turned the place over to Antipas, as they eventually had, they actually supplied food for the residents and encouraged large communal meals and a sharing of tasks as a way of maintaining some sort of discipline and order. Now, however, the residents were dependent on the generosity of their relatives in bringing food and on the honesty of the guards in delivering it.

What was surprising in the camp was its air of normalcy: people went about their business, cooking and cleaning, carrying water, even farming a bit of field there, with only the slightest sense of hush and shame at their afflictions. Clearly Yeshua had brought an air of hope to the place. He encouraged cleanliness and had set up special areas of segregation to monitor various ailments and work towards a cure; and he treated people from an entirely medical point of view, with none of the condescension that the priests in Jerusalem showed in sending the afflicted off to their quarantine, nor indeed with the least concern for their uncleanness. When I asked him how he reconciled his approach with the proscriptions of the scriptures, he said merely that our forefathers had found their own way of expressing things that could not otherwise have been understood then.

When he had finished his rounds in the camp proper, he led me down to the caves. This was where the worst cases took refuge, those without hope. The whole mountain face at Arbela was riddled with these caves, which were accessible only by a steep footpath, one that here and there required you to scrabble against the rock face; already as we neared the end of it there was an overwhelming stench of putrid flesh, people moving like wraiths against the caves' darkness. It was from here that Antigonus, the last of the Maccabees, had fought Herod the Great, Herod finally resorting to swinging grappling hooks down into the mouths of the caves from above in order to drag his enemy out from them. But for the lepers who had now retreated to them, the caves had become their permanent homes, not because they had been forced into them but because shame had driven them there. So it was that once their disfigurements had rendered them hideous they repaired from the barracks above to this forsaken place, where they lived out their final agonizing years wondering what sin of their fathers or themselves had brought this horror on them.

Yeshua was surely the first visitor from outside the camp whom many of these people had seen in months or years. He told me they had shunned him when he'd first come, out of shame and their concern for his own purity. But now at his approach they came together quite openly, gathering on a little rock shelf that jutted out from the cliff face. It was an astounding sight, these dozens of lepers congregating there, men, women, and even some children, many of them so gnarled-limbed and deformed they were hardly recognizable as human. But what was surprising in lepers was that as putrid and corrupt as their outward form might be, their mental faculties were not affected in the least, so that you were suddenly astounded to hear from out of their mass of rotting flesh a perfect human voice. Thus it was that Yeshua did a most simple and amazing thing: he sat himself down amongst these lepers and conversed with them as if their affliction counted for nothing in his eyes.

This was no doubt what Yeshua had wished me to witness—the utter contrast in these people between the outer person and the inner one, a theme he returned to again and again in his teaching. He liked in particular to tell the story of the pious man and the sinner who went to the temple to pray: the former used the occasion as an opportunity to list all his virtues, while the latter, not even daring to look up to heaven, merely begged the Lord's mercy. The sinner, of course, was the hero of the tale, for his inner humility made him more worthy of God's love than the other's outer piety; and the story always went over well with people, who saw in it, I imagined, a sanction for their own laxity. I, however, always felt sorry for the poor pious man, who was stuck with the rigour of his discipline and self-denial while the sinner was left free to sin again.

But sitting among the lepers I did not feel quite so cynical. For the longest time, not even aware I was doing it, I stood well back from the circle they had formed around Yeshua, so repulsed was I by their smell and their hideousness and so accustomed to keeping lepers at a distance. But perhaps it was their own unthinking acceptance of my aversion, even as they sat conversing in the most normal fashion with Yeshua, that shamed me, that brought home to me not only how quick we all were to judge by appearances but also how deeply ingrained were the prejudices that got passed on to us. It was second nature in a Jew to see in a leper's affliction a sign of hopeless corruption. But it took only a few minutes among them to see they were merely average sorts of beings like the rest of us, made perhaps more humble and timid by their isolation but still recognizable as people you might have passed in the streets of any village. Afterwards I could hardly remember what was talked about—the most mundane of things, what had been done in the towns for the feasts, how the harvests had been, what marriages had taken place, petty matters I would not have imagined that Yeshua would have paid the least attention to. But within a matter of minutes I was sitting there amidst the others and had almost forgotten their deformities, so much had the smallest acquaintance with their inner selves transformed my vision of their outer ones.

At one point water was passed around, and a bit of oil and bread. To save me embarrassment, one of the women brought me a separate portion that had apparently been specifically sent for from above, the bread wrapped in leaves so that no hands should have touched it and the water and oil set in pots of stone to keep them pure. But for Yeshua, I saw, no special arrangement was made, nor did he so much as flinch at taking the ladle from which the others had drunk. It seemed so repellent a thing and yet so intimate, to share with them in this way—the sight of it left a strange agitation in me that afterwards I could not shake for many days, as if I witnessed some horror. Yet it was clear that, for the lepers, it was as though he had thus taken their affliction upon himself, to share the burden of it. I thought I understood something in him then, though I could not quite have expressed it, that indeed he was like the lepers in some way, or even Rakiil, all those who were marked, though he had a prince's bearing and the looks of one. If I saw the lepers differently afterwards, it was perhaps exactly in this, in understanding in them a dislocation that was still in some sense spiritual yet not moral, which was a manner of thinking that as a Jew I was not accustomed to.

Whatever Yeshua's intentions with the lepers, however, it remained true that his treatment of them continued to polarize feeling about him, so much so that for a time it grew difficult for us to travel freely and people were forced to come looking for him at Kefar Nahum, where he would speak to them either on a hill above the town or on the beach, sometimes standing in a boat a little ways off from the shore then so that they could see him. For the core of his following, of course, the matter was merely further evidence of his greatness, and for all I could say, that was indeed the case. But as tensions and emotions rose, there seemed a danger of descending into fanaticism, with the attendant risk of calling onto Yeshua the fate of Yohanan before him.

For my part, I could no longer pretend that I might somehow be able to turn an association with Yeshua to the good of my own cause. The animosities he had aroused in the region made it difficult for me to establish relations with anyone outside his following; while within it I had found no one who seemed sufficiently like-minded to be a good prospect for recruitment. Even the faction that had split from him under Aram of Kinneret, when I tried to approach it, would have nothing to do with me: they apparently assumed at once I was a spy, either for Yeshua or for Herod, so that even when I finally managed to arrange to meet directly with Aram himself, I was left standing half the night in the woods outside Kinneret without seeing any sign of him.

It so happened that it was just around this time that Pontius Pilate arrived in Caesarea Maritima to take up his post as Judean procurator. News of his arrival would likely not have drawn much attention among the Galileans, who seemed to make their indifference to Judean politics a point of pride, were it not that as his first act, Pilate had the Antonia fortress in Jerusalem regarrisoned and had the new squadron erect around the place, secretly and by night, standards that bore the images of Caesar. When the populace awoke to find Caesar's image flying well-nigh over the temple, there was a great outcry. Almost at once a mob formed to travel to Caesarea, where Pilate had apparently remained the whole time without so much as having stepped foot outside the palace.

When word of the protest reached us in Kefar Nahum, it was my immediate instinct that I must join it, as much from shame over my long idleness as from eagerness for the cause. In any event it seemed certain that some from our own movement would be among the protesters there, and so I might learn from them how matters went in Jerusalem and if it was safe to return. At the back of my mind I knew that if I left Yeshua now, I might not find the circumstance that would let me rejoin him, and no doubt it was for that reason that I chose to leave in haste, and without explanation—not, as I deluded myself, because I feared I should be forced to lie to him, since he surely would not have required any excuse from me for my departure, but rather because I was afraid of that part of me that simply wished to remain with him. Later I had cause to regret this hasty exodus not only on my account but on Yohanan's, from whom I had been unable to hide my departure and who begged to accompany me. In the end he got only as far as Sepphoris before turning back, confessing that he feared his father's anger, since he had not sought his permission. But I later discovered that despite his early return he was severely chastised, as if he had gone off on some debauchery, though he was hardly a child to be so much under his father's yoke.

By the time I reached Caesarea on my own, the protest had already been going on for several days. I was amazed by the numbers I found gathered there, in the thousands and still growing, not only from Jerusalem but apparently from all the countryside in between. The entire square in front of the palace was filled with protesters, all the usual traffic there came to a halt; and though apparently soldiers had initially been posted at all the entrances into the square as if to hem people in, the crowd had grown so sprawling and large by now that it could no longer be comfortably contained and the soldiers had retreated to form a line in front of the palace instead.

The crowd looked made up of the simplest sort of folk, men, women, and children all mixed together as if whole families had simply stood up from their dinners and set off en masse for the capital the instant word had reached them of Pilate's sacrilege. As far as I could tell, the only leadership to speak of consisted of a few of the more radical members of the Council (certainly none of the priests were there; nor, at first, did I see any of our own people); and then, from the villages, a number of teachers and elders, each to his group. Under normal circumstances, with such a crowd and no one dominant voice, there would have been the danger of the entire affair deteriorating into factionalism. But since people had come so single-mindedly, with no motive except their outrage and no objective except the removal of Caesar's standards, there was an atmosphere in the crowd of tremendous solidarity.

It seemed Pilate had not yet made an appearance, but had sent word that even if all of Palestine gathered at his door, he would not have the icons removed. As the crowd continued to grow it appeared that indeed would be the case, that soon the whole of the country would have joined us there at Pilate's gate. But rather than being encouraged by this show of force, I felt a familiar despair. In the first place, it frustrated me how quick we were to take affront at this type of incorporeal challenge when our people were daily murdered and enslaved without our raising a whisper of complaint. In the second, what I was most struck by at seeing us gathered in such numbers was less our strength than our weakness. Not a man of us was armed; and even had we been, we would never have been so well-armed as Pilate's soldiers, who, apart from the weapons they carried with them, had engines in their garrison capable of killing whole swaths of us with a single stroke. Beyond that, even if by sheer force of numbers we were to overwhelm them, the empire would yield up an almost infinite number of replacements for them, so that in the end the sum of every last Jew scattered throughout the civilized world from beyond the Euphrates to beyond the Nile would not total a fraction of the forces that Rome could muster against us.

These were truths, of course, that our movement had always kept before it—so we had laid down our foundations, and eschewed populism, and sent our missions abroad in search of allies, all so that we might avoid the senseless massacre in which most of our uprisings had ended. But perhaps it was exactly being there in that crowd, feeling the energy of it, that I saw clearly how doomed our own enterprise was as well, just endless scheming and planning and waiting that bore no relation to the mass of people, our tiny gains promptly erased at every smallest setback. There seemed only these two extremes, either to recklessly seize the moment in the face of certain defeat, or to plan and plan so endlessly that all momentum was lost and the moment of action forever deferred.

In the square, however, the main concern by that point was with finding food. No one had been prepared for the thing to drag on like this, and what supplies people had brought with them had long been used up. There was little help to be expected on this front from the Caesareans, who were mainly pagans and regarded us as at best an annoyance and at worst a positive menace; and even the Jews who lived there seemed unwilling to show us open solidarity lest they be made to pay the price after our departure. But teams had apparently been organized to fetch food from the surrounding countryside, and these returned not long after sundown with vegetables and cheese and fruit, wine, fresh bread, all of it donated by the Jewish villages and farms around the city and parcelled out equally among us so that no one of the thousands gathered there in the square should go hungry. In addition, reeds and branches had been brought in to make booths against the cold as if it were the Feast of Tabernacles, and there was such a celebratory mood in the square that night, with fires and singing, that you would not have known if you had stumbled upon us that we had come there in anger and in protest.

It must have put a fright into Pilate, however, to look out from the palace windows the next morning and see the square taken over by our booths as though by a conquering army. Not long after sunrise he responded by calling out what seemed the whole of his legion, maybe some three thousand in all, who lined up practically *a testudo* in front of the palace ten rows deep, seeming fully prepared to march against us. Most of us were just coming to after the night's festivities and we stared out bleary-eyed and hushed at this apparition. But when half an hour had passed and still the soldiers had not moved against us, the crowd began to taunt them. Many of the soldiers were Samaritans, and understood perfectly well the abuse that was being hurled at them; and we would surely have descended into violence had the soldiers not been recalled as suddenly as they had been deployed, the bulk of them filing away into the palace courtyard and seemingly back to the garrison to leave only the nominal handful guarding the gates.

None of us had any idea what to make of this apparent backing down. Pilate, having only just taken up his post, was an unknown quantity to us, and whether he was showing cowardice or benevolence in withdrawing his troops we couldn't judge. But not long afterwards he sent his pages out among us to announce that he was prepared to come to terms, and that we should gather in the stadium so that he could comfortably address us. Such a feeling of elation went through the crowd then that no one thought to question the wisdom of letting ourselves be penned up like that, the whole crowd instead surging at once towards the stadium gates so that even those of us who might have resisted were swept along with the rest. Meanwhile the citizens of Caesarea, happy to have their square liberated, stood lined up in the streetside arcades to watch us pass as if we were prisoners being marched along in a triumph.

At the stadium there was a handful of troops who directed us to the arena, into which the several thousand of us were crammed like so many sheep. Pilate had already taken his seat on the tribunal—he was smaller than I'd expected, and had that bearing, at once arrogant and defensive, of someone perpetually conscious of being of second rank. It was always hard to tell with that sort what excesses they would be prone to when given power. In this case, it was also unclear whether Pilate had acted on his own in setting up the standards, or on the express orders of Tiberius. The rumour was that he so hated the Jews he had been determined to put them in their place at once by rescinding the special privileges they had always enjoyed. But if that was the case and he had acted without Caesar's sanction, then he was foolish enough to be a real danger to us.

When we were all assembled, Pilate raised his hand and we fell silent. At that point there were only perhaps fifty soldiers visible in the stadium, most of them milling around the gates in what appeared to be a casual way and the rest stationed up near Pilate's tribunal. But then on a nod from Pilate the gates were suddenly secured, leaving no exit, and an instant later there was a great rattle of armour while what seemed the entire contigent of troops that had beset us that morning suddenly poured out from the wings and into the stadium's first rows to encircle us, the host of them planting themselves there with their hands on the hilts of their swords as if ready on the instant to leap over the barricade and massacre the lot of us. We all stood dumbfounded: even those of us who might have suspected Pilate's intentions would never have believed he would consider resorting to such wholesale slaughter. Either he was bluffing or he was one of those madmen that the emperors sometimes sent out to the provinces simply to rid the capital of them.

"Cease your protest and go home," Pilate said, "and I will spare your lives."

And on that signal the soldiers to a man unsheathed their swords.

This was an act of such provocation that it seemed there would be nothing for it but for us to riot, weaponless though we were and composed as much of women and children as of able-bodied men. Perhaps that was exactly what Pilate had hoped for; he could then send word back to Caesar that the Jews had revolted, and he had been forced to put them down. For a long moment then the strangest sort of tension seemed to hover over us, of outrage mingled with fear and with the simple astonishment that we could suddenly be facing our deaths. I was surprised at how little zeal I felt at the thought of such a sacrifice—it was not the way I'd ever foreseen my contribution, as a simple number in some tally of our dead.

At that instant, however, it happened that one of the leaders from Jerusalem, a young teacher by the name of Eleazar, suddenly came forward out of the crowd and had himself heaved up onto the barricade beneath Pilate's tribunal. Before the soldiers could remove him, he shouted out to Pilate that we were prepared to die rather than transgress our own law. Then, for all to see, he knelt down on the narrow shelf the barricade afforded and bared his neck to the soldiers, as if to invite their swords.

A hush fell over the stadium while we waited to see how the soldiers would respond. But since no signal was forthcoming from Pilate, they made no move. Someone else took up Eleazar's cry then, and someone else again, so that it spread by degrees across the stadium, and then, one by one, people began to kneel down in the dirt with their necks offered up, until nearly every man, woman, and child in the place was readied for the sword.

My initial reaction at the sight of such submission was abhorrence, for while there had clearly been something calculated and cynical in Eleazar's gesture—he was, in effect, simply calling Pilate's bluff—the crowd seemed following his lead in utter seriousness, as if people were truly prepared to be slaughtered there where they knelt. But even as I struggled with my revulsion I found myself kneeling with the rest, perhaps merely because I feared being taken for a coward if I did not; and in kneeling I had a sort of revelation, for what I felt was not a sense of submission but of sudden power. The most an enemy could take from you was your life; offer that to him freely, and his hold over you was gone. So it was that the ten thousand of us kneeling there in the sand, our lives at stake, suddenly seemed to be the ones who instead were holding Pilate for ransom: he could only submit to us or have us killed, though in so doing only take that which we had willingly given over to him.

I could hardly have described the feeling that went through the stadium as we knelt there except to say that it was as if we had all of us for a moment been bound up in a single will. The fear that had been palpable when the soldiers had first appeared had completely vanished; and if it had happened at that moment that Pilate had given the signal and the soldiers had descended on us, I would have wagered that not one of us would have flinched before the knife. As it happened, however, the signal didn't come: Pilate merely stood staring out at us as dumbfounded as we had first been at the sight of his soldiers. He had reckoned us the merest savages, to be frightened off our beliefs at the first hint of any threat; instead, he found us willing to die over a matter that must have seemed to him almost trivial.

After a few minutes, Pilate, pale with anger, got up from his seat and left the stadium, leaving us kneeling in the sun and the soldiers watching over us with their weapons still bared. For perhaps an hour we remained at that standoff; and then again, as suddenly as they had come, the soldiers withdrew and the message came through from the palace that we were free to go. This time, there was no rejoicing: under the leadership of Eleazar and a few others, we marched in almost total silence back to the palace square—where our booths, in the meantime, had been knocked down—and sat ourselves on the paving stones as if we were prepared to remain there until the end of days if we weren't granted our original demand. We could see Pilate watching us from the palace windows; no doubt he had hoped that after he'd released us we would simply pick up and go, happy to escape with our lives, instead of stubbornly returning to torment him. When sunset came and we began to rebuild our booths and distribute what food we had remaining, he must have made a decision to cut his losses, for he sent his pages out again to announce to us that the standards would be removed.

It was doubtful whether any of us in the crowd had ever quite believed that the matter would end in this way, that without violence, and by sheer force of will, we would achieve our goal. The normal expectation in protests of this sort was that there would be skirmishes or at least arrests, that the matter would be appealed finally to the governor in Damascus or to Rome where it would fester for months or years before any decision was made—in short, that our people would still in the end be made to suffer every indignity while the administration, even if it had massacred scores of us, would at best be only mildly reprimanded. That we were walking away now with what seemed total victory left us a bit stunned at first—it was as if we hadn't quite understood why in this case things had turned out differently. Somehow Eleazar, either by stroke of genius or of luck, had rescued us, had found the way to save at once both our honour and our lives. I remembered a story I'd heard as a young man of a similar protest in Alexandria, where the Jews, to save their quarter from attack by fellow citizens during some dispute, had simply lain down in the path of the approaching mob; faced with the prospect of having to trample a mile of them, the mob had eventually turned tail and headed home. At the time, the strategy had struck me as foolhardy and craven. But now I saw the matter differently; I saw the power there was in confronting the enemy with the spectre of his own barbarity.

Since it was dark by the time of Pilate's announcement, most of us bedded down in the square for the night and only set out for home the following morning. We were a haggard lot by then, seeming more sombre and chastened in victory than we'd been in adversity. No one dared to rejoice until we'd seen with our own eyes that the standards had truly been removed. For my own part, I believed that Pilate would keep to his word—surely he wouldn't risk another confrontation of the sort he'd just been through. Nonetheless, it was my plan to follow the crowd back into Jerusalem, as much, however, for the cover it provided for my return there as out of concern for the standards. I could not go any longer without some news of our group; it did not bode well, I thought, that I had recognized none of them amongst the protesters.

It was exactly then, however, on the road out of the city, that I finally met some who were familiar to me, two young men whom I knew by the names of Rohagah and Yekhubbah. They behaved strangely towards me, hardly meeting my eye, and it was only by pains that I was able to learn from them that I was under question because I had not yet returned to Jerusalem. I was outraged at this. I said to them that surely they'd had word of me from Tyre.

The elder one, Rohagah, though they were neither of them much more than boys, said, "From Tyre we heard only that you had left in the night, and given no message," which was untrue.

The two of them were types of a new recruit that I did not get on with, and who hardly differed from Zealots in the narrowness of their thinking and the severity of their manner. Towards me, their sort were disdainful and thought me untrustworthy because they regarded me as a foreigner, and hence tainted by the ways of the world.

I said to them that in any event I was just then on my way to Jerusalem, and that surely I had been wise to await the proper moment for my return rather than risking bringing further suspicion on us in the midst of the reprisals.

"Then you should not come at all, if you're under suspicion," Rohagah said, stupidly, it seemed to me.

I might have thrashed him. We stood there in the middle of the road not speaking until Yekhubbah, seeing my anger, said awkwardly, "They're planning an action for Jerusalem," though it was clear from Rohagah's look that he had overstepped his bounds. "They only want to take care."

I was amazed at this. Surely it was foolishness to proceed with an action in Jerusalem when we could not be certain of any of the outposts; if Pilate did not crush us, the Syrian governor surely would.

I said, "I'd heard the reprisals had left us decimated."

"Those who were lost have been replaced," Rohagah said, which chilled me, for I understood him to mean that he and his lot had now got the upper hand.

He had been good enough to leave me a way out.

"Perhaps you're right that I should wait," I said. "You'll tell the others that I'm looking to our work in Galilee."

"Of course."

And when they had gone I felt a tremendous relief to have escaped them.

I realized then how loath I had been to return to Jerusalem from the start; understanding the situation there made me infinitely more so. The truth was that once I had got caught up in the spirit of the protest, I had hardly given a thought to Jerusalem, or to our cause; rather it had always been to Yeshua that my mind had gone back, and to what he might make of the thing, and to what I would say to him if I returned to him. It seemed my experience in Caesarea had changed my view of things in some important way, like a shift of light that made you see some object differently, that made you reconsider what you thought its nature to be. The object, in this case, was our freedom, which I had always imagined was a thing that had to be wrested away from our enemies like a trophy or prize. But in the stadium, when we'd been kneeling there, it had seemed something more subtle than that, not to be captured or won but somehow called into being, conjured up like a spirit.

Thus it fell out that I did not go on to Jerusalem as I had planned but rather left the crowd where the road forked north to return to the Galilee. While I was stopped in Sepphoris the word came through that Pilate had in fact kept his pledge, though no one in that city, filled with Greeks as it was, showed much interest in the event. Later, of course, Pilate would make us pay dearly for this early leniency, never missing an opportunity to put us in our place. But at the time the victory seemed a significant one, not least for the method by which we had brought it about.

On my way out of Sepphoris I could not resist the urge to detour southward a few miles to Notzerah, the town of Yeshua's family, though I did not know what I hoped to find there. Apparently the place had been just a hamlet until workers hired on for the rebuilding of Sepphoris following the rebellion had begun to take up residence there, forbidden as they were from living in Sepphoris proper. As a result, the present town was rather sprawling and unkempt, and stretched out pell-mell along a series of irregular slopes so that it made a disagreeable impression and so that defences of any kind were impossible. All the buildings showed signs of haste in their construction; several that I noticed had upper storeys that lay collapsed in ruins above the main one, so that it was easy to surmise they had been added on in the shoddiest possible manner as the town's population burgeoned. Ironically these were the hovels that the craftsmen who built the splendours of Sepphoris had had to return to every evening. At the height of the construction the town must have been a bustling one; but now I found it half-deserted, many of the houses abandoned and an air of desuetude hanging over the place. In the surrounding region the town had a reputation for roguery and dishonesty, though also, apparently, for the beauty of its women, which, however, I saw scant evidence of during my own visit.

I asked about Yeshua. People knew at once who I meant, though at first I wasn't certain we were referring to the same man, so different was the image people gave out of him from the one I had come to have. As it turned out, he had left the town long before, only a matter of years after his family had come there from Egypt; and from the sound of it, the townspeople had been glad to see the back of him. He'd had airs, people said, the town couldn't abide him; or they said he'd gone mad and run off, and his family hadn't been able to bring him back. Of his current ministry, which most of them had heard about, they were dismissive—what kind of a man, they said, and him the eldest son, left his widowed mother and siblings without a further thought to them.

About his family they were more generous: they were good people but kept to themselves. The father, who had died not long after coming to the town, had been a stonemason; but not much more seemed to be known about him. Since his death the family had been supported by Yeshua's brothers, who worked at odd building jobs as well as farming a plot of land outside the town bought by the father just after his arrival.

This was not the background I would have guessed for Yeshua, whom I had imagined the son of a clerk, at least, or a merchant, to judge by his education. No doubt this explained the town's dislike of him: he had acted above his station. I would have liked to have met some of his family, to get a clearer notion of him, but I did not know what I might say to them, or if they would welcome me. Instead I contented myself with a view of his home, which I was directed to, in the hope I might catch a glimpse of some brother of his in passing.

The place was built on a steep incline that led down to one of the little valleys the town was folded into, clinging there precariously, I thought, though it looked of slightly sturdier construction than many of the other houses in the town. It was double-storeyed, the bottom floor built directly into the hillside and seeming to function as a stable, with a little courtyard out front, and the second one reached by a narrow stone stairwell, though apparently opening out at ground level in back. There was nothing particularly distinctive about the place—it seemed the house of a family that had done neither excessively well nor excessively poorly, that was not remarkable in any way, except that it had produced this Yeshua who was either a madman, as the townspeople had it, or a saint, as his followers did.

While I stood staring at the place from across the street, a woman emerged from the stable into the front courtyard and looked out at me—his mother, I presumed, though she did not look nearly as old as I would have expected, her hair pitch-black and her eyes blacker still. She was the first woman I'd seen in the town in whom there was any sign of an intrinsic beauty, though it was clear from her look, which had something of the Arab to it, and from her bearing, which was that of a city woman, that she did not belong to the place, and that indeed she would gladly have kicked the dust of it from her heels. She held my gaze an instant, though distractedly, with a sort of hollowness that seemed to suggest her life had failed her in some way. I was almost tempted to go to her, to bring her some word of comfort: I come from your son, who sends his greetings. But as abruptly as she'd come she turned away and retreated into the shadows, and I saw no more of her.

I returned to Kefar Nahum. After the tension and ferment of Caesarea, the town seemed like the end of the world, hopelessly backward and remote, and Yeshua himself perhaps the madman, after all, that his fellow townsmen had reckoned him to be. I began to speak to him of the events in Caesarea but he was strangely distant and cool, treating me as if I had betrayed him by going off or by daring to learn things that might compete with his own teaching. Then several times he went out of his way to show favour to Kephas at my expense, even though Kephas, to his credit, was clearly shamed by such pettiness. For my part, I took the matter much more to heart than I would have admitted—I had come back from Caesarea in a sort of agitation, on the verge of some insight, it seemed, that I owed to Yeshua's example; yet he had spurned me as if to say that I'd understood nothing, that we walked in different countries, that I was still too hopelessly far from any real grasp of things for him to stoop to instruct me.

I might have simply gone my own way then except that I lacked not only destination but means: at my departure, to repay any debt I owed, I'd left the bulk of my remaining funds to the common purse, which I'd left behind for Yohanan's brother. The purse had now been given over to Matthaios again, with no suggestion it would be returned me; and so I was in some measure held hostage there, unless I chose to hire myself out in the streets for my living. It was as if while I'd been gone some enemy had worked every means to put me at a disadvantage should I return. Had I foreseen the reception that awaited me, I might just as soon have gone back to Jerusalem after all, where at least I was known and felt of some use, while here it seemed that for a few days' absence I had become a stranger.

There had been some changes while I'd been away. Yeshua had added a new disciple to our inner group, a pagan they called Simon the Canaanite, the first heathen he'd included among us; and he made it clear to all of us that he was to be treated as an equal, even though in so doing he seemed merely to emphasize the man's difference from the rest of us. In the end, of course, none of us could shake the tinge of condescension that marked all our exchanges with him, particularly as he himself had the cringing manner of someone used to abasing himself for the sake of fitting in. Apart from the fact that his addition to the group brought our number to a portentous twelve, as if we were the twelve tribes reborn, the sole reason for his presence seemed to be to further rile the powers already set against us.

It had never been any secret that Yeshua considered his mission to extend to the heathens. But until now his proselytizing had always been seen in the same light as that of the Pharisees, aimed simply at winning converts for the Jews. Simon, however, had remained uncircumcised, and though he would surely have submitted to the knife at once had Yeshua required it of him, Yeshua seemed to want to make an example of him. The thing was never spoken about openly, of course, but as the rumour of Simon's condition spread, the matter threatened to be an even more explosive one than that of the lepers. At every gathering a question would come up about the covenant; and Yeshua would use his usual evasions and riddles to avoid confronting it directly. Then when someone asked him outright if some different sign would replace circumcision in his new kingdom, Yeshua said it was only the weak of faith who required a mark of their covenant. On that occasion there were some in the audience who were ready to stone him on the spot had they not been restrained by the people around them.

In the end, however, the matter resolved itself quietly: it seemed Kephas and some of the others went behind

Yeshua's back and convinced Simon to have the thing done. Yeshua was furious when he found out, railing at us that we were as simple-minded and faithless as the rest. Kephas took all the blame on himself, not daring to put up the least defence; but the truth was that he'd probably saved the lot of us, because once the word had got around that Simon had been circumcised, the tension at Yeshua's gatherings dropped and the questions ceased. Even Yeshua, in the end, seemed content to let the matter rest—it wasn't time, was his favourite refrain to us now, a sort of blanket forgiveness for our great ignorance.

There was something slightly disturbing in this refrain, and in the hints he had begun to drop that there was some moment we were moving towards when all the criticism and misunderstanding that now confronted us would fall away. It was as if he could no longer bear his own contradiction, that he so openly courted controversy and dissension in all he did, seemed in fact to thrive on it, then counselled love and forgiveness towards those who hated us as a result. So he had hatched this notion that even our enemies, in the end, would be won to us. As I discovered, he seemed willing to go to some lengths to prove his point on the matter—a few weeks after my return, for instance, I learned that in my absence he had somehow worked a reconciliation with that same Aram who had earlier split with him over the question of force. It was only by chance that I heard of the thing, from Yohanan, who had always been my faithful informant but had kept somewhat shy of me since my return, on account of the grief he had suffered; as I understood the matter, Yeshua had managed to win Aram back mainly because of Aram's fear, however unjustified, that Yeshua would turn him in as a rebel.

So Aram had renounced his views and come meekly back to the fold, and Yeshua had been able to show his great mercy in accepting him. But to me it seemed a manipulation—surely Yeshua had merely preyed on his insecurities, which I myself had seen ample evidence of in my own frustrated overtures to him. Indeed they continued to manifest themselves even now: still unconvinced of my own trustworthiness, Aram kept well wide of Yeshua after my return, so that in the end I never even so much as laid eyes on him.

I now understood, however, some of Yeshua's coolness towards me, for Aram had surely told him of my attempts to contact him, which must have made it seem that I had been courting his enemies behind his back. If I had known of the thing at once, I might have found the way to smooth it over. Yet the truth was that I held the whole matter against him, and could not bring myself to go to him now as if in apology. At any rate, it was seldom that I found myself in private audience with him any more, on account of the women, who having rejoiced when I had gone, as they no doubt hoped for good, now found the way to keep him from me at every instant, and so to keep alive the disaffection between us.

It was perhaps inevitable that in the light of these tensions I should begin to see Yeshua differently, and I wondered now if I had not earlier been as besotted with him as the rest. The contradictions in him that before had made a sort of sense now seemed held together only by the strength of his character; and his contentiousness, at first engaging, suddenly appeared so much theatrics, directed as it always was at petty local despots and leaders rather than at our true enemies. It was this that most struck me, though I still had the cold in my bones of my meeting with Rohagah and Yekhubbah, that I had deluded myself into believing I might find with him some better way. Perhaps it was exactly that I expected more of him now when before he had been merely a diversion, and so I judged him more harshly. Yet it was a bitter disappointment to have returned, as I thought, to a sage, and to have found instead someone arrogant and petty and vain. All the exhilaration I had felt in Caesarea had drained away from me—now I had neither one thing nor the other, nothing to hold me here with Yeshua yet nothing to return to.

Yeshua's growing popularity had made him increasingly bold. In the towns we went to there were a number of elders and teachers who had trained under Pharisees of the school of Shammai; and these Yeshua had begun to take a particular pleasure in baiting and goading. Yet while it was true that many of them, in those towns, took their superior learning as an occasion for condescension and sententiousness, others were among the most pious and respected members of their communities. Yeshua did not always take the trouble to separate the one from the other, nor was he without duplicity in decrying Shammai's excessive legalism, which he seemed to use as an excuse for his own laxity towards the law. The attitude had begun to wear off on his inner circle as well, some of whom, for instance, openly flouted the sabbath now by travelling from their villages to join us for evening prayers in Kefar Nahum. When Yeshua was challenged over these matters, he shrugged them off.

"How can you fault them for coming to pray with their teacher?" he said.

"They have teachers in their towns."

"And if the Messiah came," Yeshua said, "would you tell them to keep to their towns rather than worship him?"

This kind of provocation struck me as foolhardy, particularly as there was no shortage of fanatics attached to him now who might be inclined to take such statements literally. But while logic suggested that his insolence would increasingly marginalize him, in fact the opposite seemed to be occurring—the more brazen he became, the more the crowds grew, even if half of them came merely for the spectacle and many of the rest out of superstition, hoping that some good fortune would descend on them by being near him or that some ailment they had would fall away. So his rise had begun to resemble that of the usual charlatans and false prophets, for whom it could truly be said that the more outrageous their promises and claims, the greater their sway over the people. Yet with Yeshua there remained this distinction: that for all his irreverence there was always a core of truth in whatever he said. Perhaps even now this was why I did not simply leave him—there was still that sense at the back of my mind of some answer he might hold to me, like some intractable nut he had cracked open.

Once, just among the group of us, Yaqob put a question to him about Simon's circumcision, still troubled, as we all were, by how Yeshua had handled the matter. It was my suspicion that Yeshua's views were even more radical than he had dared to say, or than any Jew could accept. But he answered Yaqob now by citing Hillel's reply to the heathen who wished to learn all the law in an afternoon, that its sum was to do to others as you would have them do to you. It was one of the few times I heard Yeshua cite an authority, unlike those teachers who could not so much as put on their shirts without quoting the Torah; though it was typical that he should choose a teaching that even in its day had caused no small amount of bafflement, and that indeed had helped Shammai in gaining ascendancy over Hillel. Now, however, Hillel's meaning seemed obvious enough—wasn't there more virtue, in fact, in a single kind act than in the keeping of every covenant and code?

With regard to Simon, anyone could see that circumcision or no, it would have been hard to find a more faithful proselyte: it was not only that he hung on Yeshua's every word but that he set all his teachings into almost immediate practice, with an earnestness that would have put even the most pious of Pharisees to the test. It happened, for instance, that not long after he'd joined us he heard Yeshua in one of his sermons chastising those hypocrites who made a great public show of their praying; and for some time thereafter we could not get him to join us in our prayers on the beach, so frightened was he of falling into the same hypocrisy. To ward off the least possibility of pridefulness he even went so far as to deny that he prayed at all, though we would see him stealing off to some closet every morning and hear his whispered offerings. So it seemed true that his circumcision had not the least bearing on his piety, though it was the work of a Samson for any Jew to separate the two in his own mind.

When Passover approached there was an assumption amongst Yeshua's followers, many of whom had abandoned their teachers in the towns on his account, that he would lead their pilgrimage to Jerusalem. It was in my own mind, however, to advise him against any journey into the city, because I feared that the action Yekhubbah had hinted at was imminent, since it was always for the feasts that such things were planned, to take advantage of the crowds then. I travelled into Tiberias to see what news I might gather there and in fact was very troubled by what I heard. It seemed there had been a spate of assassinations in Jerusalem, though there was much confusion over these—some said it was the Romans who had hired assassins to root out any remaining rebels, others that the rebels themselves were purging their own ranks of those suspected of any betrayal during the reprisals. I did not know what to make of these rumours, what to discount in them and what to believe, or whether they showed us under siege or on the assault. On my own account, remembering my exchange with Rohagah, I had cause enough for concern—surely if they were attacking those under suspicion, I must number myself among the threatened.

Afterwards I was unsure how to proceed. While I wished to protect Yeshua from risk, I did not want to bring any more to myself or to break the oaths I had made to the movement by revealing what I knew. But in the end it was Yeshua who one night took me aside from the others—it was the first time since my return from Caesarea that he'd sought me out in this way—and led me out to the lakeshore to speak. It was a moonless night and pitch black, but he insisted on rowing out onto the lake in one of Kephas's fishing boats, which struck me as peculiar and even frightened me a little. I had the instant's foolish thought that he intended me harm in some way, as if I had misunderstood him until then; though the truth was that for all that he preached peace, there had always seemed this side to him that was volatile and unpredictable and slightly sinister.

He rowed us out in silence a little ways from the shore. In darkness that lake had something of the oppressive to it, since you were still somehow aware of the mountains pushing in on every side, with only the small light of lamps here and there from the shore.

He said to me, "We did not expect you back from Caesarea."

I did not know how to respond.

"And yet I'm here," I said.

It seemed some matter weighed on him but he wouldn't broach it.

"You didn't go down to Jerusalem."

"No."

"Is there a warrant for you there?"

I was surprised at this. So it seemed that was his concern, that I would compromise him should I travel with him to the city.

"Surely if there were a warrant," I said, somewhat arrogantly, "they would have made the day's journey to fetch me here."

We were silent. I was angry now, and had lost the will to warn him of what I knew. There seemed something unreasonable in this and yet I thought surely he knew what I was when he asked me to join him.

Finally I said, "I hadn't planned to accompany you on your pilgrimage," which was the truth, given my situation then.

After this he tried to make light of the matter. He asked me about Jerusalem, but only to flatter me, I felt, broaching subjects that I thought were of no concern to him—who the power-brokers were in the council, what the mood of the people was. But then he asked about the troubles in the city, of which he'd heard, and I could not feign ignorance.

"They say the rebels are killing their own," he said.

"Whatever the killing," I said, "there's sure to be more of it soon enough."

But I didn't go on, nor did he press me, rowing us back to shore in silence.

In the night I repented that I had not given him a clearer sign of the danger to him in Jerusalem, since whatever anger I bore him, I couldn't wish on him the massacre that might result should there be an uprising. But the following morning he surprised us all with the announcement that he would not be going to the city for the feast after all but rather into retreat, giving as his excuse his wish to worship free from the crowds. He would be taking with him only his usual retinue, Yaqob, Yohanan, and Kephas; the rest of us should feel free to celebrate in our own homes, since, as he said, God didn't live only in the temple that he could only be worshipped there.

His followers didn't know what to make of this, and were greatly disappointed, while his detractors were quick to denounce him and to say he preached sacrilege against the temple. But I wondered if he hadn't understood more than I had thought, and had taken my warning without however pressing me into betrayal. It occurred to me now that perhaps it had been concern for my own safety rather than his that had made him ask after the warrant against me. But still I couldn't find the way to make amends to him before his departure, so that when he left there remained the same strain between us that there had been ever since my return from Caesarea.

As it happened, the feast passed with no report of insurrection. But when Yeshua and the others returned to Kefar Nahum I learned in secret from Yohanan that Yeshua had led them into Jerusalem after all. They had put up in Bet Aniah with one of Kephas's cousins, and any time they had gone into the city Yeshua had made them cover themselves with their cloaks lest they be recognized by any of his followers. All this might have seemed sensible enough, and in line with whatever warning he'd understood from me, except for some peculiarities in his behaviour that Yohanan described to me. For instance, there were many parts of the city Yeshua avoided as if he had enemies there; and then at the temple he had refused to inscribe himself in the rolls for the temple tax, claiming exemption because he carried no coin. On that occasion he had argued so fiercely with one of the temple priests that they had nearly come to blows, and Yohanan and the others had had to spirit him away to save him a beating from the crowd. Afterwards he had not entered the temple grounds again, and it had been left to Yohanan and the rest to bring the lamb for its blessing.

I had no idea what to make of this behaviour and wondered why he had travelled to the city at all, or why, after the pains he had taken to conceal himself there, he should then have risked a public argument. As it was, a number of his followers who had gone to the city on their own had recognized him and could not understand why he had deceived them. But Yeshua held to the story of his retreat, saying he had been to Mount Tabor. As Yohanan told me, there was at least some truth in this—they had spent the night there, on their return.

All of this seemed the sign of a creeping strangeness in Yeshua, one that was all the more alarming because it appeared finally to have attracted the attention of the authorities to him. Until this point he had seemed protected by the relative insignificance of his following and the apparent respect in which the Roman captain Ventidius held him. But now it grew clear that someone had taken note of him, whether because of his altercation in Jerusalem or simply on account of his increasing brazenness, because it happened that certain narrow-eyed sorts who had obviously been sent out from Tiberias began making appearances in Kefar Nahum, asking questions here and there or lingering at the edges of the crowd when Yeshua preached wearing an air of innocence that seemed exactly to trumpet their sinister intent.

In Jerusalem such matters were handled much more delicately, the knife already inserted and removed before the least suspicion was aroused. But these men seemed hardly to bother to mask themselves. Indeed, when I slipped a few coins to one of them, he admitted at once that he had been sent by Herod Antipas, to keep an eye on the upstart Yeshua. Clearly what had happened was that Antipas, who was not known for keeping an eye on the happenings of the Galilean countryside, had finally got wind of Yeshua's ministry, and was anxious now to head off the rise of another holy man whom the Romans might later compel him to kill.

For my part, I believed there was a real danger from Herod's men. But Yeshua played with them in a way that seemed unwise, saying any number of things that could be used against him should someone have a mind to twist his words. Antipas was not some village elder, whom he could get the better of by a clever turn of phrase; and Pilate and Rome stood behind him, who not all the peasants of Galilee could stop should they decide to remove him. It had been easy enough, after all, to do away with Yohanan, who had had a greater following and not so many enemies.

But when I brought these concerns to Yeshua, he dismissed them.

"They hire scribes to write down what you say so it can be used against you," I said, which I had seen one of them do.

"Should I stop telling the truth, then?"

"The truth has nothing to do with it. You provoke them."

"Why are you so timid," he said, "when you are the one who wants to chase them all into the sea?"

So he made the thing appear simply a matter of staying true to his beliefs. But the fact was the more he was threatened, the more he became reckless. This seemed especially the case since his return from Jerusalem, so that I suspected there was more to what had happened there than Yohanan had been able to tell. I remembered Yeshua in Tyre, how ill at ease he had been with the crowd, and thought perhaps he had travelled to Jerusalem on his own so that he might again test himself outside the world of fishermen and farmers. But it seemed he had fared even worse in Jerusalem than he had in Tyre.

As part of their strategy, Herod's spies spread many calumnies about Yeshua, some of which had a sufficient element of truth to take hold. So, for instance, they began to cast aspersions on his morals, on account of the women in his group. I had often warned Yeshua of the ill-advisedness of going about like some desert chieftain, with all his wives in tow, and he had laughed off my criticisms as if it did not matter to him what people made of these women. Yet it was exactly the accusations against them now that seemed the thing he took most to heart. In his typical way, however, he did not simply counter them but rather raised the flag higher, and ensured that the women were always with him now whenever he appeared in the streets. This had the odd effect of once more increasing the size of the crowds who came to see him, as many were anxious to catch sight of the eccentric holy man and his concubines; and again, in the unpredictable way of these things, the rumours of his indiscretions seemed only to raise his authority with much of the peasantry, particularly the Syrians, who apparently had begun to see in him some remnant of the fertility cult they had had in their Asherah before the Jews had forced them to abandon her.

All this was a matter of great irony, I thought, for though Yeshua had always been happy enough to eat and drink well when the occasion arose and to surround himself with young women, he had often struck me as someone almost entirely lacking in desires, as if his physical nature was merely so much baggage he carried, that he might slough off at its first inconvenience to him. Though he did not encourage fasting, for instance, he himself sometimes did so for days, as if simply by oversight; and though I had never heard him advocate sexual abstinence, which was the case with many of the cults, he had never shown any particular favour to one or the other of his women or given reason to believe he might choose one as his wife, so I might almost have wondered, if it were not so uncommon among Jews, whether his desires did not run in another direction. For these reasons, I felt no cause to believe there was any substance to the rumours against him. But exactly because there was so little in his teaching that reflected this ascetic side of him, it went unnoticed. Instead people made much of the feasts he went to at the homes of his wealthier patrons and how he never refused a glass of wine, so that it seemed entirely reasonable to believe as well that he kept his women with him for his pleasure.

Thus many who had followed him before, and who counted themselves pious, now grew uneasy with him; while others who had ignored him suddenly thought him a Bacchus come to life, and began to come to him to bless their crops or cure their infertility, which appalled him. Sometimes a dozen or more would already be awaiting him at Kephas's gate when he arose; sometimes at his sermons above the town he could hardly be heard for the clamour people made to be attended to. In the midst of these there were the usual ill who continued to come, and whose numbers had grown, so that more than once it happened that seeing the crowds waiting in ambush of him he would steal away with a few of us and leave them in the lurch.

"If someone comes with only the truth, it's not enough for them," he said, growing bitter. "They have to have wonders."

So he grew increasingly reclusive, and even those times when he tended to the sick he appeared worn out by the effort, as if his healing had become a drain on his own vital force; because while at the outset his healing had appeared the natural complement to his ministry, it now began to seem an obstacle to it, and so he lost the heart for it. In this matter as well, however, logic was confounded: rather than diminishing his reputation, Yeshua's growing reluctance to cure seemed instead to have the effect of enhancing it. As what had once been freely offered became more inaccessible and rare, so did the stories grow of the wonders that Yeshua was capable of and of the miracle cures he had brought about. Thus the blind and the lame appeared at the gate, and those close to death, filled with hope; and thus we were forced to turn them away. For Yeshua, there seemed no way out: the less he appeared in public, the more the rumours of his potency grew; but if he should come out and simply tend to people in the usual way, they felt disappointed, as if some sin of theirs or some failure of faith had kept him from using his powers to the full.

On one occasion an old cripple who had had his relations bring him across the lake from Sennabris was so insistent on being seen that he had himself lifted up on his stretcher to the roof of Kephas's house and lowered down by ropes into the courtyard. Kephas was ready to chase him and his people away at the end of a stick. But Yeshua was impressed by his persistence, though the man freely admitted it was skepticism and not belief that lay behind it: he wished to put to rest the rumours of Yeshua's abilities.

"You're right to be skeptical," Yeshua said. "Only God has that sort of power."

"Then why do you allow such lies to be spread about you?"

"I can't control what people say."

"Ah," the old man said, "you're like the ugly girl who to hide her ugliness never leaves the house, so the rumour spreads she's in fact very beautiful and the suitors begin to line up at her door. When her sister accuses her of deceit, she says, 'I can't control the lies people tell about me.' But in the meantime she doesn't mind being thought beautiful."

Yeshua took all this very well and indeed seemed enlivened in a way he had not been for many weeks. He and the old man ended up talking together at great length, and parted friends. The man promised to return to Sennabris saying he had found not a miracle worker but something much rarer, a man of wisdom.

This was the sort of thing that most pleased Yeshua: a reasoned discussion that ended with his interlocutor won over to his point of view. In this he revealed himself to be at heart a teacher—not a mystic, not a cultist, not even a healer per se, but merely what he had presented himself to me as from the start, someone with a few plain truths he wished to impart to people. Indeed, this was the Yeshua that I had been drawn to, and that I now missed. If things had been different, if the need of people hadn't been so great or if he himself hadn't had that special air to him, the quality of being chosen or marked that seemed almost to stand outside him like a second person, then he might have simply lived out his life in Notzerah or Kefar Nahum with his little following and his bit of renown. As it was, however, the mood of the times went against him, so that though he preached peace, yet he would not be left in it.

It was around this time that one of the women in our group, Ribqah, from Migdal, took seriously ill. She was a girl of little means and of questionable virtue whom Yeshua, however, no doubt exactly because the world held her in such low regard, had always kept very close to him. He had suffered much criticism on this account even from his own people, and Herod's spies had been quick to make use of the thing to further discredit him. Thus when she was struck down it was taken as a sign, in the way the peasants did, and the matter assumed a much greater importance than it merited.

It was mid-morning when word came to us that she was ill. A group of us set out at once from Kefar Nahum for her village, which was some five or six miles down the lakeshore. When we arrived there we were directed to a salting shed on the beach, and were surprised to find her simply spread out on a table next to a heap of entrails from the night's catch. Yeshua was livid.

"Why hasn't she been brought inside?"

But her father couldn't seem to fathom Yeshua's anger.

"We wanted to keep an eye on her while we worked," he said.

She had suffered a bite of some sort while she'd been walking along the beach, no one knew from what. The bite, on her shin, had already formed a suppurating abscess and had bloated her leg. Yeshua brought her to her bed and treated her as best he could, lancing the abscess and drawing blood from her in the hope of draining the poison. But within the hour she was dead. When the life passed out of her, Yeshua wept. It was a long time before we could get him to leave her so she could be dressed for burial.

"I did nothing for her," he said.

Afterwards he kept up his mourning for many days, holed up in his little room at the back of Kephas's house. The entire time he neither ate nor washed, his forehead still smeared with the dirt he had put there when Ribqah had died. He seemed to be mourning his own impotence—for all the wonders people ascribed to him, he had been unable to save one of those closest to him. So it was that whenever he heard there were supplicants at the gate, he would at once slip out by the back way, and be gone for many hours.

We were all of us worried for him at the time, and wondered what would become of him. With each day that passed without food he seemed to grow more wild-eyed and less reasonable, so that we feared he would descend into madness. The only one of us whose presence he would suffer then was Andreas, from whom he took water at least and who would cling to him to comfort him without the least affectation or reserve, so that tears would come to Yeshua's eyes. Indeed it was Andreas, I thought, who was the thing that held him to the world then, since he was such a child and could not be put off, whereas the rest of us hardly dared to go near him.

For my part, I wondered, seeing the depths he had fallen into, if I had ever really understood him, since he seemed such a stranger to me in that state, and more defeated even than when I had first met him at En Melakh. Clearly it was not only the matter of Ribqah that had undone him, for there were any number he had not cured and more than one who had died in his arms. Rather it seemed he had lost his way, as if he himself was no longer certain what he must be to people or as if the second person he was, which was his public one, had somehow split away and left only this ghost of himself. Afterwards I thought it had been a mistake for even those of us closest to him to have avoided him during that time, and to have failed to reassure him. But in my own case I no longer felt sufficiently in his confidence to believe I could reach him in any way.

After many days in this state he finally called us together at Kephas's house and said he would be leaving us for a time, he could not say for how long. Among the twelve there was a great sense of destitution at this, and it seemed only by force of will that the women were able to keep themselves from wailing aloud. Yet because we didn't know the state of his mind no one dared to beg him to stay. Perhaps he took offence at this, or indeed had been awaiting some sign from us of our support for him, because he left the house at once then to be alone again.

When he'd gone I said, "We must find the way to accompany him, when he goes," and I could see there was some relief at the suggestion, since the notion apparently hadn't occurred to any of the others.

It was agreed that three of us would go with him. Kephas put himself forward to lead the group, but it was the height of the season for him, and his mother-in-law was ill and near death, and we rightly discouraged him from going off on a sojourn of uncertain destination and length. It was the same with Yaqob and several of the others, so that in the end we were left with Yohanan and Simon the Canaanite and also myself, because no one, I supposed, had been quick enough to voice an objection to me.

I went out in search of Yeshua then and found him on the beach just outside the town. He had walked out along the breakwater there, which sat low at that time because of the rains, so that he seemed to hover on the surface of the lake.

I told him the plan we had made, and who would accompany him. He did not put up any objection but seemed surprised, perhaps even disappointed, with whom we had settled on for the purpose.

"So you see how the last are first," he said, which was a saying of his, meaning that Simon and I had been the last to join the twelve.

I, however, felt a throb of anticipation at the journey, though I would not have foreseen this. Perhaps what drew me was simply the prospect of leaving Kefar Nahum, which had begun to be a prison to me. But it was also, I had to admit, the chance of being in close quarters with Yeshua again, for it seemed now I had missed him in these past weeks and months as if he had been away from me, and I wished for his return.

Yeshua wasted no time now in setting out, rousing us before dawn the next morning and saying nothing of our destination except that we would be heading north towards the Syrian highlands. We followed the Jordan Valley road as far as Lake Huleh and then crossed over at Thella into Philip's territory, though there was not so much as a tollgate there to mark the passage. I had never made this trip before and was amazed at the lushness of the valley, particularly around the lake. There were all manner of trees and vegetation, reeds three times as high as a man, birds and animals of every sort, as if we had stumbled upon the first site of creation.

From there on, it was clear that we were in foreign country. The landscape became increasingly rugged and wooded; the villages we passed were like little pagan fortresses, high-walled and forbidding and seeming cut off in some absolute way from the rest of the civilized world. All along the roadside were shrines to the local gods, little altars in the middle of nowhere or strange, demonish faces carved into the cliffs or just arcane agglomerations of rocks and stones that only the slightest bit of order distinguished from the random rocks nearby. It was hard to believe this land had formed part of old Israel, so completely had it reverted. As it turned out we were lucky to have Simon along with us—he spoke the dialect, and helped to mitigate the instinctive distrust that most of the locals felt for Jews.

We put up for the night in the woods just outside Paneas, or rather Caesarea Philippi, as Philip had now renamed it. Simon warned us that we would be much safer in the town; but Yeshua, who had hardly spoken the entire trip, refused to pass through the gates. In the morning, Yohanan and I went in to fetch some food and managed to steal a glimpse of the cave of Pan where the Jordan began. The entire site was dominated now by Herod the Great's temple to Augustus, one sacrilege laid over another; though at least the worship of Pan had the virtue of being rooted in the honest feelings of the people. Even that early in the morning the shrine was already filled with pilgrims, some of them caught in fits of ecstasy. Niches carved into the cliff face were filled with idols; everywhere were offerings of food and garlands and coins and bits of silver and gold. Yohanan, who had never seen such a sight, was very affected by the visit—no doubt he had never imagined that pagan gods could inspire such a level of devotion.

Though Yeshua had not told us as much, it was clear by now that we were headed up Mount Hermon. Simon appeared to grow agitated at this prospect—the mountain was a site of worship for his people, and he seemed to fear some vengeance from his former gods for his desertion of them. His panic increased when in the woods we passed a group of acolytes of Pan writhing and moaning in the morning fog. So his conversion had not quite taken after all; later it came out that what he had feared the previous evening when we'd slept in the open had been not the threat of thieves, as we'd thought, but rather of Pan visiting mischief on us in the night. All of this he tried to hide from Yeshua, of course, only reluctantly confiding in Yohanan and me when his fears began to get the better of him.

Though well worn by pilgrims, the road up the mountain was not much more than a sheep path, irregular and stony and steep. We passed an altar where a sacrifice was in progress, the smell of blood heavy on the air; it occurred to me that we were not far removed here from our own forefathers, slaughtering their lambs in the high places of Canaan. But Yeshua continued forward in his single-minded manner, always slightly ahead of us, seemingly unmoved by the strange, pagan atmosphere of the place, the sense that a thousand spirits hovered around us. The higher we went, the more alien and savage our surroundings became; but Yeshua did not even so much as look back at us, climbing the slopes with the agility of a mountain goat while the three of us struggled to keep up. At one point a patch of mist cut off our view of him entirely and Simon, in a fit of panic, shouted out to him.

We found him waiting for us in a clearing.

"I was afraid we'd lost you," Simon said.

"And what would you do then?"

The hardness in Yeshua's voice made Simon redden.

"I would look for you."

"How long? An hour? A day?"

"Until I found you," Simon said, and I saw there were tears in his eyes.

By sunset we had reached the point where the wooded slopes of the mountainside began to give way to barren rock. There was still a bit of snow at the mountain's peak, which gave a bitter chill to the wind that blew down from there, and as we had not brought any tents Yohanan and I suggested we spend the night in a little temple nearby, a crude construction of wood and unfinished stone. Yeshua, however, would have none of it, and insisted we build huts from what branches and saplings we could scrounge together. We built a separate one for him and then, a little apart, a large one for the rest of us, since Simon had made it clear that he was too frightened to sleep alone. Yeshua retreated into his own the instant darkness fell, declining to share our supper. A while later we heard sounds from his tent that we took at first for sobs, but he was merely praying. Nonetheless, Simon was thrown into a panic again, and edged up to his hut.

"Master!" he said.

"What is it?"

"Ah! I'm sorry. We thought—I was frightened."

Silence.

"Master, we're wondering why you've come here," Simon said.

"What is it to you, why I've come? Is it such a burden to keep me company?"

We passed a miserable night. A fog had set in that chilled us to the bone; and then all night long Simon plagued us with his fears, growing more and more crazed. I gathered that in his mind the gods that had peopled his old life had not so much vanished with his conversion as been transformed into demons, all of them now intent on his destruction. To be fair to him, there was something about the place that inspired this kind of madness; and then in the middle of the night, as if his worst fears had materialized, there was a great crashing in the underbrush and wild animals of some sort—we were never able to determine what they were—encircled our camp. For the longest time we sat huddled in our tent trying to keep silent while the animals rampaged around us; Simon, despite our imprecations, finally broke down and began whispering atonements to his old gods, believing the animals to be demons that had been loosed upon us. It seemed only by some fluke that the beasts didn't knock down our flimsy hut and make off with us. Then, as suddenly as they had come, they were gone.

We went out at once to check on Yeshua: his hut was empty. Simon let out a wail at this discovery. But there was no blood nearby, so far as we could tell, nor had there been any sounds of struggle; it was possible, therefore, that he had simply fled. Clearly we had to wait until morning to begin a search, given the fog and the dark and the danger of falling prey to the very beasts we had just been saved from. But Simon had grown frantic, weeping and lamenting as if the entire blame for the calamity fell on his own shoulders, and before Yohanan or I could stop him he rushed out into the dark, calling out for his master. We tried to chase after him to bring him back, but within a matter of paces we already seemed in danger of losing our way.

We had no option except to wait, huddling once more in our little tent. The time seemed interminable; at one point we heard distant sounds in the underbrush again, called out, got only an animal moan in return, and decided to repair after all to the little temple nearby, shoring up a small pile of stones inside as ammunition and stopping up the entrance with a few boulders and rotting logs. The place was drafty and dank, with a smell of lamp oil and smoke and old blood; we tried to build a fire but couldn't get it going. Out of sheer exhaustion and cold we finally fell asleep, only waking when the first light had begun to show through the mist.

Our first priority was to look for Yeshua—we reckoned that if he had fled, logic would have sent him along the treeless upper slopes of the mountain, where it would have been possible to run in the fog and dark without fear of obstruction. We set out along the rough path that led up towards the mountaintop, able to pick our way even though the fog was so thick at first that we could not see more than half a dozen paces ahead of us. Then, as we rose higher, the fog began to thin and the light to grow stronger. We had not gone very far, however, before we heard shouts in the distance: Simon. He was coming down the path towards us.

"I've found him!" he was saying. "I've found him!"

He emerged finally, breathless, out of the fog.

"He's on the mountaintop!"

"Is he safe?" I said.

"Yes, yes! He's with the others!"

"What others?"

"Come and see!"

He was babbling. We tried to calm him but couldn't get much sense out of him.

"Come and see for yourselves!"

We followed him up. Soon we had risen above the fog into brilliant morning light. It was as if we had entered the heavens: at our feet the fog stretched, a great cloud spread out for as far as the eye could see; then, before us, bathed in light, the snow-covered peak of the mountain. At the very peak we could make out the figure of Yeshua, alone.

"They were there before!" Simon said. "I swear it!"

Angels, he said they were, all in white; who knew what trick of the fog and light and of his own fevered mind had induced in him this vision. From what we gathered, he believed they had interceded to save Yeshua after the demons had carried him off to the mountaintop.

"I assure you I came up here entirely on my own," Yeshua said, when we reached him. It turned out he had been there most of the night, and had not even been present when the animals had attacked. As to our own miraculous escape, he put it down to God or blind luck.

"If there had been angels, I would have been the first to see them."

But he didn't manage to shake Simon of his belief; and later, of course, when we returned to Galilee, it was Simon's version of things, being the most fantastical, that seemed at once to gain currency.

Yeshua showed no particular joy that we had survived our attack, and indeed I had the impression he might just as soon have had us devoured and been rid of us. What seemed of greater concern to him, when we returned to the camp, was that we had been so foolish as to leave our sack of food within easy reach, and the animals had made their supper of it.

"So it seems you'll keep me company in my fast," he said, and thus gave us to know he would not give up his retreat, though we were without food and at the mercy of the wild animals.

There was no thought of abandoning him. But a plan had to be devised to keep safe our own lives. In the end it was Simon, again, entirely calmed now that he'd seen that Yeshua's magic was greater than that of his demons, who proved indispensable: it turned out that for all his fanciful notions he understood a thing or two about the wild, pointing out, for instance, that most animals would be loath to leave the wooded lower slopes of the mountain for the barren ones higher up. Accordingly we moved our camp to the mountaintop, where the air was colder but actually less damp than on the slopes; and for added security we built a little fortress of mud and branches and stones for the three of us, then a smaller one, again, for Yeshua, which, however, as far as we could ascertain, he seldom used. It was Simon also who found a spring for water, and who fashioned traps so that we were never in want of meat; and though with each day that passed there seemed less and less to distinguish us from the wild beasts, it was also true that our survival no longer ever seemed in serious threat.

As it happened the retreat lasted many days and weeks, so that we had only the moon to tell us the time and sometimes could not even say for certain which day was the sabbath and which was not. Yeshua, at first, had little to do with us, and would take his food apart if he ate at all and spend his time praying alone on the mountaintop or wandering in the woods or caught up in some little project that would then take up all his energies. Once he borrowed a knife from Simon and spent the entire day carving and whittling away at a log he had dragged up from the forest; and when evening came and we dared to look at what he had done, we saw he'd carved our own three likenesses, Yohanan and Simon and myself, so amazing in their accuracy that even Yohanan and I, despite our unease, stood a moment speechless at his skill.

"But, teacher," Yohanan said finally, "it's forbidden."

"You're right. Burn it."

And without further ado he had us throw the thing into the fire.

But after some time it seemed he slowly came back to himself. It started with his joining Simon on his morning rounds to his traps, which pleased Simon no end, and had him instructing Yeshua in every detail of how he set the traps out, and laid the bait, and studied the animals' habits so that he knew how such and such a placement or such and such a trick would catch them up. We'd see the two of them go off every morning like seasoned hunters, and hear Simon's chatter, and somehow all seemed right with us again. By then Yeshua had begun to join us for our meals and the small, crazed glint of his fast had left him, so that he began to seem happy with us out there in the wild, with no one to pester him or make demands. What I understood then was that he was not one of those who felt his very existence threatened if he did not have the adulation of the crowds, but rather someone who felt most himself exactly alone like this with his few friends and unremarked, and who suffered leadership only because he could not find the way to avoid it. For my part, I felt we had returned at last to the simple friendliness there had been between us at the outset, uncomplicated and unfraught, when we had often talked into the night in Kephas's courtyard or on the beach.

Once, when we were alone, we came to discuss Ephesus and he asked after my family, the first time he had ever done so. I told him then that my parents had died in the famous fire there some ten years before, during the riot against the Jews. I was already in Jerusalem then, finishing my studies; when I returned to Ephesus to settle my father's affairs I saw that the entire block where we had lived had been reduced to cinder.

"It affected you deeply," Yeshua said, which was not what I'd expected.

"It changed the course of my life."

"Because you blamed the Romans for what had happened."

"In short, yes."

I expected an argument from him, how the Romans protected the Jews, how they everywhere granted us special privileges; it was not the Romans, after all, who had burnt my father's house but the ignorant masses, who hated us exactly for our special treatment. I did not know what to put against this logic except the arguments I had made to myself as a young man—that a Jew must be free, and did not go on bended knee to ask for privileges, and that until the bond to Rome was broken we would remain the target of the world's persecutions, because we claimed to be chosen yet were in chains. But I did not know if I believed in these arguments as I once had.

To my surprise, however, Yeshua said only, "I'm very sorry for your parents' deaths," and did not challenge me, for which I was grateful.

In the end, his silence on this matter did more, perhaps, to question my convictions than any argument from him might have, for I understood in the wake of it how my hatred of Rome was as much a loyalty to the memory of my parents as a reasoned stand. I remembered my anger when I'd learned of their deaths, how I had wanted a target for it—I had been an easy prospect then for whatever cause or creed had first got hold of me, and might just as soon have become a Zealot. For the truth was that there were not many of those I'd met in the movement then who had struck me as men of great integrity or vision, and had I not been so blinded by rage and grief, I might not have been so quick to follow them. I wondered what I would have made of a Yeshua, had I met one then, how different the course of my life might have been. Yet it was likely I would not have heard him, or given him any heed, when even now it seemed always that I fought him in some part of myself and could not give in to him.

After we'd been on the mountain for some time it began to happen that some pilgrims who had made their way up to the place for their own ends got wind of the holy man who had pitched his camp there and began to seek him out. These were to a one pagans, mainly locals but also from as far away as Damascus and Tyre, and I was certain it was Simon who had somehow managed to spread the word among them, though he denied this. Usually they brought little offerings of food with them, which Yeshua, despite their taint of idolatry, authorized us to accept. But he did not grant them much of an audience, and then was uncompromising in his treatment of them. When they asked him the path to wisdom, he told them to follow the one true God; and when they asked after their own gods, he said they were phantoms, inventions of their own errant minds.

"But your own disciple here says they're demons," one of them said, referring to Simon.

"He's a child, and so he understands things as a child would," Yeshua said, at which Simon, however, beamed and took not the least offence.

I was surprised at how much these visitors indulged him—he had pitched camp, after all, on their own sacred ground, then had the audacity to blaspheme their gods. But most of them took this in stride, though I could not have said if they simply assumed he was mad or were genuinely drawn in by his strange air of authority.

One day a man from Sidon arrived, a wealthy merchant of some sort, with an entire entourage of slaves and a gilded litter that bore his sick daughter, whom all his doctors had been unable to cure. He had taken her to the shrine at Caesarea Philippi, again without success; but while there he had heard of the holy man on the mountain, and so had come to him to try his fortune. Yeshua's first reaction was to chastise the man for dragging his poor daughter across the countryside when she would have been much better off at home in her own bed. But then he set to work on her, draping her in a dampened cloth to bring down her fever and cooking up a pungent brew from a plant I was unfamiliar with that he found on the mountain slopes, small-leafed and bitter and brilliant green. Within a day her fever had begun to abate and her colour to return. Her father was ecstatic—he offered Yeshua a permanent place in his household, all the riches he could ask for, a temple dedicated to his god.

"Will you worship with me there?" Yeshua said.

"I have a dozen temples already to worship in. But if you want, I'll join you in your own as well."

"And if I asked you to come only to mine?"

The man laughed.

"Now your price is too steep."

When they'd gone, Yeshua fell into low spirits again.

"They were only pagans," Yohanan said, to console him. "Why should you trouble yourself over them?"

But Yeshua turned on him.

"Wasn't Simon a pagan? Do you think our god looks after only the Jews and doesn't concern himself with the rest? Is he just some little wood nymph to make an idol of, who lives in his little cave?"

The outburst silenced us, and left Yohanan red-faced with shame. But Yeshua's anger had surely come from his own divided mind: he seemed both to resent the help he gave to the heathens and yet unable to find the way, within his own philosophy, to refuse it.

We all feared the incident would send Yeshua spiralling back to the depths. But he recovered quickly enough, and even seemed heartened in the end, for he began to greet the pilgrims who came to him with some of his old humour and open spirit. Then one day, without any warning to us, he said the time had come to go home. At the news, Simon was so happy he began to scamper around like a foal and turn somersaults, until we were all in stitches. As for myself, I was pleased enough to be leaving the wild; yet already I regretted the loss of the closeness we had had there, with our fires and our makeshift meals and our men's unthinking camaraderie.

We spent the first night of our return journey at Caesarea Philippi. This time, however, we took rooms in the city proper, with alms the merchant of Sidon had given us. There we attended the baths, and walked through the city streets until late in the night. Yeshua spoke about his childhood in Alexandria, the first time I had heard him do so, and described some of the wonders he had seen including the Pharos, whose light, he said, could be seen halfway to Rome. When Yohanan asked which city was greater, Alexandria or Jerusalem, he surprised us by naming Alexandria, saying Jerusalem was the home of one great nation but Alexandria the home of many. He had never seemed so simply a man among men to me as he did that evening—we might have been soldiers on furlough, taking the town in, wending our way towards some final tavern or brothel to spend the night.

But already by morning, as we approached the border, he had begun to retreat into himself—I understood now the extra skin he put on to be with his followers, to become the teacher, the healer, what he must be to them. He had grown distracted and quiet with us; at Lake Huleh, where we stopped to refresh ourselves, he did not join us in the water, though he had bathed with us like any common Greek only the night before. The lake seemed to have a different aspect after our trip up the mountain, more pagan and desolate and wild, not part of God's creation at all. I thought of what Yeshua had said, how our god was not some creature in a cave like the gods of the Greeks. But it was true that I had always thought of him in that way, perched above his little promised land not bothering himself with what went on beyond it, the whole insignificant pagan world. What a paltry deity it suddenly seemed I had made for myself compared to Yeshua's, in whose dominion a place had to be found not only for us handful of Jews but for this savage lake, for the acolytes writhing in ecstasy in the forests of Mount Hermon, for the rich merchants who made temples to the gods of every nation.

We were not far past Thella before we began to draw a little crowd of hangers-on of those who knew Yeshua. I was surprised to discover that tales of the miracles he had wrought on Mount Hermon were already circulating, along with Simon's story of the angels; it was amazing to me, this hunger people had for wonders, and the speed with which they published them. I had almost forgotten the stature Yeshua had with many of his followers—alone with us in the woods he had appeared fallible and mortal and unsure, but here the adulation of his disciples seemed instantly to raise him up. The cloud under which he had departed appeared to have dissipated; it was the usual way of these things, that a scandal that one day was on every tongue, and seemed insurmountable, was all but forgotten the next.

Because Yeshua stopped to speak with all of those who came up to him, our progress was slow. By sunset we had not yet reached Kefar Nahum, though by then some of the twelve including Kephas had got wind of our approach and had come out to meet us. We were still on the river then and I suggested we cross over to Bet Zayda on the other shore, where we could rid ourselves of the crowd and get a decent night's rest. But Yeshua, to our surprise, said we should camp there in the fields so that he could be with his followers. There were perhaps fifty or more who chose to stay with us; a great fire was built and some of the women were sent into a village nearby to fetch food for us all with what was left of the alms we'd had from the merchant of Sidon. Yeshua stayed up teaching well into the night, seeming his old self in a way but also changed, more circumspect and controlled. Perhaps it was simply that I had seen him miserable and out of sorts and so understood now what he hid, and the struggles in him, which he would not show his followers.

Out in the open there with our fire it seemed we were not so far from the pagan places we'd left behind, with the bit of woods nearby and the smell of smoke and the cool air off the lake. Even the disciples who had gathered were at bottom not much different from the heathens who had come to Yeshua seeking they knew not what, some magic solution to their dilemmas or some potion or charm against the world's ills. I knew Yeshua did not encourage them in this and yet it was his lot to inspire extreme reactions in people, and to raise their hope, and to touch the need that was bottomless in them. So I had the sense that he was lost to me again, because his people had claimed him, and he could not be simply a man or a friend as I wished him to be.

The truth, however, which it seemed the others had always known, was that I'd had no real place with him there from the start, because of that part of me that would not quite relinquish itself, that could do no more than love him. So the others could not accept me, because I reduced to merely a man the great notion that Yeshua was to them, the notion of their own betterment and redemption. I had understood this in an instant when Kephas had come and made his greetings, and I'd seen how he ached with emotion at Yeshua's return and with the things he wished to say to him but held himself back on my account. And though I had never held Kephas to be a man of great intelligence, I wondered now if he did not see Yeshua more clearly than I did, because he understood him with his heart, while I had always striven to find the argument that would defeat him.

In the morning, because his followers would not leave him and others had begun to join them, Yeshua hardly stopped at Kefar Nahum before making for the hill above the town where he often spoke. All morning, by ones and twos, the crowd continued to grow, which surprised me, given how divided and in disarray his following had seemed at his departure. At one point the crowd had swelled to such a number, well up into the hundreds, that Ventidius arrived with some men from the Roman camp to see if there was any trouble. But seeing Yeshua teaching peacefully there, he quickly withdrew.

It was towards midday that I noticed someone eyeing me nervously from the edge of the crowd: it was the same Yekhubbah whom I had met at Caesarea. My heart fell at the sight of him—my first thought, given the news I had heard out of Jerusalem, was that he had been sent to accuse me as a traitor.

"I've come to call you back to the city," he said when he had taken me aside, making it seem he came in good faith by naming the lawyer I had reported to in the city administration as one of those who had sent him. Yet he wouldn't meet my eye.

"What of your friend?" I said, meaning Rohagah. But he answered only that Rohagah awaited me as well, and thought I might be of use.

I wasn't sure what to make of him. It seemed he had been waiting for me there for many days, which did not bode well. But perhaps he had simply not known what to do, being sent to fetch me by his betters and finding I had gone.

I did not know what path to take. Yet in the end my way was clear, because though with Yeshua I felt quickened in a way I had not for many years, still I didn't belong with him, while in Jerusalem, even if I was vilified by my own people, at least they were my own. I was certain that this time I would not find the way to return to Yeshua if I left, and so did not know how to part from him.

"We'll go in the morning, then," I said to Yekhubbah.

But Yekhubbah would not be put off.

"It would be better to leave at once," he said, which did not boost my confidence in him. "You may say that your family has need of you."

I realized then that he would not leave my side, and that therefore there was no thought of speaking frankly with Yeshua. Indeed I did not wish to speak to him at all, with such a one as this at my elbow.

"Then let's go immediately," I said rashly.

"You don't wish to take your leave?"

"No."

He was clearly bothered by this but didn't know what to do.

"We'll go, then," he said finally.

It happened that I still had my few things along with me from our retreat, so there was nothing for us to do but set out. Yeshua had a crowd around him then, and I saw that Yohanan too was in the midst of it. Only one of the women noticed me there at the edge of the crowd and caught my eye, with that coldness the women reserved for me.

"I've heard troubling news from Jerusalem," I said to Yekhubbah.

"There are many lies being spread," he said. "In Jerusalem you'll learn the truth."

And it was on that comfortless note that I set off with him towards the Jerusalem road.

It took us three days to reach the city. From the outset Yekhubbah was tight-lipped and anxious, which raised my concern; though what news I eventually loosed from him only raised it further. He referred to Rohagah as one of our leaders, which confirmed my fears—surely all was lost, if we now looked to such as him to set our course.

When we reached Jerusalem, however, I found the situation much worse even than I had imagined it. Yekhubbah led me at once to Rohagah's quarters in the lower city, where there was much toing and froing and many whispered words; and I saw how the others deferred to him, and the fear in them.

To me, he said only, "It was good of you to return, now that we have need of you," in a tone devoid of inflection.

However I was not invited to speak to him again for many days, nor was I given any mission, and it seemed that those I had known before in our cause were at pains to avoid me. When I asked after my former contact in the city administration, whom I had trusted, I was told he had left the city for Alexandria; my other contact, following his arrest, had been deported. So I was alone, with no one to turn to. It was only by chance once, at the temple, that I met someone who was willing to speak to me, a pock-faced tanner named Abram whom I had known only in passing, and never much trusted because of his boasting manner. Now, however, fear seemed to have humbled him.

"We've done a better job killing our own than the Romans ever did," he said, and he described how it was not only those suspected of betraying us who had been killed off but even several of our own leaders, whose deaths had been arranged by those who opposed them, then blamed on the Romans. To do the work the *sicari* had been hired, named after the daggers they used—they would attack their prey in a crowd and slip off before they'd been noticed. So the old leaders had quickly been done away with and no one dared to oppose the new, because of their ruthlessness.

I had no way to gauge the truth of these accusations, since even to repeat them was a danger. But I grew increasingly uneasy in the wake of them, watching my back each time I stepped from my gate and feeling spied on at every corner. I had put up at a cousin's house, since I had abandoned my own when I'd left the city; but he knew nothing of my cause and so found me increasingly peculiar, because I made no effort to reopen the shop I had run in the bazaar, nor did I leave the house at all for days at a time, afraid as I was for my life. When Tabernacles approached, he said to me that his brothers would soon come in from the countryside for the feast and I must give up my bed, and so made it clear that he wished to be rid of me.

I sold off some of the inventory from my shop then that I had put away before my departure and took a room in a boarding house near the Dung Gate. There I passed the time of the festival, hardly daring to go out into the crowds, which were thick then because the year of Jubilee had been proclaimed, yet not wanting either to leave the city, for I was determined to do nothing that could be used against me. Then when the feast had ended and the city had emptied again, I was finally called back to Rohagah. This time we met in the upper rooms of the old school building that his quarters stood behind, and that served to mask the many comings and goings. There were several others present whom I did not recognize and whose faces I could hardly make out, since it was night and the room was dimly lit.

Rohagah said, "Because there have been many traitors among us, we must make sure of you," and I understood that I had been brought to stand trial before them.

I might simply have flouted them then and gone my way, and so at least kept my dignity. Perhaps it was only cowardice that kept me from doing so, since I surely had reason enough to believe by then that they would take my life if they saw the need. But the truth was also that I did not wish to give them that satisfaction. They thought my kind could not be trusted, that we would not lay down our lives for our nation, simply because we had been abroad or had read more than the scriptures or had shown ourselves open-minded towards the customs of the world. But I wished them to see it was not a crime to seek education and knowledge, nor did it make you a traitor to your people.

As it happened my trial lasted many days and weeks, and was as much in the silences I endured as in the interrogations. Thus they would ask about some obscure episode in the past, often hardly memorable, as if it had given rise to the suspicion over me; and when I had accounted for every action and cleared every hint of doubt they would make as if they had acquitted me and assign me some little mission in the city. Each of these, however, was more insignificant than the last, and seemed only to push me further and further to the margins of their work, until finally after weeks had passed I would be called in to them again and they would recommence their questions. The chief accusation against me, as I gathered, was that I had been the one to betray Ezekias, since I had fled then and had been so long out of communication; but even this seemed only an excuse for their general distrust of me. In the meantime I was kept in the dark about their activities and so learned only the barest rudiments of the great action they had put their hopes in, which was set for the coming Passover. In this, at least, it appeared they had planned well: because of the Jubilee the crowds would likely number into the hundreds of thousands then, who, if they rose in revolt, would easily overwhelm the few thousand who guarded the Antonia fortress.

Towards the end of my interrogations I was several times asked about Yeshua, who I was surprised to learn was well known to Rohagah and his group. It grew clearer to me now why they had sent for me: they wished to know if Yeshua might be of use to them, having somehow formed the opinion that he was a firebrand and a rebel. I ought to have disabused them at once of any hopes they had on this front. But either out of pride or sheer contrariness I somewhat encouraged them in their notions, even if only by ambiguities, since I did not want to make it appear that I had merely been biding my time with Yeshua, which would have given force to their accusations against me. I soon had cause to regret this strategy, however, because Rohagah was quick to call my bluff.

It seemed his informants were much more extensive than I had imagined, and had learned that Yeshua planned a pilgrimage with his followers for the Jubilee Passover.

"You must find the way to put yourself among them again," he said, "so that you can turn them to us at the right moment."

I was at a loss. It was on my lips to blurt the truth, and be blunt about the sort of man that Yeshua was. Yet in those few words I would have undone all the work of the previous months, since I knew Rohagah was angry at having proved nothing against me and would take the least chance to have me convicted. So I let my silence give him cause to believe I would do the thing, when I could not.

It was only a matter of weeks then to the Passover. The mood in the city was one of great expectation, and already the streets had begun to fill and barricades were being built to control the crowds and every corner was being swept and scoured, so that God should not find us derelict. Yet it did not seem now, after all, that Rohagah and the others had judged our time well, or that we remained anything more than the merest anomaly in the city's life, or that there was any stomach in people for insurrection, when all their thoughts were on feasting and profit. It was true the Roman procurator was hated, and that he had already committed many other offences large and small since the first one of the standards; yet he did not much occupy people's thoughts. Indeed, returning to the city after an absence from it, and living as I had amongst the peasants and fishermen of Galilee, I saw now how prosperous the Jews of Jerusalem were despite their foreign yoke, and how they lived well and ate well, and perhaps thought of the Romans as a godsend after the many abuses they had suffered under their own rulers.

Some days after my final meeting with Rohagah a messenger came to me at the boarding house where I was still staying to give me instructions to set out for Galilee. There I was to insert myself again amongst Yeshua's men and join them in their pilgrimage, though saying nothing, of course, of our plans; once back in Jerusalem, I was to report for further counsel. I knew very little at that point of what Rohagah and the others had in mind—an attack on the fortress, I assumed, and then perhaps the formation of some makeshift battle force once the armoury had been breached. It was all madness, of course, I saw that, and was amazed that Rohagah and his cronies did not: we would all be slaughtered, either quickly and cleanly at the outset, or more slowly and more disastrously. In the process our cause would be set back many years, and many innocents who knew nothing of us, and perhaps did not even care what we stood for, would be slaughtered along with us. So I did not know what to do, for if I did nothing I would be killed, yet perhaps also if I fled; and if I said nothing to Yeshua he would march his own lambs into the slaughter, yet if I warned him, I still put him at risk.

I regretted now that I had ever come back to Jerusalem, and had not simply turned tail at the sight of Yekhubbah and
set out for the hills. And I thought, We have been deluded from the start, the old guard as much as the new, not because of this failed plan or that, or this or that schism, but because of our great irrelevance. Yeshua, with his few hundred, had never made that mistake—he sought to bring along with him only those who understood him, and made no claim to the rest. Meanwhile, we with our dozens imagined instead

that we spoke for the whole of our race, when they cared nothing for us, nor we, for that matter, for them. No doubt it was exactly this fear that drove the likes of a Rohagah, that we were powerless and insignificant and small, that history would erase every trace of us. Or perhaps it was the greater fear of every Jew—that God had deserted us, that he would no longer descend from the heavens to redeem us from our humiliations, and we, like an army whose commander had deserted, were merely skirmishing towards our doom.

Many years before, when I travelled once to Rome, I was taken by the strange contradictions I found there in the worship of their gods, who seemed at once revered as the authors of human fate, yet also disrespected and mocked at every turn in a manner no Jew could ever countenance. It seemed that at bottom their gods were regarded as no better than mortals, except for their bit of magic that gave them power over us, and worship of them was not so much devotion as simple appeasement, in the way we flattered a tyrant to save our necks. I saw in this at the time a sign of our own superiority—how much greater our own god from whom our entire moral order flowed, who was so much above us we could hardly fathom his ways. There was the famous story of Pompey's surprise upon entering the Holy of Holies at finding it not bedizened with all manner of riches as he'd expected but empty and barren as a grave: it was beyond the scope of the pagan mind, we had been taught, this sense of a thing larger than their own imaginations, unrepresentable. Yet how truly different was our god, in the end? What we called inscrutable in our own god, we called simple fickleness in theirs; and while our god, for all his greatness, had made our people insignificant and weak, the Romans, who debased our temple and committed every sacrilege against us, ruled the world. What sense could we make of such an injustice, and how could our god, in the face of it, seem what we believed him to be? When I thought of the splendours I had seen in Rome, the great palaces and public buildings that were just the tiniest fraction of what the empire had built throughout the civilized world, it seemed the sheerest folly, while we struggled here for our few wretched acres of promised land, that we should imagine our god the one true one. And if he were, then surely we must surmise that we had displeased him in some final and absolute way, that he should so plunge us down and give such solace and strength to our enemies.

Though a man barely of middle age, I had often had the feeling I had come up against the brink of things, had reached the end of every path. As a young man, I believed I would define who I was through my actions; when that failed, when I became involved in what revealed itself as an endless process of deferral, I hoped at least for wisdom. But wisdom, too, eluded me. I had visited a dozen nations, and heard tell of a hundred philosophies; but what had most struck me in this was how little of value there was in the world, how men were deceitful and base and would espouse to you the loftiest ideals in one breath and contradict them in the next. When the chaff was sifted from things there seemed only further chaff, the same tired notions, the same predictable vice. Thus when I considered what it was in Yeshua that had held me to him, it seemed exactly the hope of something new: a new sort of man, a new way of seeing things. I thought, If there was a single person who had found the way to speak the truth, perhaps the rest was worthwhile; if there was someone whose vision was truly more than hope for his own gain or greater glory, then perhaps God had not made us simply animals, a pestilence the world would be well rid of. I thought of the times in which we lived, of the murders and massacres, the kings who thought only of their treasuries and the bandits who robbed and killed the innocent in the name of justice; I thought how miserly and mean even the common people had become, so that in every village the gates were slammed shut against any stranger and the poor died of hunger by the road. Perhaps, then, we were truly at the end of days as some of the madmen in the desert preached. But there was in Yeshua that quality that made one feel there was something, still, some bit of hope, some secret he might reveal that would help make the world over. Tell me your secret, I had wanted to say to him, tell me, make me new. And even now, though I had left him, I often saw him beckoning before me as towards a doorway he would have had me pass through, from darkness to light.

BOOK II

MIRYAM OF MIGDAL

WE LIVED IN MIGDAL and made our living curing the catch that the fishermen brought in from the lake, salting it or smoking it depending on the season and where it would go. Some of it we sold as far away as Jerusalem, though also north to Paneas and the highlands, where my mother was from. My father, of course, was a Jew, from the south, which was how I was raised; but my mother he found in the mountains when he first came here as a young man. In all the years she'd been with him she had never taken to the ways of the Jews, had never sat down with us to pray or accompanied us to the assembly house. Her own people, she said, had lived on these lands since the world was created, and had got on very well long before the Jews arrived with their one true God.

Our house was just off the waterfront, not far from the smoking sheds and the harbour. Though my father was a trader, it was modest enough, with only a bit of stonework above the lintel to set it off and a tessera floor in black and white at the entrance. But as there were just the five of us there, my two sisters and I and our parents, with no other family to crowd us in, we seemed to live in wealth, so that my friend Ribqah, who had hardly a corner to call her own, imagined our home a great palace. For my own part, I might not have minded the furor of a fuller household, and also the presence of boys, whom my mother, some said out of spite, had refused to offer up. She had us three girls all in a row, with not much more than a year between us, and then of a sudden ceased her childbearing as if a spell had been cast on her. Nonetheless, my father loved us all and showed us kindness.

Though I was the eldest and had long been of marriageable age, I had no suitors. My sisters had inherited our mother's beauty, and were both betrothed. But I was plain, like my father. It wasn't true, however, that no one had ever asked for my hand—in the beginning there were several who had come, nervous young boys whom my father had rounded up from one place or another. They would stand near the smoking sheds and look at me while I worked, and I would pretend not to notice them. In the end I always found some reason to refuse them, which my doting father indulged, so that eventually the word went around that I had got only the worst of my mother, which was her wilfulness, and the men stopped coming. It wasn't that I disliked these men—since I had hardly spoken a word with any of them, I couldn't in fact feel one way or the other. Perhaps I was afraid that they'd grow tired of me, or that I'd be barren and they'd divorce me, and couldn't bear the thought of such humiliations. But it was more than that—when I imagined myself as a mother or bride, it seemed a sort of death, though I didn't hate these things and couldn't say what other future it was I intended for myself, since there was none.

After Yeshua came to us, however, the question of my marriage ceased to seem important. The first time my father invited him to our home I made the mistake at the start, from how my father deferred to him, of imagining him another suitor, though he was still haggard and thin then from his time in the desert. But Yeshua was nothing like the other men who had come. For one thing, he wasn't a child—that was clear from the look of him and from his bearing, which was proud and erect, as if he knew his own mind. He came into our house entirely without pretension or affectation and at once made himself one of us, though our household was without distinction and we ourselves, because of my mother, somewhat outcast. My father offered him our good chair, a fine thing of leather and carved oak that had been a gift from a merchant my father had dealings with. But Yeshua refused it, saying he hadn't come to our house to place himself above us.

My father had met him outside the Tiberias gates, where he had been preaching. This was in the time just after the arrest of the prophet Yohanan, who, because he had spoken against Herod's marriage to his brother's wife, Herod had put away. During his travels my father had often passed Yohanan's camp on the Jordan and had been taken with his teachings, and hearing Yeshua defending him and calling himself his disciple, he had been moved to invite him to our home. For several days then, since he had just come from the wilderness and had nowhere to keep himself, Yeshua stayed with us in Migdal, sleeping in our courtyard. But then we heard that the neighbours had begun to chatter because there were unmarried women in the house, and my father arranged a place for him with one of the fishermen he knew up the coast in Kefar Nahum.

So attached had I already become to Yeshua by then that the day he left I shed tears and could hardly keep my mind on my work, certain I would never see him again, though he had promised to return. It was difficult to say what had so drawn me to him—not merely a girl's infatuation with novelty, for all that my life had been sheltered until then. Rather it was as if a door had suddenly opened, or a passage been granted to a country you'd hoped might exist but had never quite dared to imagine. I could smell the air of this other place on him, feel the wind of it, see its different sunrise, and felt inside me the sudden sure thought that I must travel there with him. While he was with us, he had come to me one night on the beach, where I often walked before sleeping, and talked to me in such a way as no man had ever spoken to me before, as if every subject was permitted; and though I could hardly recall afterwards what it was that we had discussed, still it seemed to me then that he had reached inside me with his words to touch the inmost part of me.

The day he left the mat where he had lain in our courtyard still lay on the ground when I came in from the smoking sheds, and I would have taken it then for my own simply to remember him by had it not seemed shameful to. But then the following week, when I had all but given up hope of his return, he suddenly appeared in the harbour one morning in the fishing boat of Shimon bar Jonah, to whom my father had entrusted him. My heart was so full at the sight of him that I ran out to greet him like a child, and I could see that Shimon was embarrassed for my sake. But Yeshua embraced me openly, the first time any man had ever done such a thing.

You see, I've kept my promise, he said.

He had Shimon tie up the boat and then invited my family and me to have breakfast with them on the beach, as the fishermen did. It was from that morning that Yeshua came to call Shimon the Rock, because he sat in such stony silence at the scandal of being there in the open with three unmarried women. That was how we thought in those days, the women as much as the men. But Yeshua came to change us all, even Shimon, whom the four winds couldn't move when he had set his mind to a thing.

It was not long afterwards that Yeshua began his meetings in Kefar Nahum. In the beginning there was just a handful of us who attended—our family in Migdal, which was to say, however, mainly my father and me, since my sisters' betrothed were quick to forbid them; then Ribqah, who I invited and who came against her father's wishes; then Shimon and his brother Andreas and a few of those that Shimon knew in Kefar Nahum, including Yaqob bar Zabdi and his brother Yohanan. We'd meet on the beach or in Shimon's house or in our own and discuss Yeshua's teachings, and Yeshua always encouraged us to ask him questions or even to contradict him. Many of us were alarmed at this, not least the women, since we had always been taught to hold our tongues, and indeed often enough we didn't know at all how to respond to him, because his ideas flew in the face of what we had heard in the assembly house or from our elders. For myself, who had been raised a Jew yet had never dared to ask what a Jew was or what was our teaching on such a thing or another, it was a revelation to me that these matters could be put to the question at all, and required a mind to piece them together.

That Yeshua kept us women with him made him many enemies and caused much dissension even within our following. More than once it happened that some young man who had heard him preaching in the streets and been moved to attend one of our meetings instantly fled at the sight of Ribqah and me; and even Shimon, at first, seemed on the verge of bolting at every minute, barely able to settle himself and sometimes rising to pace so that the meeting could hardly go on for the distraction he made. But Yeshua, though he listened patiently to every argument, didn't relent. When the men argued that women were of weaker mind than men, Yeshua replied that it would be wrong therefore to exclude them from his teaching, when they must have greater need of it; when they argued that they were more given to evil, Yeshua said it was exactly those given to evil who concerned him. So he confounded the men's arguments and left them without a response, though so strong was their resistance to our presence that they seemed to feel cheated by Yeshua's logic.

Then one evening Shimon said, You're saying that the women are like us fishermen and peasants. No one bothers with us because they think we're nothing, and that's why you've come to us. And Yeshua agreed that Shimon had understood him.

That was an important moment for us—once Shimon had been won over the other men, who looked to him for leadership, grew more accepting. For Shimon, the evening marked the beginning of his great loyalty to Yeshua, and he always seemed to carry with him afterwards the small shame of that first doubt he had shown. As for Ribqah and me, our relief was unbounded, since every day we had feared expulsion—that would have been the worst thing, to have the door opened to us, then be turned away. Later people said that we women clung to Yeshua as we did only because he indulged us and showed us respect above our station. But that was not the case. Rather we stayed with him for this, that he let us see it was no sin to.

It seemed all of us in that first time of coming together had such moments of understanding when a difficult thing, an impossible notion, grew suddenly simple and plain like a knot that had unravelled. In the assembly houses we heard only of laws we couldn't keep or couldn't understand—how we women, for instance, must bow our heads and cover our lips and spend half our lives behind closed doors, though we weren't the princesses of Judea who could afford such luxuries but must daily work alongside the men. But Yeshua didn't come to us citing this law or that to beat us with, or invoking our ancestors to make us feel insufficient. Rather he made it seem that we ourselves were a beginning, and could see things anew.

Not long after we had settled the controversy of the women, another arose that proved to be my own test. One evening, while we were meeting at Shimon's house in Kefar Nahum, it happened that Yeshua's mother and one of his brothers appeared at the gate from their town of Notzerah. Shimon's wife Shua came to us and announced them, saying that they had heard of Yeshua's presence in Kefar Nahum and had come to fetch him home. But Yeshua refused to see them. Shua, a timid woman, was so taken aback at this—as were we all—that she couldn't bring herself to confront them.

Miryam, Yeshua said to me, because I was closest to him, go to the gate and send them away.

But what shall I tell them, I said.

Tell them I'm already home, and so there's no need to fetch me.

None of us knew what to make of this. Until that moment Yeshua had never spoken to us of his family, nor had any of us thought it our place to ask after it. But I couldn't imagine what crime they had committed to bring out such contempt in him. I went to the gate and his mother and brother stood waiting there completely silent, his mother in a shawl so that her face was barely visible and his brother slightly behind her. The brother was perhaps a few years Yeshua's junior, but was broad-shouldered and dark-skinned and rough and didn't resemble him in the least. His mother, however, was clearly his flesh and blood—there was that same fineness of features, and also a bearing that they shared, as if they had descended from princes. So strong was the sense of her presence, of some force that she carried with her, that I couldn't bring myself to address her.

We've come all the way from Notzerah, she said. We want only a word with him.

But I told her he wouldn't see them. Because she didn't reply, I felt compelled to add, He won't give a reason. He says he's already home.

She looked at me then and asked, Are you his wife, and I said, He has no wife, but felt a deep shame at the question, I couldn't have said why.

We stood a long moment in silence. It was growing dark and I could hardly make out their expressions. I asked them where they would spend the night and the brother, who hadn't spoken until then, said they had already taken a place at the caravansary at the edge of town.

If I could offer a bed, I said.

But his mother said, There's no need. And they set off into the dusk.

The incident affected me deeply. I didn't see them again, but later heard that they left promptly at dawn the following morning. Afterwards people said they had come for Yeshua because they'd heard he was preaching in the streets and had assumed he'd gone mad. But that was not what I had seen in his mother. I couldn't say what I'd seen, perhaps only a mother's sadness. But it was more than that, it was some kind of knowledge she had, and I couldn't look at Yeshua afterwards without seeing his mother's face, the sense of futility in it when I'd told her he wouldn't come.

When we questioned Yeshua about the incident he grew angry with us. Why do you trouble me over this, he said. It was the first time we had seen him this way, and many of us were frightened.

Yaqob said, But the law tells us to honour our mother and father.

The law also tells us that a man leaves his mother and father, Yeshua said.

But that is to marry.

And so I've married you, Yeshua said. Now my followers are my family.

Afterwards, when the group of us spoke privately, it was clear that none of us had been able to follow Yeshua's meaning. But most of the others had so put their trust in Yeshua by now that they ascribed their confusion to their own ignorance, even Shimon and my own father. I was very disturbed by this—I thought that if they had seen his mother as I had, they wouldn't so easily accept his argument. Also, I couldn't think what it meant to be his family, if I had to choose then between him and my own, which I could never do. There were my sisters, for instance, whose betrothed had forbidden them to follow Yeshua; and there was my mother. I didn't believe Yeshua could make her abandon her ways when so many other inducements had failed, though she had never said a word against him.

So sharp was my fear that I would be called on at some moment to make a choice that for a time I ceased to attend our meetings, making one excuse or another and even trying in various ways to keep my father from them, terrified that he might one day reject us for Yeshua. My father was surely confused by this, for I didn't explain my reasons and indeed couldn't bring myself to say anything to him against Yeshua, since I knew his loyalty to him and still retained the greater part of my own. But one evening while I was walking on the beach Yeshua suddenly appeared beside me, saying he had spotted me from the fishing boat of Yohanan and Yaqob and come over to me, though I couldn't see the boat near the shore.

Have you chosen to leave us, Yeshua said, and I was instantly put off balance by his candour. I began to protest, but as I couldn't lie to him said, I'm only a woman, what difference could it make if I stayed or left. But I was at once ashamed to have said this, since it went against what he'd taught us.

He told me a story then of a shepherd who left behind ninety-nine sheep to go searching for one that was lost. Surely the ninety-nine are more important than the one, I said. But he answered, Wouldn't the shepherd who gave up on the one also give up on the others, when the time came. I couldn't follow his argument and fell silent, and so we kept walking along the shore until we were quite far from the village. A cloud passed across the face of the moon and for several minutes I couldn't make him out at all in the dark, could only hear his breathing beside me and the sound of his footsteps.

He asked if it was because he'd sent his mother away

that I'd left him, and when I agreed that it was, he said I couldn't know what had passed between him and his mother.

But you were angry with us, I said. You encourage us to question you, then grow angry when we do.

He said, You're right to reprimand me, and then explained what he had meant when he had called us his family. He used the example of Ribqah, whose father Urijah was little better than an animal and suffered her to attend our meetings only because he was afraid she would accuse him before the elders of the abuses he had committed against her. Yeshua seemed to know these things though he could hardly have learned them from Ribqah, who even to me spoke of them only in the most veiled terms.

If Ribqah goes against her father in following me, he said, surely you don't believe her to be sinning, and I agreed that I did not.

Her father is a godless man, I said.

But still he's her father.

He doesn't act like a father to her.

And so Ribqah is justified in defying him.

Yes.

And we who love her and accept her, aren't we more her family than her father will ever be?

When the argument was put to me in this way, I saw at once that Yeshua was right. Yet still I resisted him.

Is your mother godless then like Ribqah's father, I said.

No, not godless. But she tries to keep me from God's work. I was silent and he added, as if he knew my thoughts, You mustn't think I would ask the same sacrifices of my followers as I ask of myself.

My own mother is a heathen, I said. Surely one day you'll ask me to leave her.

It's true that sometimes we have to make a choice. But I'm not the one who'll ask you to choose.

Who, then.

The moon was out again. We were near the outskirts of Kinneret and fishing boats were visible in the moonlight as they set out from the harbour for the night's fishing. I wondered what the men in the boats would say, to see a man and a woman walking alone on the beach in the night as we were. I myself could hardly believe it was so.

You needn't fear for your mother, Yeshua said. There are many ways to worship.

But there's only one God.

Yes, but perhaps he has many faces. Don't think it's our mission to close people out. Our mission is to include them. To find the way to include them.

In the end, even though I hadn't understood him, I agreed that I would begin to attend our meetings again. Then somehow it came to me what he'd meant, not as a single phrase I could have put into words but as a feeling that washed over me. It occurred to me, for instance, how in all the years we had lived in Migdal, the teacher in the town, Sapphias, had never once so much as exchanged a greeting with my mother while Yeshua had joked with her and broken bread and chosen her home, whose threshold Sapphias would never deign to cross, as the seat of his mission in the town. I had never blamed Sapphias for his actions, for I'd always believed he did merely what the law required. But now I saw things differently. I understood that for Sapphias the law was a wall; while for Yeshua, it was a gateway. That was what he'd meant when he'd said he wasn't the one who would make us choose—it was we who had to choose, who stood before the gate and had to open it. Somehow I hadn't understood this simple thing, that choice was exactly what couldn't be forced on me, for whatever was forced wasn't a choice.

These were the things that we learned from Yeshua, things that weren't taught in the assembly house even to the men and that finally couldn't be taught at all in the way we understood teaching, but could only be discovered in oneself. Later, when he was with the crowds, people often said his meaning was unclear, or twisted his words and held them against him. But for those who had ears to hear, as he said to us, his message was plain enough. He spoke often of God's kingdom, and people imagined he meant to make himself king of Israel, or that the end of days was at hand, or that we must wait until death for the kingdom to come to us. But those who listened could see that the kingdom was neither one thing nor the other, not a place outside of us that we must travel to like some far province or city but rather inside us in the way we looked at things, and so always there for us to bring forth. When will the kingdom come, people asked him, and he always replied, It's here. He said, Look at the trees or the birds or the lake. Look at the wildflowers that come up in the spring. The wildflowers don't feed us, people said. They don't pay our taxes. But they hadn't understood. Even those closest to him didn't always understand, and I among them, but that was our own hardheadedness, because no one before had ever said to us, Open your eyes and see.

From the very start we had our enemies, those who couldn't bear that someone should come to us saying things which they themselves hadn't thought of or who saw the devil's work in anything that questioned their own authority. In Migdal, Sapphias was quick to speak out against Yeshua at sabbath prayer, as was the teacher at Kefar Nahum, and in Korazin one of the leaders there, Matthias bar Qeynan, whose injustices Yeshua had often denounced, had taken up cause against him. Then Yeshua called down on himself the wrath of the elders of Tsef when he spoke out against one of their judgements. The incident involved the stoning of a woman, a rare event in our region and in this case one that I had the misfortune of seeing with my own eyes, since my father and I happened to be at the Tsef market the day it occurred.

Tsef had always been much looked to for wisdom in the region. But its elders were a hard and unforgiving group, all of them followers of the house of Shammai. On this day they had condemned a woman for sorcery and had led her out to the gates at the head of a mob. Afterwards they claimed it had been their intention only to chase the woman from the town. But my father and I saw that the crowd had been incited and was already armed, and the poor woman had hardly stepped from the gates before people began to hurl their missiles at her. They chased her through the market until a throw caught her leg and she fell. The rest was too miserable to relate—what had been human was within minutes reduced to a bloodied mass. My father tried to shield me but I was as if spellbound, unable to take my eyes from the woman though I'd had only the most fleeting glimpse of her before she'd been rendered unrecognizable.

I had never witnessed a stoning and was dumbfounded at the violence of it. Afterwards the elders said they had never given the order for the first stone, but also that they would have been within the law to do so, since the woman, who was well known as a sorceress, had been caught in the very act of conjuring demons against them. But when Yeshua heard of the event he was quick to condemn them.

They want to make it seem that they're both merciful and just, when they're neither, he said.

He went to the town and spoke to the people there. Most of them, because they had been among the woman's executioners, were ready to chase him away; but a few were willing to admit the woman had done no one any harm. So Yeshua stood at the gate and questioned the elders' actions, and said the blood of the woman was on them for not preventing her death. The elders quickly sent their supporters to argue with him and ridicule his position. But when these were unable to defeat him by argument, they threw stones at him to silence him, seeming ready to repeat the crime they'd committed only days before.

In the following weeks several matters were brought to light that showed Yeshua had spoken truly. It was revealed that the woman was a Syrian and had long been an enemy of the elders, who had tried to cheat her of property that had been in her family for generations. In order to get their way the elders had stirred the town up against her, using the old blood hatred that still existed between the Syrians and the Jews. It was only because of Yeshua that these things came out at all, for no one else would have dared to question Tsef's elders as he did. There followed a great debate in the region as to whether they had acted justly, though Yeshua, meanwhile, was accused of fomenting discord, even if it was the elders, as he pointed out, who had stirred people's hate. The truth was that in taking the part of the Syrians, Yeshua had no doubt helped to stave off further bloodshed, for they thus were able to see that not every Jew was against them.

Even among Yeshua's followers, however, there was some confusion as to what he intended in this matter and whether his own teachings, since he defended a sorceress, went against the law. He wouldn't answer these people directly, but asked instead how many of them had broken the sabbath in some small way, or had kept an idol or charm in their homes, or had taken the Lord's name in vain. He told the story from the scriptures of the man found gathering sticks on the sabbath who was put to death, and it was clear from the looks on his listeners' faces that not one of them was guilty of less. In this way he made people think in a manner that hadn't occurred to them before, and see how the law must be tempered with mercy or not one of us would be spared. Meanwhile I, who couldn't put from my mind the stoning and the look on the woman's face when she fell, was able to take some comfort from Yeshua's defence of her. I thought of my mother, who, though my father always rooted them out, even now made secret idols of her old gods, and I wondered how many deaths she would have suffered at the hands of Tsef's elders.

This incident earned Yeshua many opponents, especially among those who had power in one way or another and feared Yeshua would question their own authority as he had that of the leaders of Tsef. In Tsef itself, the elders issued an order condemning Yeshua's teachings and barring him from the town. But the Lord worked to turn adversity to Yeshua's favour, for there were many who hadn't heard of him before or taken him seriously who suddenly paid him attention. Often a crowd gathered now when he arrived in a town to preach, where before there had been only a handful; and our evening meetings could no longer be accommodated in my father's house or Shimon's and often had to be held in the open or in the assembly house at Kinneret, where the teacher was sympathetic to us.

Because of the attack against Yeshua at Tsef, Shimon insisted that some of the men travel with him at all times now whenever he preached. It was mainly Shimon himself who did this at first, along with Yaqob and Yohanan, whom Yeshua called his Sons of Thunder. But soon they recruited others to help them—Philip from Bet Zayda, and Thomas and Aram from Kinneret, and Kaleb and Thaddaios and Salman from Kefar Nahum. Yeshua said he was afraid he would be taken for a bandit chief, travelling with such an army of men. But as time went on he came to enjoy their company, and even took to inviting the women with him when he preached, who were mainly myself, when my father could spare me, and Ribqah, and Noadiah, the sister of Yohanan and Yaqob, and Shelomah, a woman from Kinneret. Because we travelled in such a group, and the women a bit apart, no one remarked on us and we moved about freely, as far as Sennabris along the lake and Cana in the hills. In each town we visited there was a house we would go to that Yeshua had chosen, as he had chosen our own in Migdal; and here we would meet with his followers and often share a meal.

Many of the towns we went to in this way were ones that I had never laid eyes on before or knew little of, and it was a revelation to see the different ways in which people lived, how in the hills, for instance, they ate mainly lentils and meats, which we rarely saw on the lake, or made their fires of pine instead of poplar, which gave its own particular smell. The houses Yeshua visited in these places were often enough the merest hovels, yet that hardly mattered to him—he had come to them, I discovered, much as he had come to our own, because someone there had learned of him or heard him speak at the gates, and had been moved to take him in. So he let himself be chosen and refused no one who welcomed him, regardless of their station or their wealth, and in this way seemed always to find those who were truest of heart. There was such an intimacy to these house meetings—the talk of the men, the old women past hearing, the children who Yeshua always won over, staring out from corners—that I often felt as if I had stumbled into them by the merest good fortune. Later, when the crowds grew and we were forced to meet in the open, I missed those days of courtyards and kitchens with their cooking fires and the smell of food, the sense then of some tremendous secret I had entered into.

When we were among the crowds it was clear that something had been lost, since we couldn't be sure of those who came and what their intentions were or if they understood. And from the questions that were put and the judgements we heard in the streets, we could see that despite all those who listened now, there were still few who accepted Yeshua's message. Either people couldn't make sense of him, or they thought him a rebel and were frightened, or they thought him merely clever like the charlatans in the cities and feared being taken in by him; and so while they were drawn to listen to him, because he spoke with authority, they wouldn't dare to say that they followed him. Then there were some who had followed Yohanan who began to say that Yeshua had strayed from his teachings and was not fit to call himself his disciple, since Yohanan had spoken of repentance and of

God's anger like the prophets of the past while Yeshua spoke only of God's love. Someone was sent to Yohanan's prison cell then to ask him his view and Yohanan said, Since I didn't speak like my teachers but only like Yohanan, why shouldn't Yeshua speak like Yeshua. But this only caused more dissension, as some said he had supported Yeshua while others that he had not.

Then it happened once when we were in Arbela that a leper somehow escaped from the colony nearby and came to Yeshua as he was addressing a crowd at the gates. A shout went up at the sight of him, and some picked up sticks to strike him, chastising him for not declaring himself as he approached. But Yeshua at once quieted the crowd and asked the leper his business.

I heard a holy man had come, he said, and hoped he knew the way to make me clean.

Leave that to God, someone said.

But Yeshua, to the crowd's amazement, went up to the man and removed the cowl that had covered his face. His skin was spotted with sores, festering and red.

I have a family that starves while I rot here, the man said, and Yeshua, surprising us, replied, I can help you.

He followed the man back to the colony, the crowd keeping pace behind him to see what he would do. At the gates the guards, who were Herod's men, must have taken him for a priest because they let him through without argument, and did not seem to care that the man he accompanied had escaped from under their supervision. We were all startled that Yeshua so willingly turned himself over to impurity, though those of us who were his disciples were concerned for him, while those who were not thought him merely foolhardy. An hour passed, then more, until the crowd had dispersed and only we who were close to him remained.

It was almost sunset before Yeshua emerged. Aram of Kinneret, who was Thomas's cousin, was with us then and said, Because of the leper you lost the crowd.

In the leper, I'm sure of a follower, Yeshua said. In the crowd I was sure of none.

But he's a leper. You've made yourself unclean.

Is it a greater evil to risk uncleanness or to turn down help to someone who needs it, Yeshua asked, and Aram was unable to answer him.

When we returned to the lake, Yeshua washed to purify himself, then remained apart from us until the evening of the following day, as the law required. After that we thought no more of the leper, nor did we ask Yeshua what help he had given him, for we imagined only that he had prayed for him. But when some days had passed, a man appeared at Shimon's gate while we were meeting there and asked after Yeshua. When we recognized him, we stood amazed: it was the leper from Arbela, cured.

Go to the priest in Tiberias, Yeshua told him, and have him pronounce you clean according to the law. But see you tell no one who cured you.

Those of us who'd been at Arbela were in awe at the sight of the man—it was as if some invisible hand had come down and wiped him clean. Had I not seen the change with my own eyes I would hardly have believed it possible.

Aram, who was with us, whispered that perhaps Yeshua had used sorcery. But Yeshua, overhearing him, said, If someone is well now who was sick before, where is the sorcery. Sorcery appeals to the devil, who only makes things worse. So if the man is better, it must be the will of God.

Yet it was true we were all of us made afraid by what we'd seen and for many days didn't speak of it, heeding the warning that Yeshua himself had given to the leper. But the leper, for his part, didn't hold his tongue, for it happened not long afterwards that others began to seek Yeshua out at the house of Shimon in order to be cured. The first who came, a mother with a child who had taken ill, Yeshua refused to see, making Shimon take him out on the lake by the back way. But when they returned to the house to find the mother still waiting at the gate, Yeshua did for the child what he could. In the morning the woman came back with a gift of olives and grain, saying her child was cured, and Yeshua, refusing her gift, sent her away with the same warning he'd given the leper. But the next day, instead of one at the gate, there were three, and because these too saw their ailments vanish after Yeshua had ministered to them, the numbers continued to grow.

In the towns of our region there were several who were said to be skilled as healers, both pagan and Jew. These, for a price, made infusions or balms or invested a charm or broke a curse, and so drew people in. But since our leaders didn't approve of them and accused them of sorcery, they didn't practise openly, and asked for payments that many of us couldn't afford. Yeshua asked no price for his cures and refused payment of any sort even when it was pressed on him, so that at first people doubted him on that account. But it wasn't long before it grew clear that he was more gifted than any of our own healers, though he shunned talismans and invocations and required no sacrifice or offering except thanks to the Lord. Because people had never seen such a healer before, they didn't know at first what to make of him, except that they went away cured; and I could see that his healing was no mere magic or enchantment but a sort of power that flowed through him in his very touch, and that surely must have sprung from the Lord. Sometimes he need only lay his palm on a sick child's brow for the fever to lift, or move his hands over a crippled leg for the bones to find their place, and the lame to walk again.

I had never seen such wonders nor heard their like spoken of even from Judea, and the truth was I felt a confusion now in the face of them, for this was a man I had known who had suddenly become a stranger to me in his power. I wondered why he had never revealed this side of himself to us, if he had thought us unworthy of it or imagined it beyond our comprehension. But soon enough it was clear what had deterred him, for once the word of his healing had spread he was immediately suspected of sorcery and of every manner of sacrilege. The elders of Tsef called for his banishment, saying it was only for the Lord to heal, since it was the Lord who afflicted; while others said that because Yeshua believed in life after death, as the Pharisees did, he did no favour to the sick by curing them, only delaying their journey to God.

Yeshua's answer to these charges was always that it was only by God's will that people were cured, not his own; and it was true that there were many who came to him for whom he could do nothing, though whether because of their own sinfulness and lack of faith, or because of God's greater plan, Yeshua wouldn't say. This led some to accuse him of deception, for if he couldn't cure all those who came to him, then perhaps those he did cure were merely the ones to whom

God would have tended in his own time. To these Yeshua said, Since I take no payment and ask for no tribute to myself but only to God, where is the deceit. Nonetheless there were still those who tried to stir people against him, saying that the scriptures condemned healers as devil-workers, even though they themselves often stole to them in the dead of night when they had need of them.

In the end, however, Yeshua's enemies couldn't touch him, not only because they lacked the authority but because of the immense need in our region for a healer who respected people and wouldn't cheat them. I had seen the children who were brought to him with worms in their bellies or close to death with fever and those who came with crushed limbs or fits of possession or wounds that festered and reeked and wouldn't heal. All of these Yeshua tended to, with good results, when otherwise poverty would have kept them from any healer, or worse, they would have spent their last pennies on charlatans without any respite from their suffering. I couldn't imagine how any evil could be seen in this, or how the scriptures could forbid what was clearly good, though I too had been raised to believe it was for God to see to our fates, and only devilry to try to change them. So I had thought the sick cursed and deserving of their lot, but Yeshua taught us differently. What child deserved to suffer, he said, or what family to starve because the father took ill; and indeed it was clear to me, from being at Yeshua's side, that the sick were not any more given to evil than the rest of us.

It was in this time that Yeshua began to make his weekly visits to the camp at Arbela. He went about the visits quietly at first, so even those of us close to him were unaware of them; but as soon as the matter became known he went more openly and without shame. He insisted on going alone and so we knew only that the inmates welcomed him and that many were cured. But amongst ourselves we tried to make sense of his mission there, since the law told us to shun the very beings Yeshua embraced. Shimon and some of the others said it was Yeshua's way to show us, as he taught, that we must look to the inner person and not the outer one, but in my heart I didn't agree. Though I didn't have the words to say the thing clearly, I thought it was exactly the outer person that Yeshua embraced, because he didn't disdain the lepers' rotting flesh but accepted it. It was what I had understood when I worked beside him with the sick—the imperfect flesh we were made of, the blood and the filth of it, and how Yeshua didn't shun it but laid on his hands.

Once when just a few of us were with him, and I the only woman, we were called to a hovel in the hills outside of Garaba where a young pagan girl was in the throes of childbirth. There was an obstruction and the child wouldn't come and so the husband had sent for us, and should Yeshua not have been present, the girl would surely have been dead inside the hour. Even with his intervention there was so much blood from her and such screams that I held little hope she would live. As it was, Yeshua couldn't save the infant, who was stillborn, but the girl survived. I, who stood by at every stage and mopped her blood and wiped her excrement, had never seen such a thing, nor did I think there were any men but Yeshua who would have done such work, even to save a life. I saw the sweat on him as he worked, and how he held the dead infant he had pulled from the girl, and I felt joined to him then in the very stench and mess of that place.

It seemed then that what Yeshua taught us was that we could not divide things into clean and unclean and what could be kept and what cast out, but must take all as one, and see how it made us. Indeed, it hurt me that Yeshua had never taken me in to the lepers with him, that I might also understand in my bones how their flesh was my own.

Of the hundreds who were now drawn to Yeshua on account of his cures, there were a good number who were eventually won over to his teachings, and understood in his power the sign of God's grace. But many others went away still baffled by the things he said or disappointed because they'd wished him to cure things only God could undo such as blindness or barrenness. Nonetheless, Yeshua turned no one away, be they pagan or Jew, rich or poor, nor did he require that they follow him before he cured them. When on one occasion a woman arrived secretively who was rumoured to be of the royal family, we were all certain that Yeshua would send her away, because Yohanan still lay in chains. But he saw her as he saw everyone. Afterwards it was said that this was why Herod did not dare to lay a hand on him even though he grew great, not, however, out of thanks for his service but out of fear of his power.

By now the number of those who counted themselves among Yeshua's intimates had grown to such a level that we hardly knew from one day to the next how many would arrive to take their morning meal with us or to join us on the road. But one evening Yeshua called us all together at Kinneret, some two dozen of us or more, and after we'd had our meal on the beach he didn't release us or even have us light our lamps, but kept us there as the darkness fell and the light from our fire dwindled. The evening wind had come up and brought with it a smell of woodsmoke and hyssop from the farms across the lake.

Finally Yeshua said, Some of you have turned against me.

None of us were prepared for this and we were at once thrown into confusion. Yaqob said, How do you mean, but Yeshua would only answer, The ones I'm referring to know what they've done. We sat waiting for some further word from him until the fire died and it was pitch-dark and we could hardly see the faces of our neighbours. Then Shimon said, If anyone here has betrayed you, I'll surely kill him.

There was a moment of fear then when it seemed that each of us imagined we had been the one to betray him, in some way we didn't know. I couldn't see Yeshua's face and so wasn't sure whether to take his silence as a sanction of Shimon's threat. But then he asked, Since when have I taught you to kill, and we knew Shimon had misspoken.

Even those who are against us must be granted forgiveness if they ask for it, Yeshua said, then waited in silence. But when those he referred to didn't come forward, he still wouldn't name them, saying only that they shouldn't present themselves among his brothers and sisters, as he called us, if they had their daggers drawn for him.

The following morning when we gathered for prayer it was only Kaleb and Pheroras from Kefar Nahum and Aram from Kinneret who hadn't come. Though we knew now that they were the culprits, still Yeshua would say nothing against them, which however had the effect of making us imagine them guilty of every sort of crime. As it fell out, we were not so far from the truth—bit by bit we came to learn that the group of them, under Aram's leadership, had made a pact with the brigand known as Hezron the Tyrian to deliver

Yeshua's followers to him for an attack on the Roman garrison at Kefar Nahum. Hezron kept an army in the mountains beyond Gush Halav, and was much reviled in our region for plundering the homes and farms of the innocent; for though he claimed his enemy was Rome and his cause was for the Jews, he brought more trouble to us and inflicted greater suffering than the Romans ever did. That Aram had thought to turn to Hezron's purposes the followers of Yeshua showed contempt not only for Yeshua's message but for the loyalty and sense of his followers.

The question of Rome had often been put to Yeshua, since Galileans hated any fetter and couldn't bear that Herod was Rome's vassal. But Yeshua always said to people, Didn't even the Maccabees, who were our liberators, rule as tyrants when they gained power, and end in disgrace; and didn't even Solomon, our greatest king, collect taxes for his own pleasure, and thus plant the seeds of revolt. So he said that one oppressor replaced another, on and on, and if it wasn't the Persians it was the Greeks, and if not the Greeks then our own saviours, so that we might go on killing our oppressors until the end of days, and still be oppressed. Thus he didn't support those who called themselves rebels, or the shedding of blood, since it wasn't by killing that we could come to freedom, he said, but only by cherishing life.

The fact was, however, that Aram had gone to Hezron not because he followed the rebels or believed in their cause but merely for revenge against Yeshua, having taken offence the times Yeshua had reprimanded him. It came out now that Aram had long been a scoundrel, an idler and a prodigal who was a huge burden to his family and who had been recruited to us by his cousin Thomas merely in the hope that he might be reformed. We saw now how far he remained from fulfilling that hope, and in fact the instant his plot was uncovered, he went about denouncing Yeshua and spreading lies about him. Over the matter of the lepers, for instance, he claimed he had witnessed Yeshua's sorcery in curing them; and beyond this he tried to raise people's fears by saying the lepers now flocked from Arbela to seek Yeshua out, and would soon pollute the whole of the countryside. Much of the time he went around half-demented with wine and invented every sort of thing. But still Yeshua would say nothing against him, nor would it ever have crossed his mind to turn him in to the authorities.

It was largely on Aram's account, however, that we came to the matter of the twelve. It had become clear that with so many who now wished to be among Yeshua's intimates there was always the danger that those who couldn't be trusted would insert themselves among us. Thus one morning Yeshua picked twelve of the men who were closest to him, like the twelve tribes of old Israel, he said, and named them his special messengers. Those who were left out felt slighted, and wondered why he had chosen Shimon's brother Andreas above them when he was simple, or Matthaios, who was a toll collector, or Thomas, who had brought us Aram; and indeed I myself was guilty in this, not for my own sake, since Yeshua had made clear that we women would all remain with him even though we were not named among the twelve, but for my father's. It was my father, after all, who had been the first to accept Yeshua, and who had found him his home, and I saw how it hurt him now not to be among the chosen. I was afraid he had been rejected on my mother's account. But Yeshua, seeing my distress, didn't reprove me as he might have, but came to comfort me, saying it was because he loved my father most that he had excluded him.

He's a merchant and can't afford enemies like the rest, he said. The others have only the fish to look after.

There were several of the men, however, who came to him unhappy at being excluded with whom he was harsh, accusing them of thinking only of their own glory. He asked them how many rowers fit in a boat before it sinks; and so it was with him, that a dozen men would help him while fifty only hinder, and each must be happy with the lot he'd drawn. The whole matter left him angry with us, not only because of the grumblings of those who were excluded but because a few of those who'd been chosen went so far as to boast of the fact and to lord it over the others. Then almost immediately it happened that two of the twelve were lost—one of them, Salman from Kefar Nahum, was drowned during a storm on the lake, while the other, a young man from Judea named Yishai, grew frightened at the ill omen of Salman's death and returned to Judea to his family. But Yeshua refused to fill these places from among those he'd rejected, saying none of them had shown themselves worthy.

In the midst of these troubles the rumour came to us that the prophet Yohanan had been condemned for treason and taken down to the fortress at Macherus. This was at the end of a long killing spree on Herod's part when dozens of his enemies had been dispatched, and we were afraid that Yohanan would be added to the lot, and had been moved to Macherus so the thing could be done in secret. By chance it occurred that a few of Hezron the Tyrian's men were captured around the same time; and this worked to our detriment, for when Aram learned of their arrests he began to fear that they would betray him. Such was the working of his mind that he imagined to protect himself by levelling his own accusations in turn. So he began to go about the countryside publicizing that Yeshua had been Yohanan's acolyte and saying his treasons far exceeded Yohanan's, no doubt believing he might thus barter Yeshua's life for his own should he be accused.

Thomas was the first to get wind of these things and quickly came to warn us.

Yeshua said, Should I run like a criminal then, and seem to confirm his charges.

He assured us that as he had always kept himself within the law he had nothing to fear; and it was true that whenever his enemies had tried to lure him into treason he had outsmarted them. But we knew that Herod would find the way to accuse him if he had a mind to.

In the end, because Shimon and some of the others implored him, Yeshua agreed to leave us for a time and go up into Tyre, beyond Herod's borders, in the hope of cutting short Aram's accusations. He agreed to this more for our sake than his own, lest Aram's charges bring the rest of us into risk, and said he would go openly and not by cover of night. Shimon wouldn't hear of his going alone and so at once arranged to accompany him, enlisting also Yaqob and Yohanan, though they would be sorely missed from their father's boats and Shimon himself must leave his work to a brother who was simple-minded and to sons who were still children.

For my part, I was filled with foreboding over the journey, because I was afraid it would change things among us in some irrevocable way. Already we were so different from how we had been in the beginning, and there were the crowds now, and the sick, and Yeshua's enemies who wished him harm, and each of these seemed a fence that kept me from the man who had first walked with me by the lake. When Yeshua had chosen the twelve, he had promised to keep me always at his side; but how, as a woman, could I hope to keep pace with him. I envied Shimon and the others for being men, but in my pride also thought that they couldn't fathom Yeshua as I did, and that Yeshua too had understood this.

On the day of his departure I didn't cry as I had when he'd left our home months before, nor did I take it hard that it was Ribqah's hand he held at the end and not my own. We were at the house of Shimon and he said to me, Look after your sister, and indeed it was Ribqah who shed tears, for since Yeshua had come her father hadn't dared to lay a hand on her, but with him gone who could say. Then he set off, and there were people who'd heard of his departure who were waiting for him at the gate. I saw him differently then, watching him pass through the crowd—for a moment I didn't know who he was, or how I had dared to speak to him, or whether I had dreamed the times when he'd walked with me by the lake. I was a girl then, I thought, a child. Yet only a season had passed since he'd come, hardly time enough even for barley to ripen.

During the time that Yeshua was away there was a group of us that met in my father's house in Migdal. Some of the women came, and those of the twelve who remained. But without Yeshua we seemed lost, as if nothing of what he'd taught us had stayed with us. Many times there were arguments, and the simplest matters eluded our understanding, so that even things that had been settled now seemed unclear again. Philip, who hadn't been with us in our earliest days, brought up again the question of having women among us—how was it, he said, that the women were allowed to stay with the twelve when there were men who had been turned away. None of us knew how to answer this, not even those who had been there when Yeshua had first taught us. Afterwards Ribqah was afraid we would be forced to leave the group, but it was my mother who calmed her, saying that Yeshua would put the men in their place when he returned.

With each day that passed, however, it seemed to me less likely that he'd return at all. I began to fear that God had betrayed us—why had he forced Yeshua out to Tyre, to those who had no use for him, when we here who depended on him felt his lack hourly. But my greater fear was this: that over time even our own need for him would pass. Already I could see us returning to what we'd been before—the men went out for their fishing; my father tended to his business. My own place was back in the smoking sheds, and day by day I felt something fading from me, until I began to see my life ahead of me as if Yeshua had never come to it. It was possible, I saw, to return to the old ways, even when the truth had been laid out before you, since what was familiar was always lying in wait to reclaim you.

Then one day the word came to us that Yeshua had been seen crossing back to Galilee at Gush Halav. Not much more than a month had passed since he'd gone yet I had missed him as if he vanished from the earth, and could hardly call up the image of him in my mind. Aram had come to his senses by then, and seen how he only brought risk to himself with his accusations, and so it appeared that Yeshua had timed his homecoming well. But rather than the joy I had imagined, I felt a strange misgiving when I heard of his return, fearing every sort of thing, that he had changed or no longer loved us or that I had been mistaken in him in some way and must now see the truth.

It was the end of the summer and a busy time for us, but my father called me from work the instant he'd got word and said we must make our way to Kefar Nahum to be there to greet Yeshua when he arrived. He had one of the labourers prepare our boat, then filled it with fish and provisions so that we might get ready a feast at the house of Shimon. But when we arrived at Kefar Nahum there was a large crowd already awaiting Yeshua at the gates. My father wanted to find the way to include them in the feast but I discouraged him.

There are too many, I said. And how will we know his followers from those who are merely taking advantage.

That isn't how Yeshua would have us think, my father said, but still he deferred to me, for which I was ashamed, since I knew it was only that I wished to have Yeshua alone with us, free from the crowds. It was my punishment that in the end I caused my father to be shamed along with me, though he had seen the matter rightly, because when Yeshua arrived and heard that food had been prepared, he promptly reprimanded us for not having given it out among the sick who awaited him. That was the greeting that we had from him, then, and no feast at all, for when he had finished with the sick, he said he was tired from his journey and sent us on our way.

I couldn't have borne the humiliation of this and the coldness with which he greeted us, which indeed confirmed my every fear, had it not been clear to me at once that he was not himself. At first I imagined that some calamity had befallen him along the road. But I'd noticed the fourth who accompanied Shimon and the others as if he'd made himself one of them. His look set him apart—he wasn't solid like we Galileans, but small-boned and thin and his skin as dark as an Arab's, almost black. Several times Yeshua spoke to him as he went about tending to the sick, but in a manner I hardly recognized—it was the manner of city people, who smiled and raised their voices, but behind every word seemed to hide a dozen that went unspoken.

By the following morning it was clear that along with the stranger had come an evil influence. We awoke to the news of the prophet Yohanan's death—in Migdal the word came through at dawn, out of Tiberias. My father and I immediately set out for Kefar Nahum, to find a large crowd had already gathered there at Shimon's gate to await some word from Yeshua. A wail of mourning had gone up, but though there was much bitterness among people, there was no disorder.

While we were waiting, however, I saw the stranger approaching from the far gates, which led out to the Roman camp, and not long afterwards a contingent of soldiers arrived. I didn't know what to make of this except that he was a spy who had been sent to us and had called the soldiers in the hope of provoking a riot, so that Yeshua might be arrested as the cause of it. If that was the case, he hadn't reckoned that the garrison's commander, Ventidius, a Sidonian who had lived among us for many years, was one of those whom Yeshua had won over. Thus his soldiers held back and didn't disturb our mourning, and when Yeshua emerged to address the crowd, Ventidius at once took the chance to express his own outrage at Herod's crime.

Yeshua had already begun his own mourning and came to us with his robe torn and his head blackened. At the sight of him the crowd was instantly silenced. He did not mince his words then, but spoke openly of Yohanan's death, comparing him to the ancient prophets who, like him, had been persecuted by their leaders and had seen their warnings ignored. Then he told us of the years he had spent with Yohanan in the desert—there were many, he said, who had called Yohanan a madman, and he'd had the look of one, but his madness had been that of truth, which had the appearance of madness to those who had never heard it spoken before.

When Yeshua had finished he retreated to return to his mourning, and the crowd gradually dispersed. Those of us who were with the twelve gathered outside Shimon's gate then. I thought the stranger would drift away with the crowd, but instead he inserted himself among us, and prevailed upon Yohanan to introduce him. He gave himself out as Yihuda from Qiryat, in the Negeb of Judea. But when Philip asked how many days' journey his town was from Kefar Nahum, he couldn't tell us.

It was only when Shimon led us all out to Yeshua at the lakeshore to take our morning meal with him that I understood Yihuda did not intend to leave us. Surely, I thought, he knew that some of us had seen him coming from the garrison. But when we sat for our meal he instantly took his place in our circle, rudely, so that it seemed he would eat without so much as a prayer, even though he presented himself as if he were a person of breeding. Then when we came to discuss Yohanan's death, many of us couldn't feel free because of his presence.

Yaqob, speaking cautiously, asked if we might not protest Herod's actions to Rome.

Surely you understand it was the Romans who killed Yohanan, Yihuda said, tempting us to treason. When none of us would respond, he tried to provoke us by insult, accusing us of being Rome's pawns.

We have no quarrel with anyone, Thaddaios said. It's not our way.

To our surprise, however, Yeshua took the part of Yihuda.

If we have no quarrel with anyone, then we stand for nothing, he said. How is it that Yohanan is dead, if he had no quarrel. Do you imagine our road is different from his.

We were all silenced by this. Not long afterwards Yeshua sent us away, so that only Shimon and Yihuda remained with him. The rest of us, in our disturbance, at once met at the house of Yaqob and Yohanan.

Perhaps he is a spy, I said, but the others wouldn't give me credence.

Yaqob said, The teacher has called him, as he called us. It's not right to question him.

He encourages us to question him, I said.

Not in such things. Only in his teachings. And then only to show us our errors.

The following day we learned from Shimon that Yeshua had asked Yihuda to join the twelve. I was astonished at this and that the others made no protest to Yeshua, when we stood in such threat in the wake of Yohanan's death. It seemed to me that the others had been bewitched, that they accepted Yihuda so blindly; and indeed it was true that we behaved strangely, as if we weren't what we'd been. The men all called Yeshua teacher now whenever they spoke to him—perhaps there was no evil in this, it merely showed respect, yet it seemed Yihuda whom they deferred to, as if he was the one who would judge us. But when I spoke of these things, when I said, We are changed, or, Yihuda means us harm, the men wouldn't listen.

Once he and I were left alone on the beach as I cleared the remains of our meal.

What's your name, he said to me, and I was amazed that after the many days he had been with us he still didn't know me.

I'm Miryam, I said. I imagined he would share some thought with me then, but he said only, Fetch me some water to wash, as if I were nothing.

I could not stop my apprehension then, but felt it grow larger day by day, that we had allowed this one among us not knowing him or who had sent him. After a time, I went to Shimon. Yihuda was often insolent with him, calling him the Rock to his face, which was only for Yeshua to do. But because Yihuda was a guest in his house, Shimon was reluctant to speak against him.

He is our test, he said. Even if we despise him, we have to make a place for him, the way Yeshua has taught us.

Perhaps he's an agent of the evil one, I said.

If he had been sent by the evil one, Shimon said, Yeshua would know it.

But to me it seemed Yihuda grew stronger at every turn, so that soon he would rule us.

Not long after his arrival he managed to take charge of the common purse. I didn't know what argument he had made to win this trust, or how Yeshua had given in to it when there were so many who relied on him, whether it be the sick whom he fed and purchased medicines for or the destitute, cretins and cripples and the like in the towns we went to who often enough depended on him for their very lives. None of the others made any objection to Yihuda's assuming this power—since many of them lived solely by barter, they in fact preferred that the monies entrusted to us be handled by those who understood such things. I, however, the daughter of a merchant, saw more clearly what Yihuda gained by this, and the danger in which we stood. Indeed, of the sums that came in to us from Yeshua's followers, not a small portion came from my own father, and I couldn't feel easy that this money fell to Yihuda's care.

Our meetings were utterly changed from what they had been. Yihuda was quick to speak his mind on every matter that came before us; and so he would catch Yeshua's interest and draw him out, leaving no place for anyone else. He claimed he had studied at the temple in Jerusalem, and it was true he was well versed in the scriptures and knew how to use them to his own end, so that sometimes even Yeshua was forced to defer to his greater learning. But this was no mark of piety in him, but only of cunning, since like a Greek he might support a notion one day if it suited him and refute it the next. I'd heard these were the sorts of skills one learned now in the temple, where the priests made arguments merely for their own convenience and believed in nothing but their purses. Yet I couldn't conceive that Yeshua would be taken in by such devices.

Then there was the matter of Shimon's brother, Andreas. As a boy, he had nearly drowned in the lake and had never again been right in his mind, so that although he was more gentle than most and caused harm to no one, he was also more susceptible to evil influence. Yihuda, seeing this, had promptly taken advantage of him, giving him the occasional almond or fig to win him over and then treating him like his slave. When he couldn't be bothered to join us for our meals, he had Andreas bring him his portion; if he was cold in the night, he called to Andreas to bring a blanket to warm him. To my own eyes, it was clear that Yihuda had enchanted Andreas and that he stood in peril; yet somehow Yeshua was blind to this. Before Yihuda had come, Yeshua had always treated Andreas like his own brother or son. But now he suffered Yihuda's abuse of him as if it amused him, and indeed said it was a mark of Yihuda's goodness that one so innocent should worship him.

At last, as the others would say nothing, it fell to me to speak to Yeshua. It was difficult now to be alone with him, because Yihuda hardly left him in peace; and so I had to come to him at dawn and ask him to follow me to the lakeshore.

When we reached the beach I thought at first from his silence that he was out of temper with me. But when he spoke he said, I have missed our walks, and in an instant my heart was in his hands.

I've also missed them, I said.

It was sunrise and there were many fishing boats near the shore, some returning and some going out. As a child, I would watch them from our porch and imagine that the lake they plied was the world entire, with its depths and its distant shores. But now the lake seemed small, since Yeshua had come.

Yeshua walked with me near the water.

I wouldn't think to question you, I said. But once you encouraged us to.

Yes.

I think Yihuda means us harm.

Has he offended you in some way.

No, I said, for it didn't seem right to mention how he had slighted me on the beach.

Then why are you troubled.

For your sake.

Do you think him stronger than me.

No.

Then you needn't concern yourself over him. In the scriptures, God accepted challenges even from Satan. So if Yihuda is a force for good, then we'll learn from him, if for evil, then we'll defeat him.

I was left disturbed by this, still uncertain how Yeshua could admit among us someone who might do us harm. I might have questioned him further yet he had begun to seem a stranger to me, changed as though I saw him across a great distance. Walking with him then I had a sensation almost of fear—for the first time, it seemed, I was aware of him as simply a man, as someone utterly separate from me.

It wasn't long before we women, who knew more of these things than the men, heard rumours of how Yihuda in fact did do injury to us. Because he refused to go out on the boats with the others, he often spent his days in the markets and taverns; and there, through his idle talk, he had revived Aram's lie concerning the lepers, that they had begun to follow Yeshua wherever he went and threatened to overrun us. This was hardly the case—as the lepers knew that Yeshua would come to them, they had no need to seek him out. Yet the rumours had done us no little harm, for although people had been able to see with their own eyes that they were untrue, many had been happy to judge us solely on hearsay. It was just at a time when we were laying these falsehoods to rest that Yihuda began putting questions here and there and encouraging gossip again, so that people were quick to add one exaggeration to another and to circulate every sort of lie. Thus people's fears were rekindled; and since the occasional leper did indeed arrive in search of Yeshua, people had proof enough that their fears were justified.

Around this time there was a man in Korazin who had been condemned as a leper who refused to go into his quarantine, saying the wonder-worker Yeshua would come to cure him. This was a person well known as a troublemaker, who had always sought every means for avoiding the law. But the landowner Matthias, who was Yeshua's enemy, didn't miss this chance to stir up hatred against Yeshua, and prevailed upon Korazin's elders to have him banned from the town as an evil influence. So it was that one morning we arrived at Korazin's gates to find the town guards lined up there to bar us entry, bearing knives and clubs. Such a thing had never happened to us—even at Tsef no one had dared to come openly bearing weapons. But Yihuda, instead of taking the blame on himself for feeding people's fears, at once turned it onto Yeshua.

For the sake of the few you win over among the lepers, you risk losing all the rest, he said, much as Aram had months before at Arbela.

I thought that surely Yeshua would now put him in his place. But instead he did a thing that passed comprehension: he invited Yihuda to accompany him the following day on his visit to the Arbela colony. This was a trust he hadn't shown any of the rest of us, though I, for one, would gladly have undertaken it. I was astounded now that he had extended it to this one who was such a serpent among us. So it was that the next day while Shelomah and I waited outside the gates of the colony as we usually did, Yihuda stayed by Yeshua's side. I could hardly bear this, or how Yihuda came back to us afterwards boasting about Yeshua's good work, though it seemed to me he was the one who had least understood it if it took so much to convince him of its worth.

Often now it was just the two of them who stayed late on the beach when the rest of us had gone, or who sat apart and talked in a way we others couldn't follow or of things we didn't know. It hurt me then to see Yeshua smile or put a hand on Yihuda's shoulder, as if he had not understood how Yihuda drove us apart. I thought surely the others must take offence, but even in this Yihuda was cunning, for one by one he had begun to win the rest of the twelve over to him—first the innocents such as Andreas and the young Yohanan and those like Thomas and Thaddaios who were weak-spirited, but then even Philip who was sharp-witted, but who more and more admired him and took his side. When he saw that it was only the women who still opposed him, he began to deride us in front of the others and bring up the old arguments against our inclusion, until it began to seem he would prevail against us.

I went to my father then.

He wants to destroy us, I said, and listed all the ways he had gained power over us.

But my father, no doubt still remembering how I had misadvised him when Yeshua had returned from Tyre, said we couldn't make accusations merely from appearances.

It's only that you dislike his manner, he said, and warned me of turning the blame to Yihuda, when I was the one who could not accept him.

I might simply have resigned myself then, since I had exhausted every means, if Shelomah hadn't come to me and said there were rumours in Kinneret that Yihuda had sought a pact with our enemy Aram. So it seemed I hadn't been mistaken in him, and he indeed wished to ruin us. I resolved at once that I wouldn't see us destroyed and so went to Aram, secretly.

If you plot with Yihuda, I said, though he swore he hadn't yet met with him, I'll surely turn you in as a traitor, and he knew I would do it.

It was clear to me by now that I couldn't rest easy until I had found the way to rid us of Yihuda for good. So it was that I came to do a thing that brought danger not only to me but to all of us, and that went against the teachings of the scriptures and of Yeshua himself.

As a child, I had only once been to the town of my mother, during a time when my father had thought to divorce her for refusing to accept his beliefs. But it was there I learned the ways of the pagans, for my mother's people, who were called Martu or Amurru, did not worship the god of the Jews, but Asherah and Baal. We hadn't been there long before my father missed us and came to reclaim us. But afterwards I remembered my time there as if it formed part of some different life I had led, so awed was I by the place and so different was it from what I had known. I had never been in the mountains before and felt as if someone had caged me, since everywhere were trees and bush and in every direction peaks that cut off your view. The houses were like caves carved out of the mountain face, and there was always the smell of blood from the sacrifices and of smoke, but not like the smoke of our smoking sheds, more acrid and sickly and stale.

There was a priest in the place, whom the Jews would have called a sorcerer, who every morning killed an animal on an altar just above the village. He himself dressed only in skins, and smeared himself with the blood of his sacrifices, and often spoke in a language that none of the villagers understood and that was said to be the language of their gods. His eyes would turn upwards then and his body shake like a thing possessed, and it frightened me to look at him though many in the village would join him in his fits as if they too had been taken over.

During the time that I was there it happened that a leopard came to curse the place, carrying off several children and leaving the remains of one for all to see in a clearing just outside the village. The priest said the leopard was the spirit of an enemy who had come for revenge, and required the villagers to find the beast's excrement and bring it to him. When this was done he mixed it with blood from a sacrifice and other things, including poisons and the sting of a scorpion. Three days later, the animal was found dead in the forest. The priest's acolytes brought the carcass into the village to show us that there was no mark on it, and hence that it had fallen dead only through the priest's power.

These were the things I remembered and that came to me now, clouding my mind. So it was that I began to go before dawn to Kefar Nahum, telling my father that I had been called to make the morning meal for the twelve, and to wait secretly outside the latrine near the harbour gate until finally once I saw Yihuda come to it. When he had gone I so debased myself, though it turned my stomach, as to retrieve his waste from among the rest, knowing it by its heat. I wrapped it in leaves and buried it along the beach, and then after our meal I carried it home and hid it beneath a stone in our courtyard.

In the hills outside Bet Ma'on lived a pagan named Simon who was called the Canaanite and who was known to sell remedies and spells. The local people, though they were mainly Jews, nonetheless tolerated him, because they thought him harmless and because many of them came to him for his cures. His house was little more than a hovel, a crude thing of sticks and mud hardly more substantial than the huts we built at Tabernacles, and even from the road gave off the same stench I remembered from my mother's village, of animal skins and smoke and old blood. He had cleared a bit of field that he farmed for his food and his medicines, and bartered his cures. But beyond that he lived in the bush, hunting like the people of old and living not much above the station of the animals that he killed.

I went to him one morning, veiled so he wouldn't know me, and found him working in his field. The look of him frightened me, for he was unkempt and wild-eyed, though from the distance he kept from me it seemed his own apprehension was equal to mine. I couldn't find the way to explain to him my purpose but somehow he divined it, for he said if I wished someone killed, he wouldn't do it, since it was not his way to use his magic to such ends. From his words I came suddenly to understand the gravity of what I'd undertaken, and made clear to him that it was not my intention to murder, which was against my own law as well, but only to drive someone away.

I showed him what I had brought from Yihuda and also two drachmas I had taken from my father's purse. He motioned me inside his hovel and had me set my parcel on a sort of table or altar there, where he inspected it. Besides the doorway, the house had but a single opening, at the peak of the ceiling, and all the walls were blackened with smoke and the smell of the place was overwhelming. There were little figures of clay arranged on the table and on the floor—of his gods, I imagined. I felt sick at the sight of them, for it was profanement for me to be among them and surely no good could come of it. But he said the thing could be done. Since I couldn't bear to remain with him one moment longer I said I would leave the matter to him and go my way. For payment, he took just a single one of the drachmas I had brought. This surprised me, for I hadn't expected him to be honest.

I told no one of what I'd done. But in the following days it happened that Simon's measures took effect, for first it came about that Yihuda moved his quarters from the home of Shimon to that of Yaqob and Yohanan and then that he left us entirely. Both these changes, however, caused such tension and discord among us that whatever good they might have promised was quickly belied. In the case of Yihuda's move to Yaqob's house, the matter was handled with such a degree of informality and haste that Shimon took great affront at the insult to his hospitality. He put the blame at first on Yaqob, so that for several days there was enmity between them, until it grew clear that Yohanan had made the invitation, though it was hardly his place to decide on his household's comings and goings.

The incident ought to have been a sign to us of Yihuda's growing power over Yohanan. In any event, his bad influence was soon clear enough, for we awoke one day to discover the two of them had run off together. We'd been given no warning of their departure and so I understood it was the Canaanite's bewitchment that must be at play, but also that only evil could come of evil, for we had lost Yohanan who was innocent and still not much more than a child. It was amazing to me that Yihuda hadn't also made off with the common purse—Yaqob found it on his bed, though how much had been pilfered from it, no one could say.

When Yeshua learned of the thing he seemed shaken in a way we had never before seen. Zabdi, the father of Yohanan, came to us at Shimon's house and charged that Yeshua had led his son into corruption; and when he had gone Yeshua bemoaned the humiliation we had brought onto him.

One of the twelve said, But it was you who brought Yihuda among us.

And so my own poverty is revealed to me, Yeshua said, if he who understands is the one who leaves and you, who do not, remain.

Astounded, Yaqob said, We've always followed you in your teachings, when Yihuda did not. Even now, though my brother is gone, I'm here.

So you too blame your brother's loss on me, Yeshua said.

I blame it on his weakness.

I stood in fear of my life then at the pact I had made with the Canaanite, sure that it lay behind our derangement. As soon as we had disbanded I set off at once for Bet Ma'on, praying to the Lord that what had been done could be undone.

When I arrived at Simon's house, however, I found him deathly ill and delirious, lying in his own filth in his blackened hovel. For a moment, in my desperation, I thought simply to leave him there to die, and thus free us of his spell. But by now it was clear to me that evil only fed on itself, and that even Simon's illness must be part of the evil I myself had planted in him. I ministered to him in what way I could, washing the filth from him and feeding him a crust of bread that I found. Then I returned to Kefar Nahum with all due speed to fetch Yeshua to cure him, travelling without once stopping to rest though the sun was at its height.

In my distress I was prepared to confess to Yeshua my entire crime and to throw myself at his mercy. But though he knew what nature of man Simon was, he did not ask what my business with him had been or how I had found myself at his home, but merely followed me without question. From Kefar Nahum it was a two hours' journey back to Bet Ma'on, and it would have been longer still had we not gone by the back ways, since it was impossible now for Yeshua to step from his gate without being surrounded by supplicants. Nonetheless he and I hardly spoke, nor in the end did I dare to breathe any word of the truth to him since he seemed still in the temper in which we had left him earlier in the day.

When we arrived at Simon's house Yeshua promptly set to work to cure the man, cooling him with damp cloths and making a brew for him from herbs he found in Simon's own garden. Of the filth in which Simon lived, and of the idols strewn throughout his house and even in his field, Yeshua said nothing, nor of the parcels wrapped in cloth or leaves, one of which I now recognized as my own, that lay in crude niches in the wall.

Yeshua sent me into town to fetch food from one of the houses where we were known. However, when Yeshua's followers heard he was nearby they insisted on accompanying me back to him. They were surprised when I stopped at the house of the Canaanite, and refused to come close.

Yeshua came out to the doorway and, seeing how his followers hung back, said, Your faith must be weak if you think merely breathing the air of a heathen's house will corrupt you.

A moment later, to my amazement, Simon himself appeared in the door, pale but standing, when I had left him delirious not a half-hour before.

I said to the others, He has cured him.

But my first thought was, Now my crime will be known. Simon, however, looked at me and didn't seem to recognize me, and in a moment returned to his bed.

I made some food for him and he ate it, then fell deep into sleep. It was nearly dark by this time. I said to Yeshua that he should spend the night at my father's house in Migdal, which was close, and he agreed to this, leaving Simon to the care of one of his followers from Bet Ma'on. So I thought that I had escaped with my crime undetected. But the following morning Simon, completely cured now, appeared at my father's gate not long after dawn, having tracked us down. When Yeshua came out to him he immediately fell prostrate, calling out every sort of thanks and praise to Yeshua for having saved his life and offering to serve him in whatever way he wished.

Get up, Yeshua said, but Simon remained at his feet, even kissing them. My father said, He is a pagan, not wanting Yeshua to be profaned, and Yeshua reprimanded him, saying, Isn't your own wife a pagan, who has never profaned me but shown me respect. At this my father held his tongue. But I knew he had meant that Simon was a sorcerer, and that what he praised in Yeshua was not the glory of God but only what he understood as the greater power of Yeshua's magic.

Because Simon refused to leave Yeshua's side, Yeshua ended by bringing him with us to Kefar Nahum to meet with the twelve. Those we passed on the road were startled to see Yeshua in the company of a pagan and a sorcerer. Then when we were with the twelve, Yeshua said, See how this one offers me everything though I've only cured him of a fever, when my own men can't stay with me though I promise them eternal life.

Yaqob said again, We are here, and Yeshua relented.

Then accept this man as one of us, he said, since he has shown great faith.

We didn't understand if he meant us to accept Simon only as a disciple or also as one of the twelve, which we couldn't fathom, since surely he knew of Simon's ways and that he didn't follow the one God. But because of Yeshua's mood we didn't dare to question him.

For my part, I stood in terror of the moment that Simon would reveal me to the others, for I was sure he had finally recognized me now. But he said nothing, and was timid with me as if he were the one held in threat. So a day passed, and another, and it seemed things would go well with us, since Yeshua was pleased to have converted Simon and had him sleep with him at the house of Shimon in the spot Yihuda had once had.

Then, to our joy, Yohanan returned to us, much repentant. He told us he had only wished to see the city of Sepphoris, putting no blame on Yihuda for his departure; yet neither did he say anything in his favour, from which we understood that though Yihuda had tempted him, in the end he had come to his senses. Yeshua instantly forgave him, saying it was left to Yohanan to know what sins he'd committed; and even his father was quick to pardon him, because the matter was not yet known in the town and so he'd been spared any dishonour. Thus the conversion of Simon to our cause appeared a good omen, since it had brought Yohanan back to us and kept Yihuda away. But still I couldn't rest easy with Simon among us.

I went to Yeshua directly in his quarters, the first time I had ever done so, and said, Those who condemn you will say that you too are a sorcerer if you take up with one. But Yeshua said, in a tone he had never used with me, Woman, be careful who you accuse lest you reveal your own treachery, and I knew then that he had understood what had happened between me and Simon.

At once my tears came, and my confession of what I had done.

My lord, I said, and fell on my knees in front of him, I've sinned against you and against God, and he took my hands and lifted me up and said, There's nothing you've done that can't be forgiven.

In that moment it was as if a veil had been lifted from me or as if the evil that had poisoned me was flowing away with my tears, and I understood then what it was to be forgiven, and how much evil clouded our vision until what was white was made black and even the simplest things could not be seen clearly. For now all the time of my plotting seemed like a darkness I had fallen into or like the delirium that came of a fever, though when I had been in the midst of it I had imagined, even as evil filled me, that I would be justified.

It was only because I was frightened for us, I said to Yeshua.

But he answered me, I was to blame. I held Yihuda too closely.

And he took me in his arms to comfort me in a way he hadn't done since he had first come to us. My heart gave in to him then. For many days afterwards I still felt the press of his arms against me like the bodily mark of his forgiveness.

When all of this had come to pass, it was as if after much struggle and despair I had suddenly reached the pinnacle of some high mountain, from where everything was visible. I saw now how the Lord had sent Yihuda as a test just as Shimon had said to me, and how in his mercy he had used him to save not only me but even Simon the Canaanite, who otherwise would surely never have been led to the one God. Then, because I had told Yeshua of my threat to Aram, he summoned him to reassure him he wouldn't be betrayed; but Yeshua had not so much as opened his mouth before Aram broke down and repented of everything he'd done, saying that from the time he'd left us he hadn't known anything except misery and ill fortune, and had every day feared arrest.

You only had to ask for forgiveness and we would have granted it, Yeshua said.

And Yeshua arranged among us to find him lodgings and work, since his family, by then, had long turned him out into the streets.

I would never have believed that the matter could have ended so auspiciously, seeing that even Aram had been brought back to us. But I soon saw that the twelve didn't understand the thing as I did, since they hadn't passed through my ordeal nor indeed, thanks to Yeshua's silence, did they know anything about it. Thus, while they were willing, for Thomas's sake, to suffer Aram's return to us, they couldn't bring themselves to countenance the Canaanite, whom they considered beneath them. Secretly they went to Simon and said that unless he be circumcised, they wouldn't accept him among us, at which Simon, however, grew mortally afraid. He asked if there wasn't some other way that he could show his loyalty to our god. But the others mocked him, saying he hadn't understood what it meant to be a Jew and to follow the Lord.

They went to Yeshua and said they couldn't accept Simon because he had refused circumcision. But Yeshua, seeing their contempt for Simon, grew angry.

You only talk about the outer man and not the inner one.

The law tells us there's no inner faith without the outward sign, Yaqob said.

Tell me who is more true to God, Yeshua said, the one who as an infant has done to him what he doesn't know or understand or the one who freely chooses God as a man.

No one knew how to answer him. Finally Shimon, who was deeply troubled by the matter, said, But without circumcision there's no covenant. Without circumcision we aren't Jews.

Sometimes you have to be more than Jews, Yeshua said.

Because of his anger the men wouldn't press him any further. But afterwards they argued amongst themselves. I wanted to speak in Simon's defence but felt ignorant of the law, nor did I think the men would listen to a woman on the issue.

Philip said of Simon, He's like a child, so how can he follow the master's teachings. But Shimon rightly reprimanded him, saying, Weren't we children when Yeshua came to us. Yet we've come to understand him.

Indeed we saw with our own eyes how, except in the matter of circumcision, Simon had abandoned all his old ways and embraced those of the Jews. He had gone to his old home and smashed all the idols there and made a fire of the shards, burning even his house; and he had taken a horde of coins that he had saved from selling his cures and given them in to our common purse. With the twelve, though they still held him in suspicion, he was open and honest, so that in his innocence he indeed seemed a child, as Philip had said of him. But in being a child, he showed more truly than the others the love Yeshua had taught us.

Thus I thought that in time even the matter of circumcision would come clear to us, as had so many others, along with whatever message Yeshua hoped to teach us through Simon's example. And so it might have been had not Yihuda returned to us suddenly, with as little explanation as when he'd gone, saying only that he had been to the protest at Caesarea, though a good deal of time had passed since it had ended. We were all amazed that he had dared to show his face again, but considered it beneath us to question him, waiting to take our lead from Yeshua. Yeshua, however, though distant with him, did not turn him away.

If you've come back, I hope it's to be one of us and not to divide us, was all he said, and even Yihuda seemed surprised at this, as if he'd hoped for an argument.

In the next days we all saw how Yeshua no longer raised Yihuda up as he once had, but was rather at pains to give each of us our proper place. This had the effect of bringing out a servility in Yihuda that had never been much below the surface, and of making him vie for Yeshua's attentions. Having learned, no doubt, how Yeshua had publicly praised the Jews' actions at Caesarea and the peaceful manner in which the protest there had ended, Yihuda was keen now to claim his own part in the thing, and to say how much further he had come in his understanding of Yeshua's teachings. But if that was the case, it was still no mark of distinction in him that with all his learning he had thus merely done what so many others had accomplished more quickly with none.

Out of Yeshua's hearing, however, it was soon clear that Yihuda hadn't reformed, because he wasted no time now in spreading dissension. He had taken an instant dislike to Simon the Canaanite, no doubt because he feared he had replaced him among the twelve; and so, learning of the controversy surrounding his inclusion among us, he seized the chance to prey on our confusion.

Aren't you afraid of people's anger, he asked, warning that this was a matter over which the crowd might strike Yeshua dead. And he said it was only the fact that Simon had been a sorcerer that people could see, and that he remained uncircumcised, for they were too ignorant to understand when Yeshua spoke of what was outside and what was inside a man.

The rest of the twelve pretended not to mind him. But privately they began to wonder if he had spoken rightly, and to fear for our master's life. Then it happened once in Akhbara, beneath Tsef, that some of Yeshua's old enemies sent their men to trouble him.

Is it true that you teach the end of circumcision, they said to him.

But Yeshua, knowing who had sent them, would say only that just as all things would one day end in judgement, as their own teachers taught them, so too would circumcision come to an end.

None of them had any answer to this. But not admitting their defeat, they said, Even after the judgement there will be circumcision, since that is how the Lord will continue to know those who have kept his covenant.

Now Yeshua lost patience with them.

Do you think the Lord requires a mark of faith inside his kingdom, he said. Doesn't he see into our hearts, and know us more fully than any mark can show. It was only because of the weakness of the Israelites that God gave them a mark to bind them to him, because if they'd been strong, their faith alone would have been enough.

At this the men had their excuse and began to stir up the crowd against him, saying, See how he insults Abraham and our fathers, and calling for him to be punished. Some of them went so far as to throw stones, and one of these struck him. But because Yeshua did not turn and run as they'd expected but held his ground, they lost courage.

Shimon, however, was made very concerned by these events and afterwards took Simon aside and explained to him how he had brought his master's life into danger, which until then Simon hadn't understood. In this way he convinced him to receive the mark, for the good of us all. To avoid those who hated us and spare from criticism those who loved us, Shimon wouldn't go to the teachers in our towns to have the matter looked to but only to the priest in Tiberias. Simon balked at this, thinking he wouldn't come out alive from that place, since it was believed even by the pagans to be cursed. In the end I was enlisted to accompany him to bring him comfort, for because I had been present at his cure, he showed a deep trust in me, unwarranted though it was.

So it came about that I entered Tiberias, whose gates I had never passed through though as a child I had watched the city rise up from nothing in the slopes beyond Migdal. Shimon and Simon came for me by boat but we went the rest of the way to the city on foot, to avoid the harbour tax and the risk that the boat would be stolen or ruined, as often happened there. I was under orders from Shimon to keep my face covered and my eyes downcast, and so my impression of the city was only of the noise of carts and passersby and of the blinding glare of white stone, so different from the black of our villages. I felt a double disgrace in being there, because it was Herod's place, and built over the bones of the dead, and because I knew we didn't have Yeshua's sanction for what we'd undertaken, though I had gone along with the thing because, like the others, I was afraid for his life.

Simon didn't speak a word from the time we entered the city and indeed looked even more terrified than I was at the confusion and noise, like an animal who had been brought in from the wild. Shimon led us quickly through the streets to the quarter where the Jews lived, passing by the palace, which was heavily guarded and gave onto a vast open square. There was a view out over the lake there that made it seem utterly alien from the lake I gazed out to every morning from my own front stoop, framed as it was within the city's strange white monuments and colonnades and forbidden icons.

The assembly house that we finally arrived at, though faced in limestone, was hardly much grander than the one at Kefar Nahum, with a small portal that came out to a street where merchants had their shops. Further on, however, off a courtyard covered in white paving stones, was a larger building that we were told was the home of the Levite under whose patronage the assembly house was held. The doorway was framed by two massive animals carved from rock—lions, as I imagined them, or bears, though I had never seen them—which I was astonished to see in the house of a priest and a Jew. Then a servant came to the door and I saw that the floor of the entrance hall was covered in bits of coloured stone that also formed images.

The servant was dark-skinned and spoke with the clipped accent of a Judean.

What is your business, he said, and when he learned what we wanted, and where we had come from, he at once reprimanded us for presenting ourselves at the front gate.

He sent us around to the servants' courtyard, which smelled of offal and waste. After we had waited a long while and made many enquiries among the servants who passed through there, an acolyte of the priest, a boy who could not have been much beyond my own age, finally came to us and offered his service, naming a price, however, of five denarii. Shimon, seeing the nature of the place we had come to, and how we had been treated, and the child who had been sent to tend to us, was ready at that moment to abandon our mission and return home. In the end it was Simon who bade us remain and go through with the thing, for the fact was that the grandness of the priest's home had inspired confidence in him, and so he seemed suddenly ready to suffer any chastisement for the sake of Yeshua's safety.

We required wine for Simon to drink. The acolyte said that that of the house was too fine for us, and so we were sent back into the street to purchase some, which Simon drank down undiluted. He and Shimon then followed the acolyte to an inner room from which I was forbidden. I heard Simon's screams, and a short while later he and Shimon emerged from the house alone. There was blood on Simon's tunic and Shimon had practically to carry him, for he was faint from the surgery and from the wine. It was getting towards dusk and we ought to have remained for the night in the city, to let Simon rest. But we were afraid of making our way in that place, and of the cost, and that my father, who didn't know what mission I'd undertaken, would be sorely distressed if I didn't return.

It was well past dark before we reached Migdal. Simon by then was feverish, and had not ceased to bleed, and indeed we had got him as far as Migdal only by dint of carrying him in one manner or another, either draped over the back of Shimon or with Shimon at his arms and me at his feet. We managed to put him into Shimon's boat and then I told my father that Simon was unwell and I would need to accompany him to Kefar Nahum, without however explaining to him what had happened. It was clear by then that we would need to go to Yeshua, even at the risk of his displeasure, for Simon had taken on such a pallor and was in such a delirium that we believed him close to death. I was enlisted to row along with Shimon, because the wind was against us. But even still it was midnight before we reached Kefar Nahum,
and Yeshua had to be raised from his bed.

As we'd expected, he was angry with us beyond measure at what we'd done. He didn't however waste time to chastise us but looked at once to Simon, making a proper bandage to staunch his bleeding and setting me to brew an infusion of honey and bitter rose, as we called it, to give him strength. By morning, the threat to him seemed to have passed. But when we had gathered together for our morning meal, Yeshua did not mince his words.

If those I put closest to me behave like fools, what can I expect of the rest, he said, angry not only because we had acted without his sanction, and brought into danger Simon's life, but because we had done in secret and by apparent coercion what ought to have been done freely and in celebration. We might have told him then that it was Yihuda who had planted the notion in us, and raised our fears. But Shimon took all of the blame upon himself and said the idea had been his own solely.

So the matter ended in confusion, and I was angry that Yihuda had again been the cause of error for me, and wondered if I would ever be free of his influence. This time, however, it happened that some of the others saw the thing in the same light, because Yaqob, knowing my feelings for Yihuda, came to me and said, We must find the way to send him from us. I saw he was worried that his brother might again fall under Yihuda's sway; for their father hadn't known the way to refuse Yihuda his old place at their home.

I would not scheme again as I had and told Yaqob we must go at once to Yeshua. But Yaqob grew uneasy and said we should await our moment so that we might bring a proper charge. In the meanwhile, however, Yihuda continued to stir dissension, always finding the way to make controversy with the crowds whenever Yeshua preached; and in this he was no doubt taking out his resentment at Yeshua's coolness towards him, which had clearly affected him. He chastised us, for instance, because several of us often travelled to Kefar Nahum now before sabbath fell so that we might be there to say our evening prayers with Yeshua—according to Yihuda, it was a mark of arrogance in Yeshua that he should require such devotion, since it was in the spirit of the law that the sabbath be spent near our homes. Yet he himself could hardly be bothered to pray, seldom joining us when we did so, as if it were beneath him to abase himself before us in that way.

Since he'd come back his movements had grown even more mysterious than before. He often went into Tiberias, on what missions he didn't say; and when he returned he was always in a state of great agitation, as if he had committed some crime there. Every manner of suspicion crossed my mind—that he was a murderer or a thief, or that he reported to Herod, or that he was a black marketeer who used Yeshua as his cover—but because of my earlier sin I didn't dare accuse him. Rather I prayed that he would find the way to accuse himself, and so spare us the need to conspire against him.

Then one evening, when we were at Kefar Nahum, I was sent to find him so he might join us for our meal. I searched the town, going even to the tavern, though I was told he hadn't set foot there. But passing the assembly house I saw a light through the door and was drawn to see who was inside. I didn't know why this was so, since it had been many months that those of us with Yeshua hadn't frequented the place. Thus I was startled to see it was Yihuda who had lit
the lamp there, and that he was praying on his knees in front of the Torah chest.

Hearing me at the door, he immediately turned and rose up.

What is it, he said, seeing who it was, and for a moment I couldn't answer him, so surprised was I at finding him there.

I was sent to call you to supper.

I'll be along.

And yet I wouldn't leave him.

I'll wait for you in the street, I said.

It was some minutes before he joined me, and then in consternation, for clearly he didn't see why I solicited him in this way when I had always spurned him. The truth was I couldn't have said so myself; and yet there was something I had seen in the look of him as he prayed there in the assembly house, which was his fear.

You needn't have waited, he said to me, and set off at once at a brisk pace, so that I was at pains to keep up with him.

After this I looked at him differently. I saw that if he seemed uncouth and ignorant, it was because he didn't understand us or our ways; and also how he himself knew that he wasn't one of us, and couldn't shake his unease among us. So if he stayed with us, it was because he depended on us, and if he hated us, it was also for this, because of his need.

It seemed the Lord had shown me what was inside the man as a rebuke to me, to make me see I'd been mistaken in him. Yet still I couldn't trust him, or warm myself to him, or melt the hardness I felt towards him. This was surely a failure in me, for Yeshua had taught us to love even the Syrians and the Samaritans whom all the Jews numbered among their enemies, and I couldn't love even one of our own.

It turned out that in all this time Yaqob had not been idle as I'd supposed, but had been busy sounding out the others on the grievances they held against Yihuda. Because he was forceful, most of the twelve had come around to him and found some complaint to make, that Yihuda had slighted them or had spoken against Yeshua or his mission or had made some statement that could be held against us. So Yaqob gathered the charges up and went to Shimon with them, so that they might make their case to Yeshua.

This was in the days just before the Passover, when we hoped Yeshua would lead us in pilgrimage to Jerusalem. Because there was a great deal of danger in Jerusalem during the feasts, on account of the soldiers and the crowds, we were anxious to have Yihuda away from us before our journey so he wouldn't make trouble for us. Shimon waited until Yihuda had gone off one day on his own and went to Yeshua, sending Yohanan off as well, not wanting him there to take Yihuda's side.

Yeshua, however, didn't see the thing as we did.

Someone pricks you and you say instead that he stuck a dagger into you, Yeshua said, of the slights we'd endured.

Nonetheless, he saw we were united in the matter. Then one of the twelve, one of the youngest, Yaqob bar Heleph, said, It was Yihuda who convinced us to go against you in Simon's circumcision.

No one knew what to say to this. We all saw he had put the thing more strongly than was fair, but only in his zeal, hoping to please us. So no one wished to gainsay him and cause him embarrassment.

Yeshua asked Shimon, Is this true.

But because Shimon hesitated, Yeshua thought he meant to affirm the thing.

Yet you took the blame on yourself, Yeshua said, and still Shimon couldn't bring himself to speak.

Yeshua's face darkened but he didn't say another word on the matter. But when Yihuda returned that evening Yeshua invited him to the harbour and rowed out with him onto the lake in one of Shimon's boats. We imagined he had listened to what we had told him and would ask Yihuda to leave. Some of us went out to the shore to try to catch sight of them on the water and follow their progress, but though we could hear their voices drifting over the lake, we couldn't tell what they said, nor could we even make them out in the dark.

We waited until they had rowed back to shore, and Yihuda had gone to his bed, before we dared to ask Yeshua what had passed between them.

We spoke about Jerusalem, Yeshua said, and about our pilgrimage.

We weren't sure what to make of this.

And what about our petition to you, Shimon said finally.

Yihuda has made a petition too, if not in words, Yeshua said. And it is that we accept him. So if he needs us, then it would be our failure to turn him away.

He said then that he wouldn't take us into Jerusalem as we'd planned because he hadn't the stomach to lead a multitude there. We took this as a reprimand, as if we were being punished. But perhaps it was simply that we had soured the thing for him, with our intrigue. I felt ashamed then, understanding this, and remembering how I had seen into Yihuda at the assembly house, yet still wished to be rid of him.

I spent the time of the Passover in Migdal, since Yeshua had refused to lead us and my father, on my mother's account, seldom made his own pilgrimage. Yeshua had left for Mount Tabor to make a retreat there, taking only Shimon and Yohanan and Yaqob; though we learned on their return that he had made his own pilgrimage in the end, reaching

Jerusalem by way of Samaria. The others had hardly known where he was taking them until they had arrived at the very gates of the city, and indeed had wondered that he would lead them through Samaria, where the Jews were hated. But he told them he had merely wanted to avoid running into his own disciples on the road, so that he might be free to worship in peace.

In Jerusalem, at Yeshua's request, they had gone about quietly to avoid calling attention to themselves. But despite Yeshua's intentions he ended up attracting a crowd one day in the temple precincts when he debated one of the scholars there. It was his misfortune that an enemy was among the crowd then, a teacher from Ammathus named Yibkhar whom Yeshua had once slighted. Yibkhar immediately tried to find the way to discredit Yeshua and so brought the discussion around to the question of the temple tax, knowing that Yeshua, who did not believe a man should be obliged to look to the welfare of the temple priests before that of his own family, had often spoken against it. The Judeans, of course, found Yeshua's view sacrilege; and so Yibkhar was able to turn the crowd against him, to the extent that some among it, enraged that a Galilean would question their customs, threatened Yeshua with violence.

All this would have been of no great concern, however, had the matter ended there. But Yibkhar, it turned out, was also a merchant to Herod's court, and when he returned to Galilee he began to plant lies in the ears of Herod's courtiers, charging that Yeshua had nearly provoked a riot and that he had skulked around Jerusalem hiding even from his own followers like a fugitive or a rebel. There was enough truth in what he said for him to find corroboration. So the matter must have come to the attention of Herod himself, who no doubt began to fear that Yeshua would become a thorn to him as Yohanan had been. In Kefar Nahum two men appeared at the time asking after Yeshua and putting all sorts of questions about him to people, claiming they were from a village in the north, though it was clear from their manner and their dress that they had come out of Tiberias.

Hearing of them, Yeshua went to them at once.

We heard of your fame, they said to him, and wanted to learn your message.

But Yeshua, knowing who had sent them, said, You surprise me, since usually dogs chase the fox, but you do one's bidding, for the fox was the name we gave to Herod.

For all their questions, the men couldn't find any evidence of wrongdoing on Yeshua's part. But they had heard from the townspeople how the crowds loved him, and had seen with their own eyes how he was afraid of no one. So they must have put fear into Herod, because not long afterwards a certain Chizkijah of Bersaba began to appear in the crowd whenever Yeshua preached. This was a man who was well known, for he was often in our towns pretending to be one of us in order to find out our neighbours' secrets or who of us sympathized with the rebels. Now, however, he made no effort to hide his intentions, and indeed told us openly that he had been sent to catch Yeshua out in some word of treason.

There were some among Yeshua's followers who wanted to kill the man when they heard this. But Shimon quickly went to them and called them fools, making them see that if Chizkijah spoke so openly, then surely he'd come only to frighten us. Indeed, even now it was said that Herod didn't dare to lay his hands on Yeshua after everything he'd heard about him, not only on his own account but because he'd been an acolyte of Yohanan's, over whose death Herod was now plagued with guilt. Thus we suffered Chizkijah to stay among us without giving him any provocation or cause for complaint, though at every opportunity he put questions to us about the payment of taxes or whether we honoured Herod the king.

Among the twelve, we didn't imagine that Chizkijah could be any threat to us when so many others had proved none. The truth was we all believed that Herod was foolish to employ the likes of someone as well known and disrespected as Chizkijah, and that it was only because he never came out to the countryside and knew nothing of what went on there that Chizkijah had prevailed upon him to engage his services. In Bersaba, which was Chizkijah's hometown, it was said that even his own family would have nothing to do with him, and that he had been chased away as a young man because of the debts he had accrued and because of other infamies; and even in appearance he was wretched and ugly, being humpbacked and thin-limbed and with a foul odour to him like a leper. Yeshua had taught us not to make our judgements from the appearance of a man; but Chizkijah seemed truly punished by God in his deformities, since the outer look of him was so much the mirror of his inner nature. Yet it was from Chizkijah that a great threat to us took shape, for it was exactly because no one took him into account that he was able to insinuate himself among us and cause us harm.

From the very start we were put off our guard, since it seemed so simple a matter for Yeshua to avoid the traps that Chizkijah set for him. He was quick to ask about the kingdom, saying he had heard others speak of it and wondered if it was a place of the heavens or of the earth.

But Yeshua, knowing his intentions, said, What do those you speak to tell you.

Truly I don't think they've understood you, Chizkijah said, because some say it's in heaven, some on earth, and the rest somewhere in between, at which many in the crowd laughed, for though people despised him, he was clever enough to amuse them.

Yeshua said, Then they've answered rightly, since it's all these things.

But how can it be on the earth, Chizkijah said, when the Galilee belongs to Herod and Judea to Rome.

Tell me this, who does the wind belong to, Yeshua asked him.

How can the wind belong to anyone.

Then the kingdom is like the wind, Yeshua said, which is in heaven and on earth and in between, and belongs to no one.

So Yeshua always found the way to get the better of him, and soon people gave up their fear and let Chizkijah move among us freely. And we grew used to seeing him in the crowd when Yeshua preached, and exchanging a word with everyone as if even he himself did not take his mission seriously but must show his face so that he might collect his payment from Herod.

At the time, the crowds that gathered around Yeshua had grown large, as much as several hundred. It was hard to say, then, who came and went, or what they wanted, and it was all Yeshua could do to deal with these and to tend to the sick, who continued to flock to us. Over time we ceased to pay any mind to Chizkijah at all, since he no longer put himself forward as he once had, and asked no questions. Yet he did not abandon us, for we would make him out now and again at the edges of the crowd, but looking increasingly dejected and careworn as if he had lost heart for his mission.

Soon the rumour started to spread that he regretted having made himself Yeshua's enemy, for in the course of listening to Yeshua day by day and watching him with the crowds, he had begun to be won over to him. No one knew from what source this notion had arisen, but neither did it seem far-fetched, since it had often been among the greatest sinners, as with Simon the Canaanite, that Yeshua had won his most fervent converts. Thus it happened that some of our own people, anxious for a conversion to be made of Chizkijah like that of Simon, began to take him into their homes in the hope of being the ones to bring him to Yeshua's side.

In this way Chizkijah was finally able to worm himself into the confidence of many of Yeshua's disciples. If these had been wise, they would have come to Yeshua at once, or to one of the twelve, and we would have understood then how far Chizkijah's wiles could extend. But Chizkijah convinced them to keep their silence, saying it shamed him to come openly and also might endanger his life. As he had chosen carefully, and gone to those who were blinded in some small part by hopes of the glory that would come to them should they win him over, he was thus able to work his evil in secret, biding his time and preying on people's trust until he found the way to turn one of Yeshua's greatest works against him.

It was well known throughout the region how Yeshua had saved the life of Ribqah, the daughter of Urijah, for since he had come to us her father had ceased to abuse her. But now it happened that Urijah conspired to have his revenge on

Yeshua, contracting to have Ribqah sold to a man in Migdal who was three times her years, and who already had a wife who had given him sons. When Yeshua learned of the arrangement he said he would not stand for it, and proffered twice Ribqah's bride price out of our own purse so that she might be spared a life of misery and servitude. Urijah, who in this way saw more money than he had ever laid eyes on, immediately agreed to the thing. But soon enough the matter became known, and so reached the ears of Chizkijah.

Now Chizkijah, in his cunning, didn't do as he might have done, and simply denounce Yeshua's actions in the matter. Instead he asked those who had let him into their trust for every detail of Ribqah as if he was very taken with her plight, then began to go about the towns of the region telling how Yeshua had saved her and what a great thing he had done for her. In so doing, however, he didn't omit to say in passing how beautiful Ribqah was, and how she cried when Yeshua left her, and how on some occasions in the night, when she feared her father, she had gone to Yeshua at the house of Shimon; and in this way he let the putting together of one thing and another make its own accusation, though he himself didn't say the words. Indeed, if he had said, Yeshua has taken her for his concubine, even Yeshua's enemies would have dismissed him, knowing the man he was and that he was Herod's spy. But because he came as if in praise, it happened that the first to be swayed by him, and to have their doubts, were exactly Yeshua's disciples, who couldn't see through Chizkijah's guile and so believed they had arrived at their indictment of their own accord.

Thus many things began to be whispered among Yeshua's followers that, because they passed secretly from ear to ear, we could put up no defence against; and since Chizkijah had picked his words judiciously, and had said nothing that wasn't true, those who began with only the smallest doubts saw them grow into certainties. For it was true that Ribqah was beautiful, as anyone who had seen her could attest; and it was true she could hardly bear to be from Yeshua's sight, though this could be put as much to her fear of her father as to her love for Yeshua. Then there were many in Kefar Nahum who could bear witness that on more than one occasion Ribqah had come in the night to the house of Shimon and had stayed until morning. These were the times, as she had told me, when her father had moved against her and she had been afraid for her life; and the people of Kefar Nahum, knowing what her father was and that the house of Shimon was a respectable one, had said nothing of her visits. But now the matter appeared in a different light.

By the time we among the twelve got wind of the accusations that had begun to circulate, they already seemed to have gained wide currency. Yeshua would not deign to respond to them in any way, not even to the twelve, saying only that he would not shun those he loved for the sake of a rumour and still keeping us women by his side when he preached. But eventually people began to see in his silence a sign of his guilt, so that his name, which even among his enemies had always been raised above that of the common lot, was now tainted with petty slander and the gossip of the marketplace. Many of our own followers began to say that Yeshua had indeed acted wrongly in preventing Ribqah's marriage, and that it was not his place to interfere with how a man disposed of his daughter or to beg alms so that he might turn them over as ransom. Meanwhile Urijah, seeing how the matter had gone against us, began to put it about that Yeshua had coerced him, and that it was only because Yeshua had promised to take Ribqah as his own wife that he had agreed to his payment.

For my part, I felt the coolness towards us women now at many of the meeting houses we went to, since we had all been painted in the same light, and saw the looks that went to us behind Yeshua's back, and heard the hint of condescension in the voices of those who had been our friends. Among the crowds it was worse—the men leered at us as if we had become a spectacle. I was happy enough to put up with these things for Yeshua's sake; but I saw that Ribqah, being the one who was named, took them much more to heart.

If there's no truth to the charges, you needn't concern yourself, I said to comfort her.

But to my surprise she answered, If he married me, then he would save my honour, as if to ask that I petition for her.

I didn't know what to say. I began to fear that she herself had misunderstood Yeshua's intentions, and that because he had paid her bride price, she imagined him beholden.

We aren't for marriage but something higher, I said finally, meaning she mustn't think in the old ways, of husbands and wives, when Yeshua had taken us beyond such things. But I didn't think she understood.

The truth was I held her words against her, and was afraid she had begun to imagine that Yeshua did more for her because he loved her more deeply, rather than because she had greater need. However, I didn't go to Yeshua then with my apprehensions, not only to spare Ribqah disgrace but because I didn't wish to add this concern to the many others that had beset him. For in addition to the accusations against him and the growing distrust of his own people, it had also happened now that the sick had suddenly become a plague to us, coming in ever greater numbers and expecting every sort of miracle. As it turned out it was Chizkijah, again, who was behind this—in the same guise of praising us, he had gone about the countryside exaggerating Yeshua's powers so that the sick would overwhelm us and it was certain that large numbers of them would be forced to go away unsatisfied and uncured. Yeshua could hardly bear any more to see the hordes that awaited him at every turn, most of whom came to him now not as to a man of God but as they would to a common sorcerer. Once there was a mother awaiting him at Shimon's gate with two infants, twins, already blue with death—she wouldn't accept that he couldn't help her, but railed at him and cursed him as if he were the one who had killed them.

Soon enough it happened that Yeshua was openly accused from the crowd on Ribqah's account. We were surprised, however, when he did not answer the charge but left it to hang over us in silence. No one had ever seen him fall mute in this way and not have a response to a thing. Afterwards there were some of the twelve who began to wonder privately if indeed there wasn't some truth to the accusations against him.

You're no better than our enemies to say so, Shimon said, growing angry, and because even Yihuda supported him in this, he was able to put the others in their place. Nonetheless, it seemed that the poison Chizkijah had released among us had now seeped to our very core, and we could no longer be certain even of our own perceptions.

Urijah by now had forbidden Ribqah to accompany us, saying we had disgraced her. So closely did he keep watch over her that she did not even come out to the smoking sheds to do her work and I no longer saw her even in passing. But though we felt certain Yeshua would take some action on her behalf, the days passed and he did nothing. When we asked why he had abandoned her, he said he did not wish to do her further harm.

Shimon said, Did you harm her before in saving her from her father.

But Yeshua asked how had he saved her when he had taken from her what he couldn't restore, her reputation.

For several days then he seldom left his quarters and made us turn away all those who came looking for him, even the sick. Thus, in the end, it wasn't Yeshua who went to Urijah but rather Urijah who came to him—one day he presented himself at Shimon's gate, waving the very bag of coins that Yeshua had given him for Ribqah's bride price and shouting like a madman for Yeshua to show himself.

By the time Yeshua went out a crowd had already gathered. There in front of everyone Urijah said to him, My daughter is pregnant by you. And he threw the bag of coins at Yeshua's feet.

We could hardly believe the accusation, or that Urijah, a man of so little character, should have the gall to make it. And yet everyone had seen how he had gone so far in supporting the charge as to return our money to us. My mind strained to piece the thing out—surely he had lied to say Ribqah was pregnant. Yet how would he dare, when the truth would be known soon enough.

Urijah left the town at once then, not waiting to hear any response, but Yeshua quickly set out after him with a group of us so that he might have a chance to answer his charge. By the time we reached Migdal, however, Urijah had already enlisted his cousins to bar us from his house. Indeed, by dint of shouting his accusations from his gate as we tried to approach, he managed to draw half the town into the street and turn them against us, so that even the teacher Sapphias, who had never had anything but contempt for Urijah in the past, was quick to take up his side. Yeshua demanded that Ribqah be allowed to appear to speak for herself. But Sapphias said we could hardly be expected to take her word on the matter, one way or the other. In the end, to avoid violence, we were forced to retreat back to Kefar Nahum.

Philip said to Yeshua, You must either marry the girl or put her away from us, or risk losing all our efforts.

But Yeshua was furious with him.

Why do you offer me the same choices as my enemies, he said.

That night when I returned to Migdal I couldn't rest until I knew the truth. By moonlight I went to Ribqah's window and woke her from her bed, and she slipped out to me then, though her father slept by the gate.

We went out to the lakeshore and I asked her if she was indeed pregnant. But she wouldn't look at me.

My mother says it is so, she said finally.

I stood dumbfounded. It seemed suddenly I didn't know her at all, that such a thing could be true. To my shame, I felt it like a betrayal, that she had shown herself different from me in this way when I had imagined us sisters, of a kind.

Who is the father, I said.

But she wouldn't answer me. I didn't press her because of my fear of who she might name.

I could hardly hold together my thoughts then, or imagine what to say to her. I ought to have found the way to comfort her yet it seemed that surely she had disgraced us all.

Tomorrow I will speak to Yeshua, was all I said, and then I left her.

In the morning, however, the word went out through the town that she was missing from her bed. Everyone assumed at once, as even I did, that she had fled to Yeshua at Kefar Nahum, and Urijah and some others immediately set out in a mob to fetch her back. It wasn't long, however, before the message came that she had been found in a cave up the beach near Kinneret, in a fit of delirium. Seeing her thrashing, those who had discovered her had promptly imagined her possessed, and so had sent for Sapphias. This was a mistake, for Sapphias was only too glad to have a report that lent further credence to the scandal against Yeshua and so made a great show of going out to the place, drawing half the town with him and causing delay that perhaps cost Ribqah her life.

I was among those who went out. Seeing her moaning there on the beach, still in her convulsions, I didn't waste time in accompanying the others as they returned with her to the town, but quickly set off to fetch Yeshua in Kefar Nahum. I could not keep up my pace, however, and past Kinneret had to stop to regain my breath, practically in a faint. My mind was swimming then with everything that had happened. All night I had been unable to sleep with the worry of the scandal Ribqah had brought to us, and it crossed my thoughts now in my agitation that it might indeed go better for all of us if Ribqah should die, not least for Ribqah herself. But later I had my punishment for thinking in this way.

It was mid-morning by the time I reached Kefar Nahum, finding Yihuda and a few others gathered together in Shimon's courtyard. When they learned what had happened they hastily prepared a boat, and a group of us set out with Yeshua for Migdal. The wind was with us and we made the town quickly. But when we came ashore we found that Urijah had simply laid Ribqah out on one of the tables near the harbour where the fish were gutted, though she still had not settled from her convulsions, and was working there beside her hardly minding her yet not permitting anyone else to come near her. If my father had been present, he would never have allowed such a thing. But he was away at market, and no other man in the town had dared oppose Urijah, even though it was clear from the wild look of him and from his actions that he was not in his proper mind.

Yeshua, however, didn't hold back his anger or make any allowance for Urijah's state.

Would to God you lay in your daughter's place, he said, and Urijah didn't try to hinder him as he had everyone else, but instantly moved aside, seeming relieved, indeed, that Yeshua had come.

Ribqah was barely conscious and showed no sign that she recognized any of us, even Yeshua. Yeshua had her moved to my father's house and put in my own bed there, and while the others waited by the door, I stayed next to him to help tend to her, full of remorse now that I had not shown Ribqah more comfort when I had had the chance. There was an abscess on her ankle where it seemed she'd suffered a bite of some sort, but when Yeshua went to lance it we saw it didn't resemble the bite of anything that we knew except crudely, as if a thorn or spur of some kind had been taken to the place in imitation. Then we saw the purple stains on the skin there and also on her lips, the colour of the gall that grew among the rocks on the lakeshore.

Yeshua opened her mouth. Her tongue was purpled like her lips, and bits of foliage still stained her teeth.

Finally Yeshua said to me, She has poisoned herself.

I was stunned. I couldn't believe that I had been with her only the night before and had not seen the state of her mind, that she should have been driven to such a thing. I wondered how it could have been that she had admitted to me her pregnancy, yet I'd done nothing.

I confessed to Yeshua then what she'd told me.

You should have come to me at once, he said.

I was afraid who the father might be.

But he didn't rebuke me for this.

The father has already made himself known by his actions, he said, though at the time I didn't understand his meaning.

The others were still waiting outside the room. Yeshua said nothing to them of what we'd discovered, but it was clear he had lost heart now for his ministrations, merely kneeling at Ribqah's side with her hands in his own. By now the poison seemed already well advanced—she had gone limp, as happened with gall, and had lost any sign of consciousness.

Within the hour, she was dead. Yeshua wept.

I did nothing for her, he said, and it seemed that all his mission was dismissed in this, for here was one he had apparently tried by every means to save yet she had taken her own life.

I was hardly aware of what happened next. Yeshua said nothing to the others of how Ribqah had died and so left them believing she had suffered a bite of some sort; but because of this they couldn't be any comfort to us, nor could they understand the strange mood we had fallen into. In our confusion, it was left to my mother to bring us back to our senses and arrange for the body to be dressed for burial. To the surprise of all of us, it was Yihuda who undertook to go into Tiberias to purchase linens, though in all his time with us I didn't remember that he had exchanged so much as a word with Ribqah or shown the least awareness of her.

By midday my father had returned, having learned of the tragedy on the road and hurried back to us. He took charge now of the preparations, sending for mourners and pipers. But to our bewilderment Yeshua said he wouldn't accompany us to the burial.

Surely you loved her enough to see her buried, my father said.

I love the living, he said. I'm no use to the dead.

What of the rest of us, one of the twelve asked.

Do as you wish.

Even I who knew the circumstances of Ribqah's death didn't know what to make of this—if it was a reproof to us or to Ribqah or simply that his grief had overwhelmed him. I would have welcomed his solace then, since I could not put from my mind my own guilt, which sounded in my head more loudly than the keening of the mourners.

In the end we made a poor procession, with only a handful of the twelve and few from the town except my own family and Ribqah's, her mother slack-faced with grief as if some of her had died along with her daughter. Urijah, though no one showed any remorse at this, could not be found; indeed, he had left town like a skulking dog at the first word of Ribqah's death, nor had he dared to repeat any more his charges against Yeshua. By now it had also been discovered that the bag of coins he had returned contained barely a third of what he'd been given—no doubt he had already spent the rest, and had only made a show of returning the money intact to give credence to his accusations.

My father had Ribqah put in our own family tomb, since her family had none and she would otherwise have had to be buried in the earth. We were all concerned over the matter of resurrection—Ribqah was one of the first of us who had died since we had come to Yeshua's teachings, and we were unsure whether some different custom applied in the burial of her. Afterwards there were those who had the cruelty to mock us and say we should not have closed the tomb at all, but left it open for Ribqah to walk out of it. But I wondered if indeed we hadn't failed in some important way and so doomed Ribqah to darkness, she whose life had already been one of perpetual dark.

It wasn't long before Yeshua's enemies found the way to use Ribqah's death against him, saying it was shame that had kept him from her funeral and a sign of his guilt that he had been unable to cure her, when he had worked so many other wonders. Then, only days after her burial, Urijah, who had not appeared again in Migdal but had several times been seen drunk in the streets of Tiberias, was found dead at the bottom of a cliff near the Tiberias gates. Whether he had merely stumbled to his death or willingly flung himself to it no one could say; but still there were many who were again ready to put the blame to Yeshua, saying it was grief over his daughter's death that accounted for the thing. Those of us who knew Urijah, however, could not believe that grief was behind his actions. I began to think about what Yeshua had said of Ribqah's pregnancy, and about Urijah's behaviour, yet could hardly admit to my mind the conclusion that began to urge itself on me.

I went to Yeshua then.

Surely Urijah's death was a judgement against him, I said, not able to put the thing directly.

But to my surprise Yeshua said, If a tragedy is a mark of sin, who are we to accuse others when we ourselves must be the most sinful.

Still I wouldn't desist.

If he was guilty of a crime, it must be made known, to show our own innocence.

Where is our innocence, Yeshua said, when two people are dead and we were unable to save them. Don't think there's any happiness in heaven at Urijah's death. If there's any judgement now, it's against us, that we didn't help him when we could.

So he would say nothing against Urijah, not even to clear his own name, when all along he had been amongst our bitterest enemies and a man of such evil, as it now seemed, that his crimes could hardly be named. It was difficult for me to fathom Yeshua's silence, when even the alms he gave to Ribqah's family now so that they might not starve to death were seen as payments for his own guilt; nor could I share the matter with the twelve or the other women, since they didn't know the circumstances of the thing and I couldn't bring myself to reveal them. What occurred to me again and again was my own failure, that I hadn't seen Ribqah's distress or done anything to relieve it, but had thought only of the disgrace she would bring to us. Yet it was perhaps in this that I seemed to have an inkling of Yeshua's meaning, for I realized that if I had not thought of accusation then, I would have seen what was more important. It took a great stretching of the mind, yet it was possible to conceive that we had erred in this regard even with respect to Urijah, for it was true that not one of us had ever gone to him to understand him or to try to change his ways. How differently things might have unfolded then, if we had somehow tried to win him to us even though he was despicable.

For many days after Ribqah's death Yeshua conducted himself like a penitent, refusing to eat and hardly emerging from his quarters. The twelve, on the excuse of respecting his mourning but perhaps also because they had grown afraid of his behaviour, seldom went in to him in this period or had any word with him. But I went to him almost daily, afraid he would imagine we had deserted him. The truth was that he seemed almost to wish this, that we would cease to believe in him, so that he might be freed for a time of the burden of leading us.

Once he said to me, Why do you come to me, when surely my enemies will find the way to turn even this against us. But I hardly listened to him, knowing the state of his mind then. It was a sort of test to me, as I saw it, for him to say such a thing when surely he knew by then what little store I set by the opinions of the world. Perhaps he feared that my devotion to him was so abject and blind that at the first sign of reproof from him I should feel compelled to flee; but that was not the case. So I continued to go to him every day and urge what food on him he would eat, though many days he would take no sustenance except water, and he had begun to waste away to the point where we feared he must die.

Then one evening when we were gathered together he finally came out to us, breaking a loaf of bread with us and putting some morsels of it in his mouth, though more, it seemed, to appease us than his hunger.

I have to leave you for a time, he said, since I'm no use to you.

This was the thing we had most feared. Simon the Canaanite instantly fell prostrate before him and said he would not leave his side, for he was his master now.

Then you've learned nothing, Yeshua said, and are a fool, or you would know that only the Lord is your master.

Afterwards, some of the men felt he had meant to say that he didn't want any of them to accompany him when he left. But it was Yihuda who brought them to their senses.

How can we abandon him when he needs us most, he said.

He convinced us that we must insist some of us go with him wherever he went and put himself forward to be one of the group, since of the men he was the only one without any occupation. There was some discomfort among the others at letting him take the lead like that, yet no one could argue with his logic. The truth was we had in large part accepted Yihuda by then, as our greater troubles had made him appear a smaller one; and so he was elected, along with Simon the Canaanite and Yohanan, who had offered themselves wholeheartedly while many of the others either could not leave at that time of year or were reluctant to set off for they knew not where. I saw that Yaqob, who for reasons of work had not volunteered himself, reddened when Yohanan did so; yet it seemed that much as he couldn't bear to see him with Yihuda again, neither could he be happy if neither he nor his brother accompanied Yeshua.

Listening to the men make their arrangements, I felt trapped once more in my woman's skin, like a cage I lived in. It occurred to me that if I had been married, it might have been of no consequence if I travelled amongst a group of men; and so for the first time it seemed to me there might be some freedom in marriage. In any event, I would gladly have taken the first man who had offered himself to me, should I have thus been permitted to go along with Yeshua and the others. Yeshua had said he would travel north, into the Syrian highlands—the mountains my mother was from, wild, pagan places that I recalled from my own journey there as a child. I remembered a lake we had travelled near, savage and rank; a bird that I saw there, of purest black and as large as a man, so astonished me that for many years I believed it was a god I had seen, such as we knew nothing of in Galilee.

Nearly a year had passed since Yeshua had left us for Tyre. Then, I had felt broken with the fear that he wouldn't return to us. But this time there was a part of me that almost wished for his release, that he might find some new following there among the pagans and grow old with them, bringing them to our god. For I felt that we had not proved worthy of him, that we had descended to pettiness though he had tried to raise us up, and had let the ways of the world infect us. I thought of what we had been in our first days and longed to return to the innocence we'd had then and the strength of purpose, to the way our minds had seemed opened like doors to the sun.

In the end Yeshua had never spoken to us of Ribqah's resurrection, nor had we dared to ask him. For the truth was that even among the twelve we had not fully understood his teaching on the matter, if she would rise in body or in spirit, if now or at the end of days, if she would go to the heavens or return to earth. For my own part, I didn't see how the body could rise, so quickly was it corrupted, nor how the earth could be peopled with those who had risen, since surely then from the beginning of time the number of those who had risen must be greater than all those who lived, whereas we saw no evidence of them among us. But I thought that in this as in other things, Yeshua's word could not be understood in any simple way. For as he said, we needn't die to be born again, by which I took him to mean that even in this life the world could be made new for us, if we had the eyes to see it. So I had imagined that death, then, was only a small thing, a place we could cross to as over a river, that we could see waiting for us on the other shore. Yet I could not see that place now, nor Ribqah in it; I could not see whatever life it was she had entered into. And it seemed to me that neither could Yeshua or he would not have been so broken by Ribqah's death, and so at a loss that he must leave us.

The time of Yeshua's absence was a difficult one for those of us who had stayed behind. There was confusion among the twelve as to whether he would ever return, and a few of them, led by Thomas, said we were discredited and should disband. In the end it was Shimon who held us together, saying that if what he had taught us was true it was true, also in his absence, and making us look to those of his followers who had stuck by him and to the poor and sick who came seeking help.

The fact was that after the slanders that had struck us, Yeshua's following was much reduced. We continued to go around to our meeting houses in the various towns along the lake, but often only a dozen or so would come out to us and occasionally even the meeting houses were closed against us. It sometimes felt then that all of Yeshua's work had come to nothing or that what he had feared had shown itself true, that people had come to him only for his wonders and cures or because of the force of his person and not because of his teachings. But Shimon would not desist, and he and I would often travel together to Bet Ma'on or Arbela or Ammathus and meet with our people in their homes; and we saw that despite all that had happened, there were still those whose faith was unwavering and who greeted us with love. We drew courage from these, since it seemed that if even a handful remained who were loyal, these too must be tended to, just as Yeshua had tended to the handful we were when he had first come to us. Shimon found it difficult at first to lead us in instruction, since he was a man of few words; but because he spoke plainly people listened to him, and I saw how much he had understood of what Yeshua had taught us. So it wasn't true that Yeshua's work had come to nothing, when we had only to look to ourselves who were so changed. I thought of the girl I had been when Yeshua had first come, so coddled then and innocent, when now I had travelled half the roads of Galilee, and had respect, and saw things differently.

Then some time after Yeshua's departure we heard that Chizkijah, who had not been seen for many weeks, had appeared again in his hometown of Bersaba, wearing finery and boasting of how he had been rewarded by the king for ridding the Galilee of a false prophet. We didn't believe this could be so, that he could be so brazen. But Yaqob and Shimon set off at once for the town to confront him. Sure enough, they found him drunk in a tavern, telling stories of how he had tricked Yeshua's followers and spread his slanders. Seeing Shimon and Yaqob, he didn't balk as he might have but called them to him openly, as if to take them into his confidence.

I've done you a service, he said, to free you of a charlatan.

Yaqob was ready to strike the man but Shimon restrained him.

If he was a charlatan, you wouldn't have needed lies to accuse him, Shimon said.

But I only told what was true, Chizkijah said. I only praised his good works. And he seemed pleased beyond measure at his own trickery.

We began to see now what his intentions had been—he had merely sought to return to his town in glory, decked out in fine clothes and with silver in his purse, so that he might lord it over those who had had contempt for him. In his pride he was quick to boast of what he had done, not seeing how he thus vindicated us; but in Bersaba and in many of the towns in those parts it was indeed regarded as a tremendous good work that he had brought Yeshua down, since he was seen as a menace.

In the end, however, it was Chizkijah's pride that undid him, for one morning some of our own disciples found him lying near the road outside Bersaba, mortally wounded. Their first thought was to leave him there and say nothing, since they believed God had justly punished him for his evil. But then they saw that he still clung to life and that he pleaded with them for their mercy, and so they took pity on him and carried him to the town. Because they were known as

Yeshua's followers, they were promptly accused as the ones who had brought him to his state. But it was Chizkijah himself who absolved them, declaring before witnesses that it wasn't any of Yeshua's people who had injured him but his own associates from the court, who had waylaid him on the road the previous night and beaten him with clubs before leaving him for dead in the woods. He said Herod had sent the men to teach him a lesson because with his boasting he had begun to send people's sympathies back to Yeshua, and so risked undoing all the work he had been paid for.

Would to God I had been honest when I claimed to be won to him, Chizkijah said, since he is truly a great man and I am a worthless one.

With that he died, though everyone who had heard him was very moved by his words.

It didn't take long for the news of Chizkijah's recantation to spread. Those who had turned against Yeshua on his account now saw their mistake, and were reminded again of Yeshua's eminence, that even someone like Chizkijah had truly been won to him in the end. To the twelve, however, Shimon said, Don't go around boasting like Chizkijah did, but follow Yeshua's example and hold your tongue. So we didn't vaunt that we'd been vindicated, but rather let people come to us of their own accord to admit their mistake; and this worked to our credit, as Shimon had foreseen, since we didn't come accusing or laying blame, but ready to accept all those who presented themselves. Several women who had been among those who had looked askance at me came to my home now to beg forgiveness, bringing gifts of oil and such. Remembering my own guilt with regard to Ribqah, I didn't feel any bitterness towards them as I might have, but rather felt moved that they had come to me so open-handedly, when I myself wasn't certain that I could have so swallowed my pride.

Thus Yeshua's followers gradually returned to the fold, and every calumny that had been spoken against him was withdrawn. Yet our victory felt hollow because Yeshua himself was still gone, nor had we had any word of his return. A few of the twelve travelled north to Kefar Dan, where there were many Jews, to see if he had passed through there or if anyone had any news of him. But to their surprise no one had even so much as heard of him there, though the town was little more than a day's journey from Kefar Nahum.

Then one day a prince of Sidon passed through Migdal, on his way, he said, to worship the god of the Jews at Jerusalem. He bore a large retinue of servants, and a gilded litter that carried his young daughter; and, as we learned, he owed a profound debt to our Lord since his daughter had been brought back from the clutches of death by a holy man of the Jews. We didn't need to ask more than a word from him to know that it was Yeshua he spoke of, for as he said the cure had seemed a miracle, seeing that all his own healers and priests, whether by potions or burnt offerings, had been able to do nothing for her. The girl herself was a thing of amazing beauty, with the palest skin and garments of purple and gold. When she discovered that my father and I were followers of Yeshua, she came to us and kissed our hands, which was a deep abasement of herself, and said that truly our god was a glorious one if he worked through such men as our master.

We learned from the prince that Yeshua had taken himself to Mount Hermon, which surprised us, since the Jews considered it profane. But we were overjoyed to have some word of him, and that he still lived and followed his mission.

It was in our minds to send a delegation to him at once to call him back to Galilee, now that Chizkijah had recanted. But even before we had the time to make our plans we had better news of him, for the word arrived that he had been seen on the road on his way to Kefar Nahum.

This time when my father arranged for a general feast at the gates of the town, I didn't try to dissuade him, but rather built up the cooking fires with the other women and helped to give out bread and fish to all who requested them. As it happened, however, Yeshua didn't come to the town that night but rather stopped some miles beyond it, held up by all those who had come out to greet him. Shimon and a few of the others went out to him, but it was dark by then so we women stayed behind. I was happy enough to wait until the light of day to lay eyes on him again, remembering the awkwardness of his return from Tyre and how much a stranger he had seemed then.

In the morning I left Migdal before dawn in order to be in Kefar Nahum when he arrived. Then, not long after sunrise, he appeared in the street outside Shimon's house with those of the twelve who had slept with him in the open and a band of others following behind. With his retinue he looked like some beggar king, his clothes nearly rags and his hair and beard grown matted and thick. There was hardly more flesh to him than there had been when he had first come to us out of the desert; yet he was not the same man that he'd been then, but changed in a hundred ways I knew but could not quite have named. It seemed he trailed a shadow now that he hadn't then, which was the shape of all we'd been through, something dark and looming so that he seemed larger and more estimable and more hidden.

At Shimon's house he merely asked for food and said he would go at once to the hill above the town to be with his followers there. There were several of us who were there to greet him, including the other women and some of the twelve; and so I didn't put myself forward. But he saw me there among the others.

How is your family, he said, and I answered for them. Then he took my hand and he kissed it, only that, and I had to hold my breath against my tears.

He spent the rest of the day on the hill with his followers, preaching at first, and then when the wind off the lake made it impossible for him to be heard, simply moving among the crowd to exchange a word with those he knew and give his greetings. All day people continued to come in twos and threes to pay their respects, even Ventidius from the Roman camp; and so it seemed that the slanders we had suffered under Chizkijah were all but forgotten. It was not until evening that Yeshua was able to sit alone with the twelve, on the hillside there, sharing some supper with us that we cooked in the open.

We were afraid you wouldn't return, Shimon said, and could not bring himself to look at Yeshua for emotion.

It was only now once we were all gathered together that we noticed Yihuda wasn't among us. We sent a boy in search of him but he returned without news.

He's only gone to catch us some fish, Yeshua said, to make a joke of the thing, since we had understood by then it was fear of the water that had always kept Yihuda from joining the men while they fished. Yet a note of heaviness hung among us because of his absence, as if it foreboded ill.

It was Shimon who told Yeshua what had fallen out with regard to Chizkijah. But Yeshua said he had learned of his death on the road the previous day and had mourned it, and would not say any more on the matter. The truth was that even in the midst of our troubles Yeshua had not suffered us to say any word against Chizkijah, as if he were simply some follower who had strayed rather than a man bent on our destruction. At the time we hadn't understood him; but now it seemed as if all along he had seen the truest course, that it was not by enmity that Chizkijah would be won to us in the end but by our example.

It was clear, however, that there was something changed in Yeshua as a result of what we'd been through, some small hardening in him as in iron that had passed through the fire. Simon the Canaanite told how he had seen huge ghosts in Yeshua's company on Mount Hermon, and how Yeshua himself had stood transfigured and white as if the very light of the Lord had glowed inside him. But I thought that the Lord's light could also be the dark one of a smithy, and his crucible searing. So we had passed through a difficult trial and survived, and proved our worth. Yet it seemed also that a great deal had been lost to us or taken away, and with little solace.

It wasn't long before we discovered that Yihuda had truly left us. A stranger had come in search of him, as we heard, putting himself out as one of his family; and they had set off together on the southern road. Then the days and the weeks went by, and we had no news of him. We knew this was his way, to come and go as he pleased without any word to us. Yet there seemed a finality to his departure, for it had been many months now that he had not been comfortable among us.

I was surprised that we didn't feel any great relief at his going. But while it was the case that none of us had come to love him, still we had grown accustomed to him. Through Yeshua's eyes we saw how it was a defeat for us that he'd gone.

We won't fill the place he has left, he said, to remind us always of the one we couldn't win over.

And though we were more at ease now and freer in our questions, since we didn't have Yihuda to show up our ignorance, we also understood more clearly, from the general agreement among us and the lack of debate, how unreflecting and small we often were in our own thoughts.

Now that Yeshua had been vindicated his followers were anxious to make amends with him. So the crowds began to approach their former size, and those who had avoided him tried to find the way to show their love. But Yeshua held back, and often when he came to a town, he came quietly so that instead of preaching to the crowd he might go to some small gathering of those who he remembered had stayed true to him even in adversity. It was also at this time that he began to travel across the lake into the Decapolis, finding the people there, both the pagans and the Jews, less obstinate and more open-hearted than the Galileans. He went to Gergesa and Hippus and even as far as Gadara and the villages thereabouts; and the crowds would come down from the hills at the sight of his boat to await him on the shore. Many there were like children in their beliefs, for even the Jews of those parts had fallen into superstitions and worshipped Baal or Augustus, as the Romans had decreed. Thus Yeshua's words were a tonic to them, and many people were converted. Some had never heard of the one true God, and were amazed to learn of him, and it seemed to me that these were the ones that Yeshua held most dear, those pagans who were won over from black ignorance.

Then one day a teacher came to us from Judea, a certain Yehoceph of Ramathaim, who said he had heard talk of Yeshua and wished to see him with his own eyes. He was an old man long gone grey and, as we heard, much respected in his town and in Jerusalem, where he taught and where he had known the teacher Hillel. He spent many days with us, going around to the towns as Yeshua preached and often talking with him at the lakeshore into the night until the rest of us had fallen asleep or returned to our homes. He put questions to Yeshua that those of us among the twelve could hardly fathom, about God and our will and on points of law. It humbled me when I heard them—I had never given any thought to the matters they spoke of though they seemed of such importance, and I understood then how we too were like children for Yeshua, and how he missed Yihuda, for he had been the only one of us who could challenge him.

After Yehoceph had been with us for many days, he came to some of us among the twelve and said our master was graced by God, and would prove a great leader for the Jews.

Philip said, What do the people say of him in Jerusalem.

They hardly know of him in Jerusalem, Yehoceph said, which again surprised us.

As Yehoceph put it, the Judeans paid no attention to what happened in the Galilee, because they believed nothing good came from there. But it was an evil time now in Judea, since the people no longer respected the priests, who thought only of their own gain, and so followed leaders who bent them on madness or worse.

So you must lead Yeshua to us, he said, to spread his own mission there.

How can we lead him when he always follows his own mind, Shimon said.

You have to find the way.

We didn't know what to make of Yehoceph's request. Clearly he had also put it to Yeshua and Yeshua had refused him, or he would not have come to us to sway him. But we were loath to be the instruments by which Yeshua would be sent away from us. Shimon said it was selfishness to think in this way, and that we must find every means for spreading Yeshua's teaching. Yet even in his own voice we saw that he couldn't bear that Yeshua should leave us.

There were some among the twelve, however, who began to think of their own glory, imagining the fame that would come to them for leading Yeshua into Jerusalem.

Thaddaios said, The Judeans will bow to the Galileans when they see the teacher we've brought, though he had been among the first to think of deserting Yeshua during his trials. And some of the others were swayed by him, believing that Yeshua would take them with him. We women, however, knowing that we would be left behind, argued fiercely against the thing. In any event, it was well known that the Judeans were even more stiff-necked than the Galileans, and so would be hard to win over, and also that the Romans of Judea slaughtered holy men as easily as thieves, to keep them from becoming leaders.

In the end it was Yeshua himself who cleared our minds, calling us together and asking us each in turn if he should accept Yehoceph's invitation. So he went around the circle, and one said that Jerusalem was the centre for the Jews, and so he should go, and another that he had won all the glory that he could among the Galileans, and another that it was always of Jerusalem that people spoke when they spoke of the best teachers.

When it was my own turn to speak, however, I said, You came to us because we needed you, while the Judeans have many teachers and schools.

I was sure I would be reprimanded for speaking selfishly. But Yeshua said, You're right to say that, because you talk about need while the men only talk about glory.

What about the needs of the Judeans, Philip said, who are being led astray.

If they have many teachers and still go astray, it's a matter of will, not of need, Yeshua said.

So we put the question from us for the time and said nothing more about Jerusalem. Yet it seemed a restlessness had come to Yeshua, and that he was tired of his old battles and of all the intrigues he was subject to in Galilee. For many days at a time now he would be gone into the territory of the Gadarenes or even of the Samaritans, taking only some of the men with him, while at home he seldom went into the towns where he used to preach any more except to go to those houses he knew, otherwise wandering the countryside and sleeping the night in the open like a herdsman. People said that a madness had come into him, since he often went without shoes and stayed in the cold and ate or not as the spirit moved him. But in his words he had remained lucid and clear, and no one could mistake him.

When the year of Jubilee was pronounced, some of those who liked to make trouble for us came asking if all debts should be forgiven and all the slaves set free like the old laws said, though no one followed them. To put them in their place, Yeshua answered that indeed the laws should be respected, if there was anyone who had the courage to do so, since just as God gave forgiveness to everyone who asked it, so should we. Among his followers, however, he said that the biggest debts to be forgiven were not for this or that sum of money but rather the grievances and hates we bore against other people, and so we should take the Jubilee as the chance to clear ourselves of all our jealousies and hatreds. It seemed to me this was his calling to us to move past the troubles that had beset us on Chizkijah's account, and how we had been divided then and perhaps still bore a sense of accusation against those who had gone against us.

Because of the Jubilee there were many Galileans who planned to make the pilgrimage to Jerusalem for the Passover. For our part, we dared not ask Yeshua to lead us, because he had always disdained to; but then it happened that Yehoceph of Ramathaim sent a messenger to us to invite Yeshua to join him at the feast. We knew he had invited him in the hope of tempting him, and so were very surprised when Yeshua accepted the invitation—surely, we thought, he had not forgotten his decision, that he would remain with us. When some of us pressed him on the matter, he dismissed our concerns and said it would be rudeness in him to refuse the man's hospitality.

Yet you refuse your followers when they ask you to lead them, Shimon said.

Then they shall follow me to Jerusalem, Yeshua said, and be the guarantors of my return.

As he had never before led us in pilgrimage, we were unsure now whether he meant the offer in earnest or in jest.

We asked if we should spread the word among his followers, but he would not put the thing clearly.

You may say I have been invited, he said, and they may come as my own guests.

So what ought to have been a cause for rejoicing among us instead only caused confusion, for though we were going to Jerusalem, still Yeshua refused to lead us, nor would he calm our fears with regard to Yehoceph's offer to him.

I couldn't put from my mind how Yehoceph had said that Yeshua would be a great leader to our people. Indeed this was what we ourselves had imagined when he had first come to us, that he would grow famous and be a leader to those who had none. Yet at every instance he had put off the claims of leadership, and said how only the Lord was master, and how even the prophets had not sought to lead but only to speak their minds. So I could not figure what lay ahead for him, and if he put off leadership because we had not shown ourselves worthy of him or if we were only the stepping stone for some other greatness that must come to him. I remembered a visit I had made to Jerusalem as a child, and how wondrous the place had seemed, the seat of every eminence and marvel the world might offer up. Surely, I thought, it was in such a place that the greatness of Yeshua would be made manifest, a place of learning and of God himself, and not amongst the miserable backward towns of the Galilee.

It would have been fitting for Yeshua and the man that he was that he should have gone into Jerusalem in glory, and trailed with him all those who had known his cures or been saved by his charity or affected by his words. Yet as the day for our departure approached and people began to gather with their baskets and tents on the hill above Kefar Nahum, we saw that for all the hundreds and thousands who had called themselves followers when it suited them, it was only those closest to us who had joined us. So the ingot had been fired, and the dross skimmed off until only the ore remained. In the time since Yeshua had come to us we had seen our fortunes rise and fall, and the days when the crowds had filled the hilltops and those when we were only a handful. And yet it was a fact that from the start Yeshua had never concerned himself with the numbers that had come, but only with whether they were true.

I often remembered the first days that Yeshua had been among us, and how it had seemed then that I must burst with the newness of the vision he had offered us. My head was full of questions then, because he had awakened an aliveness in me I had not felt, so that it came to my mind to wonder at everything I looked at. But over time it seemed the questions had come down to a single one, which was what manner of man was this, to so affect me, that I would have abandoned every desire had he asked it of me except the one, which was to be near him. Even his enemies granted the power of him, if only in the force with which they opposed him; for if what he said was nothing, as they claimed, and made no logic or sense, they would merely have dismissed him with their silence and not their shouts. Thus it was that everyone who heard him or laid eyes on him formed an image of him, and believed him a holy man or a madman, a heretic or a sage, with deepest certainty. Yet I who was among those closest to him, who'd been embraced by him and had walked with him by the lake, could not say what it was that formed him, and indeed as the days passed and the weeks and the years, only knew him less. So he seemed like a glimpse I'd had of something that I could not put a name to, and which always slipped from my gaze before I had a chance to know it, like the great bird I had seen as a child when I travelled into the mountains and imagined a god.

BOOK III

MIRYAM, HIS MOTHER

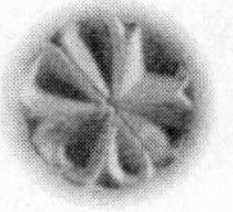

As a child I lived in Jerusalem, this in the time of Herod who was called the Great. Through many favours my father had gained a place at court, as a clerk, and he began to think how he might further advance our family's fortunes by making a good marriage for me.

Even in those days there were many Romans who passed through the court, soldiers and officials who came down from Syria or Caesarea, which Herod had built, or even from Rome. One of these, a legate awaiting orders, my father befriended and presented me to, leaving us several times alone. In the end, because I was young and did not know better and because he threatened me with harm, I was forced to yield to him. I was never able to forget the smell of him—he did not smell like a Jew but had a perfumed odour underlain with a stench like rancid fat. After that time I was able to bear many things, because I knew always that the worst thing was behind me.

The legate did not take me as his wife as my father had planned, but abandoned me the moment he had received his commission. When he had gone it grew clear that I was with child, and so was disgraced. My father beat me when he discovered this, though as I said to him, It was you who put me in his way, which silenced him. To save me then from being outcast he began to search for a husband for me, asking among the lower orders, for surely no one of our own station would have had me.

As it happened there was a mason employed at the temple works by the name of Yehoceph who was in search of a wife. He was an old man, three times my years, who had put another wife away from him for barrenness and did not want to repeat his error. So it was an advantage to him that I was with child, because I had proved myself fertile, and also that I was young, being not yet fifteen years. Nonetheless, to make up for the dishonour of me and the expense of being saddled with a child not his own, he asked much above the usual dowry, all in coin, and offered no bride price. It cost my father all his small fortune to satisfy him, in which however I took some bitter consolation, for he had ruined my life in the hope of advancing his own ambitions.

We were married quickly, at Bet Lehem, which was Yehoceph's town. Of my family, only my father and mother were present and my brothers and sisters, who were young and did not understand why matters had been done in such haste, and with such unhappiness. They thought that surely Yehoceph must be the groom's father when they saw him, so ancient did he look, and I confess how my own heart fell at the sight of him, for I had not so much as laid eyes on him until then. It was the hardness of him that I could not bear—he seemed made of the same stone that he worked in. I was in the full flower of youth then, and had had my hopes, only to be coupled to such hard, unyielding flesh. However, that first night he came to me and said that because he judged me unclean, he would not lie with me or put any hand on me until I had brought forth my child, for which I was grateful.

We shared a house with his brothers. Though Yehoceph was the eldest, he was the only one without sons and so had taken for himself the poorest quarters, which were no more than a cavern cut out of a rock face that rose up at the back of the courtyard. In Jerusalem, living near the palace, we had thought ourselves poor because of the many riches that surrounded us, and that we had no part of. But the floors had been tiled at least, and the walls plastered and adorned, while here there was nothing between us and the earth, and we lived no better than the animals in the stable.

Until I had given birth I was not allowed so much as to step out from the house's gate, to keep hidden the untimeliness of my condition. So day and night were spent in the gloomy damp of our cave, without company since the wives of Yehoceph's brothers would hardly deign to address me and also kept their children from me. Yehoceph neither encouraged them in this nor reprimanded them, and so behaved, as he no doubt imagined, with fairness. It was exactly this fairness in him that most embittered me—for instance, he said to me that until I had produced an heir for him he would use no part of my dowry except to pay whatever expenses we incurred for the child I produced, so that the dowry would remain intact should he need to return me to my family. Thus he made clear to me that I was no more than a slave he had hired to make his heirs, and that he was ready to put me away from him as he had his first wife should I fail him in this. Never once did he ask after the father of the child I carried. But I imagined this was not to spare me embarrassment but only to keep me from plying him in any way for forgiveness.

In any event, I saw him but a few moments in a day at the time, since in the mornings he left an hour before dawn to make his way to the temple works and in the evenings did not return until well after dark. As I was not allowed to prepare any food but my own, he took his evening meal with his brothers, and so by the time he came back to me in our hovel he was ready for sleep. Once, I remember, he brought a fig for me that he had purchased somewhere on the road, and for a moment then my heart softened to him and I asked him how his work had been, and how the temple progressed. But mostly I kept myself hard to him, out of pride: he thought himself my saviour, I imagined, but was only ignorant and ungenerous and dull-minded. It didn't occur to me in those days that he might fear me—I was a child, after all, what power could I have over him. Not the power of the flesh, surely, for he had held true to his word to lay no hand on me, and not once even in accident had his skin touched mine. Even the fig he had brought me he set between us for me to collect, lest our fingers brush each other's. It was the sort of man that he was, or seemed to me then, scrupulous like someone who had room in his thoughts for only a single notion.

When at last the child was born, Yehoceph came to me and said we must leave the town, for the truth was becoming known and his brothers stood in peril of dishonour. In my pride I said, It must be circumcised like any Jew, for it was a male, though I did not know if the law allowed this. But Yehoceph said it was my own concern and so I made arrangements in Jerusalem, naming Yehoceph as the father. When the thing was done, Yehoceph told me again that we must go. But I insisted we wait until after the thirty-third day, so that I might make my sacrifices. This time Yehoceph said, The child is a bastard and can never enter the assembly. But this only hardened me, and seeing my stubbornness, Yehoceph gave way.

So it was that after the thirty-third day he led me to the temple, and again my pride would not suffer me to purchase only pigeons or doves but I must have a lamb for the burnt offering, which I paid for from my dowry. I did not know why I insisted on these things, or why Yehoceph allowed them, for we both knew they were for nothing. Yehoceph, perhaps, was happy enough to let the world think the child was his own, and so save himself from scandal. Yet I knew that was not his way, that he did not court such open deceit, and thus that in some respect he indulged me. Perhaps it was the actual child that moved him, for it was beautiful and gentle, though again, as I later thought on the matter, it seemed there must have been some small part of fear in him, that he did not know what this child was or where it had come from.

The following morning we left Bet Lehem, before dawn. Yehoceph brought with him only his tools and a cloak, while I was made to carry our provisions, for because the child had been born and the time of my purification had passed, I was no longer unclean in Yehoceph's eyes. Yehoceph had not told me our destination, nor had I brought myself to ask it of him, and so I hadn't known whether to prepare myself for a journey of a day or of many. But as I had only my dowry to think of, and no other possessions save the dress I wore and the one I had been married in, it made no great difference. It was only the child I was concerned for, in the heat, for it was coming to summer, but we followed a stream the first day that had not yet run dry and so I was able to bathe him.

Now that I was purified Yehoceph wasted no time in claiming his due from me, the first night of our journey, in a caravansary where we had taken a place outside Betogabri. We had only a corner to ourselves, beneath an arcade, and the child was awake. But the moon was new and so we had the cover of darkness at least. Yehoceph did not speak or ask my leave but merely forced himself on me as we lay there beneath his cloak, his skin rough against mine like the hide of a goat. I had thought that in marriage the thing would prove less cruel than it had in sin, but that was not the case, nor did I feel less sense of violation.

Beyond Betogabri the hills gave way to lowland. I knew nothing of that country, since in all my life I had not travelled twenty miles out of Jerusalem, and was surprised at the fields that we passed and the orchards, for I had always thought only wilderness lay in those parts. The child, however, looked sickly from travelling in the heat and was not feeding well, and it occurred to me that it might die from the journey. We would be free then, I thought, could simply turn and retrace our steps to Bet Lehem, and no one would be wiser. Except we would only return to our hovel and I would be tethered still to Yehoceph, with nothing then that was my own, that set me apart from him.

On the third day, we came to the Western Sea. I had heard it described to me as a child, but no description could have prepared me for that first vision of it. We had come out of a town, Azotus, where we had joined to a caravan, and the road crested a dune and at once the blue of the sea lay spread before us. I could not have said what feeling I had in that moment—disbelief, perhaps, as though some trick had been played on me, for in my thoughts I had imagined that as wide as the sea might be, still the other shore must by force be always visible. But here the water stretched to the horizon as if the world had ended suddenly, as if we had come to its very precipice. All the notions I had held until then seemed changed in some way by that vision—what was it to live in Jerusalem, or Bet Lehem, when the world held such strangeness and wonders.

We travelled on for many days after that, so that I lost count of them, and I learned from those we had joined with that we were headed into Egypt. Some of these were from Ptolemais and Tyre and it was difficult to speak to them, so different was their language from our own. But we were all Jews, for Yehoceph had made certain of that. Because Yehoceph and I were strangers to them, people took us for what we appeared to be and asked us no questions, so that it seemed briefly that we had shed our old lives and the troubles that had burdened them. At the border, where we were made to sign the registry, it was Yehoceph this time, to save us trouble, who named the child as his own. We needed a name for him then for we had not chosen one, and since we were hurried I chose the first that came to my head, Yeshua, which was my brother's name.

We ended our journey in Alexandria. So much had happened by then that I seemed a different person from the one who had set out—I had seen the varied customs of people, and the varied ways in which they spoke, so that finally I wondered how I had managed in the world until then when I had known so little of it. All these thoughts I kept to myself, of course, for Yehoceph was not curious in this way, and indeed it was likely he would not have understood me had I tried to discuss such matters with him. There was an old couple who travelled with us, from Emmaus, who I sometimes saw with their heads bent in discussion as if they truly took comfort from one another, and I thought then at how hardly a word had passed between me and Yehoceph the entire journey, and at all the years of silence that still lay before us.

It was only as we approached our destination that Yehoceph brought up any question with me, taking me aside from the others one evening as if to discuss a thing of great import.

Because of the child, he said, with the air of having weighed this matter for many days, you shall pay the expenses for the journey from your dowry, for otherwise we should not have needed to make it.

I might have said to him, We should not have needed to make it had you not married me, but held my tongue.

It was night when we arrived in Alexandria, so that I saw only the lamps that lined the central boulevard and the great arcades there. For the longest time this was all I knew of the city proper, for we went at once to the district set aside for the Jews and did not emerge from it for many months. In the Jewish quarter there were many splendid homes as in Jerusalem, but also many hovels, and it was to one of these that we made our way, the house of a cousin of Yehoceph by the name of Yirmeyah who had lived in the city for many years. He gave us a room at the back of his courtyard for which we paid rent, and we shared our meals with him and with his children and his wife, an Egyptian woman as dark as an Ethiope who spoke neither Hebrew nor Aramaic.

As it fell out, there were problems at that time between the Jews and the Alexandrians, for the Jews had petitioned Augustus for all the rights of citizens but the Alexandrians opposed them. So it was that Yirmeyah said to Yehoceph, You have come at the worst time, since there is no work for Jews with the Greeks, but only with other Jews. Thus Yehoceph came to work for his cousin, at half the pay he had earned at the temple and doing many jobs that were difficult for a man of his age, since Yirmeyah, to keep him employed and so earn his own commission, contracted for every sort of work that came their way, whether it be carrying bricks or laying pavement or digging latrines.

We went on in this way for some time, though it did not seem just to me what Yirmeyah paid us for Yehoceph's work nor yet what we paid him in rent, for once our lodging and board had been accounted for, there was next to nothing that remained to us. In the end I spoke to some of the other women of the quarter and discovered from them that Yirmeyah cheated us, taking advantage because we did not know the ways of the city and spoke no Greek. I went to Yehoceph and said, Your cousin is a thief. He seemed ready to strike me then, because he could not imagine that one of his own family would cheat him. But because I would not retract my accusation Yehoceph agreed to bring it to Yirmeyah, since he judged it fair that he respond to it.

Yirmeyah, however, did not dispute the charge but immediately made his own.

You have defiled my house with a bastard, he said, though we had told him nothing of this matter. So we saw that my sin had followed us from Judea and we were to be cursed by it.

There are many who would have turned you away, Yirmeyah said, but I took you in, so to make it seem that he had committed no crime in cheating us, or that he himself was purer than we were though he had married an Egyptian.

But Yehoceph did not rebuke him.

You're right to say we defile your house, he said, whether out of pride or simply to agree with him, I did not know, and so he had us take our leave of him, and we were left without lodgings and without work.

The child was not yet six months then. Yehoceph would have had us return with it to Palestine, to the Galilee, where we were not known. But I said to him, If the truth has followed us into Egypt, then surely it will reach us in Galilee, at which he was silenced.

He might have returned me to my family then, except that I was already with child again, and perhaps carried his son. So we set about to make our way in the city, finding lodgings with Jews who were strangers to us and using money from my dowry to pay our rent until Yehoceph could find new work. Every day I feared our landlords would learn the truth of me and we would once more be turned out into the streets. But in the end they asked us no questions, and seemed to care nothing of what we were or were not except that we pay our rent. It was only to cover his own sins with our shame that Yirmeyah had put the fear in us that we would be driven away, for I soon understood that the Alexandrian Jews did not hold to every particular of the law as the Judeans did, nor were they so rigid in judgement. Indeed, in time I discovered that there were many women of the quarter who were in my own situation or worse who suffered no abuse on that account and even had respect, as I myself came to.

Around this time it happened that the Romans, to appease the Alexandrians and keep them from rioting, began to undertake many projects in the city. So it was that the foremen could no longer be bothered to ask if a worker was a Greek or a Jew, since there were many places to fill, and Yehoceph, though he had learned no word of Greek, was able to find employment in his own trade. From that time until we left the city many years later he was never without work, and though he grew old and though his bones must have rebelled at the punishment they endured, he never spoke a word of complaint. Out of his first pay he restored to me what we had spent in rent from my dowry, holding back nothing on account of the boy, since he was still feeding. Then eventually, when my first child by him proved a son, he lost his concern that I might try to get the better of him in some manner and began to bring all his pay to me for me to husband it, since as he did not drink or indulge himself in any way, he had no use for it except that it should feed us and pay our taxes.

In the end he took not a penny from my dowry for himself, though he might have, and after I had given him an heir he came to me and said that I should find the way to make the most of it, because the time would come when my son, being a bastard, would have need of it. So it was that I invested the greater part of it with a merchant in the city, holding some back for the boy's upkeep and education, and over the years more than doubled its value. Nor, however, was I content with only this surety against destitution, but, remembering how precarious was my situation and how we had once been put in the street, I also undertook to make my own way in the city and learn the Greek tongue, finding bits of work for myself at weaving or making trinkets for the Greeks and Egyptians. But in this I was no different from the other women of Alexandria, be they Greek or Jew, for they did not believe there, as in Judea, that a woman was only a chattel but that she might make her own life.

My second child, who we named Yaqob, was born to me only some thirteen months after the first and quickly grew to be his superior both in strength and in size, resembling as he did his father. For this reason, there was never a time when it was not clear to everyone that the first-born was foreign to us in some way, like some foundling we had taken in. This indeed was common enough in that city—children were often sold as infants, even among the Jews, those who had surfeit hence finding the way to satisfy those who had none. So we might have made our way, and no one taken great notice, had not the child himself seemed to carry so clearly the sense of his own difference.

I made every effort to treat the child as I did Yaqob or any of the others, when they arrived. But in some ways this made me less of a mother to all of them, for as I had learned not to show any joy in Yeshua, lest my husband perceive it or the Lord, so did I show little joy in the others, in the end no longer certain if I merely suppressed it, or had none. Nor did I profit in any way from this, since the child still held himself apart, and I would have done better simply to love each one according to its need. Yet the truth was that I always felt jealous for Yeshua in some way, and felt more allied to him than to the rest except the two girls, who at least seemed to take some part of me, while the boys were so clearly their father's sons. Yeshua, it could be said, did take from me some of his features, and there was that side of him that was subtle and frail and almost feminine. But even in this he stood apart, for there was much in him that was entirely distinct, and seemed to have no provenance. Unlike me, for instance, he was fair-skinned and fair-haired, which had no mirror even in the brute who had fathered him, who was swarthy. For this I was always grateful, since I could not have borne to look into his face and see the reflection there of his sire.

Yaqob, from a young age, seeing this difference in his brother, seemed always to seek the way to make it small. It broke my heart to watch him, how he deferred to Yeshua as if to say, You see how I honour you, how I give you your proper place, which made me love him. But Yeshua was often cold with him and put him off, and soon enough they went their own ways. From the age of five, Yaqob began to accompany his father to work to learn his trade, which Yeshua had not, and so Yaqob understood that separate paths were laid out for them, and seemed to give in at last to the difference between them. I found a teacher for Yeshua then, though he was still young, to make it appear that as the eldest that was his lot.

Until that time I had still had a hold on him, for he was seldom far from the house. This was not to say that he ever came to me as children did to their mothers or even that he obeyed me, for the truth was I seldom had heart enough to reprimand him for anything or to ask any chore of him. Rather it was as if we shared some common darkness, like people in the corner of a room while others went about their business. I felt his presence like a weight on me—he would come, stand near, and immediately the air would seem laden with the heaviness of him though he was only a child. It was the most peculiar sensation, at once oppressive and somehow comforting, as if some mantle had been laid over me.

When he began his studies, however, a distance opened up between us. His teacher, a young man of the quarter named Tryphon who was anxious for students and so had not balked at Yeshua's age, came to me not a month after Yeshua had begun his lessons and said, Your son has learned in a month what others do not in a year. I did not know what to make of this and wondered if it was a scheme to gain a higher fee. But then he brought the boy before me and made him read to me from the Torah, which he did, though with reluctance.

Perhaps your son will be a famous scholar, Tryphon said to me.

But still I did not understand.

You see we are poor and of no consequence, I said.

But Tryphon would not be put off, saying that one of the greatest scholars of the city had been the son of a fishmonger, and so had shown that poverty was no obstacle.

I was left very troubled by Tryphon's visit and did not know what course of action to take, for he had offered to tutor Yeshua privately at no extra fee in the hope that one day he would be remembered as the teacher of a great scholar. But I was frightened by the claims he had made. If false, they would only raise illusory hopes in the boy, and perhaps bring him to arrogance, and if true, they could not help but lead him into public scrutiny, and so to harm. For what good would greatness do to a bastard, who would then only be ridiculed and have his shame exposed to all, while the better course, as it seemed to me then, was to remain in every way unnoticed and to make no claim for oneself.

Thus, not long after Tryphon's visit to me, I withdrew the boy from him entirely and placed him with one of the older teachers of the quarter, Zekaryah, who, deeming him too young to learn with his other charges, agreed however to allow him to run chores for him, and so learn by proximity. Tryphon was put out beyond measure at having the boy taken from him, and for many days came by my house and pleaded with me to reverse my decision. I might have done well in the end to give in to him, for Yeshua had grown fond of him, and as it seemed to me afterwards, it was from this moment that he began to suppose I too was against him, and wished to thwart him. But at the time I believed I acted for his greater good. Some months later when I heard that Tryphon, having grown destitute, had left the city for Judea, I felt a relief as if an accuser had gone, though also that I had chosen a turning for Yeshua that now there was no going back from.

Zekaryah, because he did not teach the boy, did not notice anything remarkable in him, and indeed, as I had report, there were few who emerged from Zekaryah's lessons with any semblance of learning. Then once Yeshua returned home from him with his legs covered in welts. When I pressed him, he confessed that Zekaryah had beaten him because he had dared to lay his hands on the Torah. Thus I understood that the reading he had learned under Tryphon had no outlet, and felt ashamed that I had taken him from him. I would even have procured for him then a copy of the holy scriptures, had I thought it possible for a woman to do such a thing. But instead I went out into the city to a market near the Museum where they sold every manner of manuscript, and there I purchased some crumbling scrolls for Yeshua of I knew not what, making him conceal them in an empty water jar in our courtyard so that no one should wonder at them. It was only later that it occurred to me they would be in Latin or Greek, and hence foreign to him. But he seemed to make his way through them, and so must have learned the rudiments of those scripts in his brief time with Tryphon.

Then, when he had been with Zekaryah for a year, he came to me and said, with contempt, it seemed to me, You waste your money in sending me to him. But because of his tone I felt hardened towards him.

You say so because you are wilful and don't know how to be a Jew, I said.

But he answered me, It's you who say I'm a Jew, and I struck him then, in anger, I imagined, though in fact because of my fear that he had somehow seen through to the truth.

The following day he did not go to his lesson. I did not give much thought to the matter, considering it merely a moment of childish pride. But after three days he still had not gone, nor had he exchanged any word with me, but only sat in our courtyard playing listlessly with some of his brothers or scrawling letters in the earth with a stick. Even this I would have borne except that it seemed he had ceased to take his meals—I did not notice at first, because he had always moved like a shadow among us, but then I saw how he held himself back at our supper. He was not yet eight then, and I believed that like any child he must weaken and seek my sympathy. But day after day he stayed in the courtyard, until the other children began to avoid him, not knowing what to make of him there, and day after day he seemed to grow more rigid in his fast. He would sit with us at our supper, so that Yehoceph should not remark on him, but his hand would not go to the bowl.

I grew frightened then, wondering at his wilfulness, for there seemed something monstrous in it. Also I saw how powerless I was in the face of it—it appeared he had understood by then that Yehoceph had no say in the raising of him, and so that it was only a woman against him in the end.

When a week had gone by and still he had not given up his fast, I went to him and said, You shall not return to Zekaryah.

Then what teacher will I have, he said at once.

I had given no thought to the matter and was surprised, after the week we had endured, that it would be the thing uppermost in his mind.

If you wish another teacher, we'll search for one.

There's one that I know, he said. A Greek.

Surely he said this to spite me, so that I might have it on my lips to say, But you are a Jew, and choke on the words.

How can you know these things when you're a child, I said.

From Tryphon.

And I had the sense he had somehow managed the entire contest between us so that it should lead exactly to this moment, that he should put Tryphon's name, and my guilt, before me, and so have his way.

The following day I went to discharge him from Zekaryah, who appeared happy to be rid of him.

He's full of pride and undisciplined, he said to me. You would best apprentice him to a trade or no good will come of him.

I could have struck him at this, the fool, so much did my anger rise.

I will be seeking another teacher for him, I said, at which he was silenced.

So it was that my own defiance came to the aid of Yeshua's cause, since I could not bear that he should end up again with some ignorant Jew who whipped him at the sign of any intelligence.

You shall have your teacher, I said to him, which however he seemed simply to accept as his due.

The man went by the name Artimidorus. It was Yeshua who led me to him, taking me to a quarter inside the Neapolis that I had not seen before, ramshackle and poor, the streets a maze of narrow lanes so that I did not know how Yeshua could remember his way among them. Even still when we came to the house I was certain he was mistaken, for I could not believe that a teacher and a Greek could live in such poverty and filth, or that Yeshua, knowing this, would have brought me to him. The house was merely a mess of tiny rooms, each with its own family, it seemed, and in the courtyard the stink of an open latrine and of animals who wandered freely amidst the ragged infants there. It was to the smallest and, it appeared, the most squalid room that Yeshua led me, with the merest opening to let in air and light.

I was ready to turn then and retreat from the place, but Yeshua held his ground.

It is Artimidorus, he said, pulling aside a bit of tattered curtain that covered the door.

Then the man was there before us, stooping out through the doorway and blinking at the light. I had never seen the like of him, wretched and lank and black as charred wood, an Ethiopian, with just a rag for a cloak that he had draped haphazardly around himself to cover his nakedness. Yet he held himself with a dignity.

My young Yeshua, he said, in Aramaic, which disarmed me.

Perhaps we have mistaken our way, I said. We are searching for Artimidorus the teacher.

So you have found him.

He did nothing then in the way of welcoming us, which somehow made it seem that I was the one who was mistaken in my perception of him. In my confusion I did not turn and leave him as I might have, but said, I wish a teacher for my son.

I think it's your son who wishes the teacher, he said.

He turned then to wash himself as if he had finished with me, though nothing had been settled.

You may leave him with me now if you wish, he said finally.

I was at a loss. I had imagined Yeshua would lead me to some palace and the teacher demand a king's ransom, and I should be forced on that account to deny him. But this man defied every expectation.

You have not told me your fee, I said.

What was the sum you paid his last teacher.

I named it, a denarius each month.

Then I shall have the same, Artimidorus said.

So it appeared I had contracted with him, against my better judgement. Yet I saw from Yeshua's look that he was determined to stay with him.

But how shall I pay you.

How was it with his former teacher.

I was made to pay a month in advance, I said.

Then so it shall be with me.

Yet he did not come to me then to take his fee but kept on with his private affairs, rummaging through a sack he had taken from his house to pull a scrap of hardened bread from it, a crust of which he broke off for Yeshua and the rest kept for himself. In the end, I was the one who had practically to force the payment on him. But when he had taken my coins he did not put them away for safekeeping but did the strangest thing, crossing the courtyard and handing them over to one of the children there. The child, an infant, not understanding their value, immediately scattered them on the ground.

In an instant the child's mother had scrambled from her house to collect them, glancing fearfully at Artimidorus, who however paid her no mind.

In the future, Artimidorus said, you may give the fee directly to your son, so that he might purchase some texts with it.

I did not know what possessed me to abandon Yeshua to this man, who might well have been mad and could have intended I knew not what. But I had understood at least this in him, that he cared nothing for the thoughts of this world, and it was that that drew me to him, and made me imagine Yeshua safe with him. At any rate, since he showed no interest in his fee, I could not have kept Yeshua from him even had I wished to, for I was certain he would have left me rather than be barred again from following his own inclinations.

Even so, it fell out that he was as good as lost to me once he'd been taken on by Artimidorus, since he was often many days away from his bed now, accompanying Artimidorus on his wanderings. For as I soon learned, Artimidorus had no home, so that it was a miracle we'd found him that day as we had, but rather wandered from place to place, sleeping in whatever hovel was offered to him. For this reason he was in fact quite well known, being seen in every quarter, though he was seldom among the other scholars and teachers at the Museum, whom he mocked. There were many who indeed took him for a madman, because he said all manner of things and hurled insults even at the highest officials. But there were also others, I was told, who considered him a brilliant teacher.

From Yeshua himself, however, I learned almost nothing of Artimidorus. If I should ask, What philosophy does he teach, or, Does he turn you from our God, he answered always in the briefest way, and the least instructive. Of his philosophy, he said only that he taught contempt for worldly glory, and of the Jewish god, he said that they did not speak of him, either for good or ill.

What then does he say of the gods, I asked him.

He says nothing, since he says we cannot know them.

I was uncertain what to make of this, and whether to be afraid for him. But the truth was I myself did not know what to teach him, since what had seemed certain in Judea was less so in Alexandria, where there was every manner of belief even among the Jews and where even in our own assembly houses I had seen the worship of the gods of the Romans and the Egyptians.

I was not able to learn a good deal more about Artimidorus from the talk of the street, for though everyone had some story to tell of his insolence, there were few who could make any sense of his teachings. It was said that one day he preached defiance of the Romans, the next acquiescence, or that he refused the alms of the rich in the morning and in the evening ate in their homes. When it became known that one of the boys who followed him was a Jew, it was put to him whether the Jews should have equal rights, and he said then that as the Jews themselves chose to set their race apart, it should not surprise them that others did. But when he was asked who found the greatest favour in the eyes of the gods, he named the Jews, because for the sake of their god they would suffer any persecution.

The thing, however, that I could not fathom about Artimidorus was that Yeshua had chosen him, and could see wisdom in him, though only a child of eight, when so many others could not. Yet often it seemed a kind of thraldom in which Artimidorus held him, through that same power that I myself had been drawn to, the great indifference he had to men's opinions. So it was that one minute he might call white, black, and in the next reverse himself, because it did not matter to him the rules others lived by, and it was the spectre of this freedom, I thought, that drew Yeshua to him, that one might be slave to no one's judgement and remake oneself at one's whim. Except in so doing, as it seemed to me, one must also renounce all the things of this world, and so risk gaining freedom only at the cost of every other good.

I spoke with Artimidorus only once again after our first meeting, passing him by chance when I had gone to the market outside our quarter to sell the rugs I made then. It happened that he was alone, and had seated himself on the pavement and drawn a circle around himself in chalk. The purpose for this was not clear, except that it had the effect of keeping people from him, for they instinctively would not cross into the circle, which seemed to please him.

I greeted him, but when he did not reply I said, I am the boy Yeshua's mother.

I know it, he said, but it did not seem reason enough to greet you.

I knew it was his manner to speak in this way and yet I was very affected by what he said, as if he had somehow taken Yeshua away from me in that moment or erased any claim I had to him. Many years later, when Yeshua had truly renounced me, I would have cause to remember this instant and see the future laid out in it.

As it happened, however, I had Yeshua back to me not long afterwards, for that winter Artimidorus fell ill and died one night in the streets. Yeshua, because he had been home that night on account of the cold, at once blamed himself for his teacher's death, since he had not been by his side to save him.

I said to him, Surely he did not mind losing his life, when he seemed so little to value it.

But Yeshua replied coldly, You don't know what you say, and would neither share his grief with me nor relinquish it, retreating into black silence.

I could not, however, suppress a secret relief at Artimidorus's death, not only at having Yeshua returned to me but that he had been saved the life that Artimidorus offered him, of homelessness and renunciation and even of threat, for because he was outspoken Artimidorus had had many enemies. In the hope that Yeshua would cleave to me and be my son again, I remade his place for him in our home, asking nothing of him and treating him with the deference and respect due to an eldest. To the others, by now, he was nearly a stranger, as much from the look of him and his manner as from his absence from us. Yet, for my sake, they showed him what warmth they were able to and hid their discomfort.

We might have gone on in this way, and Yeshua found his place among us again, for he was still a child, had not the infant I was nursing then died. The infant, a girl—as it fell out the last child I was to bear to Yehoceph, for afterwards I did not allow him to come to me again—was some ten weeks when Yeshua returned to us, and healthy and strong. Indeed all of my children had been so at birth, and I had lost only one of them, a boy, Hosheah, at six months, to a plague that had gone through the city. But the girl had shown no sign of illness. So it was a horror to us to wake and find her dead, with no mark on her of any sort, as if a devil had taken her.

A darkness came into the house then. Yehoceph said, There is a curse on us, and we all understood him to mean Yeshua, though he would not say it. And because of the manner of the girl's death, I could not bring myself to contradict him.

In later years, as I looked back on the thing, it seemed foolishness and superstition that we should have blamed the boy. But in those days there was never a time when we felt safe from God's judgement, when we believed that the sin that marked me would escape punishment. Even Yeshua, I was certain, felt in some manner the weight of this retribution that hung over us, and his place in it, and much of his defiance of us must surely have been born of his own shame. Thus there seemed a complicity among us that this death be our expiation, and that Yeshua take it upon himself like the scapegoat.

So it was that after the child had been buried and our mourning had ended, I awoke one day to find that Yeshua had gone. He was just past ten years old then. I did not expect that I should see him again.

250 In the time after Yeshua left me I began to travel more freely in the city, expanding my work and taking commissions in every quarter. It was not that I had any true need of money then, and indeed I might have stayed in my home and looked to my children rather than wandering the streets like a common peddler. But a restlessness had overtaken me, and I could not sit still then in the small world that had been circumscribed for me, with my husband who came home at dusk and my sons who resembled him. For with Yeshua gone I felt sometimes like a stranger in my home, as if all my children, whom I loved, were yet not quite my own.

Thus, with the excuse of my work, I wandered to many places I had not seen before, and learned every face of the city. In those days Alexandria was a place of extraordinary beauty, for which it was justly renowned, but also of putrescence, which I saw with my own eyes. There were children there who were stolen from the streets and then used in the most vicious manner, and also women and men so enslaved to their lusts they would seek any means to indulge them. Then it was a place where there was not only every sort of idolatry and belief but also every kind of person, Romans and Gauls and Armenians, priests and great princes and greater thieves.

I thought at first that it was only for Yeshua's sake that I ranged so widely, that I might find him and make amends, for it was my intention then to turn over the inheritance I had set aside for him so that he might make the life that he chose and not be a beggar in the street. But as it fell out, the city was not so large as I had imagined it, nor was it so difficult to find my son. Only a matter of weeks passed after his departure from us before I received some news of him, from a woman of the quarter who had seen him, and afterwards I myself had many sightings of him, though I seldom spoke to him at any length. The first time I did so I did not offer him his inheritance as I had resolved but rather proposed to apprentice him in the trade of his choice, which caused me some bitterness, for I remembered the words of Zekaryah.

Yeshua said, There is no trade I am suited for.

Then you will be a vagrant in the street.

I am no vagrant now, he said, for I have taken myself to another teacher.

I did not know why I did not simply offer him his freedom then, and give over the money intended for him. That he was a child, surely, was my excuse, and so would unwisely squander what he had or renounce it as he had learned from Artimidorus, and be left with nothing. But it was something more than that. Perhaps it was that seeing him alive and within my reach, I was loath to give him his independence, hoping I might still find the way to bind him to me again. Or perhaps it was simply that I feared his refusal of me, for then I should truly have no power over him, and no reason more even to search him out.

With some bit of spite I asked after his teacher, believing he had spoken of one only out of pride, and if, like Artimidorus, he required no fee.

I keep his house for him, Yeshua said.

Then you are his slave.

And you are your husband's, he said to me, and he is slave to his foreman.

My anger rose then and I could not bring myself to answer him. So it was that though I had the means to save him—and as I learned I had been right to think that he lied to me, and lived in the street—I could not find the way to let him make use of them, or to move past his enmity and gain his trust. Or not enmity, perhaps, but just the habit we had fallen to, for I knew that he did not hate me but only held himself hard to me, against what threat not one or the other of us could have said.

Thus I kept up my wandering not in search of him, as I might have fooled myself into believing, but because in some way it pleased me to, or was necessary, though I did not know what it profited me or what wisdom I hoped would come of it. The truth was that through Yeshua some doorway had been shown to me that I would not otherwise have come to, for in seeing how he cut his bonds to the things of this world, and did not think twice about living in the streets and going his own way, I was put in doubt about my own verities and arrangements. So my restlessness had come to me, and I thought of Tryphon and how he had marvelled at Yeshua's intellect, and I wondered at the ways there were of seeing the world and if Yeshua's understanding did not surpass my own.

It was in the streets near the harbour that Yeshua kept himself. Some of these were the most wretched in the city, where there were no women except for whores and no worship of God, it seemed, except in the prayers whispered over the gaming boards. But it was also here that every sort of wise man and scoundrel washed up, vagrants from as far as the Indus who presented themselves as mighty wizards or priests but often enough were the merest charlatans. Among the educated and the rich they held little sway, for these saw through their fakery. But the poor and ignorant gathered there in large numbers, including many hopeful of cures, cripples and the infertile and even lepers, who smuggled themselves into the city through the harbour or paid off the guards at the city gates. Great horrors were performed there, as I heard, abortions as well as surgeries on Jews who wished to hide their mark, and many who went there in desperation ended up cheated of their money by those who promised wonders and cures they could not deliver. I myself had been foolish enough to come at the time of the plague to seek medicines for Hosheah, for which I paid dearly but to no avail.

Still I found I was drawn to those streets, not only on Yeshua's account and the hope of catching a glimpse of him, but because I had indeed seen wonders there that defied belief. For instance, there was a healer there, a surgeon, who with my own eyes and before many other witnesses I saw revive a man from oblivion by drilling a hole in his skull. The man had fallen from a building and crushed his head, and had the surgeon not agreed to look to him he would surely have been buried by evening. But there, before all of us, he burrowed through the man's very bone, thus releasing from his head a great quantity of water and blood, and moments later the patient opened his eyes like someone brought back from the dead.

I heard tell of other such miracles, those who cured lepers, others who, with surgery, cured the blind. Whether such powers came of God or the devil, I could not say. Surely they seemed directed to the cause of good, even if there were many who were made to pay much above what they could afford, and many others who died under the surgeon's knife or under some cure that had poisoned them. But it seemed to me there was much that was unnatural in what happened in those streets, and partook of powers that mortals should not take to themselves. It was said that in the city's schools even the corpses of the dead were butchered so that the ways of the body might be known. But I thought that the body was God's temple, and the ways of it were his mystery and not to be understood by the likes of men.

As for Yeshua, he was perhaps drawn to this quarter as any child would be, in the hope of seeing wonders. Indeed, often I thought of him next to Yaqob his brother, who though not swift of mind was also thoughtful enough in his way. Yet Yaqob knew nothing except cutting stone, for he had worked all his life at his father's side, while Yeshua, as I imagined, had witnessed all the wonders of the world, and the horrors, for all these could be seen in that quarter of the city. There were prophets there, and those who read entrails, and magicians from Meroe who charmed snakes or even gave themselves over to their venom, falling into a trance. Then also there were performances, one heard, that could not be described—every lewdness was practised in them, and sometimes children or slaves were dismembered or simply murdered on the stage, all for the amusement of the spectators. These were savageries learned from the Romans, with their circuses and their shows, who though they had many gods yet were godless, for because the emperor called himself God who was only a man, therefore his citizens had lost their faith.

For much of his time, I discovered, Yeshua made his living like any street urchin, running errands or working the ships at the port or begging alms as he had with Artimidorus, though, like him, he would not take money but only lodging and food. But he also had not lied to say he had a teacher, for indeed he had many, and often apprenticed himself for a month or three to this one or that, and did their business for them. To judge from how he moved from one to the other, it seemed he could not bear any of them for any great time, or that they themselves could not put up with him, for often, as I heard, he was let go for arrogance. But surely even then it might have been that he grew bored with them, or that his knowledge increased so quickly they feared it would surpass their own.

Because of the market near the ships I found sufficient reason to visit the quarter frequently. It was not hard to find Yeshua then for he was well enough known, and I needed only to ask in the street and soon enough he would come to me. I would have food for him, wrapped in leaves to keep it warm, which he ate in the open. We did not speak a great deal—I asked how he did and he said well, and sometimes I offered him money, which he refused. He did not ask after Yehoceph, or his brothers and sisters, and I did not ask the thoughts that ran through his head. Yet even then there was something between us like a grief we had shared or a secret that had not quite been spoken, and I remembered how it had been with us when he was small, the weight I had felt settle over me in his presence. It was the weight of his own single-mindedness, it seemed to me now—I did not know what he intended for himself, or what the Lord intended for him, except that he saw that thing always visible before him like a distant point he must reach.

I imagined at first that though people knew him, he lived solitarily, for that had always seemed his nature. But I came to learn this was not the case. Indeed, there was a whole band in that quarter, children of the streets like himself, who had begun to look to him as their leader, and whom he organized to salvage food from the ships that came into port or to choose their corner for begging so they should not conflict with one another, and slit each other's throats. So it seemed he had made a life for himself on his own, and had his family of the streets to replace the one he had left. It hurt me to see this, for he had found his place among beggars when he could not in his own home. Hearing sometimes how people spoke about him in the street, the affection he was held in and his eloquence and good humour, I had the sense he saved for me only the worst of himself, so little did the child they described seem to resemble my own.

I could not have said how long we might have gone on in this way, meeting only in the streets, or if in the end his path should have so varied from mine that he would have been lost to my life. But it so happened that the troubles there had been between the Alexandrians and the Jews erupted again. There was an incident, a brawl, where a Jew killed a Greek over some slight, and then the riots began, where Jews were murdered in the streets and those with shops outside of our quarter had them burnt to the ground.

It was in the midst of this that Yeshua returned to us, in the dark of night. He had somehow got caught up in the riots and taken a knife to his chest—from his pallor it was clear he had lost a great deal of blood, and it was a wonder he had made his way to us, for shortly after his arrival he fell into a swoon and did not rise again for several days. I thought then that he would not survive, and rose every morning with the same terror in me, that I should find him dead. But after a time he came around. At first he was not certain where he was or how he had come to be there, and it moved me to see the need in him and his helplessness.

You have come to your home, I said, and he did not contradict me.

Wounded and frail as he was he seemed a child again, and eventually even the other children began to go to him, wondering, I supposed, that he was their brother and yet lived so differently from them. His sisters brought his food to him so he would not need to get up from his bed, and Yaqob, who because of the troubles could not go to work, sat with him during the day and talked to him so unaffectedly, of this and that, the jobs he had done or the doings of the quarter, that I felt my heart in my throat at how he still accepted him. Yehoceph, for his part, kept his silence, and because we all lived in those days in mortal fear and every Jew looked out for every Jew, I could not imagine that he would turn Yeshua out into the street.

Yeshua had said nothing of what had happened, nor had we dared to ask him. But from the talk of the quarter we knew a Jew had been slaughtered near the docks the night Yeshua had returned to us, dragged out from his shop by the mob though he had lived peacefully in that part of the city for many years and indeed had been married to a Greek. A few who had seen the thing said it beggared the mind for brutality, since the mob had been in a bloodlust and had literally torn the man limb from limb before the horrified eyes of his children and wife. Eventually we were able to learn that it was there Yeshua had received his injury, for when he was up and about someone recognized him as one of those who had tried to stay the crowd's fury, and been attacked in their turn for their pains. So the story went around the quarter that Yeshua had risked his life as a Jew and he was seen as a hero, though he still would not talk of the thing. Among our neighbours there was surely some surprise that he should return to us in glory in this way, for after his years in the streets they had no doubt imagined him the merest wastrel. I dared to feel a mother's pride in him then, that despite the life he had led he had still brought himself honour, though I did not know if he would leave me again the instant the troubles had ended.

During that time there were many of us in the quarter who billeted in our homes those who, on account of the riots, had been forced from their own. Among the ones we ourselves put up was a young scholar of the city named Gedalyah with whom Yeshua, as he recovered, had many discussions. Gedalyah told him the story of Pompey's capture of the temple when the Romans first conquered us, and how even as they were being slaughtered the priests continued in their offices, valuing their allegiance to God above their own lives. So Pompey took charge of the place, and went at once to enter the most hallowed sanctuary of the Jews, the Holy of Holies, in which none but the high priest was permitted. For he imagined that vast riches lay within, and also that the great god of the Jews, for whom so many had fought so valiantly, must be represented there in supreme splendour. But to his amazement he parted the curtain and found that the place stood empty.

He understood then that our god was not some idol like those of the pagans, Gedalyah said, but so greatly surpassed any likeness we might make of him as to defy representation.

This story seemed to affect Yeshua deeply.

It was how my own teacher Artimidorus used to speak about God, he said.

The riots had ended by then because the Jews had all been consigned to their quarter and forbidden to leave it. It happened, however, that a group of young Jews, still enraged at the murders that had been committed and the damage to our property, stole out of the quarter one night, though it was heavily guarded, and breached the old city wall by way of the canal. From there they set a fire just inside the Gate of the Sun so that several buildings were burnt, including some homes. By morning the news of the fire had spread, and a mob had formed to march on our quarter and destroy us.

As it fell out it was the sabbath that day and we were in the assembly house near our home when the word reached us, Yehoceph and I and the children and also Yeshua, who had recovered. We came out to find the streets already thronged at the news, the more so because of the many who had been driven into the district on account of the riots. Large numbers had made their way into the streets leading out of the quarter in the hope of fleeing but had been turned back by the soldiers there, who, seeing the crowd we had formed, were loath to release us. So people thought we should be trapped there in the streets like animals and slaughtered, for no one trusted the soldiers to protect us.

My own family had ended up in the great square where we held our market. It was my thought that we return to our house, where we might at least conceal ourselves and avoid the mob. But Yehoceph said that for all we knew our house would be burnt to the ground, and that we should stand with the rest. In any event, there would have been a danger that the children would be separated from us if we had tried to make our way through that crowd, or that in the growing panic they would have been injured.

Many of the men had begun to arm themselves, heaving cobbles up from the pavement to use as weapons. Yehoceph and Yaqob were quick to join them in this, helping to smash some of the larger paving stones so that the rubble from them might be used as well. But just when it seemed certain that the matter would come to violence, a teacher of the quarter by the name of Menasheh began to go around and remind us of the sabbath, and how the Maccabees, when they were attacked on that day, did not offer resistance but willingly gave themselves over to death. He said if we gave battle, we too would surely die, women and children along with the men, for the Greeks outnumbered us and no doubt carried weapons, and the soldiers also would turn against us. Better then that we should lift no hand and at least die innocent, and let heaven and earth bear witness, as was written in the scriptures, that we were killed without pretence of justice.

Yeshua had not yet picked up any stone.

Menasheh doesn't remember that Mattatthias chose to fight when he saw his brothers killed, he said to me, or the Jews would have been wiped from the earth.

But still he would not arm himself. Yaqob, seeing this, said, People will look to you for your example, because they think of you as a hero.

But Yeshua seemed appalled at this.

Let them look to their own minds, he said.

The truth was that there were many of us in the crowd, particularly among the women, who were ready to heed Menasheh's advice, not so we should be slaughtered there like lambs but in hopes that the soldiers, seeing us peaceful, would feel obliged to defend us. Throughout the square now there were those who had begun to take up Menasheh's call, and many of the women had turned to their husbands to try to make them see the horror of what they'd undertaken. I put my own plea to Yehoceph, urging peace on him for our children's sake. I saw him look to Yaqob then, and notice how his heart was no longer in the thing after Yeshua's reprimand. Without a word to me he ceased his work and bid Yaqob do the same.

We were wrong to merely follow the crowd instead of our conscience, he said to Yaqob, which astonished me, since it seemed he deferred to Yeshua.

By now those counselling peace had gained the upper hand, so that, one by one, people had begun to set aside their weapons. Then the word reached us that the mob had passed through the Gate of the Sun and was drawing near, and Menasheh went around saying we should sit down in the street wherever we found ourselves, to show we would make no defence. The pavement was broken up where we were and Yaqob and Yehoceph needed to clear some bits of rubble away before we could sit comfortably. Yeshua helped them in this. Then, when we all took our seats in the dirt, I saw Yeshua hesitate instinctively as if it seemed forward to join us, before finally settling between me and Yaqob. I could feel the heat of him next to me, and remembered, for what seemed the first time in many years, the infant he had been, and how I had held him. The strangest feeling passed through me then, having him near—we were in that crowd, my family, facing death, for all we knew, yet in that moment it hardly mattered for we were all together.

We were packed thick in the square by then, perhaps five thousand or more, with thousands again in the streets coming off it. A silence fell over us as the last ones took their places on the ground, and there was a smell of our sweat and our fear, and our deaths seemed to hang over us. Then in the distance we heard the din of the mob as it approached. I thought of the problems I had concerned myself with in my life, and how little they had mattered in the end. My youngest was but four at the time and I took him in my arms and we sat and waited, silent, as the shouts grew closer.

It was then when our fear was greatest that some of the women began to sing.

Sing to the Lord, they cried, for he has covered himself in glory, horse and rider he has thrown into the sea.

It was the Song at the Sea that proclaimed our victory over Egypt. Slowly the women's words spread among us, to ten and twenty and then across the square to the five thousand of us, and then to the thousands more in the streets, like a fire that had spread. In the end our singing drowned out the sound of the approaching mob and helped to put out our fear, so that even when our attackers were upon us and it was clear that the soldiers would not hold them back, at once giving way before them, we did not give up our place.

From where we sat in the square what we saw was a teeming mass that seemed to spill back in every direction, with clubs raised above it and fisted rocks and charred beams that had no doubt been taken from the site of the previous night's fire. However, seeing us in the street making no defence and only singing, the mob did not know what to make of us. A few rocks were hurled in at us, and sticks, which because we were thick on the ground found their mark. But when still we did not make a move or give up our song, the mob faltered.

Lord, who is like you, we sang, so mighty in holiness, who like you among the heavenly powers.

And indeed it seemed to us that the Lord heard our prayer and worked a miracle then, for the soldiers, seeing perhaps that they did not have the excuse of the crowd's fury to explain their inaction, finally started to move in to disperse it. There were some scuffles and a few of the more vicious had to be beaten back with the soldiers' sticks. But when the mob saw that the soldiers were in earnest, they began to turn away. It was not long before the bulk of them had turned back towards the city and the soldiers had reformed their line of defence, so that even those who lingered behind could not make their way to us.

For the longest time we remained sitting there in the streets, scarcely able to believe that our slaughter had been averted. Then finally we wiped our sweat and began to return to our homes.

Yeshua stayed beside me as we made our way through the crowd.

Mother, he said, when the others could not hear him, I was wrong to reject the Jews, because I am one of them.

And because he had made this repentance, and called me his mother, I could not stop my tears.

It seemed my good fortune then was more than I deserved, that out of the tragedy of the riots I had had Yeshua returned to me. I thought that Yehoceph would surely not send him from our house now if he chose to remain there, after all we had endured together, and so I was innocent enough to imagine that we might at last find peace with each other.

But that very evening Yehoceph came to me and said, We cannot remain in this place, for he judged it foolish to have made so many sacrifices in the name of his sons only to have them murdered in a foreign country.

It was my first thought then that it was for nothing, after all, that Yeshua had come back—I could hardly command him now to follow us out of the country, when he had already been so long on his own, nor could I make any argument to Yehoceph that he still had need of us. I might have questioned Yehoceph's decision but lacked the heart to, for though I was loath to leave a place where I had known such freedom, neither did I wish to see my children annihilated or all our property destroyed. In any event it was clear that Yehoceph had already set his mind.

I need to settle my affairs, was all I said to him, meaning my dowry, and thus the matter was decided.

So it was that more than a dozen years after we'd left it, we prepared to return to our homeland. Yet I could not have said by then what home it was, when in Egypt I had borne eight children, including the two I buried, and had had work, and had understood the smallness of the world I'd left behind, so that I barely remembered any more the child who had set out.

What we had departed from as a single kingdom under Herod had, after his death, undergone many changes and divisions, so that the country we returned to was scarcely recognizable as the one we had left. There had been uprisings and revolts, where whole cities had been burnt to the ground, and there were also territories, as we heard, that were run solely by bandits. In Judea, after many troubles, Herod's son Archelaus had been banished by the Romans, who had set up their own ruler and committed many desecrations. Thus Yehoceph had no wish to return there, not only because we were known but because he did not wish to be a slave in his own land after being one for so long in another's.

We came to choose the place we had rejected years before, the Galilee, under Herod Antipas, who at least called himself a Jew, though eventually we learned that his own desecrations often exceeded those of the Romans. At the time, the word had spread that Herod planned a great city on the shores of the Sea of Kinneret, to be his capital.

Yehoceph judged there would be work in the place for many years and thought it good, for while he himself was old, he had four sons whom he needed to settle.

In the end there were nine of us who returned, because Yeshua, though I had not had the courage to hope it, chose to travel with us. I was careful not to show my joy at this or say anything in the way of encouragement, fearing these would be the very things that would drive him away. He said to me that if he was a Jew, he should see the land of the Jews, and so know himself. But the truth was he had grown close to us during the troubles. As for Yehoceph, I did not even broach the matter with him, but merely pretended to take it for granted that Yeshua would accompany us.

We stopped for three days in Jerusalem. This was a mistake, since Yehoceph, wanting nothing to do with my own family, immediately set off to Bet Lehem with his sons to show them to his brothers, leaving Yeshua behind with me and the girls. I saw how much Yeshua took this to heart. On the journey Yehoceph had warmed to him, because Yeshua had been careful always to defer to him and show him respect, though clearly his superior in intelligence. But when we entered Judea, Yehoceph seemed to remember at once all the old proscriptions. From the black mood Yeshua fell into at being left behind I gathered he still had not understood what he was, though I did not know what other rift he imagined kept him separate from us. It seemed almost wilful, this blindness, when he was otherwise perceptive, and when even as a child he had come so near to the truth. Later I began to think it was precisely this denial that let him remain my son—he would not look at the thing directly so that he need not condemn me for it outright, but only hold it over me.

I had had no word of my family in all my time in Egypt. So I was reacquainted now with my brothers and sisters, and learned for the first time that my father was dead. I gave over some of the dowry I had saved to my mother then, for my father had left her without any means and so she lived like a tenant in her own house, at the beck of my brothers' wives. My brothers, for their part, showed little joy in seeing me, and I understood now that they blamed me for the loss of our fortune. To Yeshua, one of them said, You may sleep in the servants' room. It was all I could do then not to leave that instant, which I refrained from only on my mother's account. I ended by making my own bed and my daughters' in the servants' room as well, which in any event was empty, to make it seem we slept there only for lack of other places.

Yeshua, however, understood the insult nonetheless, and the following morning I awoke to find he had gone. By evening, he still had not returned to the house. As I could not go searching for him in the dark, I spent a sleepless night, believing every sort of thing, that he had been denounced or had chosen to abandon me again or that he had been murdered in the streets, though surely he was safer in Jerusalem than he had ever been in the streets of Alexandria. In the morning I set out at sunrise in search of him and finally came upon him at the temple, listening to some of the teachers who stood discussing in the temple courts.

I felt a chill then, seeing how his own ignorance was a danger to him, for, by law, bastards were prohibited from the temple precincts, on pain of death.

One of the teachers, when he saw I was the boy's mother, said, Your son is a blasphemer, since he claims there is more wisdom than what is written in the Torah.

I remembered then how rigid in belief the Judeans were, though often enough in hypocrisy, it seemed to me, and wondered that I had not discouraged Yeshua from coming to a place where he could only be an outcast. For with a word, if the truth of him was known, men such as these could ruin his life.

Taking him aside, I had no chance to express any happiness at finding him but said, You're a fool to speak your mind so openly here.

He stayed silent at this and I instantly repented, realizing that the worst thing was that I should drive him, through his defiance, to remain here in Jerusalem.

It's just that you are a boy, I said, and they cannot endure that you should be wiser than they are, which indeed was the truth.

He finally agreed to return with me to my family's house, and I said a room had been prepared for us off the inner courtyard, where some goods had been removed. For my sake, I thought, he pretended to be satisfied with this.

Since I could no longer bear his silence on the matter, I asked if he would accompany us on the rest of our journey.

I do not think I can know the Jews by the ones I've seen in Jerusalem, he said, at which I was relieved. And in the morning he presented himself with me and my daughters at the Damascus Gate so that we might join Yehoceph there for the journey north.

We went up by way of Perea to avoid the Samaritans, travelling with a band of traders who were well armed against the brigands who hid in the hills. In the end, we reached the shores of Kinneret without incident. Yeshua, I saw, was very taken with the lake, as indeed we all were, for after the many miles of desert we had passed through, from Egypt and from Jerusalem, and after the grit that had lodged itself between our teeth, it seemed the very seat of paradise, lush and green then with the spring. We all seemed to feel a lifting, a sense of arrival, for the air itself appeared more pure than what we had left and the water more blue than even that of the Western Sea.

At Sennabris, Yehoceph enquired about Herod's new city. But we learned that the work had nearly ceased, for it had come out he had chosen a burial ground for his site and so his workers, except for the Greeks he had brought in, refused to proceed. Yehoceph was bitter at this, for we had made the journey there at no little trouble and expense. To worsen the matter, he was unwell—a fever had come to him after Jerusalem, with the damp and the cold that had met us there, and he had not shaken it. He was somewhere near sixty now, as I reckoned, and each ailment that came to him I thought might be his last. When we were settled in the caravansary outside the Sennabris gates I sent Yeshua into town to fetch a doctor for him.

You imagine we're still in Alexandria, where there are doctors, he said, and I heard the note of contempt in his voice for Yehoceph now, after Jerusalem. Nonetheless, he went into town with the coins I had given him and returned with a brew that seemed to give Yehoceph some comfort.

From some of those we met we learned there was work for masons at Sepphoris, which Herod had rebuilt after the revolts and continued to use as his capital while he awaited his new one. We went on there at once, and Yehoceph was able to find work for himself and Yaqob at least, even if not at favourable wages. Since Jews at the time were still forbidden from taking up residence in the city, we took a house at Notzerah nearby, which once, as we heard, when the building at Sepphoris had progressed most rapidly, had been an active town, but now seemed decrepit and half-deserted.

Yeshua had remained with us as far as Notzerah. But it was clear that after Jerusalem a bond had been broken, and I saw it chafed him to stay with us, and knew in my heart that he would leave. In Notzerah there was no occupation for him, nor any life that might seem familiar, and while he travelled into Sepphoris on a few occasions, where there were schools and educated men, I saw it bothered him to go into the town seeking amusements when Yehoceph and Yaqob sweated there in the sun for their daily pay. Again I could have told him of the money I'd set aside, so that he might have attended a school in Caesarea or Ptolemais on the coast. But if he should have asked why there was money for him and not the others, or indeed why I had so long withheld it, I could not have answered him.

In the end he came to me and said he would seek work on the lake as a fisherman, and I had nothing to say to prevent him from this. As I later heard, he returned to Sennabris and joined a fleet there for a season but then moved on, some said into the Decapolis, others north into Tyre. As he did not return home in this time or send any word of himself, I could not judge the truth one way or the other, and eventually I stopped asking after him entirely, to avoid the shame of being his mother yet not knowing his whereabouts, but also because I could no longer stand to hear of him, when it was clear he had cut his ties. It was strange that in Alexandria, where we had been so at odds and where there had been every influence to drive us apart, we had remained together in the end, whereas here in our own homeland he had slipped from me as if by merest chance, so that it seemed my own failure that I had not found the way to hold him close or that there had been a part of me, which wanted rest, that had been content to set him free.

Without Yeshua it appeared that our lives were made simple, that we formed a family like any other and so had truly begun again, even if Notzerah was the very end of the earth, full of goat herds and the ignorant, and Sepphoris, the few times I visited it, looked hopelessly dusty and small after our years in Alexandria. There was a quality of the air in those parts, because of the woods and the hills and because we were far from the sea, which I had grown used to, that made it seem we were lost to the world, remote from the places of import. But over time I grew at home in that remoteness, and the restlessness I had felt in Alexandria began to fade. In Notzerah, because we had come from far away and from a great city, people looked at us with respect, and there was no one who wondered at my past or took me for anything different than what I seemed. So I became simply a mother looking to my children, and my days were spent at the river and at the well. With my dowry, in the end, to keep it safe, I purchased an olive grove near the town, not trusting the merchants in those parts to invest it, but neither daring to keep it in my home for fear of bandits.

We had not been in the Galilee much over a year before Yehoceph passed on. A small illness took him over one day seemingly so trifling that he did not even let it keep him from work, but later Yaqob and some of his fellows needed to carry him home and by evening he was dead. It surprised me then the grief that went through me, for I had not imagined

I loved him. Indeed, perhaps I had not, except that I had been with him some fifteen years, and had borne his children, and he had spared me, as I saw now, a life surely far worse than the one he had given me. Never once had he raised his hand against me or asked of me anything it was unreasonable for a man to ask of his wife, and the fairness of mind I had detested in him as a bride had in the end stood me well in all my years with him. On his deathbed, when he understood his time had come, he did not say to me, I command this or that, or, Look you follow my wishes, but rather held his tongue and said only the wages that were owed to him at his work, by which I understood his trust in me.

When he had died I felt his loss in many ways, not only because of his wages and because there was no longer any man in the house but because it seemed to me that in his death I did not understand any more what it was to live on this earth. For here was a man who had worked all his days even to the final one, and who had known little comfort from his wife, whom he had married in disgrace, and yet somehow he had taken meaning from the things of his life, which was only in the birth of his sons and the thought of their prospering. But what was it if each generation sacrificed every pleasure in this way, for its sons, for then each son would sacrifice in turn, and there would be no joy on the earth.

As to myself, I was but thirty then and yet an old woman, for my husband was dead and I had no prospect of another and my daughters would marry in a matter of years and my sons find their work. So for several months I could not find it in me to leave my home, I who had wandered every quarter of Alexandria, nor could I smile or take any pleasure in my children. I thought of my own childhood in

Jerusalem and how the world had seemed different, the feast days and the market days, the great run of time that had seemed to stretch before me like very eternity. The strangest things came into my memory then—the smell of dill in my mother's kitchen, or how clear the air stood on a winter morning, or the sound the mules made in the earliest dawn outside our gate. Everything had seemed full of a promise then that had come to nothing in the end, that had slowly been stripped away from the world.

It was Yaqob, finally, seeing how unhappy I had become and understanding me more than I knew, who came to me and said he would seek out Yeshua and bring him home.

Why seek him out when he has abandoned us, I said.

Because he is the eldest, Yaqob said, and our father is dead.

I might have preferred then the stupor I had fallen into to reopening the wound that Yeshua was for me. But Yaqob was determined, and I could not bring myself to forbid him. The truth was I had little hope that he would find Yeshua, or that finding him, would be able to bring him home—we had lost our chance when we had first come from Alexandria, and I did not think we would see one another. Even then he had been like a restless animal that suffered itself out of loyalty to stay with its master but in the end must run wild.

After only three days, however, much to our surprise, Yaqob returned to us with his brother. He had found him at Sennabris—it seemed he had returned there for the high season.

I might have shown some pleasure then but did not dare to, since I did not know in what spirit he came, or if he would stay with us. But he said to me, If there's work for me, I am here to take the place of the eldest, to show that he would stay.

I could not find the words to answer him.

I have purchased a field for you, I said in the end, like a girl with a trinket, since it was all I could offer.

So it was that Yeshua returned to us, and was part of our family again. In the beginning, none of us could escape the strangeness of his presence or how he was different from us in his looks and his manner, so that there seemed a silence that spread around him like a pool, and even the kinship I had felt with him against the others when he was a child appeared to have faded, and they were the ones now I felt allied with. But true to his word he took his place among us, and together with his brothers worked the olive grove I had purchased and rented land for barley and wheat. And for a time it began to seem that in the death of Yehoceph I had after all found a new life, since I had my son at home with me now without my husband's shadow and the darkness that had dogged me for so many years seemed lifted. As to the others, because Yaqob accepted Yeshua, so his brothers did, and my daughters were happy to see him with us on my account. Even the people of the town found nothing peculiar to remark in his presence, for just as they had thought it fitting, when he was on his own, that with so many sons in the house he should have gone his own way, so they thought it fitting now, after Yehoceph's death, that as the eldest he should return.

At the olive harvest we purchased a mill to make our oil and set it at the edge of our grove. While the others shook the fruit from the trees, I helped Yeshua to press it, tending the olives while he guided the wheel. In those weeks it seemed we grew together again, because of the silence of the hills there and the air and the sky and the rhythms our bodies fell into, which were deeper than speech. In his exertion I saw Yeshua was as beautiful as any Greek, fair-skinned and fair-haired, and it took my breath sometimes to look at him and know he was my son. There was that part of me that wished to dote on him now, to make up for what I had denied myself, and indeed sometimes I felt that because I had never known the love of a husband, I was drawn to him with all the excess of emotion I thus had not spent. Once in the market, because I had kept young, it in fact happened that he was mistaken for my husband, which shamed him. But I was strangely pleased at this since it seemed I thus possessed him more, or that he was bound to me not by blood but by choice.

None of these things, however, did I say to him or in any way make apparent, instead simply showing him a mother's love, in my deference to him and the care I took in the things that touched on him. But where with my other children I was equitable and calm, with Yeshua I knew only extremes, so that there seemed little difference in the end between the restraint I had shown towards him when he was a child for the sake of shame and the restraint I showed now to keep my dignity. For his part, he remained inscrutable—indeed in many respects he brought to mind Yehoceph, fair and beyond reprimand in every thing but sparing in any emotion. For this, I blamed myself, since I had been mother to him. But also I thought he punished me in this way, knowing that I hung on any sign of affection from him. Sometimes it appeared he went out of his way to make me see what I missed, bringing gifts for his sisters or praising them before me to show he was capable of such displays, but then presenting to me always the same dutiful forbearance.

Because of these hurts, over time, even if the very restraint I had taught him was their cause, I began to find fault with him. It was over the smallest things at first, his appearance or his manners, some tiny oversight, so that it was easy enough for him to let my censure pass. But soon enough a bitterness crept into my voice. Then after the barley harvest in the spring, because he had sold the crop without so much as consulting me, I complained of the price he had got, though it was not insufficient.

What do you care of the price, since I was the one who sweat to earn it, he said.

I lost my temper then.

You would not have needed to sweat and to work the fields like a common labourer, I said, if you had followed my counsel and taken a trade.

This was the sheerest hypocrisy in me, for I had been the one to disdain Zekaryah's advice when he had given it. Yet when I had made the complaint I could not bring myself to retract it, though I knew the stubbornness of Yeshua's mind and that he would not let my words pass. So when he had finished with the wheat as well, he came to me and said he had apprenticed himself to a shepherd.

This was the lowest thing, good only for criminals and the simple-minded.

You've done this to shame us, I said.

Yet I knew it was wrong to talk of shame to him, when I was the one who had put him always in its shadow.

With some virulence he said, I'll rather spare you shame because I'll sleep in the open, and our neighbours won't see me returning to your house in dirty clothes any longer.

True to his word, he took to the pastures then and was gone from Notzerah for many days at a stretch. Since we had little to do in our own fields at that time of year, it might have happened that no one would have taken much note of this, for though the work was low, it was more respectable than idling. But during his respites he did not come home to us as he might have but rather took to the streets of Notzerah and began to live there as Artimidorus had in Alexandria, to show everyone in the town he had left his own house. He would sit at the edge of the market or near the assembly house like a beggar, and people did not know what to make of him, since they recognized him as my son. If they went up to him and asked him what his business was, he made some reply they could not understand, like Artimidorus used to do, except that in Notzerah, where there were no Greeks and where no one had ever seen the likes of an Artimidorus, he seemed merely to have lost his mind.

When I first got word of what he did, I went to him at once.

Now it's you who imagines we are still in Alexandria, making a nuisance of yourself in the streets, I said.

But he said that he had found his trade now, which was precisely to be a nuisance, and refused to follow me home.

Thus the gloom I had felt for many years, and that I thought had passed, now came back in force, so that there were many times I wished Yeshua had never returned to us, but left us in peace. For though he would not stay with us, neither would he let us forget him, coming more and more often to the town now until his employer, I heard, set him free because he could not depend on him. Subsequently, he was in the town every day, and because he had no livelihood, he had indeed begun to beg for his food.

Once more I went to him.

Your orchard needs tending, I said, since it was coming on to the harvest again.

Woman, I don't have any interest any more in olives or barley, he said, and I could have struck him then for his insolence.

So I left him there in the street and told my children not to mind him, though I knew they went out to him and brought him food. And I mistakenly imagined again, as I had when he was a child, that he could not persist in his stubbornness but must come around to me in the end. But a number of the young men of the town, having discovered that he was not afraid to speak his mind, had begun to go to him now where he was and put questions to him for their amusement, hoping to draw from him some outrageous reply. They asked him what he thought of such and such a leader or if this or that trader was honest or if it profited them to study the scriptures when they could earn nothing by them. And because he always had an answer ready, which often enough showed some truth, he began to be known in the town for the things that he said.

It was not long, however, before he began to incur people's enmity in this way. There were those who were ready to chase him away at the end of a stick because he had insulted them or called their good name into question, and many others who said he was a bad influence, since he had left his own home to beg in the streets and often called into question what people had learned from their teachers. Then there were some, because on several occasions he had complained against

Herod and said he had little respect for the Jews, who would have had him arrested for sedition. Yeshua was quick to point out then that many of the town's leaders depended on Herod for their wealth and so feared to go against him, for they served as the contractors for his workers or as the middlemen for his goods. In this way the town began to divide between those who supported him because he spoke honestly and those who hated him for the same reason.

It happened at the time that there was a woman in Notzerah, a Jewess by the name of Ester, whose husband had run away with the brigands. After his absence had gone on a year or more she had taken another man into her house, though there was no news whether her husband was alive or dead. The elders condemned her for this and wished to drive the couple from the town, to free us from their example. But Yeshua, when the question was put to him in the street, asked what purpose it would serve to drive them away when we only forced their example on others. It seemed from this that he did not believe they should be punished in any way but merely left to follow their lusts. Yet there was a logic to his words. For as he said, it was no punishment to a thief if he was merely banished to the next town for his crimes, while in so doing we made ourselves into sinners by forcing on others the thing we ourselves could not bear.

But is it not also a sin, people asked him, to see those who commit a crime and do nothing.

Yeshua gave the example then of the child who blasphemed.

He isn't banished to strangers, Yeshua said, or put to death, but rather looked to by his mother and father, who teach him his error. So do we need to see to our sinners and not pass our work on to strangers.

There were many who were amazed at such wisdom in someone little more than a boy, and it was not long before the very youths who used to come to taunt him now came because they thought he spoke more truthfully than their own teachers. But the elders in the town were furious at the position he had taken. One of them apparently went to him and said, What authority do you have in the scriptures for what you say.

But he answered, Do you require authority for what's merely common sense, which enraged the man.

For my part, I too was surprised at the arguments he made, not because of their wisdom, since I knew the acuity of his mind, but because he had attached himself to the cause of a stranger and shown compassion for her when he showed none at home. It seemed to me then that he took her part only in argument, from the rhetoric he had learned at the hands of Artimidorus. But perhaps I was mistaken. Perhaps he showed others the affection he could not to a mother as I showed him that owed a husband, for years later I heard how he preached forgiveness and love like the teacher Hillel, though I had never known these things from him.

Some of the elders, when they saw how openly he defied their authority and the power he had begun to have over the young, came to me at my home.

He will corrupt people, they said, since he speaks outside the law.

And they told me to look to him and to take him from the streets, or risk my own name.

I began to fear that they would discover what he was, and how much greater their censure would be then and how much more severe the dishonour they would visit on all of us. And it seemed a tremendous bullheadedness in him that he should do everything in his power to keep us from an ordinary life, raising troubles for us and calling attention to what it cost me so much to hide.

I sent Yaqob to him, hoping he would fare better with him, though indeed Yaqob was one of those who thought Yeshua did well to question the elders and so had little argument to make. But then Yeshua came to me of his own accord.

Why do you try to silence me, he said, when I merely tell the truth.

But because of his arrogance I said, What can you know of the truth when you're just a child.

The truth is that you're only afraid for your own reputation, he said.

I grew enraged then, thinking how I had always thought of his protection, and still he accused me.

It's you who needs to be afraid, I said, because you are a bastard and will be chased from the town.

From his look then, from the way his spirit fell, it was clear that even still he had not yet known the thing for certain. I was mortified, for I understood he had only taunted me all these years from his own fear, and had hoped against hope, and had perhaps all his life, from the days when Tryphon had first made clear to him his talents, wondered what thing it was that conspired against him, and kept him from the path of a normal life.

Return to your home, I said. You have a place with us.

It seems I have found my place, which is in the streets, he said.

This was in his sixteenth year. He left the town then, for all I knew to join the brigands, and this time I did not go in search of him, for there was all the world to search in and no thread, as I believed, that held him to me.

I could not have said how he spent the following years, or where he reached to, or what ideas formed in his head. In the first while I heard rumours of him, that he had gone up to Sidon or Damascus or even to Rome, though it was as likely that he had simply returned to his fisherman's work at Sennabris. But then the time went by and I had no further news of him. So I thought he had passed away from the world, or found anonymity, or gone to make his fortune where he would not be burdened by his past. For my part, I had looked to settling my children, had married my daughters to men of good standing and found wives for my two elder sons, and it seemed that all had ended for the best, that I had made a place for my family and safeguarded our name. Though a widow, I was fortunate enough not to be among the poor, since the olive grove I had purchased still produced and my sons had work, one at home with me and two at Sepphoris and one at the new capital Tiberias, which after all had proceeded.

It was some years after Yeshua's departure that we heard of the rise of the prophet Yohanan, who went among the Jews preaching justice for the common people and condemning every sort of hypocrisy. Once, returning from the Passover sacrifice at the temple, we came upon his camp along the Jordan, where his followers came to be purified and receive his blessing. At the time he had grown so favoured with people that a settlement had grown up around him the size of a town, the tents stretching away in every direction.

Because many of those who came, which included women as much as men, were given to ecstasies and possessions, there was a great moaning and ululation that rose up from the place, and surely those who stumbled upon it knowing nothing of Yohanan must have thought they had reached the very city of the damned.

Yaqob, when we reached the place, said, Will we be purified with the rest, for a number of those in our company had stopped by the river to be cleansed. But I said we had made our sacrifice at the temple, and so had our purity.

We might have gone on then, except that my son Ioses came to me quietly and said that Yeshua was among the acolytes who prayed with Yohanan by the river. I could hardly believe this was so. Nonetheless I followed him through the crowd to where Yohanan's acolytes prayed in a mass at the riverbank. They were on their knees there in the shoals, a dozen or more, their hair hanging in coils and their skin darkened by the sun so that it was difficult to tell one from the next. Even from a distance, however, I made him out amidst the others, wearing like them the leather belt that marked Yohanan's followers, though so changed in appearance from when he had been with us, gaunt and black-skinned and long-haired like the rest, that it amazed me Ioses had recognized him.

I had both Yaqob's wife and the wife of my son Yihuda with me then, and also many of the townspeople of Notzerah with whom we had travelled and who had known Yeshua when he preached in the streets. So in that moment it seemed a shame to me to go to him, and let it be known to all that he was there, and then be met, as I thought, only with his rejection.

I said to Ioses, You are mistaken, and he did not gainsay me, nor did he speak to his brothers. And I comforted myself with the thought that I had acted rightly, since it would only have brought upheaval to us to have Yeshua in our lives again, when we had found peace and respectability.

While we stood there, a wealthy Judean arrived in his carriage and made a great show of passing through the crowd to reach Yohanan, people clearing a path for him because they could see he was a man of stature. When his slaves had set him down he emerged from his carriage in all his finery and said he had come to be cleansed. But Yohanan at once chastised him, and said that the servants who carried him were greater than he was.

You must come to God not in your carriage but on your knees, he said.

And taking a brand from a cooking fire nearby, he set it to the carriage's curtains, which immediately went up in flames. It took only a moment before the entire carriage was burning in front of the man's eyes, with no chance of saving it.

Those of us who stood watching were astonished to see this, and more astonished when the carriage's owner, whether in true repentance or merely to save appearances, fell down on his knees before Yohanan. Yohanan, however, did not pay any further attention to him but simply returned to those who had preceded him and who still stood waiting to be cleansed. His actions impressed themselves deeply on the crowd, not least because of the pleasure we felt at seeing the man's arrogance reduced. In the meanwhile the carriage continued to burn and the rich man to supplicate but Yohanan stayed oblivious, and even his acolytes, and Yeshua among them, did not pause so much as a breath in their prayers, as if they were well used to Yohanan's actions.

We left shortly afterwards. I was careful to keep my family from the shore lest another of them recognize their brother. But no one further picked him out. On the road there was a good deal of talk of what Yohanan had done, though as much, it seemed, from titillation as from understanding, for many had heard of his madness and were pleased now to say they had witnessed it with their own eyes. But for my part, I began to see in Yohanan's actions my own reproof. For while he had shown to us how meaningless were the pomp and opinions of this world, and the airs we made for ourselves, I had denied my own son for fear of opinion.

For many weeks afterwards I could not suppress the memory of what I had done, so that it seemed the shame of having shunned Yeshua was greater by far than any that might have come from having gone to him. And the restlessness I had felt as a young woman in Alexandria began to return to me, for I saw how my mind had been open then but had grown complacent, and how I thought only of my position now, just as Yeshua had once accused me, when before I had cared more for truth. Indeed it seemed that since Yeshua had gone from me I had put from my mind all thoughts except those of the marriage of my daughters and sons, and that the doorway he had opened for me had been closed. I thought of Artimidorus, how he had given over the coins I had paid him so that they might be flung to the earth—I remembered how my blood had quickened in that instant and I had felt alive, for it was as if he had put a knife through the very fabric of things. So it had been seeing Yohanan give fire to the rich man's carriage. It seemed fitting to me now that Yeshua had taken up with him, for he and Artimidorus were of a piece, set on their minds' trajectories, caring nothing for our petty hierarchies and rules.

I was established in the world and had reached the point where I might simply have rested and found comfort. Yet even now the trouble that had marked my life would not leave me, for my conscience would not be still until I had made peace with my son. Sometimes in these days, though I could hardly call up his face any longer, I thought of the man who had fathered him, and what had become of him, and what he might make of the child he had forced on me. Likely some war had carried him off or old age, though I could not say I regretted if God had cleared him from the earth. And yet I thought I would not have traded my son away for any price, though I hated how he had come to me, nor, after all, could I have done without the trouble he had given me, for that had been my life.

Only some months after we had passed Yohanan on the Jordan we had word he had been arrested by Herod for denouncing his marriage to his brother's wife. Of Yohanan's acolytes, it was said that some had been killed for resisting Herod's men and the rest had dispersed, fleeing into the desert. I was desperate then to hear word of Yeshua, but short of taking to the road and scouring the Judean wilderness, I did not know what path lay open to me. For weeks then I could not sleep for the thought of how I had passed him by, and for wondering if I might not have recalled him to us then, and so saved his life. But just when I thought I could not go on for the uncertainty, one of my sons, Shimon, who worked at the capital, brought me hope, saying he had passed someone resembling his brother preaching outside the Tiberias gates.

Shimon lived at Ammathus then, to be near his work, and I went to stay at his home to see if I might catch sight of the man and know if he was my son. But for many days we had no further news of him, nor indeed did he appear again at the gates of Tiberias. Then one day at his work, Shimon heard talk of a teacher by the name of Yeshua who had recently set himself up in Kefar Nahum, and who preached without charge in the assembly house there to all who were ready to hear him.

I said to Shimon, I will go ahead to see if he is the one. For the truth was I did not have the courage to go to him plainly and so wished to hide myself in the crowd to see what had become of him.

There was a boat out of Tiberias for Kefar Nahum, which collected goods at the tollhouse there. I asked among the other passengers about the teacher Yeshua but none had heard of him. Then I asked what word there was in Tiberias on the fate of Yohanan and was told that surely he would soon be set free, because the people loved him and Herod would not long risk their displeasure. I was somewhat comforted by this, for it seemed Herod had arrested him merely to show his authority, and would not trouble himself to pursue his acolytes.

I had never been to Kefar Nahum and was surprised by its harbour, nearly as large as that of Tiberias, with several breakwaters and piers. But the town itself appeared crude and poor, the streets unpaved and the houses all crowded up against the lakefront. The fishing boats were just coming in then with the night's catch, and there was a good deal of activity all along the water and an overwhelming stench of fish. It was a town of workers and of work, I saw, though also, as I heard, free from pagans, for Jews had settled it.

I went first to the assembly house, putting up the hood of my cloak to disguise myself, but found it deserted. So I asked in the streets after the teacher Yeshua and some who knew of him said I might find him in the boats on the lake, for it seemed he still earned his keep that way, while others directed me to the house of a certain Shimon bar Yonah where he stayed, but where I dared not present myself. Still others laughed at me and asked had I also come looking for heaven, which was all he preached of. So I understood he was well known in the town but also that people mocked him as they had in Notzerah.

At midday I returned to the assembly house. It was a large building for the town and the only one that bore any adornments. The teacher of the town was there, an old man by the name of Gioras, along with a handful of his charges whom he had brought to sweep the floors for sabbath prayer. When I asked after Yeshua, he said it was true he had given him a place there in the assembly house so that he might teach his followers. But they were only a handful, he said, and often they met at the house where he stayed. Of his teachings, he would say only that he spoke too often in riddles.

So people do not understand him and think him wise, he said. But I am afraid he misleads them.

When I emerged from the assembly house there were three women from the town of Korazin waiting at the door, who like myself had come in search of Yeshua. Except the man they spoke of seemed to bear no relation to the one I knew as my son. They described him as Yohanan's successor though I had seen him there in the desert with Yohanan's followers and he had seemed the least of them, lost among the pack without distinction.

He has come out of the desert to lead us, one of the women said. He cares nothing for the rich but only for the destitute and the poor, like the prophets.

I did not know what to make of these things, for every person I spoke to gave a different report. I was troubled by that of the teacher Gioras, since he had seemed in every way sensible and without guile, but also by the exaggerations of the three women, for it would go hard with Yeshua if he presented himself as a prophet and was found to be false. It seemed the sheerest recklessness to me, that he presented himself as Yohanan's successor when Yohanan lay in peril of his life.

As the sabbath was coming on, I had to make haste to reach Ammathus before dusk. So I departed from Kefar Nahum without any sight of my son and with no comprehension of his plight. From Ammathus, when the sabbath had passed, I immediately returned to my home so that Yaqob and I might confer, for of my children he was the only one with some understanding of his brother.

Yaqob said, There's no sin in being a teacher, to mean we should leave him to his task.

But how could I say to him, Your brother is false, for surely it was a crime and a sin to preach to the Jews, yet be an outcast.

It happened then that some merchants of Notzerah, returning from the kingdom of Philip, saw Yeshua preaching in the streets in one of the towns on the lake. So they must have said to themselves, Is that not the son of Miryam of our town, who used to trouble us and now calls himself a prophet. And when they came back to Notzerah they began to spread stories about him, and to say he preached only to women, and took them as his wives. Because I was held in some respect in the town, there was no one who would repeat these rumours to my face. But this only worsened the matter, since it was my children then who needed to hear them and my sons' wives who were the ones to say to their husbands, Should not your mother rein him in, for the sake of our name.

I might have told them that I hardly cared any more for our name, for the little joy it had ever given me and the great costs I had paid to maintain it. But the truth was that I could not rest now until I saw him, and so was glad of the excuse to go to him. By then every sort of rumour had spread—that he was a rebel and preached revolt, or that he could not bear those of greater authority than himself, or that he preached contradictions like a madman, and one day praised a man and the next condemned him. Indeed, I myself might have begun to fear for his sanity, for surely it was madness that as a bastard he had set himself up as a holy man of the Jews. Yet my fear was deeper than this, that as always he merely followed his will, and would admit no impediment to it.

Nonetheless I set out for Kefar Nahum with Yaqob one morning to see if we might exchange some word with him. To Yaqob I said, We will invite him home in celebration as our lost brother and son, and so be able to judge the state of his mind. But the truth was I did not know what I would say to him when I saw him. Surely I did not intend to ask him to come back to Notzerah, given the cloud under which he had left the place, nor did I think he could bear such a thing. Yet short of returning to us or at least abandoning his mission, I did not know what it was that he could grant me.

It was near dusk when we reached Kefar Nahum. When we had arranged for our sleep we went to the house where he stayed, getting directions in the street. A woman came to the gate who surely could not have been one of the wives about whom the merchants of Notzerah joked, for she was homely and simple and old.

I said to her, We have come for my son Yeshua, to invite him home with us.

She did not have the courtesy to invite us through the gate, but rather left us there in a fright as if we were thieves who had come. Some time passed before another woman emerged, or a child as I made out, for she was little more than a girl. I wished to be harsh with her, because of the insult we'd been dealt in having her sent to us, but could not find it in me.

We wish only to speak with him, I said. We have come from Notzerah.

But she said he would not come.

I asked her then, not without some spite, if she was his wife. She grew ashamed and said that he had none, though I saw that she wished it.

My pride would not suffer me to remain there, held out by a girl.

If I could offer a bed, she said.

There's no need, I said. And we returned at once to our lodgings.

I could hardly bear to spend the night in that place, but there was no thought of leaving in the dark. It seemed a tremendous mistake now to have come, only to trouble myself with humiliation, to be sent a girl to turn me away so that I might understand the fullness of his contempt.

In the morning, just after first light, I roused Yaqob for our departure.

We've learned nothing, he said, and I saw he still hoped to see his brother.

We have learned he rejects us, I said, and would not hear any argument.

While we were rolling our blankets, however, a boy came to us with fish for our breakfast and two loaves of bread, saying only that someone had left them for us at the gate.

Yaqob, still hoping to convince me, said, Surely it's Yeshua who sent them.

I saw how the fish was wrapped in three layers of leaves to keep it warm, the way I had done with the food I had brought Yeshua in the streets at Alexandria.

But to Yaqob I said, No doubt it was the girl who sent them, and still would not give in to him.

We left the town the way we had come, by the road that ran along the lake towards Tiberias. We had not gone more than a mile, however, before we came upon a gathering of some kind there at the roadside, of people who seemed stopped on their way to the fields, many with their animals or their hoes. There were two boats pulled up by the lakeshore as well, with some men there who stood a bit apart from the rest of the crowd. It was only when we came close that we saw what had drawn the crowd together, for there in the midst of them, changed again from how I had seen him in the desert, fair and well groomed but also manly in a way he had not struck me as then, stood Yeshua, preaching.

So it seemed he had preceded us on the road, as if by design.

It's my brother, Yaqob said, and I saw the excitement he felt, and the strange power his brother still held over him.

We stopped there at the edge of the crowd. Yeshua's glance went to us as he spoke but he gave no sign that he knew us, and indeed I thought that perhaps he did not, for many years had passed since he had laid eyes on us. Despite the anger in me that he had turned us away, still I was drawn in by his words, and was amazed how he spoke to these people as if he was one of them, and knew their lives and what they were. It was clear as I listened that there was no madness in him as people said, since he smiled and showed patience and for every question had a ready response. And yet there was a sort of devil in him, for though he smiled, still he was contrary, and though he was wise in his manner, still his words, as Gioras had said, often appeared to make little sense. He told the story of a Samaritan who helped a Judean along the Jericho road, but his meaning was uncertain, for some were angry that he praised a Samaritan and others could not believe him and others still were merely amused at the Judean's humiliation. For each of these he had a word and yet none of them did he answer clearly, instead merely posing another riddle or turning the questioner on himself.

There was one man who said, Better to strike the Samaritan dead than take his help, at which there was laughter. But Yeshua answered, You would take from your enemy his land or his house or his goods but not his good will, which it costs him much more to give. And it was clear the man could not refute Yeshua's argument, though perhaps as much because of its convolution as its sense.

He did not look towards Yaqob and me again while he spoke. But when he had sent the crowd away he came to us immediately, and so showed he had known us from the start. Only the men by the boat remained then, though out of hearing now, and I understood they must be his acolytes, though they appeared the lowest sort of fishermen and menials.

I said to Yeshua, A Samaritan shows love for his enemy, and yet not a son for his mother.

If I love you, he said, it does not mean I do your bidding, nor should I leave the many who love me here for the few at home.

You shame me before strangers, I said.

There's no shame to you if you're blameless, but only to the one who rejects you, if he does so wrongly.

I said, Does he do so wrongly.

But he would not answer me.

I only know that I must leave behind my old life, he said, and embrace my new one.

Yaqob, who had stood by silently, asked him then, What is your new life if you must reject your brothers and sisters to have it.

But Yeshua said, Who are my brothers and sisters but those who love me and don't pursue me in the streets for fear I'm mad.

So he rebuked us, and out of pride I could not bring myself to correct him.

I have been in the streets since I was a child, he said, and you did not object. Why then do you wish to chase me from them now.

And he left us for the boats that were waiting for him at the lakeshore.

When the boats had pulled away and Yeshua had not so much as turned his head to look back at us, Yaqob said, Let us go home, and I saw how he had been hurt. I thought then of the sons that I had and not the one I had lost, and the comfort they might have been to me, and yet how often I had neglected them for the sake of the bastard one who only brought grief.

We must put your brother from our minds, I said.

So we might have done and forgotten him except that month by month then his infamy grew, until it seemed his name was on the lips of all the Galilee.

I often had cause in those days to think back on Tryphon, Yeshua's teacher, and his prediction that Yeshua would be a famous scholar. So it might have been, had I followed Tryphon's advice and not induced rebellion in my son. I could hardly remember now what it was I had tried to save him from in thwarting him from his natural path—the humiliation of his conception, I'd imagined, except all I had managed instead was to keep that thing always before him. For if I had simply left him to his abilities, he might have been a great philosopher like some of the Jews had become in Alexandria, and even the Greeks would have respected him then and none given much thought to his parentage, in that city where eunuchs and orphans and bastards were commonplace and where no one, if they had ability, was held back on that account. Instead, because I had blocked him, he had at every turn chosen the hardest path and the least respectable, so that upon the shame of his birth he had heaped up other shames and made himself conspicuous, where I had thought only to hide him away.

It seemed now from the reports I had of him that I had erred even to make him a Jew, for he appeared neither able to take to the thing nor to reject it. So I heard how he accepted pagans among his followers, and rejected circumcision and the law, yet still proclaimed the one God. All this, I thought, must come from the knowledge of his own bastardy and of his exclusion from God's assembly, such that he sought all means to make a place for the outcast and thus justify himself. Perhaps I would have served him better if when we had lived in Alexandria, where we were freer, I had simply offered him up to the pagan gods, for surely no pagan god was as cruel as our own, who so barred a man and all his generations from the assembly of his own people.

Because of his views, because he flouted the law on one hand and claimed to affirm it on the other, there was hardly a town around the lake where he had not brought down on himself the wrath of the leadership. But he continued to attract many followers among the ignorant and the outcast, who no one else would have anything to do with and who he was able to impress with the skills and tricks he had learned as a boy in Alexandria. Soon enough he had gained a reputation as a healer and even a worker of wonders, though I imagined he did little more than apply ointments and salves, which because they did not kill his patients, so made him seem much superior to the charlatans and thieves who passed for doctors in those parts. My son Shimon in Ammathus had cause to see him from time to time as he moved through the towns on the lake, and never witnessed him do more than preach his stories and perhaps give a packet of herbs for a fever. But still the tales of him were spread around, and grew more fantastical with each retelling.

In the end, I hardly knew what to make of all the reports I had of him, if he was merely bent on destruction or truly believed in the mission he followed and the message he hoped to impart. I had never known him, even as a child, to speak frivolously or without logic and cause, and so even now imagined, for all the contradictions people spoke of him, that there must be some deeper wisdom to what he did. Yet I could not believe that only the ignorant saw through to it when those of learning could not, for the fishermen followed him and the peasants and even the toll collectors, whom everyone shunned, yet the teachers did not, nor many of the elders in the various towns, nor even our handful of Pharisees, though Yeshua preached resurrection as they did and followed their teacher Hillel. Then always there were troubling accounts of him in which I could not sort rumour from truth, for as I knew that he broke certain laws that many called sacrosanct, so was I unsure what others he might break.

One of these accounts involved a certain man of influence from the town of Bersaba by the name of Chizkijah. This was a person, it was said, burdened both with an undistinguished family and a crippling deformity who nonetheless had been able to raise himself up and gain a position at court. In the early days he had been opposed to Yeshua's teachings on various grounds, but then by dint of listening to him over time he had gradually been won to him. In this way he came to be close to some of Yeshua's intimates and saw the ways in which Yeshua comported himself in private, outside the view of the crowds. He began to be troubled then by some of the things that he saw, for there was a young woman, as he claimed, whom Yeshua tried to bend from the will of her father and take to himself for his own pleasure. Those closest to Yeshua, because of their loyalty, would say nothing of this. But Chizkijah could not hold his tongue. When he was unable to get satisfaction from Yeshua's intimates, he began to enquire more broadly amongst Yeshua's other followers, to see if he only imagined impropriety or if others saw it. So, as I heard, many who had harboured concerns but had feared to voice them had them strengthened, until finally even the girl's father confirmed them, admitting the girl was pregnant and naming Yeshua as the culprit.

These charges, regardless of their truth, would have been harmful enough in themselves, and indeed Yeshua's followers had already begun to desert him on their account. But then it happened that all three of those who were at the core of the accusations against him, the girl, her father, and Chizkijah, mysteriously died, within a matter of weeks of each other. There were those who were quick to see the hand of evil in the thing, and to say it was Yeshua's own followers who were behind the deaths. I could hardly credit that Yeshua would have encouraged murder, or even that he had had any part in the pregnancy of the girl, who indeed was well known for her behaviour. Yet it was surely possible that some of Yeshua's followers had been overzealous on his account. The entire matter left an air of corruption and threat around Yeshua's ministry like the menace one associated with the Zealots in Jerusalem, who would stop at nothing to reach their ends.

In all this time I had not laid eyes on Yeshua again, after our meeting outside Kefar Nahum. In some sense I had ceased to think of him as my son, since everything I heard of him struck me as wholly foreign to the life that I lived now. Even Yaqob by now had resigned himself to his rejection of us, and no longer spoke of him, and in Notzerah I was not so much disdained on his account as held in sympathy, as if

I had lost him in some way, as one might lose a son to illness or war. So I might have forgotten him, and dismissed what I heard as the fabrication of his enemies or simply shut my ears to it, except that there was always that part of me that could not drop the fear I felt for him and the sense of a reckoning that must come, if not from the Lord, then from his own pride.

After the scandals that hit him on Chizkijah's account, Yeshua descended into increasing strangeness. It was only the most fanatical who remained attached to him now and the most destitute, with the least to lose, so that they seemed in danger of becoming like the cults one heard of, which practised the strangest rites and held their leaders as gods. Yeshua would hardly deign to enter a town any more, but only wandered the countryside with his ragged band of followers like some brigand overlord, eating roots and wild fruit for his supper and spending the nights in caves or in the open air. No doubt he thus hoped to emulate his old mentor Yohanan, except that people only saw in this the sign of a growing lunacy, and had confirmed for them the madness they had always suspected in him.

When the Jubilee was ushered in Yeshua told his disciples that all the old laws must be respected, that their land must be left fallow and any debts they were owed be forgiven. This would have beggared many of them, who relied for their very sustenance on the bit of land they had or who could not count on their own debts to be absolved as they absolved those of others. So he thinned the ranks of his following again, as if he sought to winnow it down to some sort of purity, with no taint of compromise. I thought often in those days of his teacher Artimidorus, and how he had spoken in riddles and contradictions so that anyone trailing behind him must either conform to every intricacy of his thought or lose his way. Likewise, Yeshua had set out on a path on which many had accompanied him at first, but at each difficult turn some had fallen away until he was left with only his handful.

Toward Passover I began to hear rumours that Yeshua planned a pilgrimage into Jerusalem to mark the Jubilee. I was dumbfounded, for until now he had taken all due care to avoid the place. His followers had always put this down to his beliefs, that he did not venerate the temple like other Jews, or simply that he hated the Judeans and could not bear to be subject to them. But they could not know what was surely the truth, that he dared not show his face there for fear of being exposed. Perhaps he imagined that he himself was redeemed through the Jubilee, though even the old laws, from what I knew, gave no quarter to a bastard in this respect. But my greater fear was this, that he acted, as always, in defiance. There seemed that part of him that forever fought against what he was, and would not be governed by it, as if his bastard self was some second entity in him that he must rise over and suppress. I remembered the days we had spent in Jerusalem on our way to Galilee years before and the insults my own family had paid him then, and thought that these were the grudges he had carried all his life and that would not leave him, so that he sought always the means for their redress.

At Notzerah, a good part of the town had enlisted for the Passover pilgrimage, and indeed of my family alone, when every child and spouse's cousin had been counted, we made a battalion, and I the one who was looked to, to lead us. For Yeshua's sake, when I heard of his own pilgrimage, I considered keeping instead to my home, so that I might not be in the city to bring any shame to him, or to receive it. But I told myself there were too many who depended on me, and too little chance, from the hundreds of thousands who would be in the city then, that I should encounter him. What was truer, however, was that there was that part of me that couldn't bear the thought of him in the city without me, unprotected and at the mercy of my sin.

We were many weeks in preparation for the journey, sewing our tents and baking our bread and cakes and laying in our meat. Because of the work, I could in some measure keep at bay my fear on Yeshua's account, though every day some new scene presented itself to my mind's eye until every stone of the city accused him and every man he passed said, Is that not the bastard of Miryam. I considered that I might go to him to try to dissuade him from the journey, except that I knew I would thus only seem to oppose him again, and so would confirm him in exactly the thing I wished to discourage him from. The fact was that I was powerless over him, now as always, though whether because of his will or because I had never truly entered his thoughts or followed the workings of his mind, I could no longer say. I thought of the wonders that were spoken of him, and that I dismissed—who was to say if there wasn't more truth to them than I knew, for even when he was a child I had seen the power that came off him, and that had surpassed my understanding. And this was the thing that most pained me and confounded me, how that power had been thwarted by his birth and turned away from the greatness that might have been his due, even while it seemed his very birth that marked him and set him apart and made him in every way the thing that he was.

Those of us who made the Passover journey from Notzerah appeared a rabble as we set out, enough to fill a score of tents and more, though soon enough we came upon other companies that were larger still, so that it seemed all of Galilee had taken to the road. In the hope of making better time we chose to go down by way of Caesarea and the coast rather than by the Jordan, along the highway the Romans had built. But even here the traffic was thick, since there were not only the pilgrims to contend with but also the troops travelling down to Jerusalem from Caesarea because of the threat of disturbances, and who, when they marched by in their squadrons, would beat us back from the road so that they might pass freely.

In this way, however, I saw the sea, which I had not laid eyes on since I had travelled up from Egypt many years before. I thought it would lift my heart to see it again, but I could only think of how wondrous my first vision of it had been and the possibilities I had imagined at the time that had not come to pass. It surprised me that I could look back with fondness on those days, yoked as I was then to a man I did not love and burdened with a bastard child and setting out for I knew not where. Now I had all my children around me but that bastard one, and my grandchildren, and people who respected me, yet I felt a hollowness despite myself, as if I had missed some great mystery or chance.

On the fourth day we rose up from Lydda to Jerusalem, reaching the city at nightfall. There were many soldiers along the road there, asking the business of all those they did not like the look of and considerably slowing our progress, since the way was already crowded with pilgrims. Then when we reached the gates we saw that we would not be allowed to enter the city but must go at once to the camps the soldiers had marked out for us beneath the walls. The air had turned cold with our ascent and as we were setting out our tents, in the scant half-acre of ground that was all those of us from Notzerah had been allotted, it began to snow. I remembered the snowfalls I had seen in the city as a child, though rarely at this time of year, and how quiet the streets had become then, as if they slept. But in the fields there, all of us crowded together and the ground quickly turning to mud, it was only the cold that impressed itself on us, a chill that sank into our bones, since in the work of preparing our beds before the snow overwhelmed us, we had hardly had time to so much as build a fire.

To the surprise of everyone, the snow continued through the night. By morning it had covered the fields and weighed down the cloth of our tents, and still continued to fall so heavy and thick that the very air seemed a wall to pass through. We were able to enter the city now but the place had come to a standstill, for even there the snow had not melted away as was normally the case but had stayed an arm deep on the ground. People had to dig furrows through it in order to pass along the streets, and at the temple, we heard, it took an army of Levites to keep the courtyards clear. Despite the cold, however, people were enlivened, so that it seemed no one gave any thought to work and the festival would begin from that day. Only the soldiers looked unaffected, standing guard so unmoving on the ramparts that the snow piled up on their shoulders, their Roman pride staying them from shaking it free.

It was not until evening that the snow finally tapered off and then stopped. By then, however, the mood of festivity had been quashed, for there had been an incident at the Sheep Gate where the lambs for the Passover sacrifice were being sold. Because it was the prescribed day, there were many thousands who had been pressing in at the market there, including my son Yaqob. But the snow had hampered everyone's movements and the sales had gone slowly, so that as night came on there were many who began to panic because they had not yet had the chance to purchase their lamb. Finally a disturbance broke out, and the soldiers keeping watch over the place did not waste any time, but quickly went in with their swords and their clubs, and so killed a man. There would surely have been a riot then had not the soldiers been thick on the ground, and had not the Jews already experienced the savagery of the present procurator, who had always quelled every disturbance in the most brutal manner. So no one wished to begin what would surely have been a bloodbath, and the crowd dispersed and went home, though many were forced to leave without the chance of acquiring their lamb.

The following day there were soldiers on every corner and all the snow that had remained in the streets had been carted away, to prevent any impediments to their movements. At the temple they lined the roof of the colonnade around the entire temple mount and at the fortress, which flanked the mount to the north, they stood watch at every tower, so that should any have had thoughts of revenge for the previous day, they must surely have seen the folly of them. At midday the procurator, who always came down from Caesarea during the festivals so that he might personally safeguard the peace, had himself carried through the city like a great monarch to remind us of Rome's dominion, with slaves going before him to lay purpled cloth on the pavement so that even the air that his litter passed over should not bear so much as the scent of the muddied streets. Thus the festive mood of the previous day seemed the remotest memory and we felt the sword hanging over us, fearing that some disturbance would plunge us all into bloodshed. Even in the fields where we had pitched our tents, the soldiers stood watch, and as the snow melted away and the earth turned to muck again, it seemed we occupied some vast prisoners' camp, all of us dirtied and cold and despondent, though we had come to worship.

To avoid further trouble, allowance needed to be made for the many of us who had not been able to purchase our lamb on the appointed day. The temple officials, with the consent of the Romans, arranged for lambs that were deemed to have been purchased on the proper day to be distributed from the temple basilica, in exchange for a donation to the temple treasury. This time I undertook to accompany Yaqob to make our purchase to ensure he did not come away empty-handed again, and so fought my way with him through the huge crowds that had flocked to the basilica, and which had made of it a great market. It was there as we waited that I overheard talk among some of the women nearby of a wonder-worker who had come to the city. They joked about the man and about the stories that were spread of him, that he had built a temple entirely of snow and that he had raised from the dead the man who had been killed by the Romans the day before. Yet it was exactly in these exaggerations that I recognized Yeshua. I was surprised at the anger that rose in me at the note of contempt in their voices, though it was not as sharp as my fear. Already Yeshua had found the way to call attention to himself, though only, it seemed, to make himself a laughingstock. I was glad that the women had not named him, and so that Yaqob had not heard his brother mocked.

Because of the numbers that were in the city, I thought it might easily happen that our paths would not cross. I went about my business and prepared for the feast, and tried to put him from my mind. Then the following day I was in the Lower City with my sons Yihuda and Ioses so that they might pay their respects to one of their father's sisters who lived there. As we were passing the gates that led up to the temple I saw a man coming towards us, nearly in rags, with a motley band of some dozen or so following behind. The street was crowded then with those going up to the temple or simply passing by, but people instinctively stood aside for the man, no doubt because of his appearance, all skin and bone the way he was and barefoot and in his rags, though he came up the street as if he was king of it.

It took a moment before I realized it was Yeshua. I could hardly believe what had become of him. I stood there in his path and did not know what action to take, since it would have been shameful to turn away, yet I was afraid to make known that this was my son, for fear that someone who knew me would then know what he was.

It was Ioses again, however, who said, as he had at Yohanan's camp, It is our brother. This time I did not have it in me to dissuade him. So we stood there in the middle of the street as Yeshua came on, and he could not help but see us despite the crowds.

It was not until he was quite near that he looked at us directly. I thought then that he might simply feign that he did not know us and pass us by, and so spare embarrassment to us all. But to my amazement he came right up to us and, turning to the group who was following him, said, This is my mother and these are my brothers, as though only a matter of days had passed since he had last seen us. Then he embraced his brothers and took my hand in both of his and brought it to his lips, which in all his life he had not done.

I had no idea what to make of this and was left in confusion there in the street. But then his meaning grew clear, which I saw now was the purest self-destruction, for he had wished to announce to the crowd exactly the thing I had wished to hide for his sake, which was his parentage.

He had moved on with his ragged band to the gates that led up to the temple courts. I remembered how he had gone to the temple as a child and the trouble he had made for himself then, though without knowing the danger he was in, being a bastard. Now he knew, and still he put himself forward. Surely if the word went out of what he was, he might be arrested or worse. Yet it seemed this was the very thing that he dared—to be discovered.

Since I did not know what else to do, I continued with my sons to the house of their aunt. We had hardly settled ourselves there, however, before one of the wives I had known when I had lived with Yehoceph's brothers in Bet Lehem, and who was also visiting for the feast, came in from the streets. Finding me there, she smiled with all the malice she had held for me many years before and asked if my eldest son had come for the festival as well. So I knew that already the rumour of Yeshua had spread.

They say he is a famous wonder-worker, the woman said, trying to shame me in front of my sons, which shows even the lowest can make their way.

I would have answered her then with the venom she deserved but, for Yeshua's sake, held my tongue. I could not bear to stay on there, however, and told my sons we would take our leave, which left them in confusion, for in all these years I had never made clear to them what set Yeshua apart or what enmity I had with their father's family, or indeed my own.

As we were passing beneath the temple mount again we heard rumours in the street that there had been a disturbance in the temple courts. It was impossible to get at the truth of the thing, for some said a man had been killed and others that there had been only arrests and still others that only the temple guards had been involved and not the Romans, since it was merely that a pagan had made his way past the fence. The gates up to the courts had been closed by that point to prevent any further coming or going and so we could not make our way up to get further news. But then one of those we spoke to mentioned the wonder-worker of Galilee as among those arrested, and another confirmed this, and I knew that the worst had happened.

We returned immediately then to our tents, so that I might speak to Yaqob. He wasted no time in questioning me as to circumstance, but said we must go at once to the Roman fortress to find the thing out for certain. The streets were thick with those making their purchases for the Passover meal and even in the alleys and side streets we had to fight our way, nor did the soldiers help our progress, standing squarely in the middle of every intersection to make their presence known. Then when we reached the fortress we were not allowed so much as to mount the steps to the gate, held back by the line of soldiers who stood watch there. When we tried to question them we discovered they spoke neither Hebrew nor Aramaic, and so I needed to make my way with them in Greek, which by now was almost lost to me.

I have come to learn if my son is arrested, I said.

But they said they knew nothing of any arrest, and that perhaps he had been taken in by way of the entrance off the temple courts.

The gates up to the temple had been opened again. There was a great deal of activity in the courts, with many thousands praying or milling about while the Levites prepared the ground for the sacrifices the following day, setting out barricades to divide the crowd. But there was no sign of the disturbance that had gone on. It seemed hopeless then that we who were nothing should get to the bottom of it, when it was already forgotten.

We made our way to the fortress end of the courts and there indeed found a passage into the fortress beneath the colonnade, but it was also heavily guarded. Here the guards were Samaritans, who were the procurator's special corps.

I said to them in Hebrew, My son has been brought here, but they pretended not to understand.

Yaqob brandished some coins then, and spoke in Aramaic.

We wish only to learn the charges against him, so we might defend him.

But the Samaritans merely took offence at the coins and said that several Jews had been arrested that day, cutpurses and such, and they could not be expected to know one from the other.

I regretted now that we had shown any arrogance in our approach to them, for we were at their mercy.

We beg you, I said.

But they claimed they could not be of any service to us, and that at any rate there would be no trials until after the festival, so we might try our fortunes then.

We did not know what other options lay open to us. I still had my family in the city, but it chafed me to turn to them—I had seen them only twice since returning from Egypt, after the reception I had had from them then, and not at all since my mother's death a few years before. But I knew that one of my brothers, indeed Yeshua's namesake, had followed in my father's place and found work as a clerk for the Roman administration, and so might know the way to be of help to us. Yaqob and I went to his house and found him with his family preparing for Passover.

My son Yeshua has been arrested, I said.

He did not turn me away but told me what he could, though little that gave me cause for hope. He said that as the Romans were scrupulous in their adherence to their own laws, they seldom punished unjustly, but also that the present procurator could not be trusted. In any event, in the case of a public disturbance the procurator's power was absolute, since by Roman law any hint of insurrection was punishable by summary death.

My son is not a rebel, I said, nor has he ever counselled violence.

Yet by your own account you have hardly spoken in many years, my brother said. How then can you know what he counsels.

But it seemed he merely sought an excuse to condemn him.

I did not come to be accused but only to seek your help, I said.

He could no longer hide his enmity.

You ruined our family once, he said, and now you wish to ruin it again, by having me risk my position for a rabble-rouser and a bastard.

I regretted now that I had ever come to him, or that I had let Yaqob accompany me, to hear such things.

I said to my brother, You are truly your father's son, for he also sold me when I most needed him.

And I left his house.

In all this time I had not dared to look at Yaqob. Now, in the growing dark of the street, I said to him, Do you still wish to help your brother, now that you know the truth.

But he said, I have always known it.

I hardly knew how to answer him.

How could you.

From the streets of Alexandria, he said.

I was silenced by this. I had given Yaqob so little credit, over the years, but had only taken him for granted.

Yet you never loved him less, I said.

It did not seem a reason to.

I was glad of the dark now, which hid my tears. I asked him if his brothers also knew, but he said he had always found the way to protect them.

You did right to love him, I said finally.

And I felt comforted then, and less alone, that his love was not different from mine.

I could not bear to return to our tents, to sit there uselessly. I told Yaqob to go to the others and say we made progress, to comfort them, and then to join me again at the fortress.

I made my way to the fortress through the twilight traffic. The sun had warmed the city during the day, but with nightfall the air had turned cold again, here and there a patch of snow that had lingered in some shadow or cranny giving off its particular smell. At the fortress nothing had changed except that some of the soldiers had built up a fire on the pavement at the base of the fortress steps. I put myself close to them, to warm myself and to hear their gossip, in case anything touching on Yeshua should fall from their lips. But I could not follow the dialect they spoke amongst themselves, which hardly resembled any Greek I knew.

It was some time before I noticed another woman in the shadows at the far end of the steps. It seemed modesty or fear kept her standing alone there far from the soldiers, but finally the cold drove her closer to the fire. Her face was hidden by her shawl so it took a moment before I recognized her—it was the girl who had come to the gate to refuse me when I had gone looking for my son at Kefar Nahum.

I went to her and said, I am Yeshua's mother, and she instantly broke into tears.

So grateful was I to find a stranger who shared sympathy with me that I forgot all resentment towards her and embraced her, also falling to tears. For a moment we stood there unable to speak for emotion.

Do you have any news of him, I said finally, but it came out she knew no more than I did.

Her name was Miryam, like my own. She and some others had been preparing for the feast at a room in the Upper City when the word had come of Yeshua's arrest. All of those there had fled then except she and another woman, Shelomah, the two of them waiting for some further word. When after some hours no news had come, they had made their way back to their camp, only to find, however, that their own people had been removed from it and had left no trace of their whereabouts. So Miryam had come to the fortress, while Shelomah had gone to search the neighbouring camps for any of their group.

Even to say as much as this left her in tears again, for she feared the lot of them had been arrested. But when I pressed her it grew clear that some hundred or more had accompanied Yeshua to Jerusalem, whereas only a dozen, as I had seen, had gone with him to the temple. So we had reason to believe that some of them would be discovered still, and would have further news for us.

It was growing late now. Miryam was upset that she had heard nothing yet from Shelomah, while I wondered that Yaqob had not come to join me. We went over to the Sheep Gate, which was the gate nearest the fortress, to see if we might catch sight of them, but learned from the guards that all the entrances to the city had been closed for the night. So it seemed we were left to our own resources, and we returned to our place at the fortress steps and waited there by the soldiers and their fire. One of the soldiers, taking pity on us, asked us in halting Aramaic what our business was and assured us that if my son was innocent, he would be set free. But I was no longer certain that he was innocent or what that might mean, for by Jewish law he was not innocent but a bastard, and by Roman law was perhaps less innocent still, for he was someone who spoke his mind and accepted the yoke of no one.

I said to Miryam, I will watch while you sleep.

But she broke into tears again, and said how it had troubled her to turn me away at Kefar Nahum, and how I had seemed a woman of stature. And I saw that she did not say these things to flatter me but meant them sincerely.

I took no harm in what you did, I said, but was only troubled on account of my son.

So grateful was she at this forgiveness that she at once opened her heart to me, and sought to assure me of Yeshua's virtues and of the great things he had done. And I saw how besotted she was with him and how she worshipped him, so that she could not see him clearly. She spoke of the deed he had worked here in the city, that the women at the temple basilica had joked of—it turned out it involved a cousin of one of his followers who, in Miryam's telling of the thing, had been brought back from the very grave by Yeshua's tending to him. So I gathered she was a simple girl of Galilee, with the credulity of Galileans. Yet it was true that when she spoke of my son the wonder I heard in her voice was not so different from what I myself had felt, that sense of a doorway Yeshua stood before, to some new understanding. Except that she had passed through it, and saw things in a different light, and who was I to say that the miracle she had witnessed had not occurred, for those who had eyes to see it.

So we spoke off and on into the night, sitting there at the base of the fortress steps just outside the light of the fire, and in the end I took some comfort from her. And I thought of Yeshua's life, and where it had brought him to, but though I turned every detail of it over in my mind, I could not see the sense of it or why someone so gifted by God should be so punished by him. I thought to speak to Miryam of these things but she was only a child, nor would I risk shattering her innocence by revealing to her the truth of what he was. And yet I might have wished to unburden myself then, and say every last thing as I knew it, and so perhaps for a moment lift the stone I had carried every day since Yeshua's conception.

We sat there through the night, and kept up our vigil, until the guards changed to ones who knew nothing of us and bid us move, handling us roughly when we did not at once obey. Thus we were at a loss again as to our actions, and the sun was just rising over the walls, and it was the morning of Passover.

BOOK IV

SIMON OF GERGESA

LOOKING AFTER THE SHEEP in the back pasture I'd see his followers there on that hill, hundreds of them there were, and I'd say to Moriah, my brother Huram's wife, "I've got half a mind to join him myself." That was before the trouble between us, so she'd laugh. What I wouldn't do then to get a laugh out of her, and she needed it too, seeing how Huram was. I used to say to her, "Huram thinks it's like money, he's saving it up. One of these days he's going to have a laugh they'll hear clear across the lake. Halfway to Damascus they'll hear it." And she'd laugh again.

Our farm was just above Gergesa, in the hills over the lake, so we had a good view of things. You wouldn't think you could see much, all the way to the other shore like that, but you'd be surprised. Most days I could pick him out in an instant, the way he stood in the middle of the crowd like a stone that had been dropped in the water. And I'd say to Moriah, "He's got his sheep on his hill there, and I've got mine." Or sometimes he'd take them to the beach and go off in the shoals a bit to preach at them, and I'd swear then he was standing right on the lake, which some said he could do. I'd heard it told that once he'd hiked himself straight across the water from Capernaum to Tarichea, just walking along like that as if it was nothing.

I won't say I didn't actually wonder sometimes even at first what it might be like to join up with him and see the world, travelling around the way he did. Because in all my life I'd been only to Hippus and Gergesa and once to Gadara, and I was sick of the boys I saw every week at Baal-Sarga, our village, which was just a couple of stones thrown together, though Sargon the Great himself had chosen the spot where it stood when he'd come through to conquer the Hebrews. But there was the farm to think about—more than thirty sheep we had then and five cattle and three pigs, and almonds and olives and grapes and a bit of barley and wheat, and our parents dead. And then there was Moriah.

Huram had got her at the market in Raphanah. A whole milking cow he'd paid for her, so you'd see he must have been taken with her, if you knew Huram. But then he got her home and treated her worse than the cow he'd traded her for. It was only sons he was after—he could have had himself any girl in Baal-Sarga or even Gergesa, he was rich enough for it, but he didn't want the trouble with the families or to have to go begging. So he got a slave and said when she gave him a son he'd set her free. Not for her sake, you understand—it was only that he didn't want it said that his sons were the children of a slave.

She wasn't much more than a child herself when she came to us, like I was, so of course I was the one who she turned to. That was how we both looked at it then—there was Huram, and then there were the two of us. I'd take her around to my favourite spots on the farm, and show her the flowers that came up, and throw almonds to her from the tops of the trees. Then there were all my secret places, that I'd never told Huram about—the caves by the lake, for instance, which the brigands must have used before the Romans chased them off but which were empty now except for one that I found by accident, when my hand went through the wall that closed it up. I could hardly believe what I found there—a whole family had been buried there, to judge by the bones, all laid out with their bracelets and charms to be ready for the other side. But when I took Moriah to see them, she got a terrible fright and said it was no place for us, and straightaway she had me kill a bird for her and did her prayers and chants for those gods of hers I'd never heard of.

Not even Moriah herself could have told you where she'd come from. Before Raphanah she'd been in Damascus, where she'd had a baby though they'd killed it, since it was a girl, and before that, when she'd been small, she remembered going in a cart for quite a while and then a boat. But she hadn't known the names of places, and no one had bothered to tell her, and so one was fairly much like another. The way she reckoned things she'd done well for herself to get Huram, and I could see it was true she hadn't had much of a life before him. But still it made me boil, the way he treated her. He'd have her make us supper and then give her just our leavings for her own, which he'd scrape into the same bucket we used for our pigs, to remind her who she was. Of course I'd sneak things to her, even meat now and then, though it was a waste, because half the time she'd just burn it up for her strange gods.

When quite a while had gone by and Moriah wasn't pregnant yet, Huram began to take it out on her, beating her for every little thing and threatening to sell her off. So she'd come to me, not really crying, because she could take a lot, but just a bit sad the way she was, and I'd help her to laugh the thing out. It was around then that we started to watch for the holy man across the lake from the back pasture, to pass the time. It was also around then that Moriah began to come to me in my bed—Huram made me sleep in the stable, to keep an eye out for bandits—after Huram had thrown her out of his, which he didn't much like her in once he'd finished with her. She showed me things then, though I hardly knew what I was doing, and it got so all I thought about was her coming to me, though I was sure Huram would kill us both if he saw us.

After a while of this, Moriah was pregnant. I was young at the time but I wasn't a fool—I knew the baby was mine. So I said to Moriah, "I'll just tell Huram to give me my share of things and then we'll run off, the two of us." But Moriah, changed now, said, "Don't be an idiot." I imagined she was thinking Huram would come after us and slit our throats once he'd worked out what had happened, or maybe just that we'd be better off to wait and see if she had a son, so she could get her freedom. So I held my tongue. Moriah said, "We shouldn't see each other as much, in case he gets suspicious," and never came to my bed any more or out to the fields with me, and pretended to be a good wife. And I went along with this, believing everything would work out in the end.

It wasn't long, though, before I understood things weren't the same between us. Even if Huram wasn't around now she'd put me off, half the time treating me like a servant and saying "Don't be a child," if I tried to make her laugh. "It's just Simon," I wanted to say to her, so that things could be the way they'd been before. But I'd grown a little afraid of her now. Of course, things had changed between her and Huram as well—he didn't beat her any more, on account of the baby, and he let her set a place for herself at the table. But still it wasn't as if he ever had a kind word for her.

It was around this time that the holy man from across the lake—Jesus, his name was—started coming over to our side to see what he could make of us. I'd see his boats setting out, from Capernaum or Tarichea, or Magdala, as the Jews called it, and I'd know it wasn't fish he was after because he'd make straight for our shore. This was strange enough, for a Jew, to come out in search of us Syrians and Greeks. There were Jews at Gergesa, of course, and then there was the colony just down the beach, which had been there as long as anyone remembered and which we all just assumed was made up of Jews, though we never saw hide nor hair of them. But mostly Jesus went further down to the Gadarenes, who didn't normally have much use for the Jews, though I saw from the pasture that he got up quite a crowd whenever he was there.

Then once I looked out and saw that his boats had put up right beneath the farm. He and his men had set up a few tents and made a fire and were cooking up fish as if they were settling in for a long stay. Meanwhile they must have sent out their messengers because soon enough people started to wander in from the fields and from the villages nearby to hear what he had to say to them. There were dozens of them, coming all the way from Hippus and Gergesa, from the looks of it. And I asked myself, who were all these people to go listen to him when I was the one who'd been keeping an eye on him. So finally I closed the sheep off in one of the corrals, hoping Huram wouldn't notice, and hiked myself down the hill.

It turned out it was a feast down there, his men cooking up fish as if tomorrow wouldn't come and handing it around to every beggar who put a palm out. And in the middle of the crowd was Jesus, talking with people and asking their names and making sure they had something to eat. It was the first time I'd ever laid eyes on him from close up and it was a bit of a shock—he was wearing the cheapest kind of home-spun and just a bit of bark on his feet for shoes, which made him look like someone who had just crawled out of the woods. Then he was long-haired and bearded the way most of the Jews were, that gave you the sense it was all work and seriousness with them. But soon enough I saw he wasn't like that. There was one man in the crowd, from Hippus, who said to him, "What do I have to do to follow you?" And Jesus said back, "Go home and sell everything you've got and give the money to the poor, then you'll be ready." Everyone in the crowd broke out laughing at that, and you should have seen the look on the fellow's face, since you could tell from his clothes he was fairly well off.

Now it happened at the time that there was a madman living in one of the caves along the shore there, because he'd been thrown out from the colony down the beach. That colony—the Sons of Light or some nonsense, they called it—was all madmen, from what I could tell, but as I said they kept to themselves, and had walls all around their place, so nobody knew what exactly they did. They had some fields near the lake, and raised some sheep, but from the looks of it they hardly had time for their work, since they were always washing themselves or saying their prayers. All in all, there were maybe fifty of them, though even if some new beggar should wander in one day to join them, you could be sure that another day they'd be turning someone out, for breaking some rule of theirs that only they could understand.

It seemed one of these men they'd turned out didn't take it well, and every night when the rest of them came in from the fields he'd be waiting at the gate howling to be let in again. But the others weren't having it. By now the man was looking rough, just eating roots and so on and living in a cave the way he was. Sure enough, though, when he smelled our fish he came right over. People made a path for him fairly quickly, seeing the devil that was in him. But Jesus, when he saw him, didn't move. "Would you like something to eat?" he said, and then made him sit down right next to him. And the fellow went along with him, since it looked like the first time in a while someone had treated him with a little respect.

Everyone had gone quiet now, to see what would happen next. So after the man had had his bit of fish, which he ate right down, Jesus said to him, "What's the matter with you?" just like that. And the fellow started sobbing then, and told Jesus that the Sons of Light had turned him out because they'd caught him talking with a girl when he was in the fields.

We all thought Jesus would side with the colony, because they were Jews. But he said, "Was she pretty, at least?" and everyone laughed. Then he went on and asked how it could be wrong for one person to talk to another one, and what they could be thinking in that colony to turn someone out the way they had and to close themselves off as if it was the end of the world. "If you had a lamb," he said, "and it got out of the pen, would you let the wolves have it to teach it a lesson or would you bring it back?" And he made sense, when he put the thing that way. In the end, even the fellow himself could see he'd been lucky to get away from that lot. "Go out and find yourself a wife and forget them," Jesus said to him. And to look at the man now, calmed down after his cry, you'd think he was cured. Jesus took him down to the lake then and made him wash a bit, then gave him his own coat to wear and said to the crowd, "Who has a daughter for our man here?" And everyone laughed again.

I would have stayed on then, but his talk about sheep had started me worrying about my own. Sure enough, when I got back to the farm Huram was standing there at the corral looking fit to be tied. Without a word, he gave me the back of his hand.

"You're not a boy any more," he said, "to go playing whenever you want." And he told me I'd be spending the night with the sheep on the hill, and any one missing was out of my own inheritance.

You'd have had to know Huram to understand this was the worst thing he could think of. Huram believed there were bandits behind every bush, ever since they'd killed our parents, even though it was years now since anyone in our parts had been attacked. So he must have supposed I'd be lucky to survive the night myself, let alone save the sheep. But he was ready to make that much of a lesson of the thing, to risk even the sheep, not to mention my life. For my part, I was more frightened of the wolves, who in a night could pick off half your flock. That would be my inheritance gone—ten sheep was what I was entitled to when I married, and two cattle and one pig.

I thought Huram was a little disappointed to come out the next morning and find me alive and the sheep all accounted for. But I'd had some time to think out there, under the stars. And what I'd thought was, ten sheep and two cattle and a pig. That was all I was worth in the world, what a wolf or a thief could take from me in an hour. I got to thinking about Jesus then, and what he'd said to the rich man from Hippus, and it didn't seem such a joke any more. What was the point, to care so much about your little bit of this or that, when it was nothing. When Moriah and I had been getting along, it wouldn't have mattered if I hadn't owned my own shirt, just to be with her. So what were ten sheep, if I didn't have her.

I couldn't have said I'd worked all this out in my head but it was how I was feeling then, with Huram the way he was and Moriah so changed. And I stole down to the lake to see Jesus again a few more times, and more and more the things he said made sense to me, how it was always the lowest ones who got the worst of matters when they didn't deserve it and how people never missed a chance to put on airs and lord it over anyone who was weaker than they were. A lot of times what he said went against what you might have thought was the case, or what you'd been taught. But he had a way of leading us towards a thing as if we were ones who'd found it ourselves, taking us this way and that until finally we turned a corner and the answer sat in front of us as plain as stone.

Once he picked a man out of the crowd and asked him what god he worshipped.

"Augustus," the fellow said, because we'd had to pray to him ever since he'd died and they'd made him a god.

"Good, he was very powerful," Jesus said.

But then he started discussing with us and asked what Augustus had done, precisely. And people said he was the king of the world, and built cities all around, and when he died, or so people claimed, a cloud came down from the heavens to take him up with it. And Jesus nodded at all this as if he was considering. Then he asked, "How many of you, if you had the tools, could put up a building?" And everyone said that they could. So he went on like that, and asked if we could fight a war if we had the weapons, or make a road if we had the stones, or do nearly all the things that Augustus had done. But then he said, "Now how many of you could make a bird?" and we were all stopped by that. "How many of you could make a flower or a tree? Could even Augustus do it? Could even Augustus, out of nothing, make as much as a grain of sand?"

It was clear from this, though he wouldn't say it because it was treason, that Augustus wasn't much of a god in his opinion. And everyone was happy to hear it, because none of us had ever taken to him. But Jesus went on, "Think of the strongest god you've ever heard of, then think of one a thousand times stronger than that, and even that one wouldn't be a thousandth as strong as the real god I'm going to tell you about." We all just assumed he was talking about the god of the Jews, since that was how they always made him out, as the strongest—Yahweh, I'd heard his name was, though the Jews weren't allowed even so much as to say it. But Jesus asked who had told us there was a god for the Jews and a different one for the Syrians or the Greeks. Where was the logic in that, he said, when then they'd be battling all the time in heaven and it'd be even worse than it was on earth. And what he meant to say, and it made a great deal of sense, was that there was just the one god who ruled, the way our Hadad was always said to before the Romans came.

Soon enough it happened that Moriah had her baby, and sure enough it was a boy. Naaman, Huram called him, after our father. True to his word, Huram took Moriah into town not long afterwards to get her papers seen to for her freedom. But instead of her coming back to me the way I'd hoped, she let me know at once that she had it in for me. "Let Simon tend the pigs," she said to Huram, which had been her job, "since I have the baby to look after." And it wasn't long before every little job that she could push off to me, she did, with the excuse of the baby. I had half a mind sometimes to take the boy and make away with him, seeing as he was mine, but Moriah was like a she-wolf around him, and never let him out of her sight.

Then once I overheard her say to Huram, "Your brother looks at me sometimes the way he shouldn't." Well, I felt fairly low then. But I thought I understood all of a sudden what was going on in Moriah's head—she just didn't want to lose another child. She knew Huram would kill her and the baby too if he knew the truth, so she wasn't taking any chances—she'd make Huram and me enemies so he wouldn't trust me, and then her secret would be safe. I should have been angry, but I'd got to thinking about some of the things Jesus taught, and how all her life Moriah had been just a slave and hadn't had anything and now she had a house and a husband and a son.

Huram didn't say a word to me about what Moriah had told him, but it was clear he believed her, because I wasn't allowed in the house any more. Just like that, he didn't give me a reason. For her part, Moriah didn't come out except once in a while to do the wash, and even then Huram made her keep her shawl on, so that it reached the point where I could hardly remember what she looked like. You'd have thought that by then I'd have put her out of my mind. But instead it was like a pain in me, the thought of her and of that baby hidden away in Huram's house. I could hardly believe that she'd ever come to my bed, that that was the same girl who I had to sneak a glimpse of now when she came out to the well.

The only relief I had from all this were those times I'd go down to the lake to see Jesus—it got so that was all I had to look forward to, having something to eat on the beach with the rest of the crowd and listening to Jesus's stories. For all the wondrous things you heard Jesus had done, it was mostly to tell us these stories that he'd stop by there, about rich men who'd made a ruin of their lives or poor ones who'd done even worse, or about farmers who knew what they were doing and others who didn't. And though I didn't understand everything he said to us, still it made me feel better just to listen to him. There was a place he liked to talk about, which he said we all could get to if we wanted, that he called his god's special kingdom, and it sounded grand the way he described it, because the common folk were in charge there, instead of the kings, and the people who didn't have anything were respected, but those who had it all couldn't even get in. The way he talked about the place you thought it had to be just around the bend, some hideout in the woods that he'd set up there with his people. But the thing was he would never give a straight answer about it, as if it was up to our own heads to work out what he meant. And I thought that might be the point, that it wasn't something he could lay out for us, either that or he was just pulling us along to keep us coming back. I, for one, was ready to follow—wherever his kingdom was, it was sounding a fair amount better to me than what I had on the farm.

Then sometimes I wondered if the place he meant wasn't right there in front of our eyes. Here was Jesus, who was clever enough to have been rich or some sort of leader if he'd wanted, but instead he'd set himself up on the side of the peasants, and dressed in his homespun and slept in the open and wasn't afraid to eat his food right under the sky with the rest of us. So wasn't he living just the way he described, speaking his mind to the rich but then instantly taking in people who no one else would have to do with. It was as if he himself was his own little special kingdom, doing things his own way there, which somehow seemed to work out for him even though it was the opposite of everyone else's. He'd always say to us, what was the point of worrying whether you had enough money or if your barns were full enough—and I couldn't help thinking of Huram—when if you'd just let things come to you, you'd see you got what you needed. And that seemed to be the case for him, because if ever we ran out of fish when he came by to see us then sure enough someone else would have brought along a deer they'd happened to catch or we would all throw in whatever we had, and no one would go hungry.

By then there was quite a group of us that came by fairly regularly, thirty or forty or so. Some of these were people I knew from the farms nearby or from Baal-Sarga, and I was always afraid that word would get back to Huram through them. But the odd thing was that no one seemed to talk about these meetings outside of them, as if they were a secret we shared. Other people started to look at them that way too—it wasn't long before the notion went around in Baal-Sarga that the Jesus people were no better than the Sons of Light in their little colony. Somehow the story of the madman Jesus had cured—who was long gone by then, probably back to his family on the other side of the lake—had been exaggerated beyond recognition, so that now the man had had a hundred demons in him and Jesus had moved them into some poor farmer's pigs, who straightaway had jumped into the lake. And all of this, to the ignorant peasants who were all you found in Baal-Sarga, showed that Jesus had it in for us, and was going to let loose all his Jewish devils on the countryside.

I knew Huram had heard these stories the same as everyone, though he never said anything about them. But I noticed he'd started to keep a closer eye on me all of a sudden, so that it got harder to steal down to the beach. He kept a watch over the lake now, to see what was going on there, and sure enough any time Jesus's boats set out for our side he'd be at me for one thing or another, to muck out the stables or fix the fences or water the sheep. I won't say it was Moriah who put him on to me—maybe it was just that he'd heard something in town. But still it got to me, how the two of them, which was how I saw them now, thought they'd take away the one thing I had left. The truth was it surprised me how disappointed I felt each time I missed out on one of Jesus's meetings, though maybe it was just that I couldn't fool myself then about how bad things were for me or about some special place I was going to that would make them better.

Then one day I looked out across to Capernaum and saw people had started to camp out on the hill above the town as if they were getting ready for a journey. A while later, I saw Jesus's boats set out for our side of the lake, but headed down towards the Gadarenes, so Huram didn't pay them any mind. I went straight to my lookout, though, from where I saw what Huram couldn't, that Jesus didn't stop for the day with the Gadarenes the way he usually did but kept coming up the coast. Fairly soon I was able to piece out what he was doing—he was calling in for a visit at all the places he usually came to on our side of the lake.

It was getting on to sunset before he reached the farm. I'd already been late getting the sheep out, and should have been bringing them back in by then. But I had to hear what Jesus had come over to tell us, and left the sheep in the pasture without even so much as penning them in. I was scraped and bruised by the time I got down the hill but I managed to get there just as Jesus and his men were putting up their boats.

He'd come to tell us he was going to Jerusalem for a feast there, so we shouldn't wonder if we didn't see him. He'd put the thing lightly but there was a tone to his voice as if he wasn't sure he'd be coming back. Someone asked if we could go with him, more as a joke than anything, since none of us were Jews. But Jesus said we could join him in his boats that very instant if we wanted.

When he'd gone I felt a bit miserable, because of that tone in his voice. Then I got back up the hill and found out one of the sheep had fallen in a gully and broken its leg. There was no way to hide the thing from Huram—the poor beast was crying so much when I brought it back to the stable that he came right out.

He hardly wasted a breath then but took the thing out of my hands and smashed its head on a rock.

"That's two from your own share," he said, "to make up for the wool I would have had from this one before you got it."

Something broke in me then.

"I won't be having my share," I told him, not even knowing myself I was going to say this, "because I'm leaving to join up with Jesus the Jew."

For a moment he looked fit to be tied, and that was worth a lot to me, because it seemed the first time I'd ever had anything over him. But then a look of disgust crossed his face, as if he'd known all along it would come to this.

"Suit yourself," he said, then just turned and went back into the house.

For the next little while it felt as if a yoke had been lifted off me, so that it seemed it had been my plan all along to go off with Jesus, and I'd just needed to work up the courage. And the more I got to thinking about the thing, the more it seemed right. Who needed Huram, who I'd been just a burden to since our parents had died, or Moriah, or to see my own son grow up who I couldn't call my own—at least with Jesus I'd learn a few things and see a bit of the world, and no one could tell me my business.

But then when Huram didn't come out to me that night to change my mind, and not Moriah either, who I was hoping he'd tell, it started to look as if I wasn't quite as sure about the thing as I'd thought, and that maybe I'd said it just to be talked out of it, or to find a way to make Moriah think of me again. So I didn't sleep the whole night but lay there in my bed crying like a child, and thinking how I'd miss the flowers on the almond trees, and looking out over the lake, and Moriah, and how I might never see these things again. But I'd given my word, so there was nothing for it. And when the sun came up I took what money I had from the little I'd got out of Huram over the years, and I put on my coat, and then I set out on the road that led down towards the lake from Baal-Sarga.

The trip from Baal-Sarga to Gadara, which I'd made once as a boy with my brother, was just a day's journey, and that on a road so steep that the merchants practically had to carry their carts on their backs. So seeing that Capernaum was just across the lake and that I could have thrown a stone to it, I didn't imagine I'd have any trouble getting there before dark. What I found out, though, was that you could hardly step out of your door in those parts without crossing some border or other, or without some other business or trouble stopping you up.

I was fine until I got to Gergesa, just whistling along in the sun like that, feeling fairly pleased with myself now that I'd actually set out. But then I made the mistake of going into the town, to get some food, I thought, and to see what was what. I wasn't a minute past the gates, though, when some thug came up to me and made a grab for my purse. I managed to hit him off but he got a blow in himself and left me with a bloodied nose, and not a single soul stopped to give me a hand or say a word to me, just passing me by as if I was the one who was a thief. I had a mind then just to take myself right back home again, and it was only my pride that stopped me from doing it.

I got a cake in the market, but in an instant a fellow came up to me—and not very handsome he was, scrawny and dark and with a nose like someone had bashed it in for him with a hatchet—and he said, how would I like a game, and showed me his dice. Now, like I've said, I was young but no fool—I knew his sort. So I lied and told him I'd just spent my last cent, smiling and playing the dullard. He looked me up and down and then he grinned at me with his rotten teeth, nodding his head to show he'd seen through my dodge.

"Where're you going?" he said, so I told him about Jesus, and said I was going over to Capernaum to join up with him.

The fellow made as if he'd never heard of the man and asked all sorts of questions about him, what kind of person was he and what he did, which to be truthful I found a bit difficult to answer. Before I knew it, maybe just to impress the fellow, I started telling him things I'd only heard second hand as if I'd seen them with my own eyes, how he cured lepers and walked on water and the like. But the fellow just nodded and rubbed his chin as if he believed me, then offered to come along with me to see the man for himself, just like that.

I'd never been one to mind company, but when we got outside town and had to cross the border there into Gaulinitis I started wondering if this fellow I'd hooked up with—Jerubal, his name was—might cause me some trouble with the guards. Instead, they took one look at us and let us through without even a toll, though the people ahead of us had had to hand over half their purse. Jerubal winked at me and said, "Don't worry, they'll get their cut." And it didn't take long before I saw what he was getting at, because he had a little game going that brought him in a good penny. He'd stop along the road, and scratch out a gaming board somewhere, and then it never took long before a bit of a crowd started to gather. But here was the twist—I was his hook, because people would see me gambling there like one of the crowd and winning almost every time, and so they'd put their own money down. Then oddly enough they didn't win quite as often as I did, and Jerubal would start drawing in the coins.

I thought he managed the game with loaded dice but he said he'd be dead in an hour if that was the case, someone always spotted them. It was the board that counted, he said, every dip and swell and knowing how to play them, and then the players, they had to be played as well. He was a master at that, I had to hand it to him—he knew just when to let up to keep someone in the game, and when to push. I wasn't bad myself, it turned out—Jerubal said I had the perfect face, the kind people trusted, which was why he'd picked me out.

We didn't cover a lot of ground this way, and by nightfall we hadn't even got to Bethsaida. Jerubal had us put up at a village in the hills off the main road where the people knew him—even the children there were happy to see him, and he handed around some roasted almonds to them that we'd bought along the road. You'd have thought he was the most respectable man in the world, the way people treated him, bringing food out and laying down the mats for us, and the girls giggling behind their hands to be near him, even ugly the way he was. On his side, Jerubal was suddenly fine-mannered and polite, bending down before the elders and going off to the little hovel of a temple they had at the edge of the village to make a sacrifice. It was only after, when people started coming around with gifts for him to have their fortunes told, that I saw this was just another one of his games—they took him for some kind of wizard, though he wouldn't tell me how it was that he'd won them over. "It's like your friend Jesus," he said to me, "walking on water and the like," and I couldn't tell at first if he was fooling or not. But then he grinned at me and I saw it was his way of saying he hadn't exactly taken me at my word before when I'd told him about Jesus.

Jerubal wanted to stop in at Bethsaida the next day for a game but I convinced him to make straight for the Galilean border and into Capernaum, in the hope we'd catch Jesus before he'd gone. We reached the town with the sun at its height, a terrible stench of fish coming up from the harbour in the heat. But you could see people worked for a living there, hardly catching your eye in the street, just going on with their business. We tried to ask around for Jesus but it took a while to make sense of people's accents, and we couldn't get by in Greek because there wasn't a person we met who spoke a word of it. Finally we ended up at what someone told us was the temple, though it looked plain as a barn, for all that the god of the Jews, as they said, was so great. Then the old man who looked after the place made it seem as if Jesus was a devil incarnate when we asked about him.

"Go ask his followers where to find him," was all he said, then more or less closed the door in our faces.

All this seemed fairly strange to us—we'd come there thinking to see a great wise man of the Jews and instead were being all but chased out of town just for asking about him. Then finally someone sent us to the house of a fisherman where Jesus was supposed to be staying. It wasn't much of a place, from the looks of it, windowless and with a rough wooden gate half fallen away, and then the woman who came to the gate, as homely as a stable door, couldn't make heads or ships of us when we tried to talk to her. "You go," she said, talking like a little child. "Next town. Gennesaret." Jerubal knew the place and said it wasn't far, and so we decided to try our luck, and set off.

By now it was getting clear that Jesus and his people had already started out and we'd missed them. I was a bit relieved about that at first—who was I, I'd got to thinking, to imagine I could join up with a man like him, when all I knew was barley and sheep. But then I remembered Huram, and how I'd left, and saw I didn't have much choice in the thing.

When we were a ways from the town, Jerubal stripped to nothing to cool himself in the lake. It happened that there was a village up the way and some girls at the shore doing the wash, and Jerubal decided to have a bit of a frolic, climbing up on a rock and wagging his backside at them. Wasn't it our luck, though, that their father came out and saw what was going on, and straightaway he started coming at us, picking stones up and flinging them as he went. We hardly knew what to make of him and we started to run, over the road and into the hills. But even then the fellow wouldn't let up, so that we were well up the hillside before we lost him, scrambling the whole way through a thicket of thistles and scrub. We didn't dare go back to the shore then so we just kept going, though Jerubal looked fairly amused at what his little tail-wagging had cost us.

We came out finally to a plateau that was high above the lake. There was a sort of town built across it, but there was something not quite right about the place—the walls had a makeshift look to them as if they'd just been cobbled together, with hardly a thought to keeping the place from harm. There was one spot where there was so much rubble piled against the thing you could actually climb up on the stones and have a look over the top. Sure enough that was what Jerubal did, and I followed behind, poking my head up slowly just in case someone got a mind to fling a rock at us again or run us through.

I could hardly make sense of what we saw in there at first—there were houses and streets as you'd expect in any town, except this seemed a town of the dead, people floating around with their bodies putrid and stinking as if they'd just come up out of their graves. For a moment my blood froze, and I thought that somehow the codger on the beach had chased us right over to the other side. But then it came to me, what we were seeing—they were lepers. I'd seen my share of them in my time but it didn't prepare you to look out over a whole city of them, just going about their business as if it was any normal day.

Jerubal, though, didn't seem to mind them at all, and when someone spotted us and called up to ask us our business, Jerubal instantly started speaking with the fellow. "My friend Simon and I," he said, "are looking for the teacher Jesus to join up with him." It turned out that was the right thing to say—all of a sudden the man started calling out to everyone around that we were Jesus's followers, and it wasn't long before half the camp was standing there under the wall. Jerubal, with that crowd looking up to him, suddenly seemed to know a lot more about Jesus than he'd let on to me at the start, talking with people about what he'd done and the stories that were told of him. The lepers said that Jesus came to the camp every week, curing those he could and bringing solace to those he couldn't. And Jerubal said he could believe it, and that he'd heard he'd cured cripples as well, and even a blind man, once. "He put his hands on him," Jerubal said, "and he asked him, can you see anything, and the fellow said he could see people but they looked like trees walking around. So Jesus put a little spit on the fellow's eyes then, and everything came clear."

I doubted even the lepers believed Jerubal's stories but they seemed glad to have them, and to not have to think about their misery for a while. Jerubal could have gone on like that the rest of the day, and I didn't mind it myself, since the more you talked to these people, the more they started to seem just like anyone you might meet. But by now the guards looking after the place had got wind of us and had come around to chase us off. You could see the lepers didn't like to see Jerubal go, and they called out to him that he should pass their regards on to Jesus.

It was getting late by now. We asked the guards and they said we'd passed Gennesaret, but Arbela was close by if we wanted to put up there. Jerubal, though, asked if there were any villages nearby, and the guards shrugged and said there was one about a mile off, but it was just Amorites and bush. But that was exactly where Jerubal wanted to go, he didn't say why, and so I set off with him though it was getting dark, and we were getting deeper and deeper into the woods.

Sure enough, though, we went about a mile and there was the village. It was only a bunch of hovels in the middle of the forest, from what we could see, and people were just lighting their fires and putting things up for the night. But Jerubal made us stop before anyone saw us, and from one of his pockets, and he had dozens of them, he pulled out a kind of tinderbox and some flints. "Hold on to these," he said, and then he made us pull back from the village behind a bit of hill and got busy as if he knew what he was doing, gathering up little bundles of twigs that he tied together with bits of cloth from his own coat. Then he went up to a tree and cut into it with his knife until a honeyish resin started oozing out of it, which he spread fairly thickly on his little bundles. "Put some fire to one of them," he said to me, and I didn't have any idea what he was up to but I got out the tinder and flint and started up a little fire. When I put the flame up to one of those bundles the thing sputtered a bit, and seemed as if it wasn't going to catch, then all at once burst up like a demon. I looked at Jerubal and he was grinning. "We're ready," he said, but ready for what, I didn't know.

It was pitch-dark by then, and you could hardly see your hand in front of your face. But Jerubal said, "Climb up into that tree," pointing to a big oak that stood there, "and bring these bundles with you, and each time you hear me say, 'Out, devil,' light one up and throw it down into the village. And keep quiet up there, and don't come down until I tell you." By now I'd started to have serious doubts about what Jerubal had in mind. But fool that I was, I did what he told me and climbed up the tree, even though a dozen times I thought I was a dead man, because I couldn't see enough to know if it was a branch I was reaching out for, or empty space. Meanwhile Jerubal had painted himself up with a bit of berry juice and mud so he looked even more frightening than usual, and now he walked into the village and without any warning started keening at the top of his lungs as if it was the end of things.

In no time those villagers were out their doors, holding whatever weapon they'd been able to lay their hands on. But Jerubal didn't pay them any mind, dancing in between them as if he was in a trance and still singing his song. Then when he came to the little fire they had going in the middle of the village he stopped dead, and looked around him as if he wasn't quite sure where he was or how he'd got there, and the villagers just stood there staring at him dumbfounded.

And finally he said, "It's here," and I could hear him as clear as day, because I was up there in the highest branches of my tree almost exactly on top of him.

He had people's attention now. He waited a moment, just holding the silence, then went on to say, in a slow, solemn voice I'd never heard from him before, that he'd been tracking a devil across the bush to destroy it, and had followed it here. You could feel the tremor that went through them at that. He asked if there'd been any trouble in the village the last little while and at first no one could think of anything, but then someone said there was a boy who'd died of fever a few months back, and then there was the field that had caught fire in a storm, and then once, not long before, half the village got sick when an animal died in the well. And Jerubal nodded his head, as if to say, weren't those just the kinds of things that devil would get up to. And by now he had the whole village convinced they were infested, and that this devil was at the bottom of all their troubles.

The village headman, his brow all furrowed, asked Jerubal what they had to do to get rid of the thing, and how much it was going to cost. But Jerubal made as if he was offended and said he would do what had to be done and it wouldn't cost them a thing, because he was a priest and it was his duty. Already everyone was bowing and scraping to thank him for that, but Jerubal just held himself up as if it didn't matter what they thought. He told everyone to gather together and stand behind the fire, which I supposed was to keep the light in their eyes so they didn't notice me up in my tree. Then he drew some odd shapes on the ground with a stick, and spit on a few stones, and finally looked up into the heavens and shouted, "Out, stinking devil!" and started up his chant again, so no one could hear me clicking my flints. And it took me a moment but finally I got one of my bundles smouldering, and just before the resin caught I tossed it out of the tree, so when it flamed up it looked as if it had just appeared in the air out of nowhere.

Well, those villagers were in awe at the sight of that, hiding behind each other's shirts and falling down on their knees. Jerubal, meanwhile, had gone into his trance again, and threw himself down on the ground and started rolling around in the dirt. Finally he shook himself out of it and got on his knees and shouted up again, "Get out, you devil!" I was trembling a bit with the cold by then, and had that syrupy resin all over myself, but somehow I managed to get another one of the bundles going and I threw it out.

This one took a while to catch. I was afraid it was just going to die out there on the ground, and the game would be up. But when it was just above Jerubal's head it burst up like the other one, and it was fairly spectacular, because it looked as if that devil really had it in for him. Except that what happened next was that Jerubal's coat caught fire—some of the resin must have got on him, because it went up quickly. Jerubal, though, didn't do what anyone else might have done, roll around in the dirt again or jump in the well or scuttle off into the bush, happy to get away with his life. He just stood there, burning like that, and looked up into the sky and said, "Devil, take me if you have to, but spare this village." And then as calm as a summer day he took the coat off and threw it on the ground, and the fire went out.

All this couldn't have worked better if we'd planned it—by now the villagers were convinced that Jerubal was some sort of god, and if he'd said to them, hand over your first-born, they'd have done it. Suddenly this fellow who'd said he wouldn't take so much as a coin from them had them so they were nearly begging him to take what they had. It was the headman, after people had started to recover, who came up first—he took off two bracelets he had on and laid them in front of Jerubal. It wasn't long before everyone in the village had lined up to add some other valuable to the pile. And Jerubal stood there long-suffering and patient as if these trinkets didn't mean a thing to him, but he wouldn't be so rude as to refuse them.

If that had been the end of the matter I would have been fairly happy with all of this, and with my share of things. But then the headman got out the wine, and one of his wives brought out some bread and some meat, and before you knew it they were having a feast down there, and Jerubal was telling them stories of all the devils he'd fought and sitting warm and well fed by the fire. Meanwhile I was left biding my time up in my tree, not having had a morsel to eat since breakfast. It was the middle of the night before the last of the villagers had dropped off and Jerubal, looking sober as stone though he'd been drinking with the worst of them, finally collected up his gifts and came to my tree to whisper for me to come down. I was furious at being left up there, but right off Jerubal handed me one of the headman's bracelets to keep me quiet. Then as soon as we were out of earshot of the village, stumbling along in the dark, we both broke out laughing thinking back on the thing, and could hardly stop ourselves until we were back on the main road and halfway down to the lake.

It was getting towards dawn by then. Jerubal, the gods reward him, had thought to put a mutton chop aside for me in his pocket during his little feast, which I ate right down. We should have slept then but we were both of us too wrought up, so we just stopped for a rest in a pine grove off the road. There were the ruins there of a rough little temple that must have been abandoned a long time before, probably when the Jews took over, and a spring that came up with water that tasted sweeter than wine. We found a patch of grass to stretch out on and then just sat back and watched the sun come up over the lake. It seemed the life, with the sun on us and no worries, wandering wherever we pleased. Across the lake I could see where our farm was, and even imagined I made out the smoke from the breakfast fire, and I thought of Moriah stoking it up and of Huram waiting for his porridge. But all that seemed fairly distant from me now. We were on the road, Jerubal and I, and looking for Jesus, the wizard of the Jews, though it seemed maybe we'd already come to his special kingdom and it didn't much matter one way or the other if we actually found him.

The road we were on led us down to the town the Jews called Magdala, another fishing town though the smell was more pleasant than in Capernaum, because the salting and smoking sheds on the beach smelt like something to eat. As it happened we got some breakfast there, buying some roasted fish right at the harbour. We got to talking to people there about Jesus and were surprised at some of the things they had to say. It seemed he had taken a liking to the women of Magdala, and had even chosen a couple of them as his concubines. The thing had caused him a lot of trouble in the end—one of the women had died, no one knew how, and the story was that Jesus himself had brought the thing off with his magic to get rid of her, because she was pregnant. I didn't know what to make of any of this. Over on my side of the lake he'd always seemed upstanding and decent, not the sort to do people harm because they were trouble for him. But then who knew what he got up to when he was here with his own people.

Jerubal, though, wasn't put off at all by any of this, and seemed even more anxious to meet up with Jesus. It turned out we'd just missed him—he'd passed through just the day before, with his followers. People started to tell us then the best way to find him, but warning us to stay clear of Samaria, because they'd kill us as soon as look at us there. I was a bit surprised at that—the way I remembered it, Jesus had always had a good word for the Samaritans. But when I mentioned as much to people they said that only went to show how wrongheaded Jesus was.

We traded some of our trinkets for coin at the Magdala market and then set off down the lakeshore road again, keeping our ears open for any word of Jesus. It was all we could do when we passed the Tiberias gates to keep from slipping in there, because of all the marble and gold you could see, and the whores who stood right at the gate, and the smell of money, which I could tell was driving Jerubal mad. But you knew that if the two of us put a foot in there we might never come out. By noon we'd got as far as Sennabris, and found out at the roadhouse outside town that Jesus and his crowd had put up there the night before. We reckoned that meant we were only a quarter day's journey behind him, and could probably catch up to him by dark.

We didn't know if he'd gone straight down the Jordan or cut into Samaria the way people had warned us, and no one could tell us. We were just getting ready to set off and take our chances when someone came up to us and said another man had been there looking for Jesus, a friend of his, it looked like, who'd set out down the river not a half-hour before. A dark-skinned man, this fellow told us, and not very cordial, with the look of the city on him. Jerubal and I thought the man might know where he was going, and we set out after him.

It turned out there were a lot of people on the road at the time, all travelling down to Jerusalem for the big festival. So Jerubal and I were going up to every dark-skinned fellow we saw and asking him if he was looking for Jesus, and some of them just stared at us as if we were mad and some of them ignored us and some of them said, they'd heard of him, but they weren't looking for him. We were already halfway to Scythopolis, which was where the road branched off to Samaria, before we finally spotted up ahead a fellow in a fancy coat who was walking alone as if he didn't need anyone, and we thought, here was our man.

Instead of going right up to him, Jerubal decided to have a bit of a joke, getting up close behind him and dragging his leg as if he was lame. Then he said, in a good loud voice, "I hope we find Jesus soon, because I can't go much longer on this leg."

Sure enough our man turned right around, and as soon as his eyes were on him Jerubal instantly straightened himself and said, "Gods in heaven, I'm cured, this must be Jesus himself!" For a minute, the man stood there as if somebody had just slapped him. But then Jerubal couldn't help himself and burst out laughing, and the fellow got a mean look. "What's your game?" he said to us, and Jerubal, pretending innocence, said, "We're just looking for Jesus, the same as you."

I thought the man was going to take out the dagger I could see poking out of his belt and run us both through, then and there.

"Who sent you?" he said, narrow-eyed, as if we were spies. But Jerubal, to keep goading him, said with a grin, "Why, it was Caesar himself."

The fellow looked ready to spit.

"I don't know what you're talking about," he said finally, then turned away and kept walking.

Jerubal seemed happy enough to let him go. But I felt a panic at the thought, imagining we'd be lost out there on our own, now that we were away from the lake, the countryside starting to get a little desolate and stark.

"Please don't pay any mind to my friend, sir," I told the man, "he didn't mean any harm," and then I went on to say how we were just lowly pilgrims hoping to join Jesus, and had heard tell up at Sennabris that someone looking like him might be able to help us. So he eyed us up and down, probably guessing by now that we weren't Jews and wondering what strange breed we were. But like Jerubal had said, I had that kind of a face, that people trusted.

"I don't know where he is any more than you," he said finally, but he didn't try to stop us when we came up to walk along beside him.

We managed to get his name out of him, Judas, though it was as if he'd had to think about it first, and then getting anything else out of him was like calving an ox. But he seemed happy enough to listen to us, which put Jerubal in his element, who started talking about how he'd seen Jesus here and there, and how he himself came from a poor family—though you could hear the coins jangling around in his pockets—and had heard that Jesus was for the poor, so that made him want to follow him. And since Judas didn't stop him he went on telling more and more lies that got taller and taller. But Judas, from his smirk, was making it clear what he thought of them.

"Why haven't I seen you before," he said finally, "if you know Jesus so well?"

But Jerubal hardly paused a breath.

"So you must be one of his men, then?" he said, and Judas wouldn't admit it was the case, but you could see he'd been caught out.

He told us then he was pushing on for the night to Scythopolis, in a tone that made clear he was hoping to lose us. But Jerubal said that was exactly our plan, it was only a few miles now, not that we could have stopped in the middle of that brush in any event, where there were just the few scraggly villages along the way that would probably as soon have chased me and Jerubal into the hills as given us a bed. In the end it paid off for us to have stayed with Judas—almost the instant we stopped in at the roadhouse outside Scythopolis we saw Jesus, going around sharing some supper with his people where they'd set up their tents in a corner of the courtyard. I was surprised how relieved I felt to see him—it was starting to affect me now, being away from home. Watching him I thought about how we used to get together down beneath the farm and the good feeling we had then, and in my head it seemed years since all that had happened. But the truth was I'd seen him there by the lake just a few days before.

He had some of his women with him, who he'd never brought over to the Gergesa side, a group of them going around with him to help serve out supper. They weren't as beautiful as I'd imagined, from the way people in Magdala had talked—just country girls, they were, like the girls you'd see in Baal-Sarga, and a couple of them so shy they couldn't say a word without putting a hand in front of their mouth. Then there were his regular men, up around the cooking pit, and maybe thirty or forty tents set up on the patch of courtyard he and his group had claimed, like their own little village. After the days I'd spent on the road, I would have been happy to settle into one of those tents right then and there. But Judas, who was still beside us, stood there scowling as if he couldn't quite bring himself to join in like that. I had the feeling that he hadn't been with Jesus for some time, and was seeing all this like something he'd forgotten, and wasn't too pleased with what he saw. And for a moment I could see the thing the way he did, Jesus there with his women and his tents like some desert vagabond.

It took a moment before anyone in Jesus's group noticed Judas. When they did, it was as if a bitter wind had blown through the courtyard. The women's eyes went instantly to daggers, in that way women had, and the men went stiff, though it was harder to tell with them if they hated the man or just felt the cold seep into them at the sight of him. Then finally Jesus noticed him, and everyone watched to see what he would do.

He tried to smile then but it came out more like a grimace, and it was the first time I'd ever seen him put out over anything. He came towards Judas with an arm out to welcome him, though you could see the gesture wasn't coming easily.

"You've come back," he said to him, but right away Judas answered, "You don't look very pleased to see me." And Jesus, though I could hardly believe it, looked a little ashamed of himself.

"You're the one who left us," he said. And he told Judas they still had a place for him if he wanted it, though from the look of his people it seemed they'd be just as happy if he simply went back to wherever he'd come from.

It looked as if Judas had more to say but Jesus had already gone back to his rounds, leaving him stranded there next to me and Jerubal.

"So you've found your Jesus," Judas said to us, with a look to say it was clear we hardly knew the man, when he hadn't so much as rested his eyes on us. And the truth was it hurt me that he hadn't picked me out, though I'd hardly so much as opened my mouth at any of our meetings by the lake but had just sat at the back with my hood up, afraid as I was that I'd be recognized and the word would get back to Huram.

I had a mind Judas might just have turned around then and headed home, seeing the reception he'd got. But it looked as if he'd set his mind to make a place for himself, sitting right down with Jesus's men beside the cooking pit as if it was his due, though you could see he was watching his back. And the men said their greetings to him, a bit sullen and gruff but not turning their shoulders to him, and even the women finally passed him some food and made do.

Jerubal, meanwhile, not one to waste any time, had already got up a bit of food for us as well and had started to talk with some of the people camped at the edges of Jesus's troupe. "That Judas used to come around a while ago but they chased him away," one fellow told us. "There were some who said he was a spy for the Romans." But then we heard all sorts of stories—that Judas went in for love in the Greek way and had fallen for one of Jesus's men, which was why he'd come back, but also that he wasn't a spy at all but fancied himself a rebel, though his movement was just him and some fifty others or so who plotted and gave themselves airs but would have run at the first sign of a fight. My own feeling was that you couldn't trust him either way—there was that nervousness to him you noticed from the start as if he didn't know where to expect the knife from, which made you think he'd crossed a few people in his time, one way or the other.

We could see that some of the people in Jesus's camp were just hangers-on, there because the food got handed out and no one asked anything back for it. But there were plenty of others who you saw were devoted to Jesus, some of them, from the sounds of it, who'd been with him right from the start. It opened your eyes to talk to these, because on the Gergesa side all we'd ever seen was Jesus's little coterie. I thought that because they were Jews they wouldn't want to have much to do with me and Jerubal, but that wasn't the case. Right off they took us in, and shared their food with us, and were ready to lend us their own mats to sleep on. Then we got to talking and I saw that a lot of the stories they knew were the same ones Jesus told us over on the Gergesa side, which surprised me—I'd imagined the Jews would have their own special teachings from him or that he'd just tell them things straight out instead of in riddles the way he did us. I started to think of Jesus a little differently then. Maybe it wasn't so farfetched, someone like me joining up with him.

I would have been happy to spend the night talking with these folks, seeing that they weren't the sort to give you a crust of bread with one hand while they took your mutton with the other. But I could see Jerubal was chafing—he wanted to go into town. We knew better than to ask any of

Jesus's followers to go in with us, since all these Greek towns were cesspits as far as the Jews were concerned. But as soon as people started to turn in, I and Jerubal slipped away from the roadhouse and into the city. I'd never seen the likes of the place—there were lanterns all along the main street as if it was the middle of some festival instead of just any normal night, and then people everywhere even as late as it was, and horses and carts in the streets making such a racket you'd think you'd come to Rome itself. Jerubal said the first thing to do was to make an offering, so we went off to the temple of Bacchus, who was the god of the place, and bought two flasks of holy wine, pouring one into the bowl the priest set out for us and drinking the rest ourselves. And Jerubal said, "Bacchus protect us and keep us drunk," and as it turned out Bacchus kept up the bargain.

We started at the baths, where the attendant, seeing how rough we looked, seemed all pleased at the chance of turning us away until we came up with the required fee and he had to let us through. I'd never been in a bathhouse and it felt fairly strange, the hot water around me like a blanket and the old men lying naked beside me. Then the boy we'd hired on to look after our things said any service we wanted, he could get, so Jerubal asked for some wine and he brought a flagon of it, and then he asked to be rubbed down and we were led off to a private room where two girls rubbed oil over every bit of us. And by the time we'd left the place we were a good deal poorer in coin, but not, as they said, in spirit.

What happened next I could hardly have told you, since the first thing we did out of the baths was to head for a wine shop, and we were down to the ranker sort now so it hit us fairly hard. Somewhere we got into a game, with someone even sharper than Jerubal, and then we drank with some soldiers from Ephesus and apparently stumbled into a brothel with them, or at least that was where we were when first light broke, lying in a heap in a room that stank of piss. Seeing the light coming in through the window, I shook Jerubal awake and we headed out. We made the roadhouse just as Jesus and his troupe were breaking camp, and it was lucky we'd got to them and were able to get a bite of breakfast, because by the time we'd paid our way out of the brothel there was nothing to count in our purses but a bit of lint.

The route we ended up taking out of Scythopolis wasn't east across the Jordan into Perea, where everyone else was going, or even west to Samaria, but south right along the river valley, though there wasn't really much of a road to speak of and you had the feeling bandits would jump out from behind every rock. Jesus was walking out ahead of us all seeming in a foul mood, and I thought maybe some of his camp had got up to the same sort of mischief the evening before as me and Jerubal. But what had happened was that he'd sent a couple of his men into Samaria to collect his followers there for the trip, and the men had come back in the night saying the Samaritans wouldn't join. They had their own temple, they'd said, and didn't want any part of going down to the Jewish one. But Jesus took it hard—it seemed he'd been trying from the start to bring the Jews and the Samaritans together but couldn't find the way to do it, though from what I understood it was only this little rule or that one that made the difference between them and then just the bad blood that there'd been for hundreds of years.

After the night we'd had, Jerubal and I put up our hoods against the sun and stayed at the back of the troupe. The road we'd taken was scarred with gullies sometimes as deep as a man, and it was a struggle getting along it. Then at one point I glanced over at Jerubal and saw he was looking a little grey. I thought it was just the wine from the night before, but it was something he'd eaten—not long afterwards he suddenly retched up his breakfast, and soon enough half of the rest of us had done the same, spilling our stomachs into the river. It seemed some of the fish we had along had gone bad. We had to abandon three baskets of it there by the river for the buzzards to take, going on then hoping to reach a town up ahead where there was a place to rest. But after we'd gone on a ways, Jerubal pulled me to the back of the file and told me to slow my pace a bit, and then without warning gave my arm a tug so that I suddenly found myself lying on top of him at the bottom of one of those gullies. I hardly knew what to make of that. But Jerubal put his hand up to keep me quiet. He peered up over the edge of the gully to make sure no one had noticed we'd disappeared, then said, "We're going back for the fish."

I had no idea what he intended and was half-inclined to leave him to work the thing out on his own. But he had that grin of his, which always said, you'd be missing something to pass this up. So in the end I followed him back. And it turned out a good deal of that fish wasn't as foul as we'd thought, and the lot of it was wrapped in ferns that hid the smell. So there we had ourselves a windfall, three big baskets of fish for the taking, except I didn't see what we were going to do with it, out in the middle of nowhere. But Jerubal grinned and said he'd worked it out—there was a town we'd passed a ways back, a bit off the river. He had us run the baskets through the river a bit to freshen them up, and then we hoisted them onto our shoulders—and I was the one who got saddled with two of them—and started retracing our steps, though the sun was getting high and the heat rising by the moment.

The town was a bit further than Jerubal had led me to believe and I was nearly crippled under my load by the time we got to the place. It looked to be just a wilderness town, a bit of mud thrown together, with a few squares of field around it that took water from the river but then beyond that only scrub and waste. It was our luck, though, that there was a market going on, and Jerubal took us into it, going along on a walking stick he'd culled out of the brush so he looked like an old desert wise man. Then as soon as we were in the thick of the crowd, he started shouting, "Praise to God!" at the top of his lungs, so that it wasn't long before people had gathered around us.

The way Jerubal had it, those fish we were carrying were part of a miracle we'd seen. He had the whole story plotted out, how he and I were simply walking along the river when we came on Jesus, the holy man of Galilee, on his way to Jerusalem with his followers. They'd run out of food, and hadn't money, and thought they'd have to turn back and miss the feast. But Jesus said to his men, "Cast a net into the river," and it came out teeming with fish. And they'd been able to eat their fill and pack some away for the journey and still had these baskets left over that wouldn't keep, and Jesus, seeing us going along there, had given them over to us so that we might raise some money for the poor. "I saw it with my own eyes," Jerubal said, "and my servant here, who's never told a lie in his life, will tell you the same."

Jerubal had said all this almost in a single breath, as if to admit no contradiction. But it was clear in an instant that this was no village of Amorites, because those townspeople just stood there staring at us as if they didn't know whether to stone us or spit, probably wondering, from Jerubal's accent, what kind of foreign demons we were. It seemed they were just girding themselves to drive us from the town when suddenly a man emerged from the crowd looking as if he'd just crawled in from the wilderness, his hair and beard tangled as thistle and reaching down practically to his waist, and his shirt belted on with a raw strip of goatskin. He had the glint of a madman in his eye, and I thought the crowd would chase him off. But instead everyone cleared a way for him as if he was some sort of leader in the place.

"You mentioned Jesus from Galilee," he said, staring at us as if to burn a hole in us.

But Jerubal, keeping calm, agreed that he had.

"He was with John the prophet," the man said, which didn't mean a thing to me though Jerubal seemed to know what he was talking about. "There's a lot of us here who still follow John. He used to preach at the river."

I thought he was intending to say that we'd insulted John's name, and he'd have to avenge it.

But Jerubal said, "Then it must be his power that Jesus called on, to do what he did."

I could see the fellow considering that—now he'd be the one to insult the memory of John, to say it couldn't have happened. He seemed to strain then with the weight that was on him, everyone looking to him.

Finally he said, "Then it must be a sign of the end of things, the way John warned us, if he's giving that power to the ones he taught." And he walked up to the baskets and took the first fish himself, giving us a coin to pass on, and Jerubal stood there as if it was the most natural thing in the world that this wild man should just believe when all the rest had their doubts.

Another man would have turned to the crowd fairly quickly then and said, "Look, even John's follower took one, now do the same." But not Jerubal. He just stood there a moment staring at the crowd as if to say it was clear they didn't even believe in their own god here, then started to pack up the fish. And you could see people begin to shuffle nervously at that, and talk amongst themselves, and look at Jerubal and the fish. And finally someone came up with a few coppers in his hand and said he would take one as well, and then another came and another, and Jerubal had me collect the money as if it was a little beneath him to touch it, saying we'd be catching up with Jesus on the road to hand it over to him.

It wasn't long before half the town was lined up for their fish. It was as Jerubal had told me once, the bigger the lie, the more people fell for it in the end. And it seemed true, because Jerubal could open his mouth and you never knew what kind of incredible thing would come out of it, yet he always found the way to make people believe him. Now he was going on about how he'd worshipped Aphrodite and Baal all his life but seeing the miracle by the river had won him over to the god of the Jews, and he was going down straightaway to the temple in Jerusalem to make an offering. And people were taking him seriously, and agreeing with him that their god was great, and Jerubal happened to mention in passing that rather than eating their fish, they'd do best to hang it over their doors for good fortune, to save himself a lot of sick folks holding their stomachs and chasing him down.

Our pockets were full by the time we left town. But I was feeling a bit uneasy about that money. I asked Jerubal about the prophet John and he said the Jews had all sorts of holy men like that, who lived in caves and said outrageous things about the end of the world and who the Romans usually came along and killed off, the way they'd done with this John. I wanted to know if he'd performed any miracles but Jerubal couldn't say. "What about Jesus?" I asked him. "Do you think he does miracles?" "Of course he does," Jerubal said. "Look at us—we were just a couple of poor sots when the sun came up and now he's turned us into rich ones."

In my own head, though, I couldn't make a joke of it—I had to know what was what, all of a sudden, since Jerubal had me so turned around by now I couldn't tell the difference any more between things that had actually happened and what we'd made up. I'd been that way as a boy—I'd hear a story about some piece of wonder or magic and then it was as if I was the one who'd witnessed the thing, I saw it so clearly. The truth was you could meet a lot of people who were like that, sensible people otherwise but who, when it came to wonders, couldn't have told you what they'd seen with their own eyes, or only heard about, or invented whole cloth. That seemed the way so many stories got spread, until you'd think wonders were as common as spit.

It didn't take us long to catch up with Jesus's band again—they'd put up at the roadhouse outside Aenon, just a couple of miles on, to wait out the heat. The place was known for its waters and was surrounded with palm groves and gardens, though beyond them was desert, dozens of trees sprouting up above the town walls all in bloom then with the spring. Some were the purple-flowered ones, wispy as gossamer, that we called King's Ghost up in Baal-Sarga. I felt a pang, seeing them and remembering the lake and how green everything had been around it, next to the sun-cooked flats we'd been travelling through. But the roadhouse was fine enough, with a large pool in the middle of the courtyard and a little wine shop in one of the arcades.

With money in our purses again, Jerubal and I bought some wine for some of Jesus's followers who we'd got friendly with. But while we were standing there with our cups, Jesus himself came around to join us, instantly ordering a cup as well to save us feeling sheepish at being caught with wine on our breath. Jerubal immediately got out a coin to pay for the thing, and Jesus didn't try to stop him but just said, "Thank you," as if he meant it, and took a drink.

I'd assumed by this point that Jesus hadn't recognized me from our meetings. But he turned to me now and said, "I see you're still hiding your light at the back of the crowd, the way you used to," and I saw he'd known all along who I was.

I must have blushed then because he smiled.

"I'm glad you and your friend could join us," he said, and drained his glass and went off, leaving my head spinning. But then I remembered the money in my purse and all my good feeling left me. I'd find the way to make some sort of penance with it, I said to myself, maybe keeping just enough of it back that I didn't go hungry.

We were getting ready to set off again when a bit of an argument broke out. It seemed that the town we were at, even more than the one before it, was crowded with followers of the prophet John, and some of them had got wind that an old student of his was passing through and had come out to see who it was. But when one of these fellows heard that Jesus had been drinking with his followers, he said that John would never have stood for such a thing. Jesus, instead of defending himself, agreed that the fellow was right.

"He lived the way most of us can't," he said, "and we'll never see the likes of him again. I remember how we used to come to this very town, though it wasn't everyone here who believed in him then."

It seemed he was saying that maybe the fellow himself was one of the ones who hadn't believed, and from how his face fell for an instant, it looked as if that was the case. But then he said, though more carefully, "There are more who believe in him now because they saw he was ready to die when Herod took him. But some of those who were with him just ran off."

It was as if Jesus had been slapped—he fell quiet, and turned away, and said to his men, "Let's be going." And that was how he left the place, under a cloud, so the rest of us had to hurry to collect ourselves and straggle in behind him. It was unusual for Jesus to let anyone get the better of him and people looked confused, wondering how he could have been in the wrong. But Jesus didn't stop to explain, marching straight on into the blazing wilderness. A few miles from town, we reached a spot where the river widened and there was a bit of a ford.

"We're crossing here," Jesus said, he didn't say why, though you could see he wasn't brooking any argument.

People arranged their goods on their heads and we went into the water single file, with Jesus out front. There must have been some rain up around the lake the night before, because the current was running swiftly, and the children along with us might have been washed away if they hadn't been tied to their parents. The other side of the river was even more blasted than the one we'd left, just rubble and sand and stone and then bald white hills that stretched as far as you could see. When we'd landed Jesus led us down the shore a ways to a little resting spot where there were a few thorn trees to give a bit of shade. We all stretched out our belongings to dry, but not settling much, imagining we still had a patch to cross to get to whatever town it was we were headed to for the night. But then Jesus announced we'd be stopping right where we were.

It seemed strange to camp in that bit of wild away from any town or road. But Jesus said he had chosen the spot because the prophet John had had his camp there. I made out then the old tent pegs in the dirt, and the spots where the ground was beaten down. I had an image of the place as it must have been, with the tents all around and a young Jesus there with his teacher John. Not far from the river an embankment rose up that had a row of caves in it, and I pictured John and his men putting up there looking like the wild man we'd sold our fish to, with their hair coiled and long and the strips of goatskin tied around their waists.

We set up camp. Jerubal by now had quite a following with some of Jesus's band, and the group of them set up a tent right at the edge of the camp. I wandered around on my own for a bit, though the truth was I wanted to get close to Jesus again, still drunk with the fact that he'd known me. But then he saw me lingering near his tent and actually called me over to help with supper. I was so tongue-tied I couldn't even answer him.

"Now I've got my three Simons," he said, "like the three wise men," an old story people told. And he gave me a nickname, Simon the Wise, which left me with the strangest feeling, like he'd claimed me.

So suddenly there I was right in the thick of things, with Jesus nearby and Jesus's men at my elbow. Working with them I saw they weren't so different from me in the end, like a crew of fishermen you'd meet at the Gergesa harbour. There was Simon who Jesus called the Rock, and who I knew from the Gergesa side—he was the sort who others would mock a bit, and hardly think about, but always count on in the end. Then there was his brother Andrew, who was simple, who everyone looked after like their own—he was one of the few who seemed to have any feeling for Judas, smiling like a child whenever he saw him. I'd have thought Judas wouldn't have time for someone like him but the truth was he was gentle with the fellow and humoured him, one of the few signs I'd seen in Judas that he might actually belong with someone like Jesus.

Then there was Simon the Canaanite, who Jesus jokingly called the Zealot, nearly the same word in their dialect as a fanatical sect in Jerusalem. If there was one fellow in Jesus's circle who made me want to run, it was the Zealot—it wasn't that there was anything offensive in him, but that I saw in him what it was like to be part of that crowd and not be a Jew. Everyone said he was the most loyal of Jesus's men, yet next to the others he seemed like some dog you might find in the wild and tame, loyal just because you'd brought it in. I didn't ever want to be seen that way, as if I was some savage they'd saved, just because I had grown up hardly knowing one god from the next. The truth was, though, that Jesus didn't treat the Zealot any different than the rest—he didn't condescend to him but also he didn't go out of his way to show he was equal, and so show in that way that he wasn't.

Mary, from Magdala, was the one you noticed among the women. I'd picked her out from the start, the first night—she was just a stick, so thin you felt sorry for her, knowing not many would have her. But I would sooner have put myself in the way of any of Jesus's men than in hers, for all that a good wind would have knocked her down. All sorts of stories about her went through the camp, that she was the one who'd poisoned the pregnant girl we'd heard about, out of jealousy, or that she tried to put enmity between Jesus and those she didn't like. But it was just that she wanted to possess the man—you saw that in how she never let him from her sight, and protected him, and was the one who stood guard to see he had his moment of peace. When Judas returned, it was clear she had to bite her tongue not to curse him, though she welcomed him for Jesus's sake, even if for his sake too she might just as soon have chased him away.

When the food was ready, a group of us went around with Jesus from tent to tent ladling it out, and people lit their fires with whatever scrub wood they'd collected and the sky over the hills stretched out blood red from end to end with the setting sun, a good omen. I was afraid that when we came to Jerubal's tent we'd find him gaming, but his little group was actually at their prayers, Jerubal right there next to the others on his knees mumbling along with them as if he knew what he was saying, though he gave me a wink when I went by.

When we got back to Jesus's tent, Judas was waiting there.

"I need to talk to you," he said, in that grating way of his, as if it was just him and Jesus and the rest of us didn't matter. But Jesus, to his credit, put him off.

"You can see we're just sitting down to supper," he said.

It seemed Judas had been trying to get him alone since he'd arrived, without luck—if it wasn't one of the women who got in his way, it was some work that had to be done or just that Jesus was in a foul mood, and Judas would be forced to go off again. Now he just hung there at the edge of our circle glowering like a jackal. But Jesus seemed determined not to let anything spoil our supper, not even the insult he'd had at the roadhouse at Aenon.

We got to talking as we ate, pulling in close to the fire because the night chill was coming on, and one of the men asked Jesus about his days with John the prophet. I could see Jesus didn't like to talk about his own life that way, but he started in, saying he'd come to John just a boy, willful and quick-tempered and full of pride, but had left him a man. There wasn't anything in the world, Jesus said, that would keep someone like John from following what he believed. Afterwards people said he was hard and didn't have any mercy in him but the truth was he never turned anyone away, and the only thing he asked from people was that they should be humble in front of their god.

"You have to be blessed to meet someone like that," Jesus said. "Someone who makes you look at things differently."

He told us then what it was like when John was taken. Though the Romans had had a hand in it, it was Herod's men who came for him, about a hundred of them who marched down from Tiberias one day fully armed and carrying their flags out front, so you could see them coming for miles.

"When we got word of them," Jesus said, "John called everyone together, and there were hundreds of people here then, and said, 'Go home.' But no one wanted to go. People said they would die for him before they went, and they would have. But John said there was no point in that. People didn't really understand him then—they'd always been told it was important to die with courage, and be remembered that way. But John said, 'If you die here, you might be remembered, which will be good for your own glory. But if you leave, then what I taught you will be remembered, which will be good for the glory of God.'"

Hearing the thing put that way, people finally started to go. In the end, the only ones left behind were John and the dozen or so men he'd been training to take over for him, and Jesus was one of them. Now the argument started over again, since none of them wanted to leave, and meanwhile the soldiers were getting close and no one knew, seeing how Herod was, what exactly they would do. John, looking for a way out, said half should stay, so people couldn't say they were cowards, and half should go. And the agreement was that the ones who went had to cut their hair and take off their belts, because those were John's sign, since there wasn't any point in saving themselves if it was just for the sake of being captured later on.

They drew straws for the thing and Jesus picked one of the shorter ones, and had to go.

"We hated it, those of us who had to leave, but we'd given our word," Jesus said. "So we went into the desert, each on his own, and hoped for the best. Then the next day I went into Aenon to find out what had happened and they told me John had been taken and the rest had just been butchered where they stood."

The fire had gone low, and there was only Jesus's voice in the dark.

"I thought of finding the others then," he said, "but the truth was I couldn't have looked at them, for the shame. Then I found out that some of them had gone back when the soldiers came, and been butchered as well, so that it seemed simply cowardly that I'd gone. I didn't know if I could go on then. Here was my teacher in prison, and my friends dead, and I hadn't done anything."

He paused. A deep silence had settled over us, all of us hanging on Jesus's words—this wasn't just another story he was telling us but something that had really happened to him, and it seemed he wasn't sure what to make of it any more than we might be. Even Judas was leaning in, and looked as if he had forgotten himself for a moment.

Jesus had wandered in the desert after that, not really knowing what he was doing or where he was going. For food he ate grubs and whatever he could find or nothing at all, and for water he learned where to dig to get little seepages of it, sucking the mud in like that just enough to stay alive. All sorts of mad thoughts were going through his head then so he didn't know any more who he was or what he'd been up to in his life, and he started to see things the way people in the desert did, and what he saw were his friends who'd been killed sitting around him. But they refused to look at him, and the louder he shouted, the more they pretended he wasn't there.

Finally he ended up in a town he couldn't even have told you the name of and sat himself down in the square, thinking he would die there, people leaving little bits of food for him that he was too stunned to eat. And it happened that some of Herod's soldiers passed through the place with a prisoner they'd taken, and it made him sick to see them, because it all came back to him. He went up to give the prisoner some water where they'd tied him in the square while they ate, but he had died right there in the open without anyone noticing.

"I would gladly have traded places with him," Jesus said, "but for my sake, not his, just so it could be told that I'd been killed by Herod's men like the rest. But that was a mistake. There was a man I met there who showed me that. He said to me that if I was alive, it was so I might do some good in the world, and I saw then I'd forgotten what John had told us, that we had to carry on his word, and that I'd only been thinking of my own reputation. And this man I'd met was also the only one who offered to bury Herod's prisoner, which was a risk because he'd been a rebel. And I took heart from that, from his example, and that was what helped me carry on."

He stopped, and it was clear he'd finished. He was looking right at Judas then, though with an expression I couldn't make out, and Judas grimaced and averted his eyes and then suddenly got up from the fire as if someone had kicked him and went off into the dark. None of us knew what to make of that. Jesus looked as if he was ready to take back whatever offence he'd given, but Judas didn't return.

My head was full by then. Not wanting to make a nuisance of myself I quietly slipped off and made my way back to Jerubal's tent to get some sleep. But Jerubal had a game going, so I just draped my coat over my shoulders and made a little place for myself under the stars. As it turned out, my head was spinning so much with all that had happened to me in the past few days that I couldn't sleep. It seemed the strangest thing to me, that I should be lying there in Jesus's camp under that riot of desert stars when a few days before I'd been safe in my bed on the farm.

I started thinking then about the farm and my life there, and for the first time in years, it felt, I thought of my parents, though it seemed I had only the one memory of them now, which was the day of their deaths. The bandits who'd come then were after the horses we had at the time, though what they left behind was far worse than what they took.

I was just five then. My mother and I were in the courtyard when my father ran in with his eyes lit up like I'd never seen them. Without a word he grabbed me and put me into a basket where we kept our lentils. "Don't move," he said, and put the lid on, though I could see through the weave. He barely had time to turn around again before someone came running in after him with a broadsword in his hand and raised it over him. Then the sword came down and there was a splash of blood and everything turned strange, because there was blood everywhere and my mother was screaming and it seemed the end of things had come.

Another man had come in. All I could see from the basket was my father's back where he'd fallen, and the blood. My mother must have been screaming still, but it was as if I couldn't hear her. Then things happened very quickly again. There were the two men, big and dirty as animals, and one of them threw my mother to the ground and the other got on top of her. I couldn't understand what was happening then, what kind of crazed game this was. I would even have got out of the basket, since I had it in my mind it was because I was in there that everything seemed strange, and that I shouldn't be hiding, and should call Huram. But then

I saw my mother's face, and there was an instant when her eyes went to me in the basket, wild, and told me, stay put.

My mother was a beautiful woman. It wasn't only me who thought that, who was her son—everyone said so, even after, that she was as dark-haired and dark-eyed as a Damascene princess, though she was just a poor farmworker's girl from Baal-Sarga. But watching her with those men, first the one and then the other on top of her, it was as if everything that was pretty in her was wiped out. They hit her a few times, to make her screaming stop—after that it looked as if her jaw had snapped, and the only sound that came from her was a broken moan like nothing I'd ever heard.

I couldn't have said how much time passed but suddenly Huram was there. He was holding a sword and was already covered in blood—later I found out he'd fought one of the others outside, and killed him. He was only fourteen then, but large, and strong as a bear. It took him only an instant to see what was going on, and even before the two men had noticed him, he'd lifted his sword and brought it down on the head of the one who was standing, watching the other. There was a spray of blood, and the man fell. But Huram didn't stop—he swung at the other, who was still on his knees, and cut into his back. The man tried to turn then but a fury had taken hold of Huram, who hacked at him again and again until you could hardly see for the blood. Then the man fell forward and our mother groaned underneath him, and Huram, maddened, kicked and pawed at the mass of cut flesh he had turned him into until he had cleared him off her.

There was a moment then when Huram's eyes went to my mother's and she turned away, just wheezing there, quietly and horribly. I had a sick feeling then. I saw Huram look to our father lying dead on the ground and then to our mother again, with her ripped clothes and the blood on her and her face crooked and broken. And at that instant it was as if I could feel the tumble of Huram's thoughts in my own head, how they were churning, pushing him to what he could hardly bring himself to think. Then he raised his sword, with my mother staring up at him with a look that was half fear and half pleading for the thing, and he brought the blade down.

I must have screamed then, though I didn't know it, because in an instant the lid was off the basket and Huram was staring down at me. He went hard as stone then, realizing I'd seen everything.

I was spattered in blood that had come through the weave of the basket.

"Go out and wash yourself," Huram said, angry, as if I were to blame. And when I went out I didn't even dare to look around in the courtyard, at what my father looked like, or my mother, lying dead.

Huram spent the rest of the day and into the night getting rid of the bodies, though I couldn't have told you what he did with them, our mother and father any more than the rest, because the whole time he made me stay in the stable. By the next morning, when he finally let me back into the house, I could hardly tell that anything had gone on in the place except for a spot of dried blood here or there. It was as if the whole thing had never happened, and the truth was that the time went by and not a word of the thing was ever breathed between us, not of our mother or of a single circumstance of what had gone on that day.

It was from then that things were never right between

me and Huram. And the more time that passed the worse they got, because I'd started to say to myself that what he did to our mother was no better than what he'd have done to an animal, or just that she hadn't been worth anything in his eyes, being a woman. But I knew it wasn't like that—I couldn't have said what it was like, except that I'd understood, in a way, what Huram had done, and that made it worse. Lying there under the stars now I tried to tell myself that maybe all those horrible things had been part of some plan, the way my mother used to say that there was a plan for each of us, and that somehow that made them right. But I knew I was just fooling myself, and that there wasn't a thing that was any good about what had happened back then, and even lying there thinking back on it now almost made me want to take a knife to myself, because of the waste of it.

I woke up the next morning stiff with cold out there in the open, the stars still shining over my head and just a lick of daylight skimming the hills. The rest of the camp was quiet so I went over to one of the caves nearby to relieve myself, wanting to get out of the cold. But while I was there I heard voices, so close they might have been right behind me. It was a trick of the caves—someone was talking in another one nearby and somehow the sound was getting tunnelled into my own.

It took me an instant before I realized who it was—Judas and Jesus. So Judas had finally got Jesus alone. At first all I could gather from what Judas was saying was that he didn't want Jesus to go into Jerusalem, and that he was already risking his life telling Jesus the little he had.

But Jesus answered him, "From what you've told me, I only see greater reason to go, so there'll be at least a few of us who'll be on the side of peace instead of blood."

"Then you'll just be killed along with everyone else," Judas said, sounding angry now. "From your story last night, I'd have thought you'd want to stay alive."

"Not if it means letting other people get killed."

"You didn't seem to mind in the case of John," Judas said, but from the silence that followed it was clear he regretted saying it.

A tiredness had come into Judas's voice when he spoke again.

"I had to betray all my oaths to tell you what I did. Don't let it be for nothing."

"It wasn't for nothing if you did what you thought was right," Jesus said.

An instant later I saw Jesus walking back to the camp, and then Judas following several paces behind him. I didn't know what to make of any of this. But Jesus was already going around the camp rousing people to start up our march again. I made my way back to Jerubal's tent and told him what I'd heard in the cave, starting to think by now that it might be time to heed the signs, given all the things that had gone wrong for us so far on our journey. But Jerubal said it was nothing to fret about—there wasn't a festival that went by in Jerusalem that one group or another didn't plan some sort of mayhem, though the Romans always smelled things out and squashed them before they ever got started. Jesus, at any rate, seemed only more set on his path, hurrying us along as if we were his little soldiers. It wasn't for me to gainsay him—I'd thrown in my lot now, for better or ill.

Jesus wanted to make Jericho by nightfall, and we had to do a quick march to get past the halfway point before the sun got too hot. I hung at the back with Jerubal but at one point Jesus caught sight of me and called me up with his own little circle. I was too pleased with that to do anything more than just slip in quietly there with his other men. I was starting to feel almost at home with them now, as if I might actually belong with them, half-scoundrel that I was—it wasn't like Jesus, in any event, to keep a man out simply for being a scoundrel. There was one fellow in the camp, by the name of Aram, who had actually tried to ransom Jesus's followers to a bandit chief, and Jesus had forgiven him in the end and let him stay with the rest. You didn't see much of him, though—he'd get his food, and dart his eyes around like a thief, then steal back to whatever corner it was he'd come out of.

Judas was seeming even more of a mystery now. He'd delivered his poison, and logic would have said he'd be on his way, given the danger to him, from what I'd understood, of returning to Jerusalem. But instead, like some cur, he was sticking with us, skulking along as if in the end he wasn't any different from the others, and just wanted Jesus to love him. When we joined up with the main road, where the traffic was fairly heavy with the other pilgrims going along, he kept looking around him as if he expected the knife any moment, so that my heart almost went to him. Something happened then, when we stopped to rest once, that surprised me—Judas had sat to massage his blistered feet when Mary came, though with a face like a mourner's, and offered to rub oil on them. Judas could hardly look at her then for his embarrassment. But still he nodded and she knelt in front of him, and it was the strangest thing then, watching how gently she rubbed his sores and knowing it cost her to do it.

The sun was beating down on us by then, and with every step we took the air got dryer and the land more gravelly and bare until there wasn't anything to look at but the stones and the white hills and maybe a thorn bush here or there and a buzzard or two in the sky. For all the traffic along the road, it seemed even ten thousand of us couldn't have made an impression on that rubbly wilderness. Already from a long way off, though, you could see the walls of Jericho in the valley up ahead, surrounded by palm and balsam fields because of the springs there. It made the journey easier to see that oasis of green waiting ahead for us. At noon we put up at a roadhouse to wait out the heat and then around mid-afternoon set out on the final leg to Jericho, making for the ford at Bethabara so we could cross back over the Jordan into Judea.

When we reached the customs-house at the river, though, the soldiers there, without any explanation, made us all line up at the side of the road and then came along and searched us one by one, even the women, and went through every bit of our baggage. Judas, just standing there with the rest of us, had turned to stone, whether from anger or fear I couldn't have said. But when the soldiers came to him they took his dagger, a fine thing with a gilded handle covered in jewels. He seemed ready to make an argument, the blood rising in him, but in the end he just swallowed his words. The soldiers dumped the knife into a burlap sack they carried where they'd put a few others and told him he could collect it back when he returned from his pilgrimage. But you knew he would never see the thing again.

When they'd gone through the line of us they let us cross the ford. From there, we pushed on for Jericho, reaching it after dark, and only to find it crawling with soldiers as well. We had to line up outside the city gates and go through another search. It was clear by now what had happened—the Romans had got wind of whatever plot was afoot, as Jerubal had said they would. Judas must have come to the same conclusion because he had a bit of a wildness in his eye, like an animal that didn't know which way to turn. I noticed he wouldn't let Jesus out of his sight now, as if he had to protect him. But Jesus himself only seemed to get calmer the more chaotic things got around him.

When our group had been passed we were herded off for the night to a camp the soldiers had set up just outside the walls, since the roadhouse was filled. In the dark we could hardly see what we were doing, tripping over people because the place was swarming as well, everyone trying to stake out their bit of ground for their tents. We had to fight to get a corner for ourselves, and then it was mainly just rubble and rock, so that it didn't look like a very good night ahead for us.

Our spirits improved after we'd all settled and the food had started going around. Seeing that everyone was looked after, Jesus said he wanted to see a friend of his in town who'd taken care of him after he'd come out of the desert. Simon the Rock arranged for a little group to go with him, and I noticed that Judas just pushed in to join them as if it was taken for granted. So I did the same, knotted up with the sense that something was going to happen, on account of the soldiers.

But when we passed through the Jericho gates, all the confusion and noise from the searches and the crowds dropped away and we found ourselves on a beautiful paved street lined with torchlight and fine palaces. It turned out the place was more a retreat than a town—in the time of Herod the Great it was only his cronies who were even allowed there, and now it was mainly Romans who stayed in the town and the richer Jews from Jerusalem, who had their winter houses there. We all wondered who Jesus could know in such a place, and if it was the fellow he'd talked about the night before who'd helped him carry on after John was killed. But Jesus said, no, that was another man, although this one did almost as much for him.

I'd noticed that Judas's ears had pricked up at the subject. I'd started to suspect by now who the man who'd helped Jesus might have been, putting things together and thinking of the look that had passed between Jesus and Judas around the fire the night before, and how Judas had bolted off. At the time I'd thought he was angry but it wasn't that—he'd been ashamed. Jesus had been saying to him, see what you meant to me once, though it was clear that at some point they'd fallen out, and hadn't found the way to come together again. You couldn't imagine two men more different than Judas and Jesus, one a rebel and the other for peace, one rude and hardly willing to give you the time of day and the other one taking in every beggar who came by, but still you could see they were connected, even more than if they'd been alike. At the same time you knew it had to end badly between them, because they were both of them so stubborn and set on their path, Jesus even more than Judas.

The house we finally stopped at turned out to be one of the nicer ones, with a big pool out front and palm trees all around. Three or four fellows came to the gate straightaway to take our coats and wash our feet, and then the owner himself came out and his face lit up the instant he saw Jesus.

"Get some supper ready for my friends," he told his men.

I'd never been in a house like that—I'd thought only kings or princes lived that way, with servants everywhere and where everything looked as if it had been washed down and polished just an instant before. I wouldn't have thought Jesus would want to be caught in that sort of place, but he was calling our host, whose name was Zacchaeus, his good friend, and didn't seem to mind his servants looking after us or the wine they brought out while we were waiting for supper. Along with the wine the servants had brought crushed olives and bread and dried dates and figs wrapped in some kind of salted meat, and I could see Jesus's men were a little awkward at helping themselves, maybe because we were sitting in a beautiful courtyard with palm trees around us and jasmine and good food and wine while the rest of the group was back at our dreary camp with their same old smoked fish and stale bread. But Zacchaeus managed to put them at ease with his courteousness and his talk. Only Judas couldn't seem to settle, with a look as if Jesus had come here exactly to spite him, taking the time to feast with his rich friend despite Judas's warning and the soldiers at the gates.

I could see that everything about the place was irritating Judas, the carpets we were on, the bits of coloured stone in the floor, the glass bottles the wine had come in, which were as clear as air.

"I see your wine comes from the Romans," Judas said, barely taking the trouble not to be rude about the thing. But Zacchaeus answered politely, "I get my wine from them and my wages but not what I believe."

Judas looked down with his scowl as if this was just what he'd expected. But Zacchaeus pretended not to notice. He had started to tell us how he and Jesus had met—Jesus had been begging food at the Jericho gates when Zacchaeus had seen him, all skin and bones the way he was then, and invited him home, afraid he wouldn't survive past sunset. They got to talking then, and it was the next morning before they stopped.

"I thought I was doing a good deed for a beggar," Zacchaeus said. "But it turned out I was the beggar, since I only gave him food but he gave me wisdom."

When supper was ready we went into a large room with couches all around and a big table in the middle piled high with every imaginable thing, fruit and roasted meat and big bowls of honey and nuts. Judas looked even more disgruntled now than before, pretending it was the extravagance of the food that upset him though it was probably Zacchaeus's story, and his remembering back to when he himself had met Jesus and how things had gone wrong since then. He stood to the side now though Zacchaeus had invited us all to sit, and only at the last minute did he finally take his place on one of the couches, but right at the edge of things. Zacchaeus was telling us about his work—he ran one of the balsam farms outside the city, that the Romans used for the juice that came from the trees, which was good for medicines and perfumes.

You could see Judas could hardly hold himself in any more, listening to this.

"So you help the Romans take what belongs to the Jews," he said finally, not even bothering now to try to hide his contempt.

Everyone fell silent. It was the worst you could do, to insult a man who'd invited you to his table. Even Judas seemed to realize he'd gone too far, but there was no taking the thing back. Zacchaeus just sat there not knowing what to say, so in the end it was Jesus who had to save him.

"You mean to say that Herod the Great," Jesus said to Judas, "who planted the trees, used his profits for the Jews."

"Herod wasn't a Jew any more than the Romans are," Judas said, a bit too quickly.

"Then the trees never belonged to the Jews in the first place," Jesus said, smiling to show he was offering Judas the chance to make light of the thing. But Judas's face stayed clouded.

Zacchaeus excused himself then, apologetic, lying and saying he had business to attend to. Almost the instant he'd gone, Judas, still seething with his humiliation, said to Jesus, "I don't know how you expect your fishermen to understand you, when the people you criticize in daylight are the ones you whore for at night."

It was clear again that he'd put the thing more powerfully than he'd intended. There was a look on Simon the Rock's face then that I'd never seen before, nearly of violence. But Jesus didn't balk.

"In a hundred rebels," he said, "there are ninety-nine who never gave money to a beggar, or helped someone who needed it, or showed mercy even to their own friends, but if you had to judge them you'd let them by, because they fought the Romans. But here's a man who respects his god and treats everyone fairly, but because he works for the Romans you'd throw him to the fire."

But Judas had gone too far to give in.

"You can get away with an argument like that with your heathens in Galilee, but not in Judea," he said.

Simon and the others seemed ready to chase Judas away with their fists then.

"Why did you come back," Simon said, "if it was just to make us argue again?"

"I came back to save your lives, but Jesus doesn't seem to mind giving them up. If that's what you want, then you can march off to your deaths the lot of you, for all the good it'll do anyone."

And he got up and left the room, and we heard him yelling out to one of the servants to bring his coat.

No one spoke. For a long moment the echo of Judas's departure seemed to hang in the air. Finally someone said, "Master, what did he mean?"

Jesus explained to them then about the chance of a rebellion, telling them the risk Judas had taken in order to warn them.

"You're free to turn back," he said. "It wasn't fair of me to hold my tongue. But I thought of the bloodshed, if there was no one to counsel peace."

When he put the thing to us there wasn't one of us who said a word against him. It felt strange to me, to be part of the secret we shared now, like a pact we had made in our blood.

In all this hardly anyone had touched a bite of food. It was Jesus, finally, who leaned in and broke some bread and passed it around to us. There was a feeling amongst his men like they'd failed at something important—you knew Judas had probably been trouble to them from the day he'd joined them but at least they'd always found the way to put up with him until then, just as Jesus taught.

Zacchaeus came back after a while to look in on us, though not saying a word about Judas or all the food we'd left behind, simply having his servants put it in baskets for us so that we could take it back to our camp. On our way there, Jesus walking silently ahead of us, some of the men were whispering among themselves wondering if Judas had truly gone. But I was wondering instead if Jesus hadn't planned the whole evening to turn out just as it had—that Judas would get angry, and see how he and Jesus were different, and go off then and at least save his own life.

There wasn't any sign of Judas when we got back to the camp—he hadn't even bothered to come back for his satchel. When the next morning Jesus turned it over to me to use, I saw there wasn't anything valuable in it, just a shirt and some undergarments, and I remembered Judas's dagger, and how he hadn't liked to give it up. Maybe he'd returned for it after all, and crossed the border again, and would just keep walking into the desert until the itch in his back had gone.

All the high spirits we'd had when we first spotted Jericho were gone by the following morning. We set out at dawn, going past Herod the Great's old winter palace, half-abandoned now, and through the palm plantations that flanked the city. But then the road started into the barren hills, with just rubble and scree up on one side and more rubble and scree on the other. In between was the sorriest sort of riverbed, with only the odd oleander bush poking up out of it here or there, though it looked as if the river hadn't seen water in years.

From Jericho the road just went up and up, the warm breezes we'd had on the plains turning bitter and cold. In the old days, I'd heard, the road had been plagued by bandits, but now holy men came to live in the caves along it. It wasn't the sort of country I'd wish on anyone, about as forbidding and cold as I'd ever seen, and with each step we took it seemed to get more forbidding and more cold. Jesus, though, seemed in his element, walking briskly out front, his face hardened against the wind though he looked not so much soured after his fight with Judas as a little relieved.

Soon the road had climbed to follow the edge of a cliff, the riverbed snaking along far down below us and the valley walls dropping sheer on either side. It was as if someone, maybe the god of the Jews, had taken those dirty hills and split them open, trying to get at something, except they'd found only more dirt and stones. But it took my breath away, staring down into that huge crack in the earth, so deep I could barely see to the bottom of it, and then looking along the road at the little row of pilgrims crawling along the cliff edge. It made me think there was something to their god—I almost felt him in that stone, and saw what drew the holy men to the place, the world stripped down the way it was so that it must seem you were alone with him out there.

Just when you didn't think it could get colder, it did. Everyone was saying they didn't remember it cold that way, not at that time of year, and the clouds had come in so we didn't have the sun to warm us. We stopped for a rest and tried to get up a fire but we didn't have much wood along with us, and there wasn't a stick of it to be had along the roadside. Then finally the road came out of the chasm it was following to join up with one from the south and we started to see trees again, and also hawkers who'd set up for the pilgrims coming in and the occasional little village or town, walled up and huddled tight against the cold. There was quite a mass of us going up the road and you wondered where the city would put us, and if the Romans wouldn't simply say, go home. We passed checkpoints along the way where the soldiers stood watching everyone who passed and picking out anyone who looked suspicious, and we all seemed to feel the weight of their eyes on us, and to hunch a bit when we went by them.

Around sundown we came over a hill and suddenly there was the city in front of us. After the places I'd seen and the things I'd been through, with Jerubal and the rest, I'd been thinking that Jerusalem wouldn't impress me. But I couldn't have said what it was about that first view that took my breath—maybe it was being part of that column of pilgrims, some of who got right down on their stomachs and kissed the dirt when they saw the place, or just seeing the city walls the way they were, rising up the sides of the hill the city sat on as if to say, The road ends here. Then there was a bit of sun coming through the clouds so that the temple, which you could see the top of over the walls, had a glow to it from the gold around the roof as if Yahweh was in his home, waiting for us there.

It was getting late so we went straight to a campsite in a farmer's field that Simon and the brothers Jacob and John had scouted out for us, a mile or two from the city on a slope that looked out towards the eastern walls, where the temple was. We'd been lucky to find the space—the hillside was already dotted with campsites, set up in fields and olive groves and even to the edge of a graveyard. The cold had got into our bones by then and we were all just looking to get a fire up and eat our supper. But just as we were setting up our tents, it started to snow, gently at first but then more and more heavily until you could hardly see your hand in front of your face. People thought it a sign and Jerubal said it was a sign we would freeze, if we didn't get a proper fire going. I saw him eyeing some olive trees at the edge of the field but the farmer whose plot we were on had all his sons and cousins out there keeping watch on us, so we had to make do with the bit of kindling and brush they offered to sell, at twice what it was worth. You could see they'd pegged us for provincials, and were ready to take whatever advantage they could. But Jesus, when we had a fire up and our food on, invited them along to supper and they didn't seem sure any more what to make of us, if we were having them on or just didn't mind how they were cheating us.

Meanwhile the snow kept falling, making us seem lost in a wilderness instead of a hundred paces in any direction from another field and another group of pilgrims like us huddled around their own fire. But it felt warmer now, as if the snow was a house surrounding us, with its white walls all around. That might have been how Jerubal got the idea of building huts from the snow for those of us who didn't have any tents—he started packing it together and squaring it off into bricks like a mason, and slowly building up his walls. Soon he'd set his whole group to it, half a dozen of their little houses rising up in the middle of the field, and finally even Jesus joined in on one, kneeling there in the snow and mud like a boy. When he'd finished, showing us how to round the roof over so it would hold, someone joked that the thing looked as fine as the temple in Jerusalem. "Herod spent forty years making his," Jesus said, "and I did mine in an hour."

Our landlords didn't know what to make of us, playing around in the snow like children. But by and by the word of what we'd done got out and people from the neighbouring camps started coming around to see, staring at the little village we'd made as if it was some miracle. There was just the light of our fire to see by and the snow was still coming down, and for a while all of us just stood there in the snow looking on, because it was true we had never seen such a thing, those little houses all of white. The new snow was already piling on top of them so that they seemed more real somehow, to have that blanket on them like any regular house in a snowfall, though you knew that in a day or two they'd all be melted away.

The next morning when we awoke all you could see was white, even the trees covered over, the snow two fingers high on every leaf. Our little village was just a series of lumps in the snow, and even the tents were hardly distinguishable, just little hills like the mounds of insects, so that when people started digging out from them it was as if we were some colony of locusts or ants just scratching our way out of the earth. And still the snow kept coming down, though you didn't think it could go on like that, since it seemed that another day of it and we'd all just be buried alive, and that would be the end.

It was a job getting any work done in that snow. Somehow we got another fire burning—and the price for wood had already gone up from the night before—and made up some breakfast. Then Jesus sat us down and told us we had a busy day ahead, and gave out assignments. Jacob and John, who he called the Sons of Thunder, had to take a group in to buy us sheep for our sacrifice, and Simon the Rock and

Mary and a few of the other women had to go into town to prepare a room Simon's cousin had rented for us for our festival supper. The rest of us were free to join Jesus, who would be paying a visit to the temple.

After coming all that way I was anxious to get a proper look at the temple, which people used to talk about even in Baal-Sarga. So I put myself in with the group, and Jerubal said he'd come as well. In the end, there were maybe thirty or forty of us who set out. One of them was Aram—since Judas had gone he'd gotten more forward, trying every way to catch Jesus's eye. It turned out it was Judas he'd been afraid of, and the rumour he was a spy, though we might all have preferred it if he'd just stayed in his cave instead of being always underfoot now trying to get in Jesus's good graces.

We passed the sheep market, a big field outside one of the city gates with corrals at one end where the sheep were penned, and left John and Jacob there with their group. The market was already chaotic, with people everywhere and the mess from the mud and snow, and then all the sheep crying out for dear life knowing what was coming to them. A row of soldiers stood on each side of the field, looking merciless and tense, seeming ready to pull out their swords at the first sign of trouble. There were more soldiers at the gates and we had to be checked again, and then it was the same inside, with soldiers keeping an eye out from the walls and more in the street making sure the snow got cleared away. There was so much snow by then that it seemed a hopeless job, the narrow streets there near the Sheep Gate so crammed with it that people had just burrowed little alleys down the middle and piled the snow up high on either side.

The Romans had their castle just off the gate. The height of it cast a shadow like night over the street, the walls going up and up, sheer and windowless except for a few openings near the top. I'd heard the governor put up there instead of at Herod the Great's old palace whenever he came down from the capital because he knew the Jews would be happy to slit his throat. He always came for the feasts to head off any trouble then, but from the sound of things he only made matters worse, strutting around with his special guard, who were all Samaritans, and throwing it in people's faces that the Romans ruled them.

Past the castle a wide street ran along the base of the fortress and of the wall that shored up the Temple Mount. The wall was almost as high as the fortress itself, dwarfing the houses across from it and made of stones as large as houses themselves. The wall stretched away so far that you could hardly see to the end of it, stone on stone on stone so that you wondered how it could have been built. The street along it was crowded with traffic, soldiers and peddlers and people going up to the temple, but we seemed no bigger than ants next to that wall, scurrying about on our bit of business.

Part of the way along we crossed under an archway and came into a better part of the city, the streets wider and the houses more substantial. An old wall that must have gone back to when the city was smaller divided this section from the slums we'd just come from. Not long afterwards we came to a gate cut into the wall of the Temple Mount that was the start of a tunnel that led up to the top. As we were going up, Jesus warned those of us who weren't Jews that there were certain places we weren't allowed—he himself didn't hold to the rule but we ought to be careful, since we could be arrested or worse.

It took a moment for my eyes to adjust when we came out into the temple square, the white of the marble and the snow making it seem as if we'd come up into the clouds. Then when my mind finally took the place in, it wasn't what I'd expected, mainly empty space stretching away in every direction. Way off in the distance, it seemed, was the temple itself, with a little plume of smoke coming up out of it. It didn't look as impressive as I'd expected, huddled there in the middle of all that space, and this for a god Jesus said was greater than all the rest. I felt my heart sink a bit then, and saw that I'd been hoping to believe, and that Jesus wasn't one of those who thought his own the best simply because it was his own. But then the scale of things in that square skewed your view—there were thousands of people there, the groups like us that had come for their prayers and then the families and the rich men with their slaves and the dozens of servants who were sweeping up every flake of snow that fell and carting it off to a big mound they'd made behind the temple, but still it didn't seem crowded there and you could move freely, the space as big as a city.

I'd made up my mind to follow Jesus's advice and stay close to him. But we weren't up there long before Jerubal, looking around, started to get other ideas. At the southern end of the square was a huge barracks of a place running the whole width of the Temple Mount that looked to be some sort of market, hawkers shouting out from the steps and large crowds moving through the arcades. Jerubal said he just wanted a look inside and like a fool I agreed to go with him, thinking we'd come right back to our group. But we'd hardly gone a few strides before I looked back and Jesus was already lost in the shifting crowd.

Inside, the place was cavernous and cold and filled with a hollow buzz from all the conversation and noise. There were aisles and aisles of pigeons being sold for sacrifice, all lined up neat and orderly in their cages, and then a place for lambs, and another for scrolls, and in each place the peddlers stood there with the same wares as their neighbours, at the same prices, but still each seemed to be making his living. Then all along the arcades were the moneychangers, since you couldn't pay with Greek or Roman coins, on account of the images, but had to use special ones that you bought for a small commission.

At the far end of the building people had lined up in front of tables where men in scarlet robes and pointed hats took a handful of money from them and then slowly wrote their names on a scroll. They were paying their temple tax—it seemed every year they did the same, whether they lived in Jerusalem and used the place daily or came in once a year from the other side of the Nile. There were great stacks of coins just sitting there on each of the tables, and only a couple of guards in the place, the special temple ones in red and blue who had only little clubs for weapons. I saw Jerubal's eyes go to the stacks and thought he couldn't help but think how to get his hands on them, and knowing there wasn't a thing so mad that he wouldn't try it, I grabbed him right then and dragged him through the first doorway I saw. We ended up in a dim staircase going down to I didn't know where, but I just pulled Jerubal along by the elbow until we found ourselves on the street again.

We had ended up at the south end of the Temple Mount, overlooking what seemed an older part of the city, the houses black from years of smoke and their stones more worn. But there were more gates here that led back up to the temple square—the Rat Gates, they were called—and Jerubal said he wouldn't leave until he'd had a better view of the temple. It was true we hadn't even got close to the thing—I couldn't see what harm it would be, if we were careful to watch where we went. But when we came up into the temple square I got a sick feeling, because we were on the inside of a marble fence that ran all through the square to make a smaller square around the temple. I expected the guards to come rushing for us then. But no one seemed to pay us any mind, and I thought, We'll just steal a quick look and be gone.

I had a better sense now how everything on that hill, from the colonnade that ran right around it to the fence that ran inside to the courts that closed in the temple itself, was planned to make the temple a home, square inside square inside square as if each one was a room that brought you that much closer to Yahweh. With each step we took, the temple loomed up higher, looking so much larger up close than it had from a distance, a bit of sun coming through the clouds now to catch the gold all around the roof and glinting from every part. The curl of smoke I'd seen from a distance was a great billowing cloud now, rising up over the walls of the temple courtyards with a stench of burning flesh. Then while we were still craning our necks to try to get a proper view of the place, shielding our eyes from the glare of marble and gold, we were suddenly right at the courtyard gates. There were a few guards standing there in their uniforms but they didn't give us a second look, and almost without thinking about it Jerubal and I just followed the crowd right through.

It was a revelation to go through those gates. We passed through a courtyard and then there was the temple right in front of us, so large now it filled your head to look at it. A huge doorless gate opened into it that looked exactly colossal enough for a god, so high you practically had to lie on your back to see to the top of it, and then coming from inside was a golden glow, somehow dim and bright at the same time, that you almost had to turn away from, for the richness of it. I had a catch in my throat then—it seemed it wasn't until that minute that I'd understood what a god was, since I looked at that doorway and thought that whatever was on the other side was larger and more strange than anything I could imagine.

It was a moment before I took in all the activity going on in the temple's shadow, the priests and their helpers doing their work at the base and then the hundreds of men watching them from behind a railing and the hundreds of women, who weren't allowed past the first courtyard, craning for a view of things from balconies in the courtyard walls. Just to the side of the doorway into the temple was the altar, a large thing of marble perched over a massive firepit that was sending out a blast of heat and the smoke we'd seen, a ramp leading up to the altar so the priests could walk up and throw what they had to into the fire. Over on the other side was where the animals were being slaughtered, men lined up with their pigeons or their lambs and the priests' minions, all in scarlet, taking one after another and slitting its throat, collecting some of the blood in pots so it could be sprinkled up against the altar and letting the rest drain off into runnels cut into the pavement. You could smell the cold tang of blood in the air and the burning offal and the smoke, and you'd have thought the place would look worse than a stable. But instead it was spotless, without even a lick of snow to be seen anywhere near, and the few flakes still falling seeming to disappear before they so much as touched the pavement.

At a certain point I started to sense that people were looking at me and Jerubal a bit strangely. Two fellows were staring over at us and whispering to each other, and then one of them leaned in to talk to a third one, and then this one went over to speak to a temple guard who was standing nearby. Who knew how they'd spotted us—Jerubal might have been a Jew as much as anything, the way he looked, and my own beard had grown out so much since I'd left home I could easily have passed for one as well. But the guard took one look at us and he started to come over, and then one by one everyone around us stopped talking and turned to stare.

The guard looked a little wary, not mean but just wanting to do his job. But right off he said something I couldn't follow, which must have been in Hebrew, to test us. To my amazement Jerubal answered him right back, and for a moment they had a conversation going, the guard still looking skeptical but Jerubal just grinning his grin. I thought we might actually get through the thing when suddenly the guard turned to me, starting to talk though I didn't understand a thing, and that was when Jerubal leaned in close and whispered just the one word, "Run."

Pandemonium broke out then, everyone suddenly realizing we weren't Jews and sending up a shout that couldn't have been worse if we had murdered their mothers and children. They might have beaten us to our deaths then if Jerubal hadn't had his wits about him, grabbing my arm and dragging me through the crowd back into the women's court.

The women, not knowing what to make of us, fell over themselves to get out of our path, making it harder for anyone to follow. There were only a couple of gates out of the court, and all the guards were making for them to stop us there. But they hadn't reckoned on Jerubal—he headed up the stairs that led to the women's balconies instead, which no one had thought to block. And again because of all the women stumbling and swooning on those narrow stairs as we went by, it was difficult for anyone to come after us.

I was afraid we were trapped. But from the balconies Jerubal got us up to the top of the walls that closed in the temple courts, and even the walkways there had been cleared of snow, and then, as if he knew exactly where he was going, he led us along until we were right at the temple's back, hidden from everyone's view, with just the temple's back wall rising up behind us, as solid and unfriendly as the cliffs on the Jericho road, and the city stretched out in front of us. I could already hear footsteps and shouts behind us on the walls, and knew in a moment we'd be caught. But Jerubal got right up on the parapet then, and he held his arms out, and he jumped.

I might have thought this was mad, since it was far enough to the pavement to break every bone in you, except that it came to me what Jerubal was thinking—the snow. We'd seen it as we'd come in—this was where the temple workers had piled up the snow they'd carted away from the square, behind the back wall of the temple courts. I didn't have time to think, so following Jerubal's example I climbed up on the wall and closed my eyes and jumped as well. It seemed I was in the air a long time, and it was more pleasant than I would have imagined, as if I were floating. But then I hit the snow and went a good ways into it, and I felt the shock through every part of me.

We could hear the crowd on the wall run past the spot we'd jumped from, simply assuming we'd continued to the other side of the temple. When we were sure they'd gone we burrowed our way out of our mound of snow and then just slipped quietly back into the crowd and out the first gate we came to. It was all I could do to keep from running then. But out in the streets of the city we might have been anyone, just going along with the traffic, and it wasn't long before we'd passed through the city gates and were safely back at our camp amidst the olive trees.

Jesus and his group were already back at the camp. They hadn't got wind of what had happened with us and had just supposed we'd gone off on our own, and I was happy enough not to say a word of the thing, taking a place next to the little fire that was going and trying to get my hands to stop shaking. Jerubal already seemed his old self again but I didn't have the stomach any more for his adventures—it didn't seem such a joke to me, to take your life in your hands.

Simon the Rock had returned, having left Mary and some of the others to stay in town to get ready the room we'd rented. But by mid-afternoon there was still no sign of John and Jacob with our sheep. The Rock got up a group to go look for them and I joined in with it, thinking it would be good for me to get in less with Jerubal and more with Jesus's men. The snow had stopped by then and the weather had turned warm, all the snow on the ground slowly turning the dirt underneath into mud. It was a slog to get out to the highway, and then there was so much traffic on the road from the pilgrims coming in we had to move at a crawl.

The crowd at the sheep market spilled well out into the road now, the place a devil's feast of mud and jostling limbs and bad tempers. Even so, we thought our group ought to have finished long before, seeing how early they'd come. But then we saw there was a system going on—before you got to the pens you had to pass by a line of temple officials, all in their scarlet robes, who were managing the whole affair, and were letting Judeans through before the rest. We finally found John and Jacob shunted off in a corner, and it turned out they'd somehow got herded aside almost the moment they'd arrived and been left to rot there. They were fairly angry by then, waiting there in the muck since early morning with nothing to eat or drink, and there were some others in the same situation as they were, Galileans like them, who were even more angry. There was a group of them nearby, rough-looking fellows, who I could hear cursing those officials under their breaths, hating them and afraid of them and hating them more for that.

They were at the end of their patience. Finally one of them said, "I've had enough," and went over to talk to one of the officials.

"We want our sheep," he said, in the blunt way of a Galilean but also as if he was willing not to bear any grudge over the thing. And if the official had had any sense he would just have let him through—he must have known how long he and his friends had been waiting there. Instead he said, "Go back and wait your turn." But those Galileans had been waiting their turn from the break of dawn, and their turn had come and gone a hundred times over since then.

Something burst in the man then. Quick as lightning, he knocked the official to the ground. In an instant the official was screaming for help and the Romans had come in swinging their clubs, breaking the bones of anyone who got in their way. For a moment, from the commotion, I was sure there was going to be a bloodbath. But the soldiers were so quick and their clubs so well aimed that there wasn't much chance of fighting back, and people just stood there stunned as they came through, hoping to get out with their lives. We were still a bit at the edge of things, and it was easy for us to get out of the way. But others weren't so lucky. That Galilean, for instance—one of the soldiers cracked him so hard on the head he split it open, so that he was likely dead by the time he hit the ground.

Somehow the sight of a man lying there in the mud with his skull cracked seemed suddenly to quiet everyone down. The soldiers, for their part, were apparently satisfied they had their man now—their captain barked out an order and in an instant, as if it was just the one mind that controlled them all, they put away their clubs and lined up on the double in rows of a dozen or so through the crowd to keep it cordoned off and in order. And it had hardly been more than fifty breaths from beginning to end before the disturbance was over and the place was calm again, and people were already carrying away anyone who'd been hurt and even the man who'd been killed had been wrapped up in a cloak by his friends and carted off.

The Romans, though, weren't taking any chances—they were closing the market. When they made the announcement, there was so much railing from the crowd it seemed there'd be another riot. There were thousands of people still waiting there to get their sheep, and this was the special day, according to their rules, that it had to be bought. But the Romans were quick—some reinforcements had already arrived from the fort and had lined themselves up in front of the sheep pens, so that finally the crowd started to disperse. And we had to leave along with the rest, as empty-handed as them, and John and Jacob and the Rock looked miserable at how they'd failed Jesus.

To our surprise, though, when we got back to camp and told Jesus what had happened he said it didn't matter about the sheep, we'd find the way to make do. What about the laws, his men said. But Jesus, getting angry, said, "What kind of a god do you think we have, if he cares more for your sheep than for somebody's life?"

We had just started supper when a boy came running out of the dusk, gasping for breath, and said he'd been sent to fetch Jesus. Someone was sick—it turned out it was the Rock's cousin, who lived nearby in a village on the other side of the hill. It was dark by the time we got to it, just some fires showing here and there from people's yards and the occasional lamp through a doorway. With the dark the cold had come back, breathing off the snow that still lay over everything and giving a smell to the air like water from a mountain spring.

There were people standing at the roadside as we came to the house, and then two women at the door, wringing their hands.

"You're too late, he's dead!" one of them cried, but half-raving, so you didn't know whether to believe her.

Jesus went straight into the house. It was a small place and we couldn't follow, but a moment later he said we should bring the man out to the cooking fire in the courtyard to warm him. Simon and Jacob carried him and set him down on a carpet next to the fire, which one of the women, the calmer one, shored up a bit. The two women were his sisters. The younger one, Mary, was the prettier of the two, and the more level-headed. The other was Rachel, hair pitch-black and coarse as wool, who had cried that her brother was dead. And when I saw the man in the firelight, not moving and his face grey as stone, I had to think she might be right.

His name was Elazar. As near as we could gather, he'd been at the sheep market that afternoon when the riot broke out, and had taken a blow to the head. From what he'd told Mary the blow hadn't even knocked him down, just made him bleed a bit, and he'd got home fine on his own. But after a while he'd started talking some kind of nonsense, so his sisters didn't know what to make of it, and then in the middle of it he'd just sat down on the floor and passed out. They'd called some neighbours in to look at him, but when they came he'd started to shake like a devil had got hold of him, and that was when they'd sent someone down to fetch Jesus.

When I heard all this I thought there wasn't much hope. To look at the man he seemed stiff as a beam, and then when Jesus knelt beside him and put a palm up to his nose to check for breath, he didn't seem pleased with the result. He lifted the fellow's eyelids then, one and then the other, and from the way his eyes stared out at nothing, the darks of them different sizes from each other like I'd never seen, I would have said he was already dead.

Jesus, though, didn't balk at any of this.

"Get a blanket on him," he said, "and keep the fire up," and then he took the fellow's head in his hands and started to feel all around it, softly, as if it was a baby's. This went on for quite a while, and we all stood there holding our breaths. And looking at Jesus intent the way he was, I had the feeling that he could save the man, that he could bring him back.

As if to spite us then, the fire suddenly cracked and a big ember flew out onto a bit of the fellow's leg that wasn't properly covered. Mary reached out quickly to brush it away. But the man's leg hadn't moved at all. The ember had sat there long enough that I could smell the skin burning, yet there hadn't been so much as a twitch in him. Jesus, though, hadn't seemed to notice, still feeling around the fellow's skull. Then finally there was a point when he seemed to find whatever it was he'd been looking for—suddenly he grew even more intent, and closed his eyes as if he was sending them down to his fingers to see. There was a strange moment then, the light from the fire dark and red and making shadows so I wasn't sure any more what I was seeing—it looked as if Jesus had put his fingers right down inside the man's skull, right through the bone like that, and after he'd felt around in there for a bit, something gushed out from the fellow's head into Jesus's hands, dark and alive. Rachel was standing close by and she sucked in her breath, surely thinking it was some devil that had come out of him. And I thought the same, because when Jesus tossed the thing into the fire it sizzled and squealed there like something dying.

For a moment then Jesus knelt there with the fellow's head still in his hands looking down on him grimly as if he was thinking, Too late. And that was when it happened, and we all of us saw it, that the man simply opened his eyes, and was alive.

We all stood there speechless. At first Rachel looked even more frightened than before, seeing him come back to life like that. But then realizing what had happened, she fell down on her knees kissing her brother and calling out to her god to thank him. Soon everyone was down on their knees with her, and the only one who didn't seem to understand what was going on was Elazar himself, who was still lying there with his head in Jesus's hands blinking his eyes as if wondering how we'd all come to be in his courtyard.

Jesus got Mary to bring out some cloth so he could bandage up Elazar's head. He looked tired, as if the thing had taken a lot out of him.

"Do you know who I am?" he said to Elazar, to see if he had his senses back. And Elazar got a big grin and said, "You must be the son of god himself, if you brought me back from the dead." And there was a pause and then everyone laughed, even Jesus.

After Jesus had bandaged him, Elazar sat there in front of the fire and had something to eat, and told us what it was like to be dead. And what it had seemed to him, the way he remembered it, though it was already slipping from him, was that he was in a cave and there was a group of people in with him around a little fire, though he was the only one standing up. And he was saying to the rest, I'm going out, because he could see at the entrance to the cave that it was sunny and bright outside, and didn't want to sit in the dark. But everyone was saying, Don't go, and he couldn't make sense of that. At the time he'd thought he was just having a dream but now he knew that wasn't so, since a lot of the people in the cave were the very ones sitting at the fire with him now.

He pointed at me.

"I could see this fellow and I've never even met him before," he said. Everyone laughed at that, though I wasn't sure why—it gave me a chill to think I was there in that cave with him when he was dead.

Jesus said something similar had happened to him once as well, when he'd been knifed during a riot as a boy. But he'd seen a lake instead of a cave, and had thought, I should walk off into the water, though he knew it would kill him to do it. In the end he'd actually set off, and had walked under the waves seeing all sorts of things he'd never have known were there, fish and rocks of amazing colours and shapes. And when he came to again he didn't know if his god had been saying to him that that was what his heavenly kingdom was like or just that he should open his eyes, since most people looked at the world and all they saw was grey like the surface of the lake, but some people saw underneath.

The Rock was so relieved to see his cousin alive again that he said we should bring him back to our camp and have a feast for him. But Jesus said he needed his rest, and made us promise not to spread rumours of what we'd seen, since all he'd done was a bit of medicine and the rest had been the work of his god. It was no use, though, his being modest—we'd all seen the thing with our own eyes.

In the end, the story travelled fairly quickly. Not that everyone believed it—most Jerusalemites, for instance, couldn't imagine someone from Galilee doing such a thing, and then it was almost every day for them that some charlatan came along to the city claiming this or that. But by the next day the word about Jesus had started to spread, with the handful on one side ready to believe in every wonder and the handful on the other who thought Jesus should be thrashed as a fraud. And then there were those in between who just laughed to themselves about the holy man of Galilee, who built temples out of snow and brought his friends back from the dead.

By the next morning a warm wind had come in and most of the snow had melted, the fields just one big sea of mud. Our little huts had wasted away by then into the strangest shapes, rounded and stunted like the stubby limbs of lepers, so that it almost frightened you to look at them.

While we were having our breakfast, an old greybeard came along to our camp looking for Jesus. He was a dignified sort, and well dressed, and had somehow managed to pass through all the muck without getting a speck of it on him. When Jesus saw him he went right to him and kissed his hand, clearly knowing him. But his men had grown wary, lurking nearby as if to hear every word while Jesus and the fellow talked.

His name was Joseph. I gathered he ran a school of some sort in the city, and wanted Jesus to come see it. All this seemed innocent enough except for the dark looks on the faces of Simon the Rock and the others.

"I'll come with some of my men," Jesus said, as if to appease them, and it was set that he'd go around later in the day.

Joseph wanted to introduce Jesus to a friend of his near there who owned the local olive press and Jesus went off with him, taking only Simon and John and Jacob. He'd hardly been gone a few instants, though, before two young men showed up, long-haired and a bit savage as if they'd just walked out of the desert, and said they'd come searching for the man who'd raised someone from the dead. It wasn't long before a family showed up who'd come from Elazar's village, and then a cripple who came along on his crutches. But our landlord, seeing the crowd that had started to gather, got his hackles up and went over to ask them their business. Hearing the story of Elazar from them, he started thinking he had some sort of conjurer staying on his land, and he chased off the lot of them and then came up to Jesus's men.

"You'll have to move on," he said, bald-faced like that. "I have my own people coming in."

We hardly knew how to answer him.

"Where will we find another place?" one of the men said, because you could see that all the fields around us were already taken, with more pilgrims still coming in.

But the fellow just shrugged his shoulders and said it wasn't his business, and if we had an argument we could make it to the soldiers.

While we were still wringing our hands over what to do, Jesus came back in a foul temper over some argument he'd had with Simon and the others about Joseph. It didn't help his mood when we broke the news to him about the camp, and how we'd allowed the people who'd come looking for him to be chased off. He sent a few of his men out then to see if there was any place for us at a camp the Romans had set up on the other side of the city, and said the rest, if we needed, could move to the field of Joseph's friend. John and Jacob he again charged with finding sheep for us, then he said that for himself he planned to keep his word to Joseph, and visit his school.

It turned out it was only the two Simons among his men who were left to go with him, and seeing me lingering nearby

Jesus told me to join them. I couldn't do less than hurry to fall in. Jesus set a quick pace and the three of us just followed quietly behind, hardly daring to speak because of Jesus's mood. Then even before we got to the city gates we saw how tense things had become after the riot the previous day, with soldiers everywhere, stopping people on the least suspicion and searching every basket and pocket and sack until you thought they'd crack open your eggs to see if you'd hidden any stones inside. We were all of us on edge thanks to Judas's warning—any minute, we thought, the slaughter could begin.

In the city, every speck of snow had been swept up and carted away. Then as we were walking along the wall of the Temple Mount, a line of soldiers marched through and practically knocked us off our feet to clear us out of the way. It turned out the governor had decided to parade himself through the city—we could see his gold sedan descending the steps of the fortress, servants running in front to run a purple carpet where he was going to pass. About fifty of his special Samaritan guard went ahead of him, their feathers flying and their breastplates stamped with eagles that were sacrilege to the Jews, and already as they approached you saw people in the crowd holding a fist to their chest with the first finger out, to show defiance. I got just the one glimpse of the governor himself as his car went by—he looked like a boy, fat-cheeked and mean like the children of the rich who got their pleasure from mistreating the slaves.

The procession left a bitterness in the air you could taste, as if the city had been contaminated. All the decorations that had been set out for the feast, coloured banners and bangles and great painted torches set along the streets that would be lit on the actual night, seemed suddenly out of place. But we moved on past the Temple Mount into the older section of the city and some of the tension seemed to die away, the little winding streets full of cooking smells, and fires burning in every courtyard.

After a series of twists and turns we came finally to a shady square where some children were playing. Off to one side was a gate that led into a courtyard, and in the courtyard was a little pool with a fig tree overlooking it. Under the tree, sitting on a mat with three or four fellows my own age dressed in brown robes, was Jesus's friend Joseph. He got up when he saw Jesus and made his four charges get up as well and kiss Jesus's hand.

"So you've come," he said to Jesus, and you could see he was pleased.

He had his charges bring food and a bit of wine. It turned out the school wasn't much more than what we saw right in front of us, the courtyard and then a handful of small rooms that came off it. The other teachers weren't around—they had their jobs in the day and only taught at night. Joseph looked a little embarrassed now about how humble the place was, after the trouble he'd gone to to get Jesus to come to it. He said they got some money for rent from the Jewish council but were hoping for more, since they wanted to keep their teachers during the day but didn't like to charge fees.

Jesus said, "If the truth could be bought, even kings would be wise." But I could see that the Rock and the Zealot were a little surprised at the place, and had been expecting something grander.

It happened now that one of the boys we'd met when we'd come in, and who'd gone off, returned trailing a thin, narrow-eyed man dressed in a fine coat of the same scarlet as the robes of the temple officials.

"I brought Zadok to meet Jesus," the boy said. But it was clear Joseph wasn't pleased to see him. It took only an instant to understand what was going on—the boy must have been some sort of spy for the man, who it turned out worked for the council. Sure enough Zadok took one look at Jesus, in his old shirt and coat and without any shoes, and said, "So this is our Galilean," in a tone as if Jesus was some shoddy animal Joseph wanted to sell.

From there the tone of things only worsened. Jesus had gone to stone, standing there not saying a word, while Zadok went on talking only to Joseph as if Jesus wasn't there.

"I wonder if you knew your Galilean was a great magician," Zadok said. "I heard he was going to people's graves last night and raising them from the dead."

I could see Joseph was caught out by this, and hadn't heard a word yet of the rumours going around. His eye went to Jesus but it was plain Jesus wasn't going to stoop to answer the man.

"You can't blame him for the lies people spread," Joseph said.

You knew Jesus could have put Zadok in his place in a moment—I'd seen him do it a dozen times before with his sort. But the longer he stood there silent, the more Zadok seemed to be in the right.

"I suppose we have enough teachers in Jerusalem that we don't need to go looking for wonder-workers from Galilee," Zadok said finally. Then he added, almost offhandedly, "Though I hear the man isn't a Galilean at all but a Jerusalemite, at least on the mother's side. On the father's side it's not as clear."

He looked Jesus in the face then for the first time.

"Who was he, your father?" he said. "I might have known him."

He stood there in front of Jesus, giving him time to answer, but still Jesus didn't say a word. The silence grew eerie then. But Zadok just smiled an unfriendly smile at Joseph, and said he had to go.

Joseph was full of apologies the instant Zadok left, even though his spy was still there. But at the same time everything felt different now.

"Even if they take this place away from us we'll find another one," Joseph said. "I know some people who'll help." But there was something in his voice that said he didn't quite believe this.

Jesus had remained standing where he was with the dead stillness he had.

"It was my mistake to come here," he said now, "and to bring any shame to you. But it's not because of what I've taught or what I've done but because of something I can't change, which is that I don't have any father but my god, and am a bastard."

Joseph went white as marble. We all stood in silence, and it seemed the walls of the place might fall in. I don't think any of us had followed what Zadok had been hinting at and so we were stunned, as if one man had been standing in front of us and had suddenly become another one.

Joseph couldn't meet Jesus's eye. It seemed his mouth was struggling to come up with some sort of utterance but without any success.

"I'm sorry to have brought any trouble to you," Jesus said, and then he kissed Joseph's hand and went out.

The rest of us stood there not knowing what to do. You could see Zadok's spy was itching to run off to tell Zadok what had happened, and Joseph turned to him and said, "Get out and don't come back."

It was the Zealot who finally started out after Jesus, with a panicked look. I followed after him and then heard the Rock coming up behind, though it was all we could do to make our way through those twisting streets. The Rock had a look of amazement as if the world had fallen away underneath him—it seemed beyond the scope of his mind, that the man he'd just seen revealed to him was the same one he'd trusted and followed.

We only caught up to Jesus towards the Temple Mount. He hardly seemed aware we were behind him, just making his way single-mindedly through the traffic. We couldn't even be sure where he was headed and I was relieved when he went out the gates and made for our old camp. We found things in total confusion there—our landlord had already sold off our place to another group, who'd knocked down our tents and started putting up their own. To make matters worse, there was space for only half of us at the Roman camp, which in any event had been reduced to mud pits by the melting snow. John and Jacob, however, had got our sheep, who stood there in the mud bleating to the heavens.

For Jesus, though, the chaos turned out to be a godsend, because it took all of our minds off what had just happened. He set to work sorting things out, dividing the camp and sending half of it straggling off with some of his men to the new campground. Of the rest he sorted out those who had some family in town they could go to, and sent a few others to stay with Elazar and his sisters, and a few more to the room in town where Mary and some of the other women were putting up. That left a straggling band of some forty or so, including us three Simons, who somehow had ended up huddled together there at the edge of the field as if some yoke held us together.

Jesus set off with us for the house of Joseph's friend. I thought the Rock might just stay behind sitting hunched in that field, from the way he was looking, or let us go on our way and then start off back home. But at the last minute he went to the load of goods there was to move and like an ox took up twice his fair share, though he wouldn't meet anybody's eye. The Zealot, on the other hand, couldn't keep his eyes still, looking anxiously from the Rock to me and back again, trying to get some message as to what we should do.

We had to cross a long stretch of muddy fields, up one slope and down another, but then the road we were on got rockier and more solid and the going easier. The place we came to was a large country house in the middle of an olive grove, perched well up the hillside and with a view out over the whole of Jerusalem. The owner wanted to put the lot of us up inside his house, but Jesus said no, we only wanted a corner of field, insisting on the thing so that the man gave in. No doubt Jesus didn't want it said that he'd taken advantage, if the word got back from Joseph of their falling-out. Still, the owner went so far as to kill one of his own sheep for our supper, sending it out already roasted and prepared so we couldn't refuse it.

By the time we'd eaten it was well past dark. We'd hardly had time to think with the work of settling ourselves, and not the Rock nor the Zealot or I had spoken a word since we'd come from the school. But when supper was through and people started preparing for sleep, Jesus came to us and led us into a little moonlit garden that came off the back of our host's courtyard, a walled-in cranny of a place hidden away there like a secret, with oleander and jasmine and dozens of flowers I couldn't even have named. In the middle of the place was a pool so deep you couldn't see to the bottom of it, and in the corner an ancient olive tree, gnarled and twisted and bent like an old wise man.

I didn't have any idea what Jesus planned to say to us. But once we were inside he didn't say a thing, simply sat us down on some stones there and passed around a flask of water he'd brought in. I could see the Rock was desperate to get some word from him, but still he just sat.

"You cheated us," the Rock said finally, spitting it out.

Jesus took in his anger but still sat there dignified, in the way he had, like a rod that wouldn't bend.

"Was there anything I taught you that wasn't true?" he said, and the Rock couldn't bring himself to answer him.

Jesus went off to the corner of the garden then, leaving the three of us sitting there, and got on his knees to pray. He had that intensity he got when his mind was set on a thing, until it seemed he'd brought his god right there into the garden with us by the force of his will, to be called to account. I felt ashamed watching him, because you could see the emotion in him, as if he saved for his god all the things he wouldn't show to the rest of us.

He stayed praying a long while. The Zealot looked miserable now that the Rock had declared his side—he'd hoped we were together and would stand by Jesus, and felt betrayed now and lost. But when Jesus came back to us, there was a fire in him. We shouldn't expect him to come begging for forgiveness, his look seemed to say. By now it was clear he wasn't going to ask us for anything at all—it was up to ourselves, to make up our minds about him.

We went out to the camp. I'd lost track of Jerubal and his group by then and didn't have a tent, and Jesus called me in to share his own. Suddenly I was lying there right next to him, feeling the heat of him against me, and it was the strangest thing, thinking of him as someone with a body like the rest of us. He had a smell to him just like anyone, and a slow rise and fall of breath, lying there asleep with his arms outstretched looking as unprotected as a child.

When I awoke the next morning Jesus was already gone from the tent, his place cold beside me. My mind had been racing the whole night, after everything that had happened, so that it seemed I hadn't slept at all. Then at the back of my mind I had a niggling anxiousness about Jerubal, who I hadn't seen since the previous morning—I had a bad feeling about that, and wondered if he even knew what had become of us when we'd changed camps.

Outside, it was cloudy and damp and threatened rain. I kept watching Jesus to see if he'd changed, what he planned to do differently, but it seemed he was just going to carry on the same as before. After breakfast he said he was returning to the temple, and I was surprised to see the Rock move in to go with him—it seemed he couldn't leave him, still waiting for the sign that would make things clear. With the Rock joining him, and the Zealot as well, it seemed I was pulled along by force, hardly wanting to get near the temple again but drawn into the secret group we formed, as if my lot was tied in with it now.

It was a small band that set out, we three Simons and then Andrew, who the Rock was keeping close to him now, and Aram, and a few others I hardly knew. The Rock and Andrew brought up the rear, and you could see Andrew was more skittish than usual, sensing something was wrong, lagging a bit so that his brother had to hold his arm to keep him moving along.

A road led down from the farm to a city gate at the south end of the Temple Mount, where Jerubal and I had come out after our visit to the temple market. If anything, the mood in the city seemed even tenser than it had the day before, everyone grown irritable now, the soldiers and the citizens alike, and the air felt stifling and thick as if the clouds were pressing down on us.

The traffic was heavy along the street at the base of the Temple Mount. But as we were going along there, the crowd seemed to open suddenly, and a woman stood stopped in our path. Two men were next to her but it was the woman your eye went to, small and fine-featured and slender but planted there like an island, all the traffic shifting its flow to give her her place. She was looking at Jesus, with eyes as bottomless and dark as the pool in the garden where Jesus had prayed, and it took just an instant to see they were connected, and feel the force that passed between them.

Jesus went up to her. There was a tension between them as if it were a wall or a wind, so that it hardly seemed they could stand face to face. But Jesus turned to us and said, "This is my mother and these are my brothers," as if there was nothing remarkable in this, and then he took the woman's hand and brought it to his lips.

All the movement around us seemed to stop for an instant, and it was hard to say what was in the woman's eyes, surprise at what Jesus had done but also a hundred other things, and you saw how she looked him over in his ragged clothes, with his ragged band, and wondered at what he'd become. For a moment then it seemed that the feeling between them had to find an escape, and that what stood between them would crumble. But she had the same look of unbending will as her son, and the two of them stood there without a word, and finally Jesus turned and walked on.

He didn't look back at us but made straight for the Rat Gates. I felt a panic then. But somehow I just got caught up with the crowd and before I knew it I was going up, with that sick churning in my gut again, the crowd so thick around me and the passage so dim and tight that it seemed impossible to turn and make my way back. When we came up into the square it was the same, people jammed shoulder to shoulder so that I could only follow along, trying to stay close to Jesus in the hope I'd be safe with him. I saw now there were soldiers stationed all around the top of the colonnade and outside the fence as well, the whole place seeming like kindling ready to burst into flame, the people jostling and all the shouting and flaring tempers and then the soldiers standing guard with their fists on the handles of their clubs, ready to put us down at the least sign of any disturbance.

Jesus was heading straight for the temple. There was a defiance in him, and it occurred to me he probably no more belonged on that side of the fence than I did, being a bastard. I thought what Zadok or his like would do if he was discovered and it started to seem that was Jesus's intention, to throw the thing in people's faces. I imagined him going to stand right in the temple door and shouting, Here I am, to make people accept him, showing them the foolishness of using this rule or that to judge a man instead of the evidence of their own eyes. He had it in him, to do such a thing. But then I thought of the temple with all its workers and courts and crowds, and the speck we were in the huge construction of it, and knew the Zadoks of the place would simply have called out the temple guards then as if Jesus was nothing, and had him carted away.

In the end, the trouble that came to us was simpler than that—someone in the crowd recognized Jesus as the one who'd built the snow huts in the olive fields. In that throng that might have amounted to nothing more than a finger or two pointed at him before we moved on, except that we were stalled at the moment and there was time for people to take notice. Someone repeated the joke then that had somehow gone around about Jesus building the temple in an hour and someone else took offence, saying it was sacrilege. It took only an instant then, in that packed swarm, for an argument to start up. And it wasn't long before people were shouting at one another, everyone at the edge of their patience at being stuck in the crowd and at the oppressive air and soldiers all around desecrating the Jews' holy space.

Someone fell somehow in the crowd and a panic went through it, people starting to jostle and shove to try to get free until we were swaying like a wave. It seemed chaos was about to break out. Then without warning someone was howling beside me at the top of his lungs—it was Andrew. He'd started to flail, wildly, people falling back to get clear of him and his brother trying to grab hold of him to calm him. By then everyone was scrambling, trying to make sense of what was happening, and the soldiers assumed a riot had begun and leapt over the fence to put it down.

It took only a few moments for the soldiers to make their way through the crowd to us. People were in an uproar at the sight of them on the wrong side of the fence but they kept coming, swinging their clubs. I hardly knew what was happening by then. But somehow Jesus and a few of us had ended up cut off from the crowd when people had fallen back, and then one of the soldiers seemed ready to go for Andrew, and Simon knocked the man down. The soldiers were on us in an instant. I felt a blow to the head and things went dark, and then I was being dragged along with my arm wrenched up behind me and all I saw was a haze of blood and all I heard was a dull thundering. There was a whimpering beside me and I made out Aram's voice, terrified and pleading, then heard a thud, and quiet. Finally we went through a gate and the muted roar of the temple square fell away, and I knew we were in the fortress.

My heart was pounding. It seemed this couldn't be happening, that it didn't make sense. But I could taste the cold stone of that fortress and feel the rough pavement under my feet and see other soldiers moving past, with their soldier's stink and the rustle and clank of their gear. There was a flash of daylight from a courtyard but then right away we were marched into a narrow passage where the soldiers had to stoop to get along, with uneven walls of crumbling stone and a sewer smell and just the barest bit of light from lamps along the way. We seemed to be descending—right into the earth, from the looks of it, the walls getting damper and more oozing the further we went and the stink got stronger. I thought of the Rat Gates at the Temple Mount, but here the rats were real—I could smell them in the sewer air and hear them scratching and twitching ahead of us in that narrow shaft.

When we stopped we were in a space like a cave that seemed as if it had just been hollowed out of the dirt and rock. The only light was from a couple of sputtering lamps up against one wall, the smoke from them hanging in the air. It was the first time we'd stopped since the soldiers had taken us, and that I was able to look at the others—they'd taken Jesus and Aram, and the two Simons.

Jesus looked the worst of the lot, his ear bloodied and a purpling lump above his brow. But the instant he was able to look the soldiers in the face he said, in Greek, "There's been a mistake." For his trouble he got a blow to the back of the neck, and the rest of us got the same, to make us kneel. In all this not a word had been said to us in any language we could understand.

Two brutes who had been lurking in the shadows came towards us now carrying manacles and leg irons. They were dressed in plain sackcloth and big and ugly as beasts, with a smell to them of excrement and something worse, as if they'd started to rot. In an instant they had us shackled, joining Aram and the Rock and me in one group and Jesus and the Zealot in another, hammering the pins into place with a mallet. I thought they'd hand us back over to the soldiers then, but without a word the soldiers turned and departed the way they'd come. It came home to me then how bad things were for us—here we were at the end of nowhere at the mercy of these animals who didn't know if we were killers or rebels or just petty thieves, so that it seemed we'd been thrown to the bottom of a pit to be forgotten.

The two got us to our feet using wooden prods with the ends sharpened to points, as if we were goats they were herding. One of them held each of us in turn while the other frisked us for purses, though the only one they found was my own, which they pocketed. Then they marched us forward to a rusting iron gate at the far end of the cave that gave onto darkness, looking like a passage into the very bowels of beyond. In the light of a lamp near the gate I noticed shapes etched into the floor with bits of bone scattered over them—we'd interrupted the two at a game of jackals and hounds.

They took us through the gate, one loping ahead with a lamp and the other prodding us from behind. The stench that hit us then stopped my breath. We were in a man-wide corridor with cells coming off it, and you could feel the excrement under your feet and see the runnels of it coming from under the wood doors of the cells and pooling in a trench that ran along the middle of the corridor. That was the only sign of anything human in the place—otherwise it was quiet as death along there, and all you could hear was maybe the faintest wheezing of breath like a wind blowing in from the other side.

The warder in front opened a cell door. I wanted Jesus to say something to give us hope, but in an instant the warder had shoved his prod hard against Jesus's side and pushed him and the Zealot into the cell, clapping the door shut and ramming the bolt into place. We seemed lost then, with Jesus gone. Aram and the Rock and I were shoved into the next cell over, finding ourselves suddenly in total dark, tangled in a heap in our chains so that we could hardly get free of one another. The cell didn't seem to stretch more than a few paces in any direction and we kept banging up against stone, so that we ended with our limbs all entwined and our bodies hunched against whatever piece of wall or ceiling or floor we could lean up against for support. To make matters worse, the floor was pitched towards the door, to keep the excrement running out, and was so soiled with old filth you couldn't keep a grip on it against the slope.

I couldn't have said how much time we passed in there. At one point Aram started his moaning again, but dreamily, as if he was muttering in his sleep, so that it seemed he hadn't yet recovered from the blow he'd got. Finally he slumped up against me as if he'd drifted off, and then for the longest time we just crouched there in that stinking cell in total silence. At one point one of our gatekeepers came along and passed a little saucer of water through a portal at the bottom of our door and shone a bit of light in so we could drink, the Rock and I sharing what was there since we couldn't wake Aram. But then hours went by, and nothing happened. It was impossible to sleep in there but also to think or talk or do anything, because every bone in you hurt and you could hardly breathe for the stink and you were as hungry and thirsty and tired as you thought you could get. But still at the bottom you had the feeling that as bad as things were, they might get worse.

Then out of the darkness I heard a voice, strange after all that silence, and it took me a moment to realize it was the Rock.

"We've been in here a while now," was all he said, in that fisherman's way, as if he was sitting at home waiting for supper to come instead of rotting there at the bottom of a hole with no hope. He was quiet again, and then he asked me where I came from. It was the first time he'd ever put a question to me. I told him about the farm and he wanted to know how many sheep we had, and did we plant barley or wheat, and did we ever go fishing on the lake. And talking that way with him, casually as if we were sitting under the stars or sharing a drink of wine, I almost forgot for a few instants where I was, and it became a little bearable to be there in that place.

By and by, without any push from me, he got to talking about himself, about his two boys and his girl and the one girl who'd died not long after she was born, and about his two boats, and the size of them, and how many fish they could hold when they were full. And then he got on to Jesus, and how Mary's father, who he'd had a lot of business with, had come by one day and said there was a teacher he knew, and could Simon put him up. And how it had seemed to him then when he'd got to know the man that he wasn't like anyone he'd ever met before, and when he talked you had to listen, and the things he said made you feel all of a sudden as if you'd been sleeping all of your life until he had told you, Wake up.

I'd never known the Rock to string together so many words that way, and it changed my view of him, to hear the thoughts that went on in him. But still he seemed a bit of a child, the way he'd been so taken with Jesus—seeing all the wonders that Jesus had started to do, curing lepers and chasing away devils, he and some of the others, though they'd kept it to themselves, had started to think this might be the saviour the Jews had been waiting for. It didn't take a wise man to see the Rock's hopes were too high—Jesus had his few hundred who followed him but from inside that cell the number seemed paltry, and even if the lot of them had banded together they couldn't have saved him from where he sat now.

A lot of things looked different from inside that cell. There was Jesus's god—out in the open, when you were standing in the golden glow of his temple door, you felt overwhelmed with the greatness of him. But a few hundred paces away, his temple was nothing and you were in a Roman dungeon, not at the centre of the world but just the smallest scrap at the edge of the empire. Everyone knew how the Jews had only been beaten all their years, and beaten again, back to Sargon the Great. Who, then, was their god when he'd given them only fifty acres of desert and rock for their home and let a teacher who praised him every day of his life end up locked up like a common criminal.

The Rock, though, was ready to put all the blame to Jesus now—he had made a mistake, he said, since Jesus could never be a saviour for the Jews, being a bastard. And he'd kept turning the matter over in his head and still had to think that Jesus had cheated them, and got his power not from their god but from the devils, and so had been cast down in the end.

I didn't know what to say to him. Everything about Jesus had started to skew in my head by then, how he was always turning things around as if he wasn't any different in the end from the Sons of Light, preying on people's weaknesses and warping their minds to accept all his strange notions and ways. Someone like Huram would have spotted a Jesus from miles off and stayed clear—the way things had been was the way they should be, and anyone telling you differently had his eye on your freedom or your purse. But I thought of the comfort I'd taken from Jesus, and the thoughts he'd opened me up to, and how in front of my eyes he had raised a man from the dead, and it seemed a grave loss to me that I should stop believing in him now, at a time when believing in something was all I could look to for hope.

I hardly knew how I passed the time after that, or if there was any thought in my head except that I had to get out of that cell, or die. It was as if I'd been dropped into a well and was drowning there in the water and dark, hanging always just an instant from choking. Then just when I imagined I would have to smash my own skull for relief, the door opened and one of our warders was standing there. Without a word he grabbed my arm, since I was nearest the door, and dragged me into the corridor, pressing me to the wall while his partner dragged out Aram. They knocked the pin out that connected Aram to the Rock and pushed the two of us, joined at the leg, out through the gate, though we were so numbed and cramped and stiff by then we could hardly stand.

One of them led us off then through a maze of tiny passageways, each one as close and stinking and dim as the next. At the back of my mind I was hoping that any minute we'd turn a corner and be at the front gates, and our warder would just push us out into the street and say, On your way. But it seemed just as likely that they meant to kill us. I wasn't pleased at the thought of going out with Aram—one look at him when we got to the other side, and the spirits would send the both of us off to the rankest swamps. He was fully alert now, his eyes darting with panic, and I could see the spot on the side of his skull where he'd been hit, the hair there clotted with blood.

We moved upwards at some point, to judge by the air, coming eventually to a wide corridor with doorways coming off it. Our warder jabbed us through one of these into what seemed a largish room, though the light was too dim to see into the corners. Two men sat behind a table, one bearded and narrow-eyed and thin, with the look of a trader you knew would get the better of you, and the other dwarfish and a bit humpbacked, though a standing lamp burning behind them made it hard to see them.

The bearded man grew angry at our warder for bringing us in two at a time, but the warder just shrugged him off. It took me a moment to understand what was going on with them—the fellow at the table was a Jew. I saw now the little box he had strapped to his arm, that Jews kept their prayers in, though it seemed strange for him to announce the thing that way in such a place. He told us to kneel and made us say our names, which the humpback beside him copied down on a scroll. It was the first time in my life, as far as I knew, that anyone had ever done such a thing, written down my name, and it gave me the strangest feeling, as if I'd been fixed there on that scroll for all time.

What happened next was hard to follow. The examiner didn't make any accusations but just began to put questions to us matter-of-factly on one thing and another, where we were from and how we'd got to the city and who we were with, now and then coming back to things we'd said as if to confirm them. But each time he came back to a thing, though often it was innocent enough, he'd seem to give a small weight of suspicion to it. In Aram's case that had the effect of tripping him up—he'd say one thing and then contradict it, lying in the way of someone who had something to hide and didn't know what it was that would betray him.

The examiner pretended hardly to notice Aram's mistakes. But slowly his attention shifted entirely over to him, almost as if in a friendly way, as a Jew to another. He seemed especially interested in Jesus, already aware he was among the arrested and wondering what he taught and who his followers were and so on. Aram, to his credit, called him a man of peace and said he owed him a debt for his help, and he would have done well to stop at that. But the examiner, by way of stoking Aram's natural boastfulness, encouraged him to tell what he knew more intimately. It was here that Aram showed he was a fool—he began to relate bits of gossip then to show off his authority, the scandal Jesus had had with his women and the enemies he'd made and the like, as if he'd forgotten we were in a Roman prison. And the examiner just let Aram go on like that, with nods and half-smiles, until Aram's tongue grew looser and his stories broader, and he made the mistake of mentioning Judas.

The examiner's back straightened at the name. He gave a nod to the humpback to write and then his questions grew more pointed—what did this Judas look like, and where did he come from, and how did he and Jesus meet. Aram was seeming a little alarmed—he'd mentioned Judas in his same loose-tongued way, even boasting that he'd thought him a spy, and must have been frightened now at what he'd started.

"Was he with you on the journey?" the examiner asked him, and Aram said he'd left us at Jericho. When the examiner pressed him for a reason Aram couldn't say why, but mentioned the confusion there and the searches.

It was clear Judas was known to the man. There was a new energy to him now and he seemed anxious to move on, and he rose suddenly and called a guard in from the corridor. Aram seemed as surprised as I was when he had the guard remove Aram's shackles.

"What's going to happen to me?" Aram said, afraid at being singled out. But the examiner said, "I'll take care of you."

The examiner took him away then. I had a sinking feeling, seeing them go off. Meanwhile I'd been left to the guard, who motioned me up and led me back into the castle's maze of passageways. I was sick at the thought of going back to my cell. But suddenly the guard shoved me through a gate and into the out-of-doors, where I saw it was the dead of night, and for a moment I thought that I'd got my wish and was free, and my heart jumped to smell the air and see the stars above my head.

When my eyes adjusted, though, I saw we were in the castle's courtyard. In the dark it looked to be just a large empty square, cold like the underside of a stone, the castle walls looming up in every direction. There was a fire in a corner, and some soldiers around it warming themselves, and then some paces away a kind of wheeled cage of the sort you might keep animals in during a spectacle, which my keeper pushed me off towards. When we got near I saw it was full of men, seeming heaped there as if someone had just driven the thing through the streets and hauled people in to fill it. They were mostly asleep, one up against the other, and there was a smell coming off them that carried in the night air, a human stink of excrement and sweat that was almost reassuring now.

Before my guard shoved me in with them he took a dipper of water from a barrel near the cage door and handed it to me. Stale as it was, I was grateful for it. Then the cage itself seemed the finest palace after the cell I'd been in—there was air blowing through and a view of the stars and those bodies to keep you warm, and I wedged myself in between two of them and settled in for sleep. I felt a bit of hope then. It seemed the first time since we'd been arrested that I could manage to clear my head. I thought how different things looked at the end of this day than they had at the beginning, and how that morning I'd been sleeping next to Jesus in our olive grove as innocent as a lamb, the way it felt now. Then I thought back to what I'd been on the farm before I'd set out, and it seemed I'd been just a child then. I'd come chasing after Jesus looking for his special kingdom, where all my troubles would be done, and instead had ended up in a Roman prison. And I had to ask who Jesus was who could lead me on such a luckless journey, and if he wasn't the devil the Rock had said, or if there was something in all this I'd take away and understand that would make it seem worth the passage.

It seemed I'd hardly closed my eyes before it was morning. Some of the guards came around to throw water on us to wake us, then lined us up in rows in the courtyard and gave us all a scoop of water to drink and a small loaf of barley bread, the first bit of food I'd had since the morning before. We were a motley lot, I saw now, lined up there in the grey of dawn, some beggars and some in good coats, some looking like they'd been dragged from their own comfortable beds just that morning and others like they'd been holed up in that cage for weeks. I couldn't make out Jesus or any of the others in the group. But when they started to lead us away I got a flash of a familiar face, and was just able to assure myself, before we passed back into the castle, that it was Jerubal.

I felt a thrill go through me—my first thought was that it was sure now that we'd be freed, since I'd never known any hardship that Jerubal hadn't been able to find the way out of. But then we were back in the castle's dark corridors and the thing didn't seem so certain. I couldn't get another look at him since we were being marched in a file, up a rough stairway and into a strange hall with a large room on one side, separated from us by a marble rail, and a series of barred cells on the other, which the guards put us into as we came up. There were window slits at the far end of the cells, angled narrowly into the stone, and people made for them at once, desperate for a view of the outside. I managed to get my own glimpse—we had a view right out over the temple square, the temple itself rising up almost directly in front of us. Though it was early, the square was already crowded, people starting to line up with their sheep to get them blessed for the feast. I almost envied those sheep then—at least they knew what was coming to them.

It was my good luck that among the last few they shoved into my own cell was Jerubal. "It's Simon the Wise!" he said when he saw me, with his grin, and I thought I'd break into tears then at seeing his face. He said he was in for next to nothing, just for taking the side of a hawker in the street who the soldiers had been harassing—it looked as if they were going around picking up any beggar they could lay their hands on, to show the governor they'd squashed the plot. Half the men in our cell, he said, were the same as him, pickpockets and the like who'd been hauled into the castle and whipped until they'd confessed to being rebels. He showed me the welts on his own back but said they hadn't got anything from him, so he thought he was safe.

"By tonight we'll be out having our mutton like everyone else," he said. And to hear it from him, I could almost believe it was true.

We passed a long while in that cell, the only sign of activity the sound of footsteps and chains as more prisoners, it seemed, were brought into the adjoining ones. Jerubal and I took our turns at the window—the crowd had grown vast now, separated into groups by wooden barricades, and people had started moving triple file into the temple courts to slaughter their sheep. It was an amazing spectacle, the people coming and coming and the priests, all in coloured robes now, moving back and forth to splash blood against the altar and toss bucketfuls of entrails into the fire. And the lines stretched all through the temple square, snaking around the barricades, so you saw it would just go on and on and on.

Some of the temple assistants had lined up along the ramparts of the temple courtyard and started to sing, their voices carrying above the hum of the crowd. The men in our cell got down on their knees then and started mumbling along with the words. One of the guards called for quiet, but the men kept up their singing. It must have hurt those men, to be captive here and see almost the whole of their race gathered out in the temple square. There was nothing in my life to compare to such a thing—the festivals in Hippus or Gergesa seemed only amusements next to this, an excuse for drinking, offered up to gods whose names changed each time the emperor did.

At some point there was a sudden flurry of movement on the other side of the marble rail. Slaves had come in carrying lamps and chairs and even incense pots and statues of the gods. With the light you saw the room was finer than it had seemed, with painted pictures on the walls and coloured stone on the floor. A few men in white shirts drifted into the room, checking things and looking important and yelling at the slaves, and then the corridor started to fill as well, with some of the governor's Samaritan guards and other men, more unsavoury-looking, who came strolling past the cells peering into them as if they were picking out live-stock. There were assistants along with them toting scrolls in every pocket, and I wasn't surprised when my and Aram's examiner showed up as well, with his humpback.

Things got confusing then. Without warning it seemed there were a hundred things going on at once, men being pulled out of the cells and scrolls being passed from the scribes to the examiners and back again or sometimes over the railing to the men in white. Then a trumpet sounded and another line of Samaritans filed in, on the far side of the railing, and behind them came the governor himself, though in a plain linen robe as if he'd just got up from his bed. The men in white bowed so low their shirts touched the floor when he came in, though the examiners were more half-hearted, as if he didn't matter as much on their side of the rail. Meanwhile a curse went up from one of the cells at the sight of him and quickly spread to the rest, though some of the Samaritans banged their clubs against the cell bars, smashing the fingers of anyone clinging there, until people had quieted down.

One by one, then, men were dragged out of their cells to face the governor. If they'd made a confession—and you'd see a scroll being handed over to one of the men in white—they'd hardly have a chance to so much as say their names before they were dragged away again, though they might be so bloodied and blue that it was clear the thing had been beaten out of them. More than a dozen were taken away like that. Most of them seemed people who had just been taken off the street, the way Jerubal had said, one whose indictment said he was just a baker in the lower city, another a tanner. And the whole time there was a babble of talk going on, the examiners speaking Aramaic and the men in white Greek and the prisoners crying out when they were convicted and the soldiers shouting for quiet.

When they'd finished with those who had confessed they moved on to the ones who'd been betrayed. Now the charge sheet was just the statement of some witness who didn't even appear, and each of them read almost exactly the same, how so and so had conspired against the Romans and had consorted with certain men—and there was a shifting group of names that was given—who were known to be rebels. After three or four men had been dispensed with in this way, Aram's examiner moved to the front and Jesus was brought out from one of the cells.

It looked as if he'd passed a hard time, his face swollen and black and his coats in tatters, lines of blood showing where he must have been flogged. It seemed an obscenity to see him reduced like that, so that I could hardly bear to look at him. But still he cut a figure, standing there in front of the governor straight-backed and not afraid to look him in the eye. One of the men in white asked for his name and he gave it as Jesus of Galilee. Then he said straight out, speaking directly to the governor, "You're either a fool, if you believe what you've heard here is the truth, or a scoundrel, if you're only pretending to."

There was an uproar from the cells at this, because Jesus was the first one who'd had the courage to speak his mind. One of the Samaritans hit him with his club, but the shouts only grew louder then. Jesus in all this simply stood there and said nothing, though the blood oozed from his lip where he'd been hit.

We all thought the governor would simply have him carted away. But he had taken on a bitter sort of smile as if to say he would indulge the man, to show he couldn't be bested by a Jew. He looked to one of the men in white and said to him in Greek, "Ask the man what he means to say by the truth."

But Jesus answered back, in Greek as well, "Don't ask for something you can't understand."

The governor's smile faded then.

"What do you mean to say by that?" he snapped. But Jesus wouldn't answer him.

The governor was furious. He called the examiner up at once then to read the charges. But the examiner looked uneasy—instead of reading out the same charge as the rest, he said the man's only crime, from what he could learn, was that he had associated with a certain Judas of Keriot, a suspected rebel.

"Isn't that crime enough?" the governor said to him.

"We could get no confession," the examiner said. "They say he teaches peace."

"Do you defend him because you're a Jew?"

The governor didn't wait then for the examiner to present evidence but turned at once to Jesus.

"The charge is treason," he said. "How do you answer it?"

But still Jesus stood there and wouldn't say a word.

Everyone had gone silent, waiting to see what would happen. The silence had the effect of making the governor look more of a fool—there was nothing he could do to make Jesus bend to him.

Finally, almost spitting the thing out, the governor said, "Take him!" and one of the guards led him off.

There was another uproar from the cells at this, and the Samaritans banged their clubs against the bars again. The governor sat there pretending to take no notice—he'd made his decision, and his word was the law. If he was nervous at what Jesus had said, that the trial was a farce, he wouldn't show it.

It was just as the din was dying away that Jerubal said, loud enough for everyone to hear, "If it's the truth the governor's after, the truth is he's an ass."

Everyone broke into laughter then. But the governor wouldn't be made a laughingstock again—in an instant, white-faced with anger, he had Jerubal hauled out from our cell and brought before him.

"Say your name!" he said to him.

Jerubal, though, without even pausing, said, "Jesus of Galilee."

There was more laughter, but muted now—it seemed he was going too far. It was clear the governor was almost ready to have him run through on the spot for his insolence. One of the men in white said to Jerubal this wasn't a joke, and to say his name if he valued his life. But Jerubal, as calm as still water, said again, "It's Jesus of Galilee."

Who knew what was going on in Jerubal's head then, to be so brazen when there couldn't be any good in it for him. For a moment it seemed no one on the Roman side quite knew what to make of him, even the Samaritans standing dumb, not sure if they should strike him or let him be. The governor, exasperated, finally said to him, "Fool, do you want to die?" But Jerubal just stood there and didn't answer him.

The governor scowled then as if he'd lost his appetite for the whole affair. But finally he gave the smallest nod and the guards took Jerubal away.

We all fell quiet at that, stunned somehow at the way the thing had soured. Even the governor was put off—he got up from his chair now and ordered his slaves to clear the room.

"What about the rest?" one of the men in white asked, and the governor said, "Just flog them and let them go." And he gathered his robe and left the room, so that his Samaritans had to scramble to follow.

For a moment it was as if he'd sucked all the air out of the room along with him. No one was sure what to do, not the examiners or the men in white or the guards who were left behind, and those of us in the cells couldn't say if we'd heard right and would be freed or were just going to be left to rot there. But finally someone gave an order and the cells were opened and we were marched back down to the courtyard, where we were lined up in front of a whipping post to wait for our forty lashes, under a sky too cloudy to tell the time of day.

I was in a daze by then, hardly certain what was what, and it was a while before I noticed that the Rock and the Zealot were ahead of me in the line. I managed to catch the Rock's eye but he turned as if he couldn't bear to look at me. The Zealot had that stare animals got when they'd been caged too long, clouded as though their will had died. He was about the only one who didn't flinch when they whipped him, taking his strokes as if he deserved them.

Afterwards they made us wait in a corner of the courtyard before letting us go. I'd never been flogged before and felt as if my back was on fire. I went to the Simons but for the longest time we just stood there together without speaking. The Rock looked ashamed now at what he'd said to me about Jesus in our cell.

"Maybe they'll let another group out later on," he said finally, as if he hadn't understood yet what Jesus was probably in for. But the Zealot seemed to know better, his eye catching mine then with the black look of no hope.

The truth was neither of them had followed the trial well, not speaking much Greek. They hadn't gathered it was Aram who'd betrayed Jesus and assumed it was Judas, since his was the name they'd made out during the charges—I ought to have set them straight then but didn't want to admit I'd knelt there beside Aram while he'd sealed Jesus's fate, and hadn't done anything. There was no sign of Aram in that courtyard—it looked as if he'd been the one, in the end, that they'd just taken to the gate and let go.

I kept turning over in my mind what had happened to Jerubal. Here was a man who knew every trick for saving his skin, yet he'd just stood there on his pride as if he hardly cared for his life. It turned out it hadn't been for nothing—what they'd done, he and Jesus together, had probably saved the rest of us. It was as if they'd planned it, to offer themselves as the victims. But it seemed too much to imagine that Jerubal could think in that way, or that something of Jesus had come off on him until he had reached the point where he'd said, This is the cup I won't swallow.

I'd already set my mind to what I would do the moment they let me out of the gates of that castle, which was to leave the city and head for home. That was the plan I'd made when I'd been in my cell with Aram and the Rock, thinking back then to what the flowers would be smelling like on the farm, and how the barley would be coming up for harvest, and to the son there who was mine, even if I couldn't claim him. And I could see that as bad as things had been for me there, they'd since gotten a hundred times worse, and it was seeming the wisest advice to give a man that he stay home and tend to his own business.

Didn't it happen, though, just when I could taste freedom on my lips, the lot of us standing there in the courtyard not even minding the whipping we'd got as long as they let us go, that one of the captains gave an order and a few soldiers came around and started picking men out of the group. I could see they were going for younger ones so I hunched myself and put my head down. But sure enough one of them grabbed me and pulled me out, and then we were made to stand there, the six of us they'd picked, while the rest of the group was led off towards the gates. Simon the Rock could hardly bring himself to look back at me for the shame of leaving me there, and then when the gates opened up and I saw the rooftops of the city, and the holiday banners hanging from windows and the smoke coming up from people's fires, it brought tears to my eyes. But we got just that smallest glimpse of the outside before the group had gone and the gates were closed again, leaving us stranded there with our guards.

We were put back in the cage. We tried to find out from the soldiers why we'd been kept behind, but they pretended not to understand us. Night was coming on and they brought some stew around for our supper, with actually a bit of meat in it, or at least some gristle and bone. But all I could think was how Jerubal had said we'd be having our mutton by then. I got to speaking a bit with one of the other men in the group and he said most of those who'd been sent down would probably get sold off as slaves, and end up in Rome or the like. That made me feel better—I thought Jerubal would be in his element in Rome and would wind up at the emperor's house, or instantly find the way to be freed.

The group of us didn't talk much—for one thing you never knew who might be a spy, and then the others saw I wasn't a Jew and kept their distance after that. But with some of those men you could see the soldiers hadn't made a mistake in bringing them in—they had a look in their eyes as if they were ready to slit a Roman's throat the first chance they got. It was probably just good luck for them that they hadn't come up in front of the governor. One of them, not much more than my own age, with just a wisp of beard like a goat, had that air that sent the cold up you, and I could see the others were a little afraid of him, and were watching what they said as much on his account as on mine.

I didn't sleep much, because of the whipping. Well into the night I could hear the feast going on on the other side of the walls, a thin echo of music and singing and talk that gave me an ache. In the morning we got some food again and then they took us into a storehouse off the courtyard, full of manacles and stocks and a big pile of raw timbers, some longer and some short. They made us carry a stack of these into the yard, half a dozen of each, and then we just sat in the courtyard waiting, one of the guards watching over us. I didn't have any notion what was happening but I'd noticed the others were looking grim. I asked one about the timbers; he looked at me as if I'd just crawled from my mother's womb.

"They're crosses," he said, his voice dead.

It was dreary out, grey and clammy and damp. Then while we sat there a drizzle started up, and our guard let us move against the wall to keep dry. Not long afterwards they brought a line of prisoners out into the yard, chained up in a row, and my heart sank when I saw Jesus was there, and then a couple of men behind him, Jerubal.

I could hardly believe what I was seeing—these were the ones they meant to crucify. In the rain the whole lot had a miserable sameness to them as if they deserved to be together, wretched and battered and worn down. There were seven of them, all from the trial—two looked like genuine thugs and two others were Galileans and one a foreigner, so that it seemed they'd picked this set so as not to raise people's sympathies, only their fear. Even Jesus, put in with that pack, didn't look much of a Jew, fine-boned and fair the way he was, and with Jerubal added in you had the sense it was only outsiders and renegades who wanted revolt, and not upstanding Jews. The group of them had been washed a bit to get the blood off them so you couldn't tell how badly they'd been treated. But still they made an ugly sight, and half of them with a dead, crazed look in their eyes as if they were too stunned even to understand what was happening to them.

They were taken to the whipping post and unshackled and stripped to be scourged. What we'd had the day before was nothing next to what these got, the whip split to a dozen strands tipped with nails, each lash taking flesh with it. But it made it better for them, in the end—the scourging started them dying, to shorten the time that they hung. I thought Jerubal would be flayed to the bone but he seemed to hold up as well as the rest, though naked like that in the rain he looked as rickety and frail as an old man.

They let them put their shirts back on afterwards, so as not to give offense when they marched through the streets, then shackled them again and hung placards around their necks stating their crimes, though I couldn't read them. Afterwards they brought the group of them over to the timbers. I was still by the wall nearby, and from up close I could see the whipping had taken more out of Jerubal than I'd been able to tell from a distance. Then he caught sight of me and I hardly knew what to do—I almost wanted to turn away, to save him the shame of being seen like that. But he actually winked at me then and gave me a bit of a grin, as if to say, he had a plan.

With their irons on, all the group could manage to carry were their own crossbeams. It was why we others had been held back—to carry the uprights. They'd made a mistake in the numbers, though, and only planned for six, and the captain of the guards, who looked nervous and green, shouted to his men to recruit another helper from the streets. There wasn't any question of the soldiers helping out—they thought it a curse to carry the crosses. In the end they managed to round up a foreigner for the thing, an Egyptian who was promised a denarius for his trouble, and after he'd hauled two more timbers from the storehouse everyone took up their load in the rain, and we started out.

The soldiers had lined themselves up on either side of us like a wall, riding the prisoners hard to keep them moving.

Another row of soldiers stood at the bottom of the steps that came down from the fortress gates, so that as we came out to the street we seemed an army moving in. In that crowd I hardly noticed at first that Jesus's two brothers were standing off to the side with one of the women from Jesus's troupe, Salome. They caught sight of Jesus in the line, but I couldn't read what was in their faces then, confusion or horror or simple incomprehension. Almost at once one of the brothers hurried off with Salome, but the other followed behind us, keeping a distance as if unsure what his place was.

A crooked avenue rose from the castle stairs into the bazaar, and we started along it in the rain. It went up in steps, with grooves cut into them for the merchants to move their carts, and it was a job for that gang to get along them, chained and weighed down as they were and the pavement slick with wet. The shops along there were closed since it was still a holy time for the Jews, but when the word went around of the prisoners coming through, people started to poke their heads out of their doorways or over their rooftops. From an alley we went past someone spit at one of the soldiers, then disappeared before anyone could grab him. But mostly we moved along in an eerie peacefulness, because of the hush of the rain and the sleep still in people's eyes and the sight of us passing through with our battalion of soldiers and our line of men heading for death.

With the soldiers flanking us there wasn't room for people to follow alongside. But soon enough a tail had started to form behind us, mainly of boys at first but then others. Jesus's brother was keeping pace but still hanging back, falling in behind the rest. Then after a while I noticed the second brother had joined up with him again along with another who looked older. This one looked clearly broken, chafing like a tethered animal at the back of the crowd as if he might surge forward at any moment to get Jesus free.

Salome had come back as well, with two other women in veils against the rain—Mary and Jesus's mother. It was strange to see them together like that. They looked like mother and daughter, both small and dark and with eyes that burned into you, the same wildness in them then as they searched the line to make out Jesus there, hoping against hope it wasn't true. When they picked him out, his mother's eyes went dead and she turned away, but Mary's only got wilder. It was the different way they saw him, as a woman and a mother. I thought of his mother outside the Rat Gates, and the look in her eyes when she'd seen Jesus with his followers and his dirty coat, and knew she must blame herself now since she'd made him what he was.

We were getting tired with our loads, which seemed heavier by the instant in that rain, so I was sure my back was about to break. For the prisoners it was worse, after the flogging they'd got, the backs of their shirts just a wash of blood. Then just as we were coming to where the street jogged around towards one of the city gates, Jerubal slipped and fell, crumpling like a sapling under the weight of his beam. For an instant I thought he'd planned it, that it was part of some scheme. But right away the soldiers were on him to get up and I saw it was real, because the minute he tried to right himself he fell again in a heap, screaming with the pain.

Jesus was chained behind him and in the confusion managed to drop his beam and crouch to him before the soldiers could stop him.

"His leg's broken," he said, feeling around the bone there. The captain looked as if he didn't know what to do, and Jesus said, "I can help him."

The street had widened there near the gate and a crowd had been able to form around us, watching. The captain, not wanting to appear an animal in front of it, gave a nod to Jesus and had his men undo his and Jerubal's irons. Jesus called for a stick from the crowd and someone passed him a walking stick, which he broke in half. Then he started to shift the bone around gently with his hands while Jerubal, hardly seeming to feel the movement, sat there on the wet pavement. After massaging the thing for a few moments like that, Jesus tore a strip off his own shirt and used it to tie the two halves of the stick to Jerubal's leg as a splint.

The crowd had fallen quiet, watching Jesus work there in the rain. He hadn't done any miracle, maybe just what any doctor would do, but still they could see there was something in him, that he wasn't what they'd expect in someone condemned. I saw his mother looking on, still at the back of the crowd, and how she watched him as if she was seeing him for the first time. Likely she hadn't known anything of him but the stories people told, and so had been afraid he'd become a delinquent or worse. But now she saw him with Jerubal, not just the skill he had but the dignity.

Jesus helped Jerubal up and called for another walking stick from the crowd, which someone passed in, and Jerubal managed to limp forward a bit with it. But he looked helpless now. Seeing him seemed to bring home to me suddenly that all this was real, that Jesus and Jerubal were headed for the cross and no trick or plan would save them. It was a solace that they had each other, at least—I saw that Jesus was stronger than Jerubal and Jerubal needed him, that Jerubal had stepped beyond what he could manage but Jesus was ready for this, as if all his life had prepared him for it.

There wasn't any thought of getting Jerubal's crossbeam onto his shoulders again, and the captain of the guard was looking more and more distraught at how the march was going. His eye went down the line of those of us in back and quickly settled on me.

"Tie it to his upright," he said to his men, and they scrambled then to join Jerubal's beam to my own. We started up again but looking less impressive now than when we'd set out, the soldiers churlish at the setbacks and the steady downpour and the imposing line of fetters and chains that had joined the prisoners broken now where Jerubal had been unshackled and was hobbling along on his cane.

We passed through the gate. There was a bit of a hill there rising up beneath the city wall where they did the executions, just an outcropping of mealy rock with the yellowed look of old bone, ringed round at the base with a stone fence and completely bare except for a couple of bushes and withered trees. Off to one side, closed off behind its own low wall, was a small graveyard with a few humps of tomb carved into the chalky stone where the convicts were put after they'd died. There were a few soldiers on the hill carving out holes for the uprights, or more likely clearing old ones, since you could see the place was already riddled with holes from the regular killing the Romans probably did there.

We were marched in through a small gate in the stone fence, half the soldiers staying behind to keep watch over the crowd and the other half staying with the prisoners. The hill didn't rise up more than forty paces, but still it was hard getting up it because of the slick of dirt that covered the stone, slippery as ice in the rain. I was sweating with the effort but at the same time chilled to the bone, and so numbed I could hardly feel my legs. When we got to the top and the captain told us to drop our loads I couldn't bend enough to get free of mine, and one of the soldiers had to lift it off me.

The prisoners had been unshackled and lined up in a row facing out towards the crowd, the wall of the city rising up wet and grey behind them. They looked ready for death, rain-drenched and hobbled by their march and their shirts still dripping blood from their flogging. But Jesus hadn't lost that look of being apart. I overheard one of the Galileans then, looking already as pale as death, confess to Jesus that he was a murderer, and that he could see what a thing he'd done to take a life, now that his own was being taken. But Jesus said, "If you've understood that, you're already forgiven," which seemed to comfort the fellow.

Those were the last words I heard Jesus speak, because our group was herded away, now that our work was done. Before we were led off the hill one of the soldiers came with a bag of coins—it seemed we were all entitled to payment for our efforts. The Jews refused it to a man, not even deigning so much as to say a word but just shaking their heads. But the soldier just shrugged them off and offered to split the lot between me and the Egyptian. I had to think then—I hadn't a penny to my name, all my coin pinched by the warders in the castle. In the end I took just the denarius that was due to me, and let the Egyptian have the rest.

I saw now that the crowd looking on was not as large as it had seemed in those narrow streets—there were a few hundred in all, and half of them just urchins. It didn't seem much when I thought of the crowds I'd seen lined up in the temple square to kill their lambs, the thousands and the tens of thousands of them, so that it made what was happening here appear insignificant and small. But just beyond where we were was the camp the Romans had laid out for the pilgrims, and people had started filtering in from it despite the rain to see what was happening. It was in amidst them that I made out Simon the Rock, drifting in hunched and alone towards the wall at the bottom of the hill and looking as lost as I'd ever seen a man.

I went over to him. I hardly knew what to say to him and just stood there, and he looked at me with such a blank stare that he might never have laid eyes on me before.

I asked what had happened to the Zealot.

"He went off," was all he said, and I imagined him drinking himself half to death, or worse.

It turned out most of our group had fled at the news of Jesus's arrest, even among Jesus's inner circle, and those who had stayed Simon had sent home. It was just the two of us left and the women, somewhere in the crowd.

The rain hadn't let up. On the hill, four soldiers had set to work on the crosses with Roman efficiency, chiselling niches into the beams to lock them together and binding them with rope and nails. Then they laid them out in a row, each to its hole, to ready them for their load.

They brought the prisoners over one by one, since it was just the same four soldiers who were doing the work, two to hold the men in place and two with hammers. One of the Galileans went first, and he just took up his position on the wood on his own, with a quietness that chilled you. The soldiers took his measure, so a peg could be fastened to the upright to rest his weight on, and then his arms were stretched out along the crossbeam with a soldier holding each and the spikes were nailed in at the wrists. The first blow was the one that got a scream but it was also the easiest, since it was only flesh to pass through. Then there were just the grunts of swallowed pain and the thump of the nails sinking into the wood.

The soldiers worked their way along the line like that, thundering away with their hammers as if building some infernal machine. They showed the same efficiency they had in putting the crosses together, attaching the peg and then hammering the wrists down, in unison, and then doing the feet, one over the other, with hardly a breath in between to break their rhythm. But the more they went along the more steeped they were in blood, despite the rain and a rag they carried to wipe themselves, so that it was like a dream to watch them, where suddenly some normal, innocent thing turned into a horror. And all this, too, like the flogging, was a kindness to the men, since it helped them to die, instead of leaving them to hang alive for days while their limbs turned green and their eyes were plucked by the birds. It seemed the Romans had devised the perfect way to kill a man, with such a mix of cruelty and kindness you couldn't fault them either way.

After the first Galilean it was his companion who was up, then Jesus and Jerubal. Jesus wasn't any different than the rest, crying out with the pain—he was made of flesh like them, which was what such treatment reduced you to, just skin and blood and bone and the ache of them. It was strange to see him that way, as if all of his notions, all of his sayings and his stories, counted for nothing now, and it was only his animal nature that mattered.

Because of his leg Jerubal had to be laid out by the soldiers, who took him by the arms and leaned him back to the ground. I had to look away then, though I couldn't miss the howl of pain when they did his legs. That was the sound that stayed with me during the rest, like a wind blowing through.

It was only when the four had finished the last man that they started setting the crosses upright, two of them lifting at the crossbeam and the other two guiding the base and then heaping dirt around to secure it. The crosses went into their holes with a thump, so you were afraid the men would tear free. But there was just their cough of pain at the jolt and then they hung in eerie suspension, their feet only a few spans above the ground so it seemed that with the smallest effort they might step down from there, and walk away.

Then they were lined up on their crosses in the rain, with the grey wall of the city behind them and, above that, the black sky. Jerubal's face was already set in what looked like the rictus of death from the pain, so that there seemed hardly a trace left in him of the grinning man I'd met in Gergesa. I wanted to think now it wasn't so fanciful that he'd done the thing on purpose, to save some of the rest of us—it didn't make much sense, otherwise. Maybe he'd been Jesus's miracle, won over by him in the end like a character from one of Jesus's stories. But it was just as likely he'd made a mistake, and had never reckoned he'd be killed.

Simon and I stood there a long while after that, staring up at the hill. Eventually the crowd started to thin and I made out not far from us, hardly a hundred paces away, Jesus's brothers, and the women. I hadn't picked them out since before we'd passed through the city gate. Even now, the rain had reduced them to the same mud and grey as the rest of the crowd, so that it took a moment to notice the different air that came off them. They had shuffled into two groups as if someone had sorted them, the three brothers in one, the eldest like a bulwark in the middle of them, the three women in the other. I noticed now that the mother had an arm around Mary, the two joined under the mother's cloak as if they'd been brought to the same level, helpless like children who'd been left behind. It didn't seem to matter any more how differently they'd seen Jesus—it had come to the same thing, in the end, that neither had got what they'd wanted from him, and now they'd lost him.

A silence seemed to hang over the group of them, as conspicuous as if it was itself a sound. I thought of the funerals I'd seen in Baal-Sarga, with the keeners who were paid to mourn, and their wailing seemed a quiet thing next to this, just the drone of the rain and then nothing.

There wasn't much to see on the crosses after the first agony had passed and the men had settled into the bearable misery of it. Still, you couldn't take your eyes away, looking for the twitch of a limb or a heave of breath, any smallest sign of life. Jesus's mother was the same, and Mary beside her—you thought they'd turn away, that the pain of watching would be too great, but they stood there with their eyes fixed on Jesus as if to take in every bitter drop of his dying.

"I ought to have stood by him," Simon said. It was a long time since he'd spoken. "It was what he taught us."

I thought to say, Then you'd be there alongside him. But it seemed that was his point, that he'd rather be up there on the hill than watching from below.

Jerubal, on account of his leg, was the first to die. I could sense the moment it happened, though it was a while that he'd been hanging limp—one instant it was Jerubal on the cross, clinging to his last breath, and then just dead flesh. Jesus died not long afterwards. The rest hung on though it looked to be getting towards nightfall, when they'd have to be taken down, to respect Jewish law. The soldiers went around with a club then to smash their legs, so they'd slump and suffocate. It didn't take long after that. Even before the last one had gone, the soldiers had started lowering the crosses to cart away the dead, prying their limbs from the wood with an iron wedge and then carrying them over to the graveyard nearby and heaping them all together into one of the tombs.

Mary came over to us then, her face so emptied it cut to your bone.

"We're undone," she said, and just fell to her knees in the mud. Simon tried to gather her up and ended by awkwardly embracing her, hulking and large against her tiny frame.

"We always came to understand the hardest things with him," he said. "Maybe even this we'll come to understand."

They stood like that, Mary clinging to him, until Simon grew uneasy and said there was nothing to be done, and they should leave for home.

He looked to me to ask if I'd join them but his eyes said the opposite, wary of all I knew.

"I'll manage on my own," was all I said, and the truth was I only wanted to be alone then, and on my way.

They left me there and walked over to Jesus's family, and then the group of them set off together without looking back,

Simon and the older brother big-shouldered and tall in the middle of them but seeming reduced now, like mountains worn away.

The rain had stopped by then and the crowd had mostly gone, thinned down just to straggling groups of passersby coming and going from the pilgrim camp. I ought to have gone myself, but instead I just stood there watching the soldiers as they took the last of the men away. They propped the crosses haphazardly back into their holes to stand a little ominous and askew there at the top of the hill, to be left to rot, I supposed, or scavenged by someone low enough to make use of them. Finally darkness came on but I kept by my place, at the back of my head thinking that when the soldiers left I might get into the tomb where they'd put the dead and maybe clean Jerubal a bit and lay him out properly for the other side, since it seemed to fall to me to be the one to mourn him.

To make myself less conspicuous I moved off to a little hillock near the city gate, from where I had a good view, and huddled beneath some trees there. But I could see they'd left a couple of guards at the entrance to the graveyard, who were warming their hands over a fire they'd made as if they were settling in for a long stay. I supposed they didn't want anyone claiming the bodies, which belonged to the Romans. But still I couldn't bring myself just to be on my way.

I'd noticed a small group that was lingering in the field beneath the hill. The family of one of the other men, I imagined, with maybe the same idea as I'd had about getting into the tomb. Sure enough, as soon as the other soldiers had gone and it was just the two watching over the dead, I saw the group move off towards the graveyard and go up to the guards. There was a conversation then, though I couldn't hear it, while the soldiers, who looked Syrian, kept peering one way and the other over their shoulders to see if they were being watched. Then they hunched away from the fire towards the dark with one of the group, growing secretive and strange, and I knew what was happening—silver was changing hands. From the smoothness of the exchange I guessed that this was probably the usual way, for those who knew how things worked—you paid your fee, and got through.

Things had happened quickly after that. A couple of the men from the group rolled aside the stone in front of the tomb, and took a brand from one of the soldiers and went in. I thought they'd just come to prepare their man and be off, but an instant later they came out of the tomb with him slumped over their shoulders. I caught only that glimpse of them before the whole group crept off into the shadows, jumping the fence at the back of the graveyard and disappearing with their load into the dark. Meanwhile the soldiers just quietly rolled the gravestone back to its place, looked over their shoulders again, and returned to their fire.

All this left me a little breathless, because of the daring of it. I was happy about the thing on Jerubal's account—it was the sort of conniving that would have pleased him. But there was no thought of my doing the same on his own behalf, with the lowly denarius I had in my purse. Instead I went into the city and bought some supper in the streets, finally getting my mutton, which I ate sitting on the steps of the bazaar that I'd climbed up that morning, and in the end I even managed to find a bed for myself in an inn near the Dung Gate, sharing a tiny room with half a dozen sweating men, though I slept like the dead. Then in the morning, I bought up a few provisions with what I had left of my money, and set out. And except to eat and to sleep I didn't stop until I was back home again on the farm, and in my own bed.

Quite a bit of time has passed now since all that. Huram, when I came home, just looked me up and down as if I'd only been to market, and had kept him waiting for supper because I was late, and in fact the truth of it was, though it almost passed belief, that less than a fortnight had gone by since I'd left. But things were different between us afterwards, and he had more respect, and I saw how he'd pause an instant before telling me a thing so as to put it more as to a brother than to a slave. With Moriah it happened that not three months after I'd come back she ran off taking her son, and was never heard from, and Huram, to my surprise, didn't lift a finger to go after her, nor did her name or even the boy's ever so much as cross his lips. So it turned out that I was the one to give us an heir again, marrying a girl from Baal-Sarga who already had a child in her that I'd put there. When it came, and was a boy, I named it Huram, though I couldn't have told you why except that it seemed the proper thing.

Jesus's troupe I never had much to do with again. On the way home I'd passed through Capernaum and found out that most of them were just staying quiet after what had happened, confused by it all and afraid they'd be next. But Jesus's brother Jacob had come back with them, interested in finding out what Jesus had had to say, and he and the Rock more or less took over things and kept the inner circle together. When a few months had gone by and the Romans hadn't come after them, they started banding together some of his old followers on their side of the lake to keep up his teaching. In all of this, Jesus's bastardy never seemed to have come out—maybe that was the difficult thing, as much as the crucifixion, that the Rock had had to come to understand. It wasn't for me to say he did anything wrong not to let out the truth, when often enough it happened that a truth of that sort, that didn't mean anything, stood in the way of one that did.

Nowadays rumours still come across the lake about that band, and how they get stranger by the day so that soon they'll be worse than the Sons of Light. It was probably the shock of Jesus's death that started twisting them, and that they had to strain to make sense of the thing, and that in time, with someone like Jesus, things got distorted. Now for every little thing he did when he was alive some story gets put in its place, and if he'd lanced somebody's boil it turned out he'd saved a whole town, and if there were fifty in a place who'd followed him, now it was five hundred. Then there was the story that went around that the morning after Jesus was killed, Mary and Salome went to the grave and his body was gone. That might have had to do with the group who had come to the tomb for their relation, and somehow the story had got skewed, or maybe it had happened that the group had taken Jesus's body by mistake. But eventually it got told that he'd risen from the dead and walked out of the place, and there were people enough to come along then to say they'd met him on the road afterwards looking as fit as you or me.

For all I know, it might have happened that way—wasn't I there myself when Jesus brought Elazar back, who'd been dead as stone. The truth was it wouldn't have surprised me to run into him one day on the road, and even less if who should be with him but old Jerubal, working some wile and grinning his grin. I used to imagine sometimes that he and Jesus had had the whole thing worked out between them from the start, the broken leg and then pretending to die and then those fellows who had come by afterwards to the tomb, their own confederates, it turned out, who'd come to spirit them away. And I'd see them setting off down the road and stopping for a bit in Capernaum to pull a little joke there on Jesus's troupe about his rising from the dead before they headed off together to the ends of the earth.

It won't be long, of course, before everyone has forgotten the man, or remembers only the trouble he had with his women or how he died a criminal or that he was a bastard, which sooner or later is sure to get out. But however things get remembered, you can be certain it won't be how they actually were, since one man will change a bit of this to suit his fancy, and one a bit of that, and another will spice it to make a better story of it. And by and by the truth of the thing will get clouded, and he'll be simply a yarn you tell to your children. And something will be lost then because he was a man of wisdom, the more so when even someone like me, who when I met him didn't know more than when the crops came up and how many sheep it took to buy a bride, had come to understand something of him in the end.

It happened that I was in Gergesa once and heard someone in the market speak of a trip he'd made down the King's Highway to the southern sea, through the land of the Nabateans with their great hidden city and on through the long stretch of the desert you had to cross full of bandits and wanderers with their camels and tents. Then finally you came to the sea, which was bordered by mountains so rocky and bare you'd think the gods themselves had deserted the place.

You could go for days there, the man said, without meeting a soul, and all you saw was red rock to the one side of you and the grey of the sea to the other. But if you walked out from the shore, and put your face just underneath the water's surface, it would astound you what you saw there, because a whole other world was going on under that greyness, as rich as the one above it was lacking, with coloured fish of every sort and where even the rocks were of colours that beggared the mind and of shapes such as you wouldn't imagine in nature or the world.

Normally I wouldn't have given a story of the sort much credit, since you heard all kinds of things in the market, and hadn't I been guilty of the occasional tale myself. But I remembered the vision that Jesus had told us about after he'd raised Elazar. And for a moment it was as if some curtain had been pushed aside in my head and I had a glimpse of something I understood but couldn't have put into words, like some beautiful thing, so beautiful it took your breath away, that you saw for an instant through a gateway or door, then was gone.

I suppose Jesus was like that for me, something I saw as if in the twinkling of an eye. It was just the week or so that I was with him, in the end, and what was that but half a breath in the middle of all the years of my life. But still when I look out at the fields now or at the sheep grazing on the bit of pasture that overlooks the lake, a sort of haze seems to come off things that wasn't there before, as if I'm expecting something good to come along at any minute, though I couldn't tell you what it is. And though I'm happy enough to be at home, I'll never see the likes of the times I had then, for better and worse, when it seemed that every good and ill that could come to a man, and every wonder and devilry, had passed in front of me. I often think of the night with Elazar, and seeing him rise up—for the longest time I thought that was the greatest wonder you could do, to bring a man back from the dead, since as pleasant as things might be on the other side, still I reckoned I'd rather be alive and kicking for as long as I could on this one. But now I think of the light Elazar saw in his dream, that was beckoning to him at the mouth of his cave from what place he didn't know, and wonder what further realm there might be that we see nothing of, and that seems to call for me there in the glow that comes off the fields.

AUTHOR'S NOTE

This is a work of fiction. While it takes its inspiration from the figure who has come down to us as Jesus Christ, it does not purport to be an accurate historical representation of that figure. At the same time, I have made every effort to work within the bounds of historical plausibility, based on what is known to us of the time and place in which Jesus lived. In my research I have drawn on many sources, including the work of the Jesus Seminar and of other contemporary scholars who have tried to arrive at an understanding of the historical Jesus.

In the case of one of my characters, I have repeated an error that initially entered the Jesus tradition through the mistranslation of the Greek "simon kananites" as "Simon the Canaanite" rather than "Simon the Zealot." In the novel, the character appears as both. I chose to retain the error since it seemed a way of entering a greater truth about the Galilee of that time, its cultural heterogeneity.

For their help with this book, I am deeply indebted to Erika de Vasconcelos, Don Melady, Anne McDermid, Maya Mavjee, and Martha Kanya-Forstner.